CW00362176

PENGUIN BOOKS

BITS AND PIECES

Steve Smith's first break into the world of rock and roll came when he joined GRRR Books as Editorial Associate on the bestselling Guinness series of chart information books. Among these are the *Hit Singles Books*, *Albums*, *Book of Number Ones* and *The Guinness Book of the Sixties*. He is the author of *Rock: Day by Day*, published in 1987.

His many and varied interests include Light and Bitters, the Stranglers, Victor Canning novels, friendly Irish people, Tottenham Hotspur, draught Guinness, Be Bop Deluxe, spin bowling, red wine, the Clash, getting paid, Eddie Cochran, Monty Python and Nick Lowe.

STEVE SMITH

BITS AND PIECES

The Penguin Book of Rock and Pop Facts and Trivia

PENGUIN BOOKS

PENGUIN BOOKS

Published by the Penguin Group
27 Wrights Lane, London W8 5TZ, England
Viking Penguin Inc., 40 West 23rd Street, New York, New York 10010, USA
Penguin Books Australia Ltd, Ringwood, Victoria, Australia
Penguin Books Canada Ltd, 2801 John Street, Markham, Ontario, Canada L3R 1B4
Penguin Books (NZ) Ltd, 182–190 Wairau Road, Auckland 10, New Zealand

Penguin Books Ltd, Registered Offices: Harmondsworth, Middlesex, England

First published 1988
10 9 8 7 6 5 4 3 2 1

Copyright © Steve Smith, 1988
All rights reserved

Made and printed in Great Britain by
Hazell, Watson and Viney Ltd, Member of the BPCC Group, Aylesbury, Bucks
Typeset in 10/13pt Linotron 202 Trump Mediaeval by
Rowland Phototypesetting Ltd, Bury St Edmunds, Suffolk

Except in the United States of America, this book is sold subject
to the condition that it shall not, by way of trade or otherwise, be lent,
re-sold, hired out, or otherwise circulated without the
publisher's prior consent in any form of binding or cover other than
that in which it is published and without a similar condition
including this condition being imposed on the subsequent purchaser

CONTENTS

■ ACKNOWLEDGEMENTS

The author would like to thank the following people and organizations for their help (direct or otherwise), and for their inspiration during the making of this book:

Annabel Cottrell (BBC Enterprises Ltd), the National Sound Archives, Colindale Newspaper Library, *Record Mirror* (especially Alan Jones' 'Chartfile'), *Smash Hits*, and Steve Turner for maintaining a constant flow of light and bitters and telling me useless facts about Manchester. Thanks also to everybody who ever made a record, wrote a song or picked up a guitar and played – without whom this book would be even more pointless than it already is.

Every attempt has been made to ensure that all the information in this book is accurate at the time of going to press. However, no one is infallible, and I apologize in advance for any mistakes that may have occurred.

S.S.
June 1988

■ INTRODUCTION

Why? Why did I ever embark on this long, rocky road of rock and roll revelations? I suppose because I'd been walking around with a head full of useless rock and roll facts and I needed to get them out of my system. This *vade-mecum* (look it up!) of rock and roll is the crock of gold at the end of the tunnel.

Trivia really took off in the Eighties with those crazy Canadians springing Trivial Pursuit on an unsuspecting world and Michael Caine wandering around muttering 'Not a lot of people know that!' The word 'trivia' actually comes from the Latin *tri via* which means three roads and referred to a place just outside Rome where, at the junction of (surprise surprise) three roads, Romans met to exchange chit-chat and gossip (and not a lot of people know THAT).

Most of the titles of the chapters and most of the sections within them are song titles (except those in the *Anything That's Rock 'n' Roll* section). As an extra amusement, try to spot them and name the group or artist most closely associated with each song. Most are obvious; some are obscure. The answers are at the back of the book (pages 319–21).

This book will not make you a better person nor will it make you the centre of attention at parties. However, if you're the least bit like me and get a kick out of being able to recite a list of pop stars currently serving time in gaol, or enjoy telling people that Demis Roussos, Cheap Trick drummer Bun E. Carlos' brother and Feargal Sharkey's mum have all been held hostage by terrorists or can name John Mayall's guitarists in order, then this book might give you some Food for Thought (which was, of course, a single by UB 40).

That's why I wrote it . . . I think.

Steve Smith 1988

■ CHRISTMAS SONG

Christmas comes but once a year and when it does it brings ... hundreds of bloody records about it. Some are good rock songs but most are awful, novelty records. Here is a list of some songs you may or may not have heard of and the names of the artists who recorded them. Inclusion in this list has no bearing on the quality of the record.

'Do They Know It's Christmas?', Band Aid!
'Run, Rudolph, Run', Chuck Berry
'Ho, Ho, Who'd Be A Turkey at Christmas Time?', Elton John
'Santa Claus Is Coming to Town', Blue Magoos
'Bionic Santa', Chris Hill
'I Wish It Could Be Christmas Every Day', Wizzard
'When Santa Kissed the Fairy on the Christmas Tree', Stefan Bednarczyk
'One Christmas Catalogue', Captain Sensible
'Jingle Bell Rock', Bobby Helms
'Merry Xmas Everybody', Slade
'Oh Blimey, It's Christmas', Frank Sidebottom
'Lonely This Christmas', Mud
'A Spaceman Came Travelling', Chris De Burgh
'Christmas Prayer', Billy Fury
'A Child's Christmas in Wales', John Cale
'I Saw Mommy Kissing Santa Claus', Four Seasons
'Frosty the Snowman', Crystals
'Sleigh Ride', Boots Randolph
'Wombling Merry Christmas', Wombles
'It's Christmas Everywhere', Paul Anka
'White Christmas', Stiff Little Fingers
'Silent Night', Dickies
'Reggae Christmas', Gable Boys School Choir

'Ring Out Solstice Bells', Jethro Tull
'If Every Day Was Like Christmas', Elvis Presley
'Santa Claus Is Coming to Town', Bruce Springsteen
'I Want a Beatle for Xmas', Fans
'Father Christmas', Kinks
'I Can't Have a Merry Christmas Mary (Without You)', Jerry Lee Lewis
'Christmas from Space', Universal Energy
'Santa Claus Go Straight to the Ghetto', James Brown
'Thank You Santa', Sheena Easton
'Last Christmas', Wham!
'Wonderful Christmas Time', Paul McCartney
'Grandma Got Run Down by a Reindeer', Elmo and Patsy
'Little Saint Nick', Beach Boys
'I Believe in Father Christmas', Greg Lake
'Winter Wonderland', Darlene Love
'Must Be Santa', Tommy Steele
'Santa's Speed Shop', Surfaris
'Merry Christmas Baby', Charles Brown
'I'm Gonna Lasso Santa', Brenda Lee
'Rockin' Around the Christmas Tree', Jets
'Christmas Alphabet', Dickie Valentine
'Christmas Wrapping', Waitresses
'Son of Santa', Mojo Nixon and Skid Roper
'Santa Claus Is on the Dole', Spitting Image
'Merry Xmas Blues', Celibate Rifles
'Merry Xmas (War Is Over)', John and Yoko
'No Christmas for John Key', Fall
'Reindeer Ride', Roger Lavern and the Microns
'The Man with the Mistletoe Moustache', Paris Sisters

The famous *Phil Spector Christmas Album* was originally called *A Christmas Gift for You* and was released on 22 November 1963, the day that President John F. Kennedy was assassinated.

Brenda Lee's 'Rockin' Around the Christmas Tree' was written by Johnny Marks, who also wrote 'Rudolph the Red-nosed Reindeer', one of the most frequently performed songs ever written.

Many artists have made their own Christmas albums, including Elvis Presley, the Beach Boys, Supremes, Chipmunks, Chas and Dave, Frankie Avalon, Nat King Cole, Jackson Five, Carpenters, Ventures, Stevie Wonder, Partridge Family, Four Seasons, and Frank Sinatra.

Michael Hutchence's (INXS) first recording was a version of 'Jingle Bells' recorded for the tiny records that slot into the back of talking dolls.

The Roger Lavern who recorded 'Reindeer Ride' (in the above list) was the keyboard player with the Tornados.

If all the Christmas records ever made were stacked up in the deepest part of the Atlantic Ocean . . . who'd care?

■ PICTURE THIS

The relationship between music and moving pictures, on television or in the cinema, has long been a close one. It blossomed in the rock era so that now rock and pop music are an integral part of the majority of all films and TV programmes, whether in a leading role or merely as a bit-part incidental sound-track. This chapter looks at some aspects of that relationship.

□ Videotheque

Today the promotional video accompanying the release of a single or an LP is practically obligatory. A TV broadcast of a video is probably worth a dozen radio plays, as it reaches a larger audience and is more likely to be remembered by the viewer. The growth in the use of promo videos has occurred in only the past twelve or so years, though its roots go back further than that.

In the early Sixties a machine called a Scopietone made a brief appearance in a handful of clubs and cafés, temporarily replacing the juke-box. In fact, the Scopietone was simply a glorified juke-box with a selection of library film that would be displayed on a screen while a record was playing. Although each disc had its own film, it was not made especially for the song and, likely as not, there was little connection between the lyrics and the imagery.

Later in the decade, after the Scopietone had long since vanished, several of the more popular groups began to make short promotional films to help publicize their new records. These were the forerunners of the video as we know it, but they did not get the widespread broadcast that videos do. Perhaps the best known promo films from the Sixties are the Beatles' *Strawberry Fields Forever* and Cream's *I Feel Free*, which was widely banned because the group dressed up as monks and this was considered blasphemous by some people.

At the start of the Seventies videotape became accessible outside of the television industry and in 1975 the music business found a good use for it. Queen's 'Bohemian Rhapsody' would almost certainly have reached Number One on its musical merits alone, but the spectacular promo video made to accompany it must have been partly responsible for it staying on top for nine weeks. *Top of the Pops* viewers were used to groups performing 'live' in the studio or on in-concert type film clips. Now they saw Messrs Mercury, May, Deacon and Taylor *dramatizing* the song on their screens. The video had arrived.

After Queen showed the way, the competition followed – slowly at first, but it soon picked up momentum. By the end of the decade record companies would at least *consider* a video release with a single. Five years later a record without a video was in the minority. Even the smaller independent labels sometimes had a go at DIY videos.

At the beginning of the Eighties the video juke-box, the modern equivalent of the Scopietone, appeared in some pubs and clubs, but didn't achieve the popularity that was expected.

■ Ten outstanding videos

1. *Bohemian Rhapsody*, Queen, 1975
2. *Cry*, Godley and Creme, 1985
3. *Thriller*, Michael Jackson, 1983
4. *Sledgehammer*, Peter Gabriel, 1986
5. *Who's That Girl?*, Eurythmics, 1983
6. *Ashes to Ashes*, David Bowie, 1980
7. *Vienna*, Ultravox, 1981
8. *Addicted to Love*, Robert Palmer, 1986
9. *Reet Petite*, Jackie Wilson, 1986
10. *She Blinded Me with Science*, Thomas Dolby, 1982

Music TeleVision (MTV), an American cable TV station, brought the importance of videos to the fore. Starting in August 1981 it broadcast pop music videos twenty-four hours a day. Although it includes interviews and live footage, MTV lives and breathes videos – wall to wall and back to back. Music Box gave Britain (well, the Yorkshire area at least) its first taste of this type of programming.

Videos now seem to fit into one of three main categories. Here's a brief selection of videos that slot into each category.

■ Selected videos

□ Animated/arty

Accidents Will Happen, Elvis Costello
Close to the Edit, The Art Of Noise
Cry, Godley and Creme
Road to Nowhere, Talking Heads
Sledgehammer, Peter Gabriel

□ Exotic/erotic

China Girl, David Bowie
Club Tropicana, Wham!
I Want Your Sex, George Michael
Musclebound, Spandau Ballet
Rio, Duran Duran

□ Narrative/dramatic

Ghost Town, Specials
I Don't Like Mondays, Boomtown Rats
Invisible Sun, Police
Under Cover of the Night, Rolling Stones
Vienna, Ultravox

The BBC TV show *The Golden Oldies Picture Show* gave video producers the chance to make videos for songs from before the video age. However, they were restricted to a £1500 budget, far short of the phenomenal sums spent on commercial videos.

Michael Jackson's video *Thriller* was considered such an epic that a video called *The Making of Thriller* was released.

The first LP to have a video version (a video accompanying every track) was Blondie's *Eat to the Beat* in 1979.

The first MP to appear in a pop video was Neil Kinnock, who guested in Tracey Ullman's *My Guy* video.

A short-lived alternative to the video for LPs only was the laser disc, which appeared in the late Seventies. A 12-inch encoded disc was read by a laser and produced sound and vision on a TV screen. This relatively expensive medium was soon superseded by video, but the research and technology were not wasted: they soon reappeared in the form of compact discs.

When Luis Cardenas made a video to promote his 1986 cover of Del Shannon's 'Runaway', he persuaded Del to appear in it as a cop.

□ Hollywood

Hollywood in particular and the movie world in general were quick to capitalize on the success of rock and roll in the Fifties; Elvis was dragged into the film studio with only a couple of hits under his belt, while in Britain Cliff Richard and Tommy Steele were soon captured on celluloid.

In the Sixties practically every beat group in town made at least a fleeting appearance in a lightweight pop film. Usually these films had some sort of plot and the groups appeared as themselves in night-club scenes and the like. However, not all film appearances by rock stars were in cameo roles. Many musicians considered themselves, or were considered by others, to be capable actors and so took roles in non-musical programmes and films, with vastly differing results.

■ Ten musicians turned actors: films

1. Sting in *Dune*
2. Mick Jagger in *Ned Kelly*
3. Bob Dylan in *Pat Garrett and Billy the Kid*
4. David Bowie in *The Man Who Fell to Earth*
5. Sonny Bono in *Escape to Athena*
6. Art Garfunkel in *Bad Timing*

7. Adam Faith in *Stardust*
8. Roger Daltrey in *McVicar*
9. Ringo Starr in *Candy*
10. John Leyton in *The Great Escape*

■ Ten musicians turned actors: TV

1. Hazel O'Connor in *Fighting Back*
2. Adam Faith in *Budgie*
3. Mike Berry in *Are You Being Served?*
4. Elvis Costello in *Scully*
5. Paul Nicholas in *Just Good Friends*
6. Sting in *Brimstone and Treacle*
7. Lulu in *The Secret Diary of Adrian Mole*
8. Helen Shapiro in *Albion Market*
9. Ian Dury in *King of the Ghetto*
10. Tab Hunter in *Barrier Reef*

□ Police and Thieves

In the Eighties the American cop show *Miami Vice* recognized the power of contemporary music in selling television. Apart from getting a renowned rock and jazz keyboardist (Jan Hammer) to provide the theme music, the producers also used rock sound-tracks (for example, Glenn Frey's 'Smuggler's Blues', and the Doors, whose music was used for a whole episode), and, most importantly, cast a number of established pop and rock stars in key roles.

■ Star roles

Phil Collins played a TV games show host.
Little Richard played a shore-line preacher.
David Johannson played himself (more or less) performing at a water-borne party.
Eartha Kitt played and purred.

Ted Nugent played Charlie, the crazy drug dealer.
The Power Station played in a night-club.
Frank Zappa played Fuente, another drugs dealer.
Iggy Pop played yet another drugs dealer.
Sheena Easton joined the show as Sonny's (Don Johnson) wife, a part turned down by T'Pau's Carol Decker.

In the Seventies Don Johnson co-wrote several songs for the Allman Brothers. In the Eighties he released his own solo material.

☐ Tribute to a King

■ Ten actors and actresses playing musicians in biographical films

1. Gary Busey played Buddy Holly in *The Buddy Holly Story*.
2. Kurt Russel played Elvis Presley in *Elvis: The Movie*.
3. Diana Ross played Billie Holiday in *The Billie Holiday Story*.
4. Lou Diamond Phillips played Richie Valens in *La Bamba*.
5. Gary Oldman played Sid Vicious in *Sid and Nancy: Love Kills*.
6. Billy Preston played jazz great W. C. Handy in *St Louis Blues*.
7. James Stewart played Glenn Miller in *The Glenn Miller Story*.
8. Larry Parkes played Al Jolson in *The Al Jolson Story*.
9. Steve Allen played Benny Goodman in *The Benny Goodman Story*.
10. Howard Huntsbury played Jackie Wilson in *La Bamba*.

■ Films featuring groups and artists in guest or cameo roles

1. Tina Turner appeared in *Tommy* as the Acid Queen, possibly one of the most mind-blowing scenes in cinema history.
2. Fats Domino, Johnny Duncan and Glen Campbell all made brief appearances in *Every Which Way You Can*, the sequel to *Every Which Way But Loose*.
3. The Nitty Gritty Dirt Band appeared in *Paint Your Wagon*, which also yielded a double-sided hit for actors Lee Marvin and Clint Eastwood.

4. David Bowie made an appearance in *Christianne F*, a film about a heroin addict, for which he also provided the score.
5. Wacky Sam the Sham popped up in *The Fastest Guitars Alive*.
6. The Pointer Sisters showed up in *Car Wash*, which was actually a vehicle for Rose Royce.
7. Country star Jimmy Buffet cropped up in the modern Western *Rancho Deluxe* performing the delightfully titled 'Why Don't We get Drunk (and Screw)'.
8. The Pretty Things made several appearances at the club in the Norman Wisdom comedy *What's Good for the Goose*.
9. Brinsley Schwarz made a very fleeting appearance in the film *Stardust*. The other band that the film was about, the Straycats (not the Brian Setzer lot), consisted of David Essex, Dave Edmunds, Paul Nicholas, Peter Duncan (later a *Blue Peter* presenter), and Who drummer Keith Moon.
10. Micky Dolenz made an appearance in the 1975 comedy *Keep Off, Keep Off*.
11. Eric Stewart (10 CC) played a youngster in *To Sir with Love*, as did Lulu. This film starred Sidney Poitier, who had also appeared in *Blackboard Jungle*, the film that was responsible for introducing 'Rock Around the Clock' to the world.

■ Sixteen groups or artists who have made guest or cameo appearances in TV series

1. The Swinging Blue Jeans as a Liverpool beat group (good casting that) in *Z Cars*
2. Hazell O'Connor as a pub singer in *Prospects*
3. The Riot Squad in *Emergency Ward 10*
4. Phil Spector in *Mission Impossible*
5. Mike Sarne as an eccentric sculptor in *Man in a Suitcase*
6. Midge Ure as a busker playing 'Streets of London' in AD 2000 in *Lenny Henry Tonight*
7. Harry Nilsson as a folk singer in *The Ghost and Mrs Muir*
8. Lonnie Donegan as a petty thief and copper's nark in *Rockcliffe's Babies*
9. Toyah as a punk (more inspired casting) in *Shoestring*
10. Adam Ant as a hired killer in *The Equalizer*
11. Commander Cody and his Lost Planet Airmen in *Police Woman*

12. Liverpool group The Touch as themselves in *What Now*
13. Phil Spector and the Boyce and Hart Band in *I Dream of Jeannie*
14. Sonny and Cher as a dress cutter and a model respectively in *The Man from U.N.C.L.E.*
15. Beatles copyists the Wellingtons as the Mosquitos in top Sixties US series *Gilligan's Island*
16. Laura Branigan in *Chips*

☐ Sing Don't Speak

■ Ten hits by actors

1. 'Wanderin' Star', Lee Marvin
2. 'I Talk to the Trees', Clint Eastwood
3. 'If', Telly Savalas
4. 'Under the Boardwalk', Bruce Willis
5. 'Love Me Tender', Richard Chamberlain
6. 'Goodbye Cruel World', James Darren
7. 'Windmills of Your Mind', Noel Harrison
8. 'McArthur Park', Richard Harris
9. 'Let's Get Together', Hayley Mills
10. 'Tammy', Debbie Reynolds

Although David Soul had been singing for years, it was only after he found fame through his acting role in *Starsky and Hutch* that his records began to sell. In all he had five UK hits, including two Number Ones.

Gary Holton, best known as an actor (*Auf Wiedersehn Pet*), was in a Seventies group called the Heavy Metal Kids. Later, he was in a group called the Actors and in the Greedy Bastards, forerunners of UK hitsters the Greedies ('Jingle Bells'). When Gary played for them the line-up was Holton, Rat Scabies, Gary Moore, Phil Lynott and Jimmy Bain. Gary also performed solo; his single 'Catch a Falling Star' was released shortly before his premature death.

Paul Nicholas, star of *Just Good Friends* among other things, was in the film *Stardust*. Under the pseudonym Oscar, he recorded David

Bowie's 'Over the Garden Wall', which is one of the earliest covers of a Bowie song. Paul also played piano for Screaming Lord Sutch. In the late Eighties he co-wrote (with Peter Davies) a screenplay for Paul Breeze's excellent rock novel *While My Guitar Gently Weeps*, a film for which Sting was rumoured to be playing the lead role; at the time of writing the project has yet to materialize.

Lloyd Grossman, the roving snooper on ITV's *Through the Keyhole*, once had a US hit as a rock guitarist. He was the man behind Jet Bronx and the Forbidden's pseudo-punk hit 'Ain't Doin' Nothin'', and he wrote for various rock publications in the Sixties and Seventies.

The Standells' member Larry Tamblyn is the brother of actor Russ Tamblyn. Among the many songs the Standells recorded is 'Wild Thing', written by Chip Taylor, who is the brother of actor Jon Voight.

Actor Norman Rossington has the unique distinction of appearing in both an Elvis and a Beatles movie: *Double Trouble* and *A Hard Day's Night*.

Joining Telly Savalas and David Soul in the list of singing TV cops is Dennis Weaver, alias McCloud in the series of that name, who has made several records. Comedian Billy Howard spotted this trend and made the spoof record 'King of the Cops' (to the tune of Roger Miller's 'King of the Road'), which featured imitations of many TV cops.

In 1972 Roberta Flack's three-year-old flop single 'The First Time Ever I Saw Your Face' became a hit after featuring in the film *Play Misty For Me* – 'Misty' being the song made famous by Johnny Mathis.

The voice-over on Michael Jackson's *Thriller* video is by Vincent Price.

☐ Baby Take a Bow

■ Ten child actors who became musicians

1. Davy Jones (Monkees), *Coronation Street*
2. Simon Le Bon (Duran Duran), Persil advertisement, *Tom Brown's Schooldays*

3. Marc Bolan (T Rex), *Orlando*
4. Brinsley Forde (Aswad), *Double Deckers, Please Sir*
5. Ricky Nelson, *The Adventures of Ozzie and Harriet*
6. Peter Noone (Herman's Hermits), *Coronation Street*
7. Patsy Kensit (Eighth Wonder), the film *Hanover Street*
8. Micky Dolenz (Monkees), *Circus Boy*
9. Phil Collins (Genesis), *Oliver!* stage show, Children's Film Foundation films
10. Steve Marriot (Small Faces), various films

□ Celluloid Heroes

■ Thirty songs with an actor's or actress's name in the title

1. 'Robert De Niro's Waiting', Bananarama
2. 'Michael Caine', Madness
3. 'Lee Remick', Go Betweens
4. 'Just Like Oliver Reed', Dentists
5. 'Bette Davis Eyes', Kim Carnes
6. 'I Just Want To Be Like Eddie Murphy', Jokerman
7. 'I Hate Nerys Hughes (from the Heart)', Half Man Half Biscuit
8. 'Jean Harlow', Tidbits
9. 'Brian Rix', Brilliant Corners
10. 'John Wayne Is Big Leggy', Haysi Fantayzee
11. 'Bela Lugosi's Dead', Bauhaus
12. 'James Dean', Eagles
13. 'Marie Provost', Nick Lowe
14. 'He Looks Like Spencer Tracy Now', Deacon Blue
15. 'Bogart to Bowie', Gary McDonald
16. 'Dear Rita Hayworth', New Vaudeville Band
17. 'Omar Sharif's Moustache', Goats Don't Shave
18. 'Tom Baker', Human League
19. 'Who Killed Marilyn?', Glen Danzig
20. 'W. C. Fields', Always
21. 'Bela Lugosi's Party', Dream Boys
22. 'Whatever Happened to Randolph Scott?', Statler Brothers

23. 'Yul Brynner Was a Skinhead', Toy Dolls
24. 'McGoohan's Blues', Roy Harper
25. 'The New John Agar', The Young Fresh Fellows
26. 'Roy Rogers', Elton John
27. 'Spike Milligan's Tape Recorder', Membranes
28. 'Linda Evans', The Walkabouts
29. 'James Dean' (different song to Eagles'), Jets
30. 'Charlton Heston', Stump

There was some obscure German group who recorded 'Build Me a House from the Bones of Cary Grant'; John Peel would remember who they were.

□ Theme One

■ Some TV themes by pop and rock artists

1. 'Profoundly in Love with Pandora', Ian Dury and the Blockheads (*The Secret Diary of Adrian Mole*)
2. 'Because of You', Dexy's Midnight Runners (*Brushstrokes*)
3. 'Big Deal', Bobby G (*Big Deal*)
4. 'In Sickness and in Health', Chas and Dave (*In Sickness and in Health*)
5. 'Turning the Town Red', Elvis Costello (*Scully*)
6. 'Hazell', Maggie Bell (*Hazell*)
7. 'Hi Ho Silver', Jim Diamond (*Boon*)
8. 'Star Cops (It Won't Be Easy)', Justin Hayward (*Star Cops*)
9. 'Jam for World in Action', Shawn Phillips and Blue Weaver (*World in Action*)
10. 'I Could Be So Good for You', Dennis Waterman (*Minder*)

■ Some spin-off records from or about TV series

1. 'I Wanna Be A Flintstone', Screaming Blue Messiahs (*Flintstones*)

2. 'Je T'Aime . . . Moi Non Plus', René and Yvette (*'Allo 'Allo*)
3. 'Nora Batty's Stockings', Compo and Nora Batty (*Last of the Summer Wine*)
4. 'Yogi', The Ivy Three (*Yogi Bear*)
5. 'Oi'll Give It Foive', Janice Nicholls (*Thank Your Lucky Stars*)
6. 'The Bucket of Water Song', The Four Bucketeers (*Tiswas*)
7. 'Arthur Daley ('E's Alright)', Firm (*Minder*)
8. 'Daddy', Pebbles and Bam Bam (*Flintstones*)
9. 'Kookie, Kookie, Lend Me Your Comb', Ed Byrne (*77 Sunset Strip*)
10. 'What Are We Gonna Get 'Er Indoors', Dennis Waterman and George Cole (*Minder*)

□ Music and Lights

Since its birth television has always had programmes for the specialist: from *The Gardening Club* (started 1956) to *The Sky at Night* (1957). Pop and rock music has not been an exception. With the dawn of rock 'n' roll came a string of good and not so good TV pop programmes starting in 1956 with *Cool for Cats* in the UK, and the inclusion of rock 'n' roll performers (for example, Elvis) on general entertainment shows in the States (most notably on *The Ed Sullivan Show* and *The Milton Berle Show*). Here are some facts about ten of the more important TV pop shows of all time.

1. *Top of the Pops* BBC (UK)

The king of them all, *Top of the Pops*, was first broadcast on New Year's Day 1964 and is still showing us all the current pop trends fifty-two weeks of the year (not to mention Christmas specials). BBC entertainments boss Billy Cotton originally saw the show as a rival to *Ready Steady Go*, but even he could not have realized that it would still be running twenty-five years later, having left all opposition – including the most recent, *The Roxy* – way behind.

The first show was broadcast from the Dickinson Road studios in Manchester. The studio was a converted church – something of a contrast to the studio *TOTP* now uses at Television Centre in Shepherds Bush, London. That début was hosted by Jimmy Saville, who would rotate in coming weeks with David Jacobs, Pete Murray and Alan Freeman. Nowadays all the Radio One DJs take a turn hosting the show in pairs. Samantha Juste was the young lady who put the records on the turntable in the early days.

The most famous themes to *TOTP* are: CCS's version of the Led Zeppelin classic 'Whole Lotta Love', which was used for most of the Seventies; Phil Lynott's 'Yellow Pearl', written and produced by Midge Ure; and more recently Paul Hardcastle's 'The Wizard'. Visual entertainment over the years has been provided by various dance troupes, including the Go Jos, Pan's People, Legs And Co., and Zoo.

2. *Ready Steady Go* ITV (UK)

The weekend started here! *Ready Steady Go* was first broadcast on 9 August 1963 and would become synonymous with the Sixties, particularly with the British Mod movement and beat boom. Every major British act, as well as several top American stars, appeared on the show during its three-year run. Cathy McGowan was the best-known presenter but several others also helped out, including guest artists the Rolling Stones. Unlike *Top of the Pops*, some more obscure acts made appearances on *Ready Steady Go*. A lot of rare footage exists from these shows and is now owned by Dave Clark, who made several appearances himself.

Various songs were used as the theme tune, including Manfred Mann's '5-4-3-2-1', and the Who's 'Anyway Anywhere Anyhow'. The last show was broadcast on 23 December 1966.

3. *6'5 Special* BBC (UK)

Making its début at five past six on Saturday 16 February 1957 and presented by Pete Murray and Jo Douglas, *6'5 Special* brought rock 'n' roll into homes right across the UK. The skiffle style title tune was performed by Don Lang and his Frantic Five, who had had a UK hit with 'Cloudburst'. Former boxer Freddie Mills often helped co-present the shows.

As well as the normal weekly shows, there was a *6'5 Special* film, a road tour and several specials, including one in December 1957 that featured the Goons.

6'5 Special was the first pop TV success for producer Jack Good. It ended on 22 November 1958, but twenty-one months was long enough to secure its place in history.

4. *American Bandstand* ABC (US)

Although broadcast locally in Philadelphia since February 1952, *American Bandstand* made its national début on 5 August 1957. It had been hosted since 1956 by Dick Clark, who still presides over this long-running show today. As well as regularly presenting all the great American rock 'n' roll stars, there were *Bandstand* specials, such as the one on 8 January 1962 to celebrate Elvis's twenty-seventh birthday, and the twenty-fifth anniversary show in 1977, which included Chuck Berry, Johnny Rivers, Charlie Daniels and many more.

5. *Cool for Cats* ITV (UK)

The first true pop music programme on British TV was *Cool for Cats*, which began on New Year's Eve 1956. It was hosted by Kent Walton (now best known as a wrestling commentator). The show featured a dance troupe gallivanting about to the latest pop sensations, which actually tended to be people like Rosemary Clooney though rock 'n' roll did get a look in.

6. *The Dick Clark Show* ABC (US)

Dick Clark was undoubtedly the King of Pop TV in the US. This new show started on 15 February 1958, the same day the latest edition of *American Bandstand* had been broadcast earlier on the *same* channel – and Jerry Lee Lewis appeared on both shows.

Dick Clark also took several rock 'n' roll package tours around the States and abroad. Just like the television shows, these caravans featured dozens of rock 'n' roll and R&B acts.

7. *Juke Box Jury* BBC (UK)

This programme ran from 1 June 1959 (although a pilot was broadcast on 4 April 1959) to 27 December 1967, and was different from other pop programmes. Here a jury of four celebrities and chairman David Jacobs listened to a selection of new releases and then voted them a hit or a miss. Each guest was asked to pass comment on the records, which could prove embarrassing, as every week one of the featured acts would be waiting in the wings. The original theme tune was John Barry's 'Hit Or Miss'.

On 16 June 1979 the show was revived for a short run with Noel Edmunds taking over David Jacobs' post, and the likes of John Lydon and Joan Collins sitting on the panel where once it was more likely to be Alma Cogan and David McCallum.

8. *The Old Grey Whistle Test* BBC (UK)

First broadcast on 21 September 1971, this was an attempt to cater for less mainstream musical tastes. The unusual name comes from the story that, in music hall days, if the theatre doorman (traditionally an old, grey-haired man) was whistling a song, then it was likely to be a popular number, presumably because he heard so many songs he whistled only the more memorable ones.

In the Eighties the show adopted the shorter name *The Whistle Test*, but on New Year's Eve 1987, with a look back at its past, the Test stopped Whistling for the last time.

Presenters have included Richard Williams (the first), Whispering Bob Harris, Annie Nightingale, Ian Whitcomb and Andy Kershaw. The most famous theme tune used was Area Code 615's 'Stone Fox Chase'.

9. *The Tube* Channel 4 (UK)

Britain's fourth TV channel, the aptly named Channel 4, launched its first pop show in October 1982. *The Tube*, broadcast live from a studio in Newcastle, quickly established itself as a suitable antidote to the constant stream of Top Forty pop spurted out by *TOTP* every Thursday night. *The Tube* (which ran for one and a half hours each week, much longer than most pop programmes) featured unknown and cult acts as well as the big hitsters: Frankie Goes to Hollywood were signed to ZTT only *after* a performance on *The Tube*.

There were many presenters; the best known are Jools Holland and Paula Yates. It was after Jools said a naughty word in a trailer for the show that the authorities began to get upset with the sometimes controversial programme. It was taken off the air later in 1987.

10. *The Roxy* ITV (UK)

In 1987 ITV launched what they saw as a serious contender for *TOTP*'s throne. *The Roxy* was hosted by David Jensen and Kevin Sharkey, and was originally planned to compete with the BBC's *EastEnders*, but ITV bosses capitulated and it was broadcast at 6.30

p.m. on Tuesdays instead. It featured a string of live bands and videos and was based on the independent radio Media Research and Information Bureau (MRIB) chart, which itself had been launched a few years earlier as a challenge to the BBC/Gallup chart. Neither ruffled the feathers of the BBC half as much as they liked to think they did and *The Roxy* was dropped in 1988 on its first birthday.

■ Some other pop TV shows

Oh Boy (1958)
Drumbeat (1959)
Dig This (1959)
Boy Meets Girl (1959)
Wham (1960)
Thank Your Lucky Stars (1961)
Shindig (1964)
Hullabaloo (1965)
Supersonic (1975)
So It Goes (1976)

■ Ten acts who have had their own TV shows

1. The Monkees
2. Marc Bolan (called *Marc*)
3. The Partridge Family
4. The Osmonds
5. Beatles (American cartoon)
6. Gilbert O'Sullivan
7. Moondogs
8. Bay City Rollers (called *Shang-A-Lang*)
9. Jacksons (cartoon)
10. Flintlock

Tony Wilson, presenter of the punk and new wave programme *So It Goes*, moved on to start the Manchester-based Factory label, which has brought us Joy Division, New Order and A Certain Ratio to name but three. As well as running the label, Wilson continues a parallel career as a news-reader on regional television.

When the Beatles appeared on *The Ed Sullivan Show* in 1964 no incidents of teenage crime were reported anywhere in the United States for the duration of their performance.

Stephen Stills was among the failed applicants for a place in the Monkees.

Bob 'Blockbusters' Holness's daughter Ros was a member of Toto Coelo, while another daughter had a UK hit with 'No No No' under the pseudonym Nancy Nova.

Sheena Easton's success began when she appeared in the BBC documentary *The Big Time* in 1980. A similarly styled programme *In at the Deep End*, in 1987 had presenter Paul Heiney directing a video for Bananarama's 'Trick of the Night'.

Seventies soul group Sweet Sensation made their break on the talent show *New Faces*. Soul songstress Patti Boulaye was the first act to get a maximum 120 points on the same show.

An estimated one-third of the world's population watched the 1973 Elvis TV spectacular *Elvis–Aloha from Hawaii via Satellite*.

Hazell Dean – disco singer and darling of the gay clubs – was one of the many singers on the appalling *One More Time* (BBC 2, 1977), which featured thirty minutes of non-stop rehashed pop songs.

□ Sold My Soul for Rock 'n' Roll

Since the dawn of television advertising (1941 in the US, 1955 in the UK), advertisers have realized the importance of product identity hooks. These normally take the form of a slogan, a jingle or a piece of music that becomes identified with a particular product. The first UK TV commercial, for Gibbs SR toothpaste, used a simple flute and violin piece, but as time went on advertisers began to get more ambitious. The first piece of TV advertising music to enter the UK charts was Cliff Adams and his orchestra's 'Lonely Man Theme', which was familiar as the music to the Strand Cigarettes advert.

The first pop music to be used for a UK advert came in 1963, when cartoon Beatles were used to plug Nestlé's Jellimalled bar. Later, the

Rolling Stones provided the music for a Rice Krispies ad that spoofed *Juke Box Jury*. In 1964 in America a group called the Hondells recorded Mike Curb's jingle 'You Meet the Nicest People on a Honda' for a TV advert for that product. As the ad was a success, Curb wrote 'Little Honda' for the group and it was a US hit that year.

In the late Sixties and early Seventies pop music began to be used in adverts quite frequently, and several tunes written specially for adverts were adapted and extended into hit pop songs. The best example of this is Roger Greenaway and Roger Cook's 1971 jingle for Coca Cola, which became the massive hit 'I'd Like to Teach the World to Sing' for the New Seekers. In 1986 the whole concept of using pop in adverts came to a head when a string of adverts for Levi jeans returned several old soul/R&B standards to the charts.

■ Ten hit singles from songs originally written for advertisements

1. 'I'd Like to Teach the World to Sing', New Seekers (Coca Cola)
2. 'I Put My Old Blue Jeans On', David Dundas (Brutus jeans)
3. 'It's the Real Thing', Fortunes (Coca Cola)
4. 'Gertcha', Chas and Dave (Courage beer)
5. 'Dancin' Easy', Danny Williams (Martini)
6. 'Rollin' On', Cirrus (Yorkie chocolate bar)
7. 'Hello Summertime', Bobby Goldsboro (Coca Cola)
8. 'Step into a Dream', White Plains (Butlins Holiday Camp)
9. 'Music to Watch Girls Go By', Bob Crewe Generation (Diet Cola)
10. 'Don't Be a Dummy', John Du Cann (Lee Cooper jeans)

Gary Numan was the original choice to record 'Don't Be a Dummy', but he was unavailable or unwilling and so former Atomic Rooster vocalist John Du Cann gained his one and only solo hit.

■ Ten hit singles used in their original version in advertisements

1. 'Let's Stick Together', Bryan Ferry (Start cereal)
2. 'Mr Soft', Cockney Rebel (Soft Mints)
3. 'Who Are You', Who (Renault cars)
4. 'Lean on Me', Bill Withers (Sheba cat food)

5. 'Tubular Bells', Mike Oldfield (Milk Marketing Board)
6. 'Money', Flying Lizards (Halifax Building Society)
7. 'We Can Work It Out', Beatles (Hewlett-Packard Organization)
8. 'You've Got the Power', WIN (McEwans Lager)
9. 'I Can't Let Maggie Go', Honeybus (Nimble Bread)
10. 'Fever', Peggy Lee (British Coal)

■ Ten hit singles adapted by advertisers to advertise their products

1. 'She's Not There' (originally recorded by the Zombies), British Telecom Radio-pagers
2. 'Bobby's Girl' (Susan Maughn), Smith's Crisps
3. 'Keep a Knockin'' (Little Richard), Bird's Eye Vegetables and Thomson's Directory
4. 'You're the One That I Want' (John Travolta and Olivia Newton-John), Kattomeat
5. 'Get a Job' (Silhouettes), Brook Street Employment Agency
6. 'Da Da Da' (Trio), Ariston washing machines
7. 'Smoke Gets in Your Eyes' (Platters), Esso Blue Paraffin
8. 'Rebel Yell' (Billy Idol), KP Peanuts
9. 'Bread and Butter' (Newbeats), Little Chef eateries
10. 'Windmills of Your Mind' (Noel Harrison), Great Mills DIY Centres

■ Five records used by Levi jeans

1. 'I Heard It through the Grapevine', Marvin Gaye
2. 'Wonderful World', Sam Cooke
3. 'When a Man Loves a Woman', Percy Sledge
4. 'Let Your Love Flow', Bellamy Brothers
5. 'Love's Great Adventure', Ultravox

In 1967 Jefferson Airplane did a series of five radio adverts for Levi.

The Beach Boys seem a popular choice for use in adverts. Their songs, or adaptations of them, have been used several times: 'Good Vibrations' (Crunchie, Sunkist Orange Juice), 'Californian Girls' (British Caledonian, Clairol), 'Do It Again' (Thompsons Holidays).

David Bowie's 'Crystal Japan' was used for a Japanese whisky advert, while Madness found success in that country advertising cars with 'Driving in My Car', and the Pet Shop Boys' 'West End Girls' was used to advertise Toshiba cars there.

Mark Price, the young boy in the famous Hovis adverts, later became a session drummer and worked with Nik Kershaw. In 1987 he joined All About Eve.

Bruce Springsteen turned down a reported offer of $3 (£1.6) million for the rights to use 'Born in the USA' in a General Motors commercial. The highest reported fee for a thirty-second advert is the $1.5 million (£830,000) Boy George got for selling gin on Japanese TV.

While filming an advert for Pepsi Cola Michael Jackson's hair caught alight. He was not seriously hurt.

Famous appearances by pop stars in adverts include Pete Murphy (Maxwell Tapes), Bob Geldof (Wilkinson Sword, milk), Roger Daltrey (American Express), Tina Turner (Pepsi) and Smiley Culture (National Westminster). In 1987 Britvic launched a mammoth advert for their orange juice. Filmed in black and white with Sixties-style scenes and props, the advert used Dusty Springfield's 'I Only Want to Be with You' and featured Dusty, the Tremeloes, Scott Walker, Sandie Shaw, Eric Burdon and others. The voice-over was by Adam Faith.

The Human League covered a Gordon's Gin cinema advert on their LP *Reproduction*.

Run DMC recorded a single called 'My Adidas'. It was uncommissioned and the sports company loved the free publicity.

□ A Little Bit of Soap

○ EastEnders

In February 1985 the BBC launched a major new soap opera in an (ultimately successful) attempt to overthrow the monopoly of viewing figures held by Granada's *Coronation Street*. The BBC's secret weapon was *EastEnders*, which chronicled the lives and times of the inhabitants of Albert Square in the East London borough of Walford. Although soap operas and soap opera stars had previously released spin-off records, it was *EastEnders* that took that line of marketing to its extremes, as the following reveals.

The theme tune was written by Simon May and Leslie Osborne, and was their second attempt; the first was rejected. For the twice-weekly programme the theme is performed as an instrumental by the Simon May Orchestra. It was originally released as a single in the UK in February 1985 and though it reached only Number 76, it spent well over a year in the Top 200.

In August 1986 Anita Dobson, who plays sometime pub landlady Angie Watts, released a vocal version of the theme tune titled 'Anyone Can Fall in Love', on which she was backed by the Simon May Orchestra. The original theme was on the B side while the 12-inch disc had an extra track, 'Julia's Theme': Julia being Julia Smith, the show's producer and co-creator. The record climbed to Number Four in the UK charts. Anita also released an LP entitled *On My Own* on Telstar Records, which included, among other things, a version of Eric Clapton's 'Let It Grow' (from *461 Ocean Boulevard*). In 1987 Anita worked with Queen guitarist Brian May.

In December 1986 the Shadows released their own distinctive version of the '*EastEnders* Theme', backed with a version of the theme tune to another popular BBC soap, *Howards' Way*. That same month the BBC released a record credited to Top of the Box that featured disco mixes of the themes to *EastEnders*, *Howards' Way*, *Dynasty* and *Dallas* under the umbrella title 'Soapy'. In 1987 a group called Micron released a scratch version of the theme that was mixed with Whistle's 'Just Buggin'' and featured rap type vocals about the goings on in Albert Square. The Button Down Brass also did their own medley version of the *EastEnders* and *Howards' Way* themes.

■ Theme recordings

'*EastEnders* Theme'/'Julia's Theme', Simon My Orchestra (BBC) Feb. 1985

'Anyone Can Fall in Love'/'*EastEnders'* Theme', Anita Dobson with the Simon May Orchestra (BBC) Aug. 1986

'EastEnders' Theme'/'*Howards' Way* Theme', Shadows (Polydor) Dec. 1986
'Soapy'/'Al's Way', Top of the Box (BBC) Dec. 1986
EastEnders, Micron (SG) Jan. 1987

In addition to these variations on the theme there are several spin-offs from the programme. These range from records actually connected with the show, through records by stars from the show, to records about the show or someone in it.

In 1986 a large part of the story-line centred around several of the youngsters in the programme forming their own band. The group originally consisted of Simon Wicks (real name Nick Berry) on keyboards, Ian Beale (Adam Woodyat) on drums, Eddy Hunter (Simon Henderson) on guitar and Kelvin Carpenter (Paul J. Medford) and Sharon Watts (Letitia Dean), vocals. The band were 'managed' by the belligerent Harry (Gareth Potter) who owned most of the instruments and equipment. The original name of the group was Dog Market but they changed it to the Banned, which Kelvin claimed was an original name. No doubt the Harvest punk group who revamped the Syndicate of Sound's 'Little Girl' in1977 would dispute that claim. The song the *EastEnders'* group were most often seen rehearsing was the Real Thing's 'You to Me Are Everything', which had recently enjoyed a real life chart renaissance. Simon 'Wicksy' Wicks left the group (as did a girl-friend of Harry, who had been helping him run things) before they entered a talent contest, which resulted in the band splitting up. One real life single resulted from this story-line, though it was credited only to Paul J. Medford and Letitia Dean. The song, 'Something out of Nothing', was written by Simon May, and Bradley and Stuart James.

A further story-line saw Wicksy, then a barman and occasional pianist at the Queen Victoria pub, compose a tune called 'Every Loser Wins', which became a favourite with the recently jilted Lofty (Tom Watt). In reality it was written by May, James and James, went to Number One and was one of the best-selling singles of 1986.

Much of the action in Albert Square takes place in the aforementioned Queen Victoria pub, where a juke-box can be heard playing constantly. The BBC tried to take advantage of this by promoting Barry Blood's soft-rock 'Killin' Time', which was released on BBC Records. Despite several juke-box plays, the single failed to chart. Other juke-box favourites in the Queen Vic included the Animals'

'House of the Rising Sun' and Dire Straits' 'Sultans of Swing'. In 1987 the Stranglers' 'Shakin' Like a Leaf' got more plays on the Vic juke-box than it did on Radio One.

Gay young record stall owner Barry has revealed his taste as Cream and John Mayall (though in real life actor Gary Hailes is much more likely to be found dancing in London's Town and Country Club). Former brewery manager Mr Willmott-Brown (William Boyde) has displayed his talent on the guitar. British R&B star Zoot Money appeared in the series as ageing rocker Johnny Earthquake, but he didn't perform. After this appearance he stayed with the BBC as musical adviser on the award-winning series *Tutti Frutti*.

Danielle Dax, actress and solo singer, previously with the Lemon Kittens, turned down a bit part in the *EastEnders* pilot.

Tom Watt (Lofty) was working on a rap version of the theme tune but was usurped by Anita Dobson's version. He also recorded a version of Bob Dylan's 'Subterranean Homesick Blues' as a single, but distribution problems meant it never reached the shops. However, the video did get a television airing and Tom could be seen gallivanting with the likes of New Order.

Letitia Dean released two solo singles and one with the group Young World before *EastEnders* started.

Oscar James (Tony Carpenter) was in the 1976 stage version of Harry Nilsson's *The Point* at the Mermaid Theatre in London.

Simon Henderson (Eddy Hunter) used to drum for the rock band Tarazara.

Gareth Potter now plays with the Welsh punk group Traddodiad Ofnus.

Wendy Richard (Pauline Fowler) remade her 1962 hit 'Come Outside' with Mike Berry, the singer and her fellow actor from the BBC comedy series *Are You Being Served?* She originally recorded the song with Mike Sarne.

Ross Davidson (Andy O'Brien) also released a single but this was after he had been killed off from the series.

■ Spin-off recordings

'Can't Get a Ticket for the World Cup'/'Right Fine Don't Panic', Peter Dean (Pete Beale) (Portrait/CBS) June 1986

'Subterranean Homesick Blues'/'I Had Too Much To Drink Last

Night', Tom Watt (George 'Lofty' Holloway) (Watt The Duck/EMI DUCK) June 1986
'Every Loser Wins', Nick Berry (Simon 'Wicksy' Wicks) (BBC) Oct. 1986
'Something Out of Nothing'/'Times Square', Paul J. Medford and Letitia Dean (Kelvin Carpenter and Sharon Watts) (BBC) Oct. 1986
'Jigsaw Puzzle', Ross Davidson (Andy O'Brien) (Spartan) Nov. 1986
'Love Riding High'/'Original Sin', Oscar James (Tony Carpenter) (10) Nov. 1986
'Come Outside'/'Give It a Try', Wendy Richard (Pauline Fowler) and Mike Berry (WEA) Nov. 1986
'London'/'Where Is Love?', June Brown (Dot Cotton) (MBS) Jan. 1987
'Dirty Den'/'Dirty Rag', Whisky and Sofa/David Rose (Spartan) April 1986
'Talking of Love', Anita Dobson (Angie Watts) July 1987
'Worlds Apart for Christmas', Michael Cashman (Colin) Dec. 1987
'I Dream of Christmas', Anita Dobson (Angie) Dec. 1987
'Lonely Boy', Gary Hailes (Barry) June 1988

For Christmas 1986 the cast recorded a 'sing along' album of old-fashioned songs, supposedly performed in the bar of the Queen Vic.

In June 1987 the Queen Victoria had a video juke-box installed. The first video played on it was Broken English's *Coming on Strong*.

In 1987 the Reverend Donald Lugg, vicar of St Paul's, Margate in Kent, wrote a hymn using the *EastEnders* theme as the tune.

The Dagmar, the Queen Vic's wine bar rival, favours Level 42 music.

Peter Dean (Pete Beale) appeared in the Sex Pistols' film *The Great Rock and Roll Swindle* as a club bouncer.

In 1988 Willy the Pug released 'The Woof Woof Rap'.

○ Crossroads

Crossroads was first broadcast in the Midlands only in November 1964 and was finally fully networked in 1972. It portrayed the lives of the guests and employees at a motel in Kings Oak near Birmingham.

The original theme tune was written by Tony Hatch and performed by the Tony Hatch Orchestra. In 1975 Paul McCartney and Wings recorded their own version of the theme, which was used on television for a time and appeared on the Wings LP *Venus and Mars*. Shona Lindsay recorded 'Goodbye', a vocal version of the theme, in 1988.

Several other songs have featured in the long-running series, which broadcast its final episode in April 1988, including the following:

'Where Will You Be?', Sue Nicholls (who played waitress Marilyn Gates) (Pye) 1968
'Born with a Smile on My Face', Stephanie De Sykes with Rain (Bradleys) 1974
'Summer of My Life', Simon May (Pye) 1976
'Benny's Theme', Paul Henry (Benny, the simpleton garage hand) and the Mayson Glen Orchestra (Pye) 1978
'More than in Love', Kate Robbins (RCA) 1981

'Summer of My Life' and 'More than in Love' were both written by Simon May, who is undoubtedly the king of British soap opera music.

Kate Robbins played a budding pop star in the series. In real life she is Paul McCartney's second cousin and is better known as a comedienne and impressionist. She also writes songs (including the theme to *Surprise Surprise*) and is married to Keith Attack, who, with his brother Tim, was in Child and later in David Cassidy's backing group.

In late 1987, after it was known the show was to be axed, an all-star cast assembled to record the farewell song, 'Cry of the Innocent'. It was sung to the *Crossroads* theme with lyrics by executive producer Bill Smethurst.

○ Coronation Street

Coronation Street started on 9 December 1960 and was fully networked on 3 May 1961. It revolves around the lives of the inhabitants of Coronation Street in a suburb of Manchester. The distinctive theme (performed on the cornet) was written by Eric Spear, who died in 1966 and thus never saw much of the thousands of pounds earned by his composition, which is the longest running theme music for a UK drama series.

Two of the songs featured in this twice-weekly soap opera were:

'Not Too Little, Not Too Much', Chris Sandford (who played Walter Potts) (Decca) 1963
'Dreaming Time'/'Moments of Pleasure', Bill Maynard (Decca) 1970

Both Davy Jones of the Monkees and Peter Noone of Herman's Hermits appeared in *Coronation Street* as child actors.

In December 1966 the cast of *Coronation Street* recorded an LP called *The Coronation Street Cast Sing at The Rovers Return*. In December 1987 they released *Coronation Street – The Album*, which included Bet Lynch singing 'These Boots Are Made for Walking', and Jack Duckworth with 'On the Street Where You Live'.

Pat and Greg Kane of Hue And Cry visited the *Coronation Street* set and allegedly got trapped inside The Rovers Return.

○ General soap and music trivia

Nick Pentelow, son of *Emmerdale Farm* actor Arthur Pentelow (Henry Wilks), is a top session saxophonist and has worked with Nick Lowe amongst others.

A song by indie band Fields of the Nephilim featured in *Emmerdale Farm* in a (failed) bid to give the programme street cred in 1987.

Clive Hornby (Jack Sugden in *Emmerdale Farm*) was in the popular Liverpool beat group the Dennisons, who hadUK hits with 'Be My Girl' and 'Walking the Dog'.

In March 1986 an LP titled *Music from Emmerdale Farm Church* was released. Proceeds went to the Save The Children Fund.

Sixties songstress Helen Shapiro had a regular part in the ill-fated *Albion Market*.

In 1987 Kylie Minogue (Charlene Mitchell in *Neighbours*) had an Australian Number One with a cover of 'The Locomotion'. Her UK career was launched in early 1988 with the Stock, Aitken and Waterman song 'I Should Be So Lucky'.

In real life Elaine Smith (Daphne in *Neighbours*), Paul Keane (Des), Peter O'Brien (Shane), and Alan Dale (Jim Robinson) formed the group Suitably Rough.

A character in *Neighbours* received a cassette copy of the Stranglers' LP *Aural Sculpture* as a birthday present (now that is trivial). Several posters advertising punk and indie bands, particularly British ones, have adorned the bedroom walls of various *Neighbours* characters. In fact a Sex Pistols' 'Never Mind the Bollocks' poster was quite clearly seen in early episodes, something Mary Whitehouse obviously missed.

In 1987 the Housemartins visited the *Brookside* set.

Several pop singers have appeared in American soaps . . . as pop singers: Apollonia and Melba Moore were in *Falcon Crest* and Lisa Hartman was in *Knotts Landing*. Rumours abounded that Linda Ronstadt would take a role in *Falcon Crest*.

Rick Springfield used to act in the American soap *General Hospital* before making music his main career.

☐ Solid Bond in Your Heart

The novels of Ian Fleming concerning the activities of Commander James Bond of the British Secret Service spawned a string of successful films starting with *Dr No* in 1962. While the 'James Bond Theme', written by Monty Norman, features heavily in these films, all since *Dr No* have had their own theme specially written for them. In most cases the music for the theme songs was written by film composer and pop instrumental combo leader John Barry, who also provided incidental music for all Bond films after *Dr No*, that one being scored by Monty Norman. Lyrics for the theme songs were generally provided by a guest lyricist and the song performed by a well-known group or artist. The table below lists them all. James Bond was played by Sean Connery for the first five and seventh films, George Lazenby for the sixth, Roger Moore for numbers eight to fourteen inclusive and Timothy Dalton hence.

Songs from the Bond films

Film	Theme song	Artist	Writer
Dr No	'James Bond Theme'	John Barry	Monty Norman
From Russia with Love	'From Russia with Love'	Matt Monro	Lionel Bart
Goldfinger	'Goldfinger'	Shirley Bassey	John Barry, Anthony Newley and Leslie Bricusse
Thunderball	'Thunderball'	Tom Jones	John Barry and Don Black
You Only Live Twice	'You Only Live Twice'	Nancy Sinatra	John Barry and Leslie Bricusse
On Her Majesty's Secret Service	'All the Time in the World'	Louis Armstrong	John Barry and Hal David
Diamonds Are Forever	'Diamonds Are Forever'	Shirley Bassey	John Barry and Don Black
Live and Let Die	'Live and Let Die'	Wings	Paul McCartney

☐ Film	☐ Theme song	☐ Artist	☐ Writer
The Man with the Golden Gun	'The Man with the Golden Gun'	Lulu	John Barry, Monty Norman and Don Black
The Spy Who Loved Me	'Nobody Does It Better'	Carly Simon	Marvin Hamlisch and Carol Bayer Sager
Moonraker	'Moonraker'	Shirley Bassey	John Barry and Hal David
For Your Eyes Only	'For Your Eyes Only'	Sheena Easton	Michael Leeson and Bill Conti
Octopussy	'All Time High'	Rita Coolidge	John Barry and Tim Rice
A View to a Kill	'A View to a Kill'	Duran Duran	John Barry and Duran Duran
The Living Daylights	'The Living Daylights'	A-ha	John Barry and Pal Waktaar

In addition to the above films there were two James Bond spin-offs. The first was *Casino Royale*, which, although based on a Fleming novel, was something of a spoof. It starred David Niven as the suave spy and the theme song, 'The Look of Love', was performed by Dusty Springfield. Other music included Herb Alpert and his Tijuana Brass with 'Casino Royale Theme' and an orchestral theme called 'Never Fear, Mr Bond Is Here'. The other film was 1983's *Never Say Never Again*, which saw Sean Connery return to the role, although the film was not made by the team responsible for all the other Bond movies (Harry Saltzman and Cubby Broccoli). The title song to this film was sung by Lani Hall.

Among the groups who have covered the James Bond theme are Johnny and the Hurricanes (Big Top 3146) and Billy Strange (Vogue/ Vocalion N 9228). John Barry's own version appears on the Columbia label (DB 4898). Covers of other theme songs from Bond movies include: George Bean, 'From Russia with Love'; Bachelors, 'Diamonds Are Forever'; Mantovani, 'You Only Live Twice'; the Scientists, 'You Only Live Twice'; and Johnny Rivers, 'Casino Royale'.

The American version of the Beatles' *Help!* LP features a sixteen-second snatch of the Bond theme.

Bond's service number is 007 (00 being a licence to kill) and was picked up in several songs, notably Desmond Dekker's '007', Nitty Gritty's '007 in Africa', and Jax 'Oh Oh Seven Licensed to Chill'. The latter is a 'house' song that features dialogue from the films.

The Pretenders supplied two tracks to the *Living Daylights* soundtrack LP under the semi-pseudonym Pretenders for 007. The two tracks were 'If There Was A Man', and 'Where Has Everybody Gone?'.

□ I Spy for the FBI

A selection of records connected with some of the top UK and US spy series of the Sixties

1. 'Secret Agent Man', Johnny Rivers (Imperial) March 1966

Written by Steve Barri and P. F. Sloan (the Fantastic Baggies), this was an American Number Three in 1966. It was about, and used as the title music to, the US screening of the British series *Dangerman*, retitled *Secret Agent Man* in the US. The series featured Patrick McGoohan as agent John Drake. The song has since been covered by Devo and Bruce Willis.

2. 'Kinky Boots', Patrick McNee and Honor Blackman (Decca) February 1964

A spin-off disc from *The Avengers* in which McNee played John Steed, the all-English investigator and spy, and Blackman played Cathy Gale, his first female assistant. Cherry Red re-issued this record in 1983.

3. 'The Man from U.N.C.L.E.', Gallants (Capitol) August 1965

4. 'The Man from U.N.C.L.E.', Challengers (Vocalion) November 1965

Just two of the multitude of covers of the theme from the US series *The Man from U.N.C.L.E.* (United Network Command of Law Enforcement). The men from U.N.C.L.E. were Ilya Kuryakin played by David McCallum, and Napoleon Solo played by Robert Vaughn.

5. '*Dangerman* Theme', Red Price Combo (Parlophone) June 1961

A cover version of the theme used on UK and other non-US screenings of *Dangerman*. This programme is hailed as innovative for its use of gadgets and is seen as a direct influence on the James Bond films; a role, incidentally, that Patrick McGoohan refused.

6. 'Main Theme from *The Saint*', Danny Davis Orchestra (MGM)

The Saint gave Roger Moore his first major spy role. It was as Simon Templar (the Saint) that Moore developed his chic, suave personality and the preference for fast cars that he would take to the role of James Bond in the Seventies.

7. 'The Baron', Ted Astley Orchestra (Decca) April 1966

In the British TV series *The Baron*, based fairly loosely on John Creasey's books, the Baron, a.k.a. John Mannering (played by Steve Forrest), was American, single and rather a good boy – a London-based millionaire antiques dealer who spent rather a lot of time solving crimes. In Creasey's books (sometimes written under the alias Anthony Morton) he is English, married, and an ex-burglar, albeit a Raffles-like one.

8. '*Dangerman* Theme'/'*Saint* Theme', Edwin Astley Orchestra (RCA) 1965

Before changing his name to the more trendy Ted, Edwin Astley was musical director on *Dangerman* and wrote the theme, which is more correctly titled 'High Wire'. He carried out similar duties on *The Saint*.

9. 'Theme from *The Avengers*', Laurie Johnson Orchestra (Pye) 1966

One of television's finest theme tune writers and performers with the best known of the various themes used on *The Avengers* over the years.

10. 'I Helped Patrick McGoohan Escape', The Times (Artpop) 1983

Showing that the influence of 'cult' TV lives on. The Times' own song refers to the British television classic *The Prisoner*, in which McGoohan plays Number Six, a former spy held against his will by unknown captors who constantly demand 'information'. The series, filmed largely in the holiday village of Portmeirion, is now highly acclaimed. The Times included former members of the Teenage Film Stars, the O'Levels, and the Television Personalities.

In 1987 the James Taylor Quartet released a mini-LP that contained versions of the '*Mission Impossible* Theme', 'Goldfinger' and Sixties ballad 'Alfie'.

Much of the incidental music used in *The Prisoner* was written specially for the series by Albert Elms, though some Bizet was also used. The final episode, *Fall Out*, made dramatic use of the Beatles' 'All You Need Is Love', and the Negro spiritual 'Dem Dry Bones'.

In May 1986 Pete Townshend married Edwin Astley's daughter Karen, a costume designer. Virginia Astley, another of the composer's daughters, was a member of The Ravishing Beauties group.

In 1987 *The Tube* filmed a special *Prisoner* spoof at Portmeirion with bands such as XTC and Siouxsie and the Banshees. XTC dressed like characters from the series for the video of their single, 'The Meeting Place'.

Dangerman and *Prisoner* star Patrick McGoohan directed *Catch My Soul*, the rock remake of *Othello*, with a screenplay by Jack Good.

As a child, Dave Stewart of the Eurythmics had a black dog called Napoleon Solo, and Shirley Holliman, late of Wham! and now half of Pepsi and Shirley, has a Dobermann called Emma Peel.

The Pretenders' October 1986 video for 'Don't Get Me Wrong' included footage of Patrick McNee as John Steed and Chrissie Hynde as a Cathy Gale type character.

David McCallum had a minor UK hit with the song 'Communication'. Third *Avengers* girl Linda Thorson had a French Number One with 'Here I Am'. Honor Blackman failed to make the charts with her 'Before Today', as did McCallum with 'In the Garden (under the Trees)'.

Splodgenessabounds recorded a little ditty called 'Simon Templar's Bum'.

Ilya Kuryakin has proved a popular subject in song. In 1987 the Cleaners from Venus (including Captain Sensible guesting on guitar) recorded 'Ilya Kuryakin', while back in 1965 Angela and the Fans (actually Alma Cogan) crooned 'Love Ya Ilya', and a group called the Crystalites also recorded a song called 'Ilya Kuryakin'.

In one episode of the American series *Get Smart* a group called the Sacred Cows performed a song called 'Kill Kill Kill'. This song was covered in 1986 by the Painters and Decoraters.

Dean Martin made a series of light-hearted spy films in the Sixties playing the character Mat Helms. At the end of *The Ambushers* (1967) Mat has to 'instruct' a new recruit in the art of seduction. He puts a copy of 'Everybody Loves Somebody' by Dean Martin (aka Mat Helm) on the record player but gets no response from the girl. He then plays 'Strangers in the Night' by his great friend and rival Frank Sinatra and is immediately pounced upon by the nubile young lady. Mat's response: 'Do you really like Perry Como that much?'

American songstress Julie London made a guest appearance in *The Man from U.N.C.L.E.* film *The Helicopter Spies*. Another *U.N.C.L.E.* film, *The Karate Killers*, featured the group Every Mother's Son performing 'Come on Down to My Boat'.

In 1987 Shannie G rapped over the *Mission Impossible* theme.

Dr Feelgood showed their interest in *The Prisoner* by calling an LP *Be Seeing You*, which is a catch-phrase in the series. The record was produced by Number Six and engineered by Number Two, two characters from the series.

Batman

MGM's *Batman* was one of the most popular of the American super-hero series. The distinctive theme was written and originally performed by Neil Hefti, and has been recorded by many others including the Bruce and Robin Rockers, Link Wray, the Gallants, Jan and Dean, the Dynamic Duo, the Riddlers, the Who, the Jam, and the Marketts.

Other Batman records include:

'Batman and His Grandmother', Dickie Goodman
'Let's Send Batman to Vietnam', Seeds of Euphoria
'Bango to the Batmobile', Todd Terry Project
'Batman and Robin', Adam West
'Batman to the Rescue', Laverne Baker
'Who Stole the Batmobile', Gotham City Crimefighters
'The Riddler', Frank Gorshin
'Batman', Wayne Denning and the Washingtons

Frank Gorshin was one of two actors to play the Riddler in the series. Leslie Gore ('It's My Party') once played a villainess in the series.

I'm the Urban Spaceman

The popular American sci-fi series *Star Trek*, which chronicles the voyages of the Starship *Enterprise*, has had references made to it in several songs. Check out the following and spot the references.

'Amityville', Lovebug Starsky
'William Shatner', Bodines
'99 Red Balloons', Nena
'Boops (Here to Go)', Sly and Robbie

'Where's Captain Kirk', Spizzenergi
'Spock's Missing', Athletico Spizz
'Space Rape', Zodiac Mindwarp and the Love Reaction
'Trini Lopez', Yeh Yeh No
'Captain Kirk's Disco Track', the Keys
'Dr Spock', 2 Vulcans
'The Ballad of James T. Kirk', the Jurassics

. . . and of course the 1987 UK Number One 'Star Trekkin'' by the Firm, not unlike a 1977 (unrecorded) song by the Norfolk Trayned Bandes.

Star Trek premiered on US TV the same week as *The Monkees*.

Sean Penn's dad, Leo, directed the *Star Trek* episode *The Enemy Within* (he also worked on *Lost in Space*).

T'Pau take their name from a Vulcan states-person in *Star Trek*.

□ Who Comes to Boogie?

And now a selection of records connected with the BBC's *Dr Who* series, the longest running science fiction television serial in the world.

1. '*Dr Who* Theme', Ron Grainer and the BBC Radiophonic Workshop (Decca)

The famous theme was written and performed by Australian-born Ron Grainer with help from several boxes of BBC tricks. The tune has been used to open the show since it was first broadcast on 23 November 1963, and was first issued as a single in February 1964. Although the basic tune has remained the same over the years, there have been minor alterations and remixes on at least seven occasions. Grainer died in 1981 and recent updates have been done by people like Dominic Glynn.

2. 'Dr Who', Mankind (Pinnacle)

A 1978 discofied version of the theme tune, this record reached Number Twenty-Five in the UK charts.

3. 'Who's Doctor Who?', Frazer Hines (Major Minor)

A single from October 1968 by the actor who was at that time playing the Doctor's assistant Jamie McCrimmon. Frazer is also well known for playing Joe Sugden in the country soap opera *Emmerdale Farm*.

4. 'Doctorin' the Tardis', The Timelords (KLF Communications)

A UK Number One from 1988 that blended the *Dr Who* theme with Gary Glitter's 'Rock 'n' Roll Part 2' and Sweet's 'Ballroom Blitz' in a hiphopish holler.

5. 'Who's Who', Roberta Tovey (Polydor)

A record from August 1965, this time by the girl who played the Doctor's granddaughter Susan in the two Dr Who spin-off movies made in the mid-Sixties.

6. 'Landing of the Daleks', The Earthlings (Parlophone)

This record was actually banned by the BBC because they felt a Morse distress signal on the record could be confusing to shipping. It was released in February 1965.

7. 'I'm Gonna Spend My Christmas with a Dalek', Go Joes

Yet another attempted cash-in, this time going for both the *Dr Who* and Christmas markets.

8. 'Who Is Dr Who?', Jon Pertwee (Purple)

The third incarnation of the Time Lord took a stab at the charts on the label more normally associated with heavy metal stalwarts Deep Purple. Jon (Pertwee not Lord) would later make his chart début in the guise of another of his television characters, Wurzel Gummidge.

9. 'I'm a Dalek', The Art Attacks (Albatross)

The New Wave got in on the act with this now highly collectable disc from March 1978. The band's vocalist was Edwin Pouncey, who is better known as *Sounds'* cartoonist Savage Pencil. Wire's Rob Gotobed was once a member of the Art Attacks but that was before this single was recorded.

10. 'Doctor in Distress', Who Cares (Record Shack)

When the BBC announced in the spring of 1985 that the programme was to be shelved for an indefinite period, a number of stars from the show teamed up with various pop stars, including John Lodge, Justin Hayward, Rick Buckler, David Van Day and Hazell Dean, to make this record. As 1985 was the year of Live Aid!, proceeds from this record went to charity.

Mention should also be made of Liverpool New Wave band Dalek I (formerly Dalek I Love You), one of whose singles was 'Dalek I Love You' but had little to do with the show; the Daleks, who recorded a song called 'This Life'; the Cybermen, who released a four-track EP in 1978; the Human League, who recorded 'Tom Baker' as the B side to one of their singles; and a 1986 group called The Brains of Morbius, which was the title of a Tom Baker-era story.

In the *Dr Who* story *The Chase* in May 1965 a clip from the Beatles' promo film for 'Ticket to Ride' is shown on the Doctor's 'space-time visualizer', showing that even the *Dr Who* production team were not averse to cashing in on Beatlemania.

The March 1983 story *Enlightenment* featured Imagination's Lee John as a space pirate.

The *Dr Who* story *The Pyramids of Mars* was filmed partly at Star Grove House, Mick Jagger's country home.

Capital Radio reggae DJ David Rodigan played a character called Broken Tooth in a story in the 1986 season.

The Rezillos, who were greatly influenced by TV sci-fi, used to take a full-size Dalek on stage with them.

Frazer Hines' brother Iain played keyboards for the Jets, who followed in the Beatles' footsteps to Hamburg.

Ian Marsh and Martyn Ware (The Human League) made their début public performance at a party performing the *Dr Who* theme as a duo called the Dead Daughters.

Eccentric musician Nick Haeffner recorded 'The Master' as a paean to the Doctor's long-time enemy.

☐ Puppet on a String

In the late Fifties the world of children's television took a new twist when the work of former film technician Gerry Anderson hit the screens. The novelty of Gerry's shows was that the characters were played by puppets. The first three shows were simple children's fantasy stories but the fourth, *Supercar*, opened up an era of puppet sci-fi. Here is a list of the theme tunes to Gerry's shows (including the later ones, which used real actors) and the artists who originally recorded them. Music was nearly always written and performed by Barry Gray.

■ Songs from Gerry Anderson programmes

☐ Series	☐ Artist	☐ Theme song	☐ Label
The Adventures of Twizzle	Nancy Nevinson	'The Twizzle Song'	HMV
Four Feathers Fall	Michael Holliday	'Four Feathers Fall'	Columbia
Supercar	Charles Blackwell	'Supercar'	Columbia
Fireball XL5	Don Spencer	'Fireball'	HMV
Stingray	Gary Miller	'Stingray' 'Aqua Marina'	Pye
Thunderbirds	Barry Gray Orchestra	'Thunderbirds'	Pye
Captain Scarlet and the Mysterons	Barry Gray Orchestra	'Captain Scarlet Theme'	Pye
	The Spectrum	'End Theme'	RCA

☐ Series	☐ Artist	☐ Theme song	☐ Label
Joe 90	Barry Gray Orchestra	'Joe 90 Theme'	Pye
The Secret Service	The Mike Sammes Singers	'The Secret Service'	Pye
UFO	Barry Gray Orchestra	'UFO'	
The Protectors	Tony Christie	'Avenues and Alleyways'	MCA
Space 1999	Barry Gray Orchestra	'Space 1999'	
Terrahawks	Richard Harvey	'Theme from *Terrahawks*'	Anderburr

Here are several other records connected with Gerry Anderson shows.

1. 'Captain Scarlet', Siouxsie and the Banshees (Track Rehearsals) 1977

This track comes from a bootleg EP of demos recorded for Track Records by the high priestess of punk. Siouxsie was one of the first Sex Pistols fans (along with Banshee Steve Severin, Billy Idol and the rest of the so-called Bromley Contingent). The Banshees were one of the last major punk bands to be signed and this bootleg pre-dates their first official release, 'Hong Kong Garden'.

2. 'Thunderbirds Are Go, '*Thunderbirds* Theme', Rezillos (Sire, LP tracks) April 1979

The punk-spawned popsters were among the many fans of Gerry Anderson as these tracks, on their live LP *Mission Accomplished . . . but the Beat Goes On*, prove.

3. 'Joe 90 Theme', Ron Grainer Orchestra (Casino Classic, B side) November 1978

Another seasoned TV theme writer and performer (*Dr Who* and *Man in a Suitcase*) with a late Seventies rendition of the theme to the 1969 series about a 9-year-old boy who could be implanted with the brain patterns of other people.

4. 'Thunderbirds Are Go!', Cliff Richard and the Shadows EP (Columbia) November 1966

In 1966 Gerry Anderson produced a full-length feature film version of *Thunderbirds*, which featured puppet replicas of Cliff and the Shads performing 'Shooting Star' (on this EP). The other three tracks are Shadows instrumentals used as incidental music in the film.

5. 'Stingray'/'Aqua Marina', Tornados (Columbia) September 1965

Joe Meek's instrumental protégés and former Billy Fury backing group with their versions of the main and end themes to *Stingray*.

6. '*Supercar* Title Number', Nelson Riddle and his Orchestra (Capitol) July 1963

The famous orchestra leader gets his baton into the theme of Gerry's first sci-fi series.

7. 'Captain Scarlet', Cass Carnaby Five (Maxwell Street) 1987

The group, named after a Gerry Anderson character, perform their own tribute to a show they all love.

8. 'Captain Scarlet', The Trudy (Primitive) 1987

Scarlet proves to be the most fondly remembered show with yet another modern tribute.

9. 'SOS', Kate Kestral (Anderburr) 1983

Kate was one of the pilots from the series *Terrahawks* but her cover was as a successful pop singer. This was one of the songs she was seen recording and performing in the series.

10. 'Fireball XL5', Flee-rekkers (Piccadilly)

Another Joe Meek-produced instrumental combo play their way through another Anderson theme.

Remember also: The Fabulous Thunderbirds, the Stingrays, Parker's Love Doll, the Angels, Secret Service, Gee Mr Tracey, Scarlett and Black, Fireball XL5, International Rescue and the host of other bands inspired by the super-marionation of Gerry Anderson.

Following the wave of Monkee mania after the success of the TV show, Gerry and Sylvia Anderson announced plans to make two series about a group called the Spectrum. The group were duly formed and signed to RCA. The plan was that their lead singer would be Captain Scarlet and he would star in both a puppet and a real life TV drama. In the end only the puppet show came about, but Scarlet was not a singer with the group. However, the Spectrum did record the end theme to the show. On 27 December 1967 they appeared on a special edition of *The Golden Shot* TV show, which also had several targets made up from *Captain Scarlet* scenes. It is highly likely that this group were the same Spectrum who released further singles on RCA in the late Sixties, but none of these were Anderson-related.

The Housemartins' 'Five Get Over Excited' contains a brief *Thunderbirds* reference in the lyric.

Dedicated to Destiny, Harmony, Melody, Rhapsody and Symphony Angels.

□ Movie Star

Elvis Presley may have been a rock and pop singer in the first place, but he was soon being fashioned into an all-round entertainer and the quickest way to do this was to put him in the movies. Between 1956 and 1969 Elvis made thirty-one fictional films, which ranged from good to abysmal. He then featured in two documentary films, which at least revealed more or less the truth.

■ **Love Me Tender** 1956 (black and white)

Screenplay by Robert Buckner from a story by Maurice Geraghty
Produced by David Weisbart

Directed by Robert D. Webb
Starring Elvis Presley (Clint Reno) and Debra Paget (Cathy), with James Drury, William Campbell and Richard Egan
Songs: 'Love Me Tender', 'Poor Boy', 'Let Me' and 'We're Gonna Move'

Campbell, Drury, Egan and Presley play the Reno brothers (which was to have been the film's original title) in this story set at the end of the American Civil War. The first three pop into and rob the US Mint on their way back from the war. They arrive home to discover youngest brother Clint (Elvis) has married Egan's fiancée (Paget), as Egan was presumed dead. After much squabbling and feuding, Elvis is shot dead and, in the tackiest of his four pre-army movies, returns as a singing ghost.

■ **Loving You** 1957 (colour)

Screenplay by Herbert Baker and Hal Kantner from a story by Mary Agnes Thompson
Produced by Hal Wallis
Directed by Hal Kantner
Starring Elvis Presley (Deke Rivers) and Dolores Hart (Susan Jessup), with Lizbeth Scott, Wendell Corey and James Gleason
Songs: 'Loving You', 'Teddy Bear', 'Party', 'Hot Dog', 'Gotta Lot of Living to Do', 'Lonesome Cowboy', 'Fireworks', 'Dandy Kisses', 'Mean Woman Blues', 'We're Gonna Live It Up', 'Detour' and 'Dancing on a Dare' (Some of these songs featured on the sound-track LP but didn't appear in the film.)

Enterprising press agent Glenda Markell (Scott) spots Elvis singing in a small country town and signs him up to boost the popularity of a country band led by Tex Warner (Corey). Elvis is an immediate success and becomes a star in his own right. However, the moral guardians of society soon protest about his hip wigglin' and, disillusioned by stardom, Elvis walks out with his sweetheart, simple country girl Susan Jessup (Hart). It does, of course, all end happily, with Markell reuniting with her ex-husband, Warner. The film parallels Elvis's own rise to fame, in places, and Elvis's parents make a cameo appearance.

■ Jailhouse Rock 1957 (black and white)

Screenplay by Guy Trosper based on a story by Ned Young
Produced by Pandro S. Berman
Directed by Richard Thorpe
Starring Elvis Presley (Vince Everett) and Judy Tyler (Peggy Van Alden), with Mickey Shaughnessy, Vaughn Taylor and Jennifer Holden
Songs: 'Jailhouse Rock', 'Baby I Don't Care', 'I Want to Be Free', 'Don't Leave Me Now' and 'Young and Beautiful'

While in jail on a manslaughter rap Vince (Elvis) is taught to play guitar by cell-mate Hunk Houghton (Shaughnessy). On his release, record plugger Peggy Van Alden (Tyler) becomes his manager and helps turn him into a rock 'n' roll star. He also falls in love with her to introduce the normal romantic ingredient to the film. This film contains the Elvis scene to end all others when he dances to the title song.

Song-writer Mike Stoller makes a brief appearance in *Jailhouse Rock*.

■ King Creole 1958 (black and white)

Screenplay by Herbert Baker and Michael Vincente Gazzo based on a story by Harold Robbins (*A Stone for Danny Fisher*)
Produced by Hal Wallis
Directed by Michael Curtiz
Starring Elvis Presley (Danny Fisher) and Carolyn Jones (Ronnie), with Walter Matthau, Dolores Hart and Dean Jagger
Songs: 'King Creole', 'Crawfish', 'Trouble', 'Hard-headed Woman', 'Dixieland Rock', 'Danny Is My Name', 'Lover Doll', 'You're the Cutest' and 'Let Me Be Your Lover Boy'

Elvis plays a night-club singer who falls in love with Ronnie (Jones), the wife of gangster Maxie Fields (Matthau). The two men set about each other both mentally and physically, and the action culminates with Fields killing Ronnie and then being killed himself, which leaves the field clear for Dolores Hart to move in on Elvis.

■ **G.I. Blues** 1960 (colour)

Screenplay by Edmund Balen and Henry Garson
Produced by Hal Wallis
Directed by Norman Taurog
Starring Elvis Presley (Tulsa McCauley) and Juliet Prowse (Lili), with James Douglas, Robert Ivers, Leticia Roman, Sigrid Maier and Arch Johnson
Songs: 'G. I. Blues', 'Wooden Heart', 'Blue Suede Shoes', 'Shoppin' Around', 'Pocketful of Rainbows' and 'Big Boots'

As soon as Elvis was demobbed in real life, he replayed his GI role on screen. Serving in Germany, Tulsa (Elvis) is bet $300 that he can't spend the night in Lili's (Prowse) flat. He has his work cut out, as the German girl is something of an ice maiden. However, once Tulsa starts twanging his tonsils, things begin to happen. This film is almost unique in that it features a scene in which Presley is out-acted by a puppet.
Norman Taurog, who directed this and several other Presley films, had been a child actor.

■ **Flaming Star** 1960 (colour)

Screenplay by Clair Huffaker and Nunnally Johnson based on a story by Huffaker
Produced by David Weisbart
Directed by Don Siegel
Starring Elvis Presley (Pacer Burton) with Barbara Eden, Dolores Del Rio and Steve Forrest
Song: 'Flaming Star'

In this basically non-musical Elvis film, Presley plays a half-breed Red Indian torn between his 'red' and 'white' sides when the two clash. This film did not go down well with Elvis fans who expected the usual plethora of songs and got only the title track.

■ **Wild in the Country** 1961 (colour)

Screenplay by Clifford Odets based on a story by J. R. Salamanca
Produced by Jerry Wald

Directed by Phillip Dunne
Starring Elvis Presley (Glen Tyler), Tuesday Weld (Noreen), Hope Lange (Irene) and Millie Perkins (Betty Lee)
Songs: 'Wild in the Country', 'I Slipped I Stumbled I Fell', 'Lonely Man' and 'In My Way'

Misunderstood Glen (Elvis), the rebellious hillbilly-cum-budding literary genius, has stirred the passions of three women: his psychologist (Lange), the high school floozy (Weld) and the quiet girl-next-door (Perkins). Initially this was filmed as a straightforward drama without any songs bar the title track. However, the relative failure of *Flaming Star* caused the producers to think again and the songs were added as an attempt to turn it into a standard Presley movie. In the end it fell somewhere in between.

■ **Blue Hawaii** 1961 (colour)

Screenplay by Hal Kantner
Produced by Hal Wallis
Directed by Norman Taurog
Starring Elvis Presley (Chad Gates) and Joan Blackman (Maile Duval), with Angela Lansbury, Nancy Walters, Roland Winters, John Archer and Howard McNear
Songs: 'Rock-A-Hula Baby', 'Can't Help Falling in Love', 'The Hawaiian Wedding Song', 'Beach Boy Blues', 'Ku-U-I-Po' and 'Ito Eats'

Elvis plays Chad, a tourist guide in Hawaii who is very popular with the female tourists. His steady girl-friend (Blackman) – the boss of the tourist agency – is very jealous of the attention Chad gets when he spends all day on the beach with the tourists. Chad's mum (Lansbury) is also unhappy with the situation, as she expects her son to stay at home on the pineapple plantation. In the end Miss Blackman secures her man and one hell of a Hawaiian wedding takes place.

■ **Follow That Dream** 1962 (colour)

Screenplay by Charles Lederer based on a story by Richard Powell
Produced by David Weisbart
Directed by Gordon Douglas

Starring Elvis Presley (Toby Kwimper), with Anne Helm and Arthur O'Connell
Songs: 'Follow That Dream', 'What a Wonderful Life' and 'I'm Not the Marrying Kind'

Toby (Elvis) and his dad (O'Connell) run a fishing business and look after Toby's adopted brothers and sisters. When a low-class casino opens up nearby, the area is flooded with undesirables and the authorities try to take the children into care. Toby sorts out the roguish gamblers with his hands and feet, and then beats the authorities in court.

■ Kid Galahad 1962 (colour)

Screenplay by William Fay based on a story by Francis Wallace
Produced by Hal Wallis
Directed by Phil Carlson
Starring Elvis Presley (Walter Gulick) and Joan Blackman (Rose Grogan), with Gig Young, Lola Albright, Charles Bronson and Ned Glass
Songs: 'I Got Lucky', 'King of the Whole Wide World', 'This Is Living' and 'Riding the Rainbow'

In this remake of a 1937 film of the same name Elvis plays Walter, a young boxer who becomes a somewhat reluctant star and is managed by Willy Grogan (Young). Grogan has the reputation of being a bit of a villain and his girl-friend Dolly (Albright) leaves him because she thinks he's using Walter. However, when the hoods try to muscle in, Grogan sticks up for his boy. Dolly returns and marries Grogan while Walter marries Grogan's sister Rose (Blackman).

■ Girls! Girls! Girls! 1962 (colour)

Screenplay by Edward Anhalt and Allan Weiss
Produced by Hal Wallis
Directed by Norman Taurog
Starring Elvis Presley (Ross Carpenter) and Laurel Goodwin (Laurel Dodge), with Stella Stevens, Robert Strauss and Jeremy Slate
Songs: 'Girls Girls Girls' and 'Return to Sender'

Elvis plays fisherman Ross Carpenter, who loses both his girl and his boat and takes a job singing in a night-club to earn enough money to buy back the boat. At the club he meets Laurel Dodge (Goodwin), a wealthy woman pretending to be poor. She secretly buys back the boat for Ross, but he finds out and makes her sell it. He then marries her and builds his own boat.

■ It Happened at the World's Fair 1963 (colour)

Screenplay by Seamon Jacobs and Si Rose
Produced by Ted Richmond
Directed by Norman Taurog
Starring Elvis Presley (Mike Edwards) and Joan O'Brien (Diane Warren), with Gary Lockwood and Vicky Tiu
Songs: 'One Broken Heart for Sale', 'Take Me to the Fair', 'Happy Ending' and 'Cotton Candy Land'

Elvis and Gary Lockwood are two plane-less pilots who get mixed up in a smuggling racket that takes them to the World's Fair in Seattle. Mike falls for nurse Diane Warren (O'Brien) and is helped in getting it together with her by a little Chinese girl, Sue-Lin (Tiu). Most of the action is set in the fairground.

■ Fun in Acapulco 1963 (colour)

Screenplay by Allan Weiss
Produced by Hal Wallis
Directed by Richard Thorpe
Starring Elvis Presley (Mike Windgren) and Ursula Andress (Margarita Dauphin), with Elsa Cardenas, Paul Lukas and Larry Domasin
Songs: 'Fun in Acapulco', 'Bossa Nova Baby', 'Marguerita', 'The Bullfighter Was a Lady' and 'El Toro'

Elvis is a life-guard cum night-club singer in Acapulco suffering from vertigo after a trapeze accident. He overcomes this fear by diving off a 136-feet-high cliff and swimming into the arms of female bullfighter Andress. (Don't blame me – I didn't write the script!)

Fun in Acapulco was the first Elvis movie to be shown in Mexico since *G.I. Blues* caused cinema riots three years earlier.

■ **Kissin' Cousins** 1964 (colour)

Screenplay by Gerald Adams and Gene Nelson
Produced by Sam Katzman
Directed by Gene Nelson
Starring Elvis Presley (Josh Morgan *and* Jodie Tatum), Cynthia Pepper (Midge) and Yvonne Craig (Azalea Tatum), with Arthur O'Connel, Glenda Farrell and Jack Albertson
Songs: 'Kissin' Cousins', 'Smoky Mountain Boy' and 'There's Gold in the Mountains'

Two Elvis roles, as the man plays Air Force Lieutenant Josh Morgan and his country cousin, blond-haired Jodie Tatum. Their paths cross when Morgan is sent to persuade Tatum and his family to relinquish some land on their backwoods property. Meanwhile Morgan falls in love with his other cousin Azalea (Craig), Tatum falls in love with Midge and they all live happily . . . etc., etc., etc.

■ **Viva Las Vegas** 1964 (colour)

Screenplay by Sally Bensen
Produced by Jack Cummings and George Sidney
Directed by George Sidney
Starring Elvis Presley (Lucky Jordan) and Ann-Margret
Songs: 'Viva Las Vegas', 'What'd I Say', 'If I Think I Need You' and 'C'mon Everybody'

Racing driver Elvis wins both the Las Vegas Grand Prix and Ann-Margret, but was unlikely ever to win an Oscar.

■ **Roustabout** 1964 (colour)

Screenplay by Anthony Laurence and Allan Weiss
Produced by Hal Wallis
Directed by John Rich
Starring Elvis Presley (Charlie Rogers) and Joan Freeman (Cathy Lean), with Barbara Stanwyck and Leif Erickson
Songs: 'Roustabout', 'It's Carnival Time', 'Little Egypt', 'Wheels on My Heels' and 'Carny Town'

Stanwyck's travelling carnival is fast heading downhill until she hires handyman and wall-of-death rider Elvis, whose singing pulls in the punters. However Stanwyck's drunken partner (Erickson) fires Elvis and the carnival heads for disaster. Erickson's daughter (Freeman) is romantically entwined with Elvis and she persuades her dad to give 'swivel-hips' his job back. The carnival is saved.

■ **Girl Happy** 1965 (colour)

Screenplay by R. S. Allen and Harvey Bullock
Produced by Joe Pasternak
Directed by Boris Segal
Starring Elvis Presley (Rusty Wells) and Shelley Fabres
Songs: 'Do the Clam', 'She's Evil' and 'Fort Lauderdale Chamber of Commerce'

Elvis plays a singer turned chaperon for a group of college girls on holiday. Shelley Fabres is the wildcat who eventually falls for Elvis's charms. This film included scenes of the Florida mountains. Unfortunately there are no mountains in Florida.

■ **Tickle Me** 1965 (colour)

Screenplay by Edward Bernos and Elwood Ullman
Produced by Ben Schwalb
Directed by Norman Taurog
Starring Elvis Presley (Lonnie Beale) and Jocelyn Lane, with Julie Adams
Songs: 'Tickle Me', 'It Feels So Right', 'Put the Blame on Me' and 'I'm Yours'

Elvis plays a handyman at a health farm overflowing with pretty ladies, including Jocelyn Lane. Some bad guys are trying to steal a treasure map that Lane possesses but Elvis stops them and marries Lane – whether it was for her or for the treasure though is another question.

■ **Harum Scarum** 1965 (colour)

Screenplay by Gerald Drayson Adams
Produced by Sam Katzman
Directed by Gene Nelson
Starring Elvis Presley (Johnny Tyrone) and Mary Ann Mobley, with Fran Jeffries
Songs: 'Harem Holiday', 'Kismet', 'Golden Coins' and 'My Desert Serenade'

Elvis the pop star is kidnapped while on tour in the Middle East. His kidnappers are treacherous Arabs who intend to kill the king. Elvis stops the assassination, marries the king's beautiful daughter and takes her back to Las Vegas.
Harum Scarum was called *Harem Holiday* in the UK.

■ **Frankie and Johnny** 1966 (colour)

Screenplay by Alex Gottlieb
Produced by Edward Small
Directed by Frederick De Cordova
Starring Elvis Presley (Johnny) and Nancy Kovak, with Donna Douglas
Songs: 'Frankie and Johnny', 'Petunia' and 'Come Along'

Based loosely on the traditional song 'Frankie and Johnny', this film features Elvis as a showboat entertainer and singer. When he gets friendly with Nancy Kovak, his partner, Donna Douglas, get jealous. During a gun routine in their act a real bullet is substituted for a blank and Elvis is shot. Luckily the bullet glances off Elvis's good-luck charm and he survives. Despite what everyone thinks, Donna didn't load the gun and she ends up with Elvis.

■ **Paradise Hawaiian Style** 1966 (colour)

Screenplay by Anthony Lawrence and Allan Weiss
Produced by Hal Wallis
Directed by Michael Moore
Starring Elvis Presley (Rick Richards) and Suzanna Leigh (Judy Hudson), with James Shigeta, Donna Butterworth and Julie Parrish

Songs: 'House of Sand', 'Drums of the Island' and 'Queenie Wahine's Papaya'

Elvis co-runs a charter helicopter service on Hawaii and makes out with lots of beautiful women. And that's about it.

■ Spin Out 1966 (colour)

Screenplay by Theo Flicker and George Kirgo
Produced by Joe Pasternak
Directed by Norman Taurog
Starring Elvis Presley (Mike McCoy) and Deborah Walley, with Shelley Fabres and Diane McBain
Songs: 'Spin Out', 'Stop, Look and Listen' and 'Adam and Evil'

Elvis is a racing-car driver-cum-pop singer with three women in his life (Walley, Fabres and McBain). In the end it is Deborah Walley who wins him, which is quite handy really, as she is also his drummer.

■ Easy Come, Easy Go 1967 (colour)

Screenplay by Tony Laurence and Allan Weiss
Produced by Hal Wallis
Directed by John Rich
Starring Elvis Presley (Ted Jackson) and Dodie Marshall, with Pat Priest and Elsa Lanchester
Songs: 'Easy Come, Easy Go', 'Love Machine' and 'Yoga Is as Yoga Does'

Elvis is a navy frogman diving for treasure. In his spare time he sings in a night-club, where he becomes romantically involved with a yoga expert. He eventually marries her after stopping the bad guys getting the treasure, which wasn't worth very much in the end anyway.

■ Double Trouble 1967 (colour)

Screenplay by Marc Brandel and Joe Heims
Produced by Judd Bernard and Irwin Winkler
Directed by Norman Taurog
Starring Elvis Presley (Guy Lambert) and Annette Day (Jill Conway),

with Yvonne Romain, Chips Rafferty, Norman Rossington and John Williams
Songs: 'Double Trouble', 'Long-legged Girl', 'Blue River' and 'Could I Fall in Love'

Elvis plays a pop singer in swinging London hired to protect heiress Jill Conway (Day) from kidnappers. He does. This film was *not* recorded on location.

■ **Clambake** 1967 (colour)

Screenplay by Arthur Brown
Produced by Arthur Gardner, Arnold Laven and Jules Levy
Directed by Arthur Nadel
Starring Elvis Presley (Scott Heywood) and Shelley Fabres, with Bill Bixby and Will Hutchins
Songs: 'Clambake', 'How Can You Lose What You Never Had' and 'Singing Tree'

Millionaire Elvis trades places with poor boy Hutchins and then battles with playboy Bixby for the hand of Shelley Fabres. Elvis wins because it's his film and anyway he invented a miracle paint for speedboats, which obviously made him irresistible to women.

■ **Stay Away Joe** 1968 (colour)

Screenplay by Michael Hoey
Produced by Douglas Laurence
Directed by Peter Tewksbury
Starring Elvis Presley (Joe Lightcloud) and Joan Blondell (Glenda Callahan), with Burgess Meredith, Katy Jurado and Thomas Gomez
Song: 'Stay Away Joe'

Elvis plays an American Indian rodeo rider with an eye for wild times and women. His attempts to bring prosperity to his tribe end in chaos in this brave Presley stab at (intentional) comedy.

■ **Speedway** 1968 (colour)

Screenplay by Philip Shuken
Produced by Douglas Laurence

Directed by Norman Taurog
Starring Elvis Presley (Steve Grayson) and Nancy Sinatra, with Bill Bixby
Song: 'Your Groovy Self'

Elvis plays a racing-car driver (again!) and night-club singer (again!), this time on the stock car circuit. Nancy is the tax inspector(ess) on his trail because he owes back-taxes thanks to manager Bixby, who has an inclination towards casinos. Elvis eventually wins her heart, though Uncle Sam still has to have his money.

■ **Live a Little, Love a Little** 1969 (colour)

Screenplay by Michael Hoey and Dan Greenburg
Produced by Douglas Laurence
Directed by Norman Taurog
Starring Elvis Presley (Greg) and Michele Cary, with Rudy Vallee
Song: 'A Little Less Conversation'

Elvis plays a photographer who is slipped a tranquillizer by Cary and goes to sleep for three days. Crooner Rudy Vallee plays his boss. Elvis gets the girl and the audience goes to sleep for three days.

■ **Charro** 1969 (colour)

Screenplay by Charles Marquis Warren
Produced and directed by Charles Marquis Warren
Starring Elvis Presley (Jesse Wade) and Ina Balin
Song: 'Charro'

A routine Western in which Elvis plays a reformed outlaw struggling to clear his name after he is framed for a robbery. It features no songs apart from the title track. John Wayne must have died laughing.

■ **The Trouble with Girls** 1969 (colour)

Screenplay by Arnold and Lois Peyser based on the book *The Chattaqua* by Dwight Babcock and Day Keene
Produced by Lester Welch

Directed by Peter Tewksbury
Starring Elvis Presley (Walter Hale) and Marilyn Mason (Charlene), with Sheree North, Nicole Jaffe, John Carradine and Vincent Price
Songs: 'The Trouble with Girls' and 'Clean Up Your Own Backyard'

Elvis is the manager of a Twenties travelling medicine show and causes all sorts of problems with his womanizing. In fact, Elvis doesn't appear until almost half-way through this film.

■ **Change of Habit** 1969 (colour)

Screenplay by Eric Bercovici, James Lee and S. Schweitzer
Produced by Joe Connelly
Directed by Michael Moore
Starring Elvis Presley (Dr John Carpenter) and Mary Tyler Moore (Sister Michelle), with Barbara McNair, Jane Elliot and Ed Asner
Songs: 'Rubber Neckin'' and 'Let's Pray Together'

Three young, attractive nuns are assigned to a slum area of the city where Carpenter (Elvis) is working as a doctor. Carpenter meets Sister Michelle when she is in plain clothes and falls in love with her. The nun is besotted with Carpenter, too, and faces a huge dilemma: Carpenter or God? Elvis *doesn't* get the girl. This was his last fiction film.

■ **Elvis – That's the Way It Is** 1970 (colour)

Produced by Herbery Solon
Directed by Denis Sanders

Elvis on stage and backstage at the International Hotel in Las Vegas. Twenty-seven songs are featured. Also features the Sweet Inspirations. Audience includes Sammy Davis Jr and Cary Grant.

■ **Elvis on Tour** 1973 (colour)

Produced and directed by Robert Abel and Pierre Adidge

Documentary of a 1972 American tour. Includes twenty-nine songs. Also features the Sweet Inspirations.

□ Put You in the Picture

Cliff Richard's film career was as long as, though less prolific than, Elvis's. It began in 1958 when he was given a part in the low-budget drama, *Serious Charge*, because the director wanted a pop star in it and Cliff was on his way up. The singer plays a teenage rebel in this controversial (at the time) film about a youth club leader accused of homosexuality. The songs in the film were re-recorded for release on an EP. They include 'Living Doll' (written by Lionel Bart), 'No Turning Back', 'Mad About You' and 'Chinchilla'. The latter was by the Drifters, which was the name the Shadows were using at that time.

Cliff's second film, *Expresso Bongo*, was released in 1960 and was based on a stage show with music by David Heneker. Cliff played singer Bongo Herbert and the songs included 'A Voice in the Wilderness', 'The Shrine on the Second Floor', 'Love' and 'Bongo Blues' (by the Shadows).

In1962 Cliff and the Shadows starred in *The Young Ones* (titled *It's Wonderful To Be Young* in the US). Cliff played the son of tycoon Robert Morley who intends to pull down a youth club to build an office block. Cliff and the youth club crowd fight the closure and win. Songs include 'The Young Ones', 'When the Girl in Your Arms Is the Girl in Your Heart', 'We Say Yeah', 'Lessons in Love' and 'The Savage' (Shadows). A new title song had to be recorded for the US.

Summer Holiday in 1963 had Cliff and the Shads, and Melvyn Hayes and Una Stubbs. Cliff and his pals work for London Transport and borrow a bus to tour Europe during their summer holiday. They bump into the Shadows, various girls and an heiress who gets a kick out of dressing up as a boy. Songs include 'Summer Holiday', 'Bachelor Boy', 'The Next Time', 'All at Once', 'Dancing Shoes', 'Round and Round' (Shadows), 'Les Girls' (Shadows) and 'Foot Tapper' (Shadows).

Cliff received his first screen kiss, from Susan Hampshire, in 1964's *Wonderful Life*, which saw Cliff and the Shads playing actors making a movie in the desert. Songs include 'Wonderful Life' and 'On the Beach'.

Excluding his appearance in the 1966 film *Thunderbirds Are Go!* (see p. 43), Cliff's next film was *Finders Keepers* that same year. Songs included the title track and 'Time Drags By'.

Two A Penny was a film made in 1968 by the Billy Graham Production Company – Graham, of course, being the well-known evangelist.

Cliff's last film to date is 1973's *Take Me High*, in which he played merchant banker Tim Matthews, who comes up with a marvellous Birmingham Burger and falls in love with a beautiful girl. Co-stars included Debbie Watling, George Cole, Hugh Griffith and Anthony Andrews. Songs include the title track.

The Shadows also provided music for the short feature film *Rhythm and Greens* (1964).

□ Saturday Night at the Movies

Now let's take a brief look at twenty of the more important, influential or representative rock 'n' roll films from the Fifties to the Eighties, in alphabetical order.

■ **A Hard Day's Night** (1964)

Screenplay by Allan Owen
Produced by Walter Shenson
Directed by Richard Lester
Starring John Lennon, Paul McCartney, George Harrison and Ringo Starr, with Wilfred Brambell, Victor Spinetti, Norman Rossington, John Junkin and Anna Quale

The Beatles, as themselves, are on a train trip to London to appear on a television programme. Paul's uncle (Brambell) is with them. They spend the whole film running around, mucking about and thoroughly enjoying themselves while their entourage struggle to keep away fans, get them to the studio on time, and so on. *A Hard Day's Night* caught perfectly the madness of Beatlemania. With hindsight, many rock historians and film buffs have credited Richard Lester's direction of scenes in this film as the birthplace of promo videos, as the Beatles do silly things to the accompaniment of their songs. The songs featured (all performed by the Beatles and written by Lennon and McCartney) include 'A Hard Day's Night', 'She Loves You', 'I Wanna Hold Your Hand', 'Can't Buy Me Love', 'And I Love Her', 'If I Fell' and 'Tell Me Why'.

■ **American Graffiti** (1973)

Screenplay by William Huyk, Gloria Katz and George Lucas
Produced by Francis Ford Coppola and Gary Kurtsz
Directed by George Lucas
Starring Richard Dreyfuss (Curt), Ron Howard (Steve), Paul Le Mat (John) and Charlie Martin Smith (Terry), with Harrison Ford, Suzanne Somers, Cindy Williams, Candy Clark and McKenzie Williams

It is the last night of the summer vacation in 1962. In California Curt, Steve, John and Terry are out on the town together before going their separate ways (college, job, etc.). *American Graffiti* is the story of the events that take place in the next twelve or so hours set against an aural backdrop of classic pop and rock songs from the first eight years of the rock era. The climax of the film is a race between John in his Chevy-powered Ford and a rival in a 1955 Chevy. Songs include 'Rock Around the Clock', Bill Haley and his Comets; 'Johnny B. Goode', Chuck Berry; 'Little Darlin', Diamonds; 'Ain't That a Shame', Fats Domino; 'Since I Don't Have You', Flamingos; 'All Summer Long', Beach Boys; and much, much more.

■ **Don't Look Back** (1965)

Produced by Don Court and Albert Grossman
Directed by D. A. Pennebaker
Featuring Bob Dylan, with Albert Grossman, Tito Burns, Joan Baez, Alan Price, Donovan, Bob Neuwirth, Derrol Adams and Allen Ginsberg

This documentary (or rockumentary as some would have it) was filmed in April 1965 when Dylan was making a two-week tour of Britain. It shows him in concert, in his hotel room, in cars and trains and in some special scenes singing his songs (notably the often shown 'Subterranean Homesick Blues' in which he shows, and discards, a series of placards bearing the songs lyrics). Songs include: 'Subterranean Homesick Blues', 'The Times They Are-A-Changin'' and 'It's Alright Ma (I'm Only Bleeding)'.

■ **Easy Rider** (1969)

Screenplay by Peter Fonda, Dennis Hopper and Terry Southern
Produced by Bert Schneider
Directed by Dennis Hopper.
Starring Peter Fonda, Dennis Hopper and Jack Nicholson, with Luke Ashew, Phil Spector and Toni Basil

Billy (Hopper) and Wyatt (Fonda) are two bikers who decide to celebrate the conclusion of a cocaine deal (with Phil Spector) by biking down to New Orleans to the Mardi Gras festival. The film documents the duo's encounters on the route, most notably that with George (Nicholson), an alcoholic civil rights lawyer. He rides with them but is murdered when they are attacked by vigilantes. The two survivors press on to New Orleans, but after the odd bad acid trip they head east to Florida. On the way they manage to upset a truck driver who shoots them dead. *Easy Rider* was among the first films to use a sound-track of previously released material. Songs included: 'Born To Be Wild' and 'The Pusher', Steppenwolf; 'If Six Was Nine', Jimi Hendrix; 'I Wasn't Born To Follow', Byrds; 'The Weight', the Band; and 'It's Alright Ma (I'm Only Bleeding)', Roger McGuinn.

■ **The Girl Can't Help It** (1956)

Screenplay by Herbert Baker and Frank Tashlin from a story by Garson Kanin
Produced and directed by Frank Tashlin
Starring Jayne Mansfield and Edmund O'Brien, with Tom Ewell, and featuring Eddie Cochran, Gene Vincent and the Bluecaps, Fats Domino, Little Richard, Julie London and the Platters

Fats Murdoch (O'Brien) is a gangster who wants his fiancée Georgy (Mansfield) to be turned into a star. He hires a publicist fresh from promoting Julie London to promote Georgy but instead the singer and the agent fall in love and marry, leaving Fats to become the hit-maker with such songs as 'There'll Be No Lights on the Christmas Tree Tonight Mother – They're Using the Electric Chair'. Frankly the plot is quite irrelevant; the beauty of this film is in the Technicolor cameo appearances from Little Richard ('The Girl Can't Help It', 'She's Got It'), Eddie Cochran ('Twenty Flight Rock'), Gene Vincent and the Blue Caps ('Be Bop A Lula') and Fats Domino ('Blue Monday').

■ Grease (1978)

Screenplay by Bronte Woodward based on an original stage show by Jim Jacobs and Warren Casey
Produced by Allan Carr and Robert Stigwood
Directed by Randall Kleiser
Starring John Travolta and Olivia Newton-John, with Stockard Channing, Jeff Conaway and Barry Pearl, and featuring Frankie Avalon (as Teen Angel) and Sha Na Na (as Johnny Casino and the Gamblers)

Sandy (Newton-John) is on holiday in California when she meets Danny Zuco (Travolta), leader of the local gang. They fall in love at first sight, though macho Danny is at first loath to admit it. This musical follows the haphazard course of their romance through a Fifties high school scenario with lots of rock 'n' roll from Sha Na Na and Frankie Avalon. Original songs written by Jacobs and Casey (plus Andy Gibb's title song) are performed by combinations of Travolta, Newton-John, other cast members and Frankie Valli. Best-known originals are 'You're the One That I Want', 'Summer Nights', 'Grease', 'Hopelessly Devoted to You', 'Sandy' and 'Greased Lightning'. A 1982 sequel, with the highly original title *Grease II*, featuring new cast members, fared far less successfully.

■ The Great Rock 'n' Roll Swindle (1980)

Screenplay by Julian Temple
Produced by Don Boyd and Jeremy Thomas
Directed by Julian Temple
Starring the Sex Pistols (Johnny Rotten, Sid Vicious, Paul Cook and Steve Jones), with Malcolm McLaren, Nancy Spungen, Tenpole Tudor and the Black Arabs

Very, very loosely based on the Sex Pistols' rise to glory, this film started production in 1978 when the band was hot, but by the time it was released in 1980, the Pistols were long gone. The original script, titled *Who Killed Bambi?* was aborted after several scenes had been shot but Temple used many of these clips in *Swindle*. Highlight of the film has to be Sid doing 'My Way'. Other songs include: 'Anarchy in the UK', 'God Save the Queen', 'Pretty Vacant', 'Holiday in the Sun', 'No Feelings', 'C'mon Everybody', 'Somethin' Else' and 'Johnny B. Goode'.

■ **Head** (1968)

Screenplay by Jack Nicholson and Bert Schneider
Produced by Jack Nicholson, Bob Rafelson and Bert Schneider
Directed by Bob Rafelson
Starring the Monkees (Micky Dolenz, Davy Jones, Mike Nesmith and Peter Tork), with Annette Funicello, Tim Carey, Frank Zappa, Jack Nicholson and Carol Doda

Although basically just a vehicle for the Monkees, this film was far removed from the British beat movies used earlier in the decade to promote the Beatles and the Dave Clark 5. It was also considerably different from the Monkees' own TV series. This collage of film clips and surrealistic sketches supposedly showed us a day in the life of the manufactured Monkees. A bit weird really, but the sound-track made it all worthwhile. Songs include: 'Porpoise Song', 'Can You Dig It' and 'As We Go Along'.

■ **Help!** (1965)

Screenplay by Marc Behm and Charles Wood
Produced by Walter Shenson
Directed by Richard Lester
Starring the Beatles (John Lennon, Paul McCartney, George Harrison and Ringo Starr), with Leo McKern, Roy Kinnear, Eleanor Bron and Victor Spinetti

Ringo has somehow got hold of a sacred ring belonging to a mystical Indian tribe led by McKern and Bron. *Help!* follows the attempts of the pair and their followers to get the ring back. Most of the plot is a world-wide chase, culminating in the Bahamas, where the ring just drops off Ringo's finger. Original songs by Lennon and McCartney, performed by the Beatles include: 'Help!', 'Ticket to Ride', 'You've Got to Hide Your Love Away', 'You're Gonna Lose That Girl', 'Night Before' and 'Another Girl'. Also performed by the Beatles, 'I Need You', written by Harrison. Original film score by George Martin.

■ **Jubilee** (1978)

Screenplay by Derek Jarman
Produced by Howard Malin and James Whaley
Directed by Derek Jarman
Starring Toyah Wilcox, Jordan and Adam Ant, with Jenny Runacre, Little Nell, Lenda Spurrier, Wayne County, Lindsay Kemp and the Slits

While Don Letts was documenting the true-life world of punk rock in his films made at the Roxy Club, Derek Jarman made a punk fantasy that had Queen Elizabeth I shifted into the punk era. Whether or not the film had any relevance to punk is debatable, but certainly the sound-track did. Songs include: 'Right to Work', Chelsea; and 'Love in a Void', Siouxsie and the Banshees.

■ **The Last Waltz** (1978)

Produced by Robbie Robertson
Directed by Martin Scorsese
Featuring Robbie Robertson, Rick Danko, Richard Manuel, Garth Hudson and Levon Helm (the Band), with Paul Butterfield, Eric Clapton, Neil Diamond, Bob Dylan, Emmylou Harris, Ronnie Hawkins, Dr John, Joni Mitchell, Van Morrison, Staple Singers, Ringo Starr, Muddy Waters, Ron Wood and Neil Young.

Martin Scorsese was assistant director on the film *Woodstock* (p. 69) and stepped right into the breach for this equally star-studded finale to the Band's career (until their Eighties reunion). Filmed at San Francisco's Winterland in November 1976, the film includes back-stage footage along with several classic performances from the artists listed above, most memorably the Band, Dylan, Starr and Wood doing 'I Shall Be Released'.

■ **Monterey Pop** (1968)

Produced by D. A. Pennebaker and Richard Leacock
Directed by D. A. Pennebaker and various others
Featuring the Animals, Booker T. and the MGs, Canned Heat, Country Joe and the Fish, Jimi Hendrix, Jefferson Airplane, Janis Joplin with Big Brother and the Holding Company, Hugh Masekela, Mamas and Papas, Otis Redding, Ravi Shankar, Simon and Garfunkel, and the Who

The film of the Monterey Pop Festival, which took place on 16–18 June 1967 and held the title of the biggest ever rock festival until two years later when it was overshadowed by Woodstock. Some superb performances include Hendrix doing 'Wild Thing' and Janis Joplin doing 'Ball and Chain'. Otis Redding is captured singing 'I've Been Loving You Too Long', a historically important piece of celluloid, as he died only six short months after it was made.

■ **National Lampoon's Animal House** (1978)

Screenplay by Douglas Kenney, Chris Miller and Harold Ramis
Produced by Ivan Reitman and Matty Simmons
Directed by John Landis
Starring John Belushi and Tim Matheson, with John Vernon, Thomas Hulee and Donald Sutherland

The king of the campus comedies: *Lemon Popsicle, Porkies* and *Rock 'n' Roll High School* all followed but never surpassed it. Faber College was the setting, 'Louie Louie' was the driving backbeat. The rivalry was between the kids of Omega and Delta houses. The fun was manic. Songs include: 'Louie Louie', the Delta's theme song, performed by the Kingsmen; 'Shout', Isley Brothers; 'Twistin' the Night Away', Sam Cooke; 'Tossin' and Turnin'', Bobby Lewis. An original song, *Animal House,* was written by Stephen Bishop, and John Belushi rendered us senseless with his version of 'Money'.

■ Quadrophenia (1979)

Screenplay by Dave Humphries, Franc Roddam and Martin Stellman based on a series of songs written by Pete Townshend
Produced by Roy Baird and Bill Curbishley
Directed by Franc Roddam
Starring Phil Daniels and Leslie Ash, with Garry Cooper, Toyah Wilcox and Gordon Sumner (Sting).

Based on the Who's 1973 double LP *Quadrophenia*, a concept LP featuring seventeen songs written by Pete Townshend, the film stars Phil Daniels as the f-f-frustrated Mod. The film captures perfectly the atmosphere of mid-Sixties Britain: Mods, Rockers, pills, dancing, scooters and fights on Brighton Beach. Sting features as an ace Mod, to whom Daniels looks up until he sees that during the day this cool face is just a bellboy at a hotel. Daniels loses his way in life and . . . well, you watch it. Songs by the Who include: 'Cut My Hair', '5.15', 'Quadrophenia', 'Drowned', 'Bell Boy' and 'Love Reign o'er Me'. Other songs on the sound-track include: 'Green Onions', Booker T. and the MGs; 'Rhythm of the Rain', Cascades; and 'Louie Louie', the Kingsmen.

■ Rock Around the Clock (1956)

Screenplay by James B. Gordon and Robert E. Kent
Produced by Sam Katzman
Directed by Fred F. Sears
Starring Bill Haley, Alan Dale and Lisa Gaye, with Alan Freed, Johnny Johnston and Alix Talten, and featuring Bill Haley and His Comets, Freddie Bell and His Bellboys, and the Platters.

Haley and his Comets are discovered playing in a small-town dance hall, and are signed up by Dale and Johnston. Alan Freed steps in as himself and helps propel the new rock 'n' roll sound to stardom despite Talten's efforts to stop him. It was the first rock 'n' roll movie and it caused riots wherever it was shown. Music was provided by Haley and His Comets (including 'Rock Around the Clock', 'Rudy's Rock', 'Rock-A-Beatin' Boogie', 'See You Later Alligator', 'Razzle Dazzle'), the Platters ('Only You' and 'The Great Pretender') and Freddie Bell and His Bellboys ('Giddy Up A Ding Dong').

■ The Rocky Horror Picture Show (1975)

Screenplay by Richard O'Brien and Jim Sharman based on a stage musical by O'Brien
Produced by Lou Adler and Michael White
Directed by Jim Sharman
Starring Tim Curry, Little Nell, Richard O'Brien, Susan Sarandon and Barry Bostwick, with Jonathon Adams, Pat Quinn, Peter Hinwood, Charles Gray and Meatloaf

Not so much a movie, more a way of life. Fans of this cult film turn up time and time again at midnight screenings dressed as characters from this weird rock musical about a 'sweet transvestite from transsexual Transylvania'. In the 'story' a newly-wed couple's car breaks down in a storm and they seek shelter at the mansion of Dr Frank N'Furter (the transvestite). For the rest of the film everybody camps it up and sings songs (written by Richard O'Brien), including 'Sweet Transvestite', 'Science Fiction Double Feature' and 'Touch Toucha Touch Me'.

■ Saturday Night Fever (1977)

Screenplay by Norman Wexler based on the article 'Tribal Rites of a Saturday Night' by Nik Cohn
Produced by Robert Stigwood
Directed by John Badham
Starring John Travolta, with Barry Miller and Karen Lynn Gorney

The movie that gave the disco craze world-wide exposure. The story is basically that of a hard-working hardware store assistant (Travolta) who flings off his work clothes at the weekends and takes to the floor of the local disco, where he dances a lot to a sound-track that includes the Bee Gees ('Night Fever', 'Stayin' Alive' and 'How Deep Is Your Love'), the Tramps ('Disco Inferno'), KC and the Sunshine Band ('Boogie Shoes') and Yvonne Elliman ('If I Can't Have You') among others. Both the film and the sound-track LP were smash hits and soon everybody was dancing.

A follow-up film in the Eighties, *Stayin' Alive*, fared somewhat less successfully.

■ Stardust (1974)

Screenplay by Ray Connolly
Produced by Sandy Lieberson and David Puttnam
Directed by Michael Apted
Starring David Essex, with Adam Faith, Keith Moon, Dave Edmunds, Ed Byrnes, Larry Hagman, Karl Howman, Paul Nicholas, Peter Duncan, Marty Wilde and Ines des Longchamp

A follow-up to the highly successful *That'll Be The Day*, which showed how Jim McClaine (Essex) broke away from his family to become a pop star in the early Sixties. In *Stardust* he and his band, the Straycats, become mega-stars but suffer from the pressures of stardom. The band leave Jim to his solo career and the film culminates with McClaine taking a fatal overdose on a live TV show. The music is by Dave Edmunds and David Puttnam, though several oldies also feature. The Straycats line-up is Essex, Edmunds, Nicholas (replaced by Duncan), Howman and Moon. Brinsley Schwarz make a brief cameo appearance.

■ Tommy (1975)

Screenplay by Ken Russell based on the rock opera *Tommy*, composed by Pete Townshend
Produced by Robert Stigwood and Ken Russell
Directed by Ken Russell
Starring Roger Daltrey, Ann-Margret, Oliver Reed, Robert Powell and Jack Nicholson, with Pete Townshend, Keith Moon, John Entwhistle, Tina Turner, Elton John, Eric Clapton, Arthur Brown and Paul Nicholas

Originally a 1968 Who rock opera, this is the story of Tommy, the little boy struck deaf, dumb and blind after he sees his mother in bed with a man who isn't his father. Tommy becomes a pin-ball champion through playing by intuition and is idolized as the leader of a religious cult. Songs include: 'See Me, Feel Me, Free Me', the Who; 'Pinball Wizard', Elton John; 'The Acid Queen', Tina Turner; and 'The Day It Rained Champagne', Ann-Margret.

■ Woodstock (1970)

Produced by Bob Maurice
Directed by Michael Wadleigh
Featuring Joan Baez, Joe Cocker, Country Joe and the Fish, Crosby Stills Nash and Young, Arlo Guthrie, Richie Havens, Jimi Hendrix, Santana, John Sebastien, Sha Na Na, Sly and the Family Stone, Ten Years After, and the Who

The rockumentary of the most famous festival of all that took place on Max Yasgur's farm, Woodstock, California, on 15–17 August 1969. The film shows the stages being constructed (to the strains of Canned Heat's 'Going Up the Country') plus several outstanding performances by some of the acts who performed there.

The original film ran for over three hours but a shorter version, called *Woodstock Remembered*, appeared on US TV in the early Eighties.

□ One Nation under a Groove

In 1956 a contest began that has been watched on one spring night each year by an audience growing to over 300 million even though it is ridiculed by the vast sections of the music industry and media. Each European Broadcasting Union member country is invited to select an act to perform a song written for the occasion in front of a live audience, usually in the country of the previous year's winner. The contest is broadcast live via satellite throughout Europe. After every participating country has performed, song juries in each of the participating countries award points: the highest scoring song wins the Grand Prix and, with a few exceptions, total obscurity within months.

■ The Eurovision Song Contest 1956–1988

1956 Lugano, Switzerland
UK entry: no entry
Grand Prix winner: 'Refrains', Lys Assia (Switzerland)

1957 Frankfurt, West Germany
UK entry: 'All', Patricia Breden (6)
Grand Prix winner: 'Net Alstown', Corry Brokken (Netherlands)

1958 Hilversum, Netherlands
UK entry: no entry
Grand Prix winner: 'Dors Mon Amour', André Claveon (France)

1959 Cannes, France
UK entry: 'Sing Little Birdie', Pearl Carr and Teddy Johnson (2)
Grand Prix winner: 'Eene Beetje', Teddy Scholten (Netherlands)

1960 London, England
UK entry: 'Looking High High High', Bryan Johnson (2)
Grand Prix winner: 'Tom Pillibi', Jaqueline Boyer (France)

1961 Cannes, France
UK entry: 'Are You Sure?', Allisons (2)
Grand Prix winner: 'Nous, Les Amoureux', Jean Claude Pascal (Luxembourg)

1962 Luxembourg
UK entry: 'Ring A Ding Girl', Ronnie Carroll (4)
Grand Prix winner: 'Un Premier Amour', Isabelle Aubret (France)

1963 London, England
UK entry: 'Say Wonderful Things', Ronnie Carroll (4)
Grand Prix winner: 'Dansevise', Grethe and Jörgen Ingman (Denmark)

1964 Copenhagen, Denmark
UK entry: 'I Love the Little Things', Matt Monro (2)
Grand Prix winner: 'Non Ho l'Eta per Amarti', Gigliola Cinquetti (Italy)

1965
UK entry: 'I Belong', Kathy Kirby (2)
Grand Prix winner: 'Poupée de Cire, Poupée de Son', France Gall (Luxembourg)

1966 Villa Louvigny, Luxembourg
UK entry: 'A Man Without Love', Kenneth McKellar (7)
Grand Prix winner: 'Merci Cherie', Udo Jurgens (Austria)

1967 Vienna, Austria
UK entry: 'Puppet on a String', Sandie Shaw (1)
Grand Prix winner: 'Puppet on a String', Sandie Shaw (United Kingdom)

1968 London, England
UK entry: 'Congratulations', Cliff Richard (2)
Grand Prix winner: 'La La La', Massiel (Spain)

1969 Madrid, Spain
UK entry: 'Boom Bang A Bang', Lulu (joint 1)
Grand Prix winner: 'Boom Bang A Bang', Lulu (United Kingdom), 'Un Jour, Un Enfant', Frida Boccana (France), 'Uno Cantando', Salome (Spain), 'De Troubador', Lennie Kuhr (Holland)

1970 Amsterdam, Holland
UK entry: 'Knock, Knock, Who's There?', Mary Hopkins (2)
Grand Prix winner: 'All Kinds of Everything', Dana (Eire)

1971 Dublin, Eire
UK entry: 'Jack in the Box', Clodagh Rodgers (4)
Grand Prix winner: 'Un Banc, Un Arbre, Un Rue', Severin (Monaco)

1972 Edinburgh, Scotland
UK entry: 'Beg, Steal or Borrow', New Seekers (2)
Grand Prix winner: 'Apres Tois (Come What May)', Vicky Leandros (Luxembourg)

1973 Luxembourg
UK entry: 'Power To All My Friends', Cliff Richard (4)
Grand Prix winner: 'Tu Te Reconnaitras', Anne Marie David (Luxembourg)

1974 Brighton, England
UK entry: 'Long Live Love', Olivia Newton-John (4)
Grand Prix winner: 'Waterloo', Abba (Sweden)

1975 Sweden
UK entry: 'Let Me Be the One', Shadows (2)
Grand Prix winner: 'Ding A Dong', Teach In (Holland)

1976 The Hague, Holland
UK entry: 'Save Your Kisses for Me', Brotherhood of Man (1)
Grand Prix winner: 'Save Your Kisses for Me', Brotherhood of Man (United Kingdom)

1977
UK entry: 'Rock Bottom', Lynsey De Paul and Mike Moran (2)
Grand Prix winner: 'L'Oiseau et l'Enfant', Marie Myriam (France)

1978 Paris, France
UK entry: 'Bad Old Days', CoCo (11)
Grand Prix winner: 'A Ba Ni Bi', Izhar Cohen and Alphabeta (Israel)

1979 Jerusalem, Israel
UK entry: 'Mary Anne', Black Lace (7)
Grand Prix winner: 'Hallelujah', Milk and Honey (Israel)

1980 The Hague, Holland
UK entry: 'Love Enough for Two', Prima Donna (3)
Grand Prix winner: 'What's Another Year?', Johnny Logan (Eire)

1981 Dublin, Eire
UK entry: 'Making Your Mind Up', Bucks Fizz (1)
Grand Prix winner: 'Making Your Mind Up', Bucks Fizz (United Kingdom)

1982 Harrogate, England
UK entry: 'One Step Further', Bardo (7)
Grand Prix winner: 'A Little Peace', Nicole (West Germany)

1983 Munich, West Germany
UK entry: 'I'm Never Giving Up', Sweet Dreams (6)
Grand Prix winner: 'Si La Vie Est Cadeau', Corinnine Hermes (Luxembourg)

1984 Luxembourg
UK entry: 'Love Games', Belle and the Devotions (7)
Grand Prix winner: 'Diggi Loo Diggi Ley', Herreys (Sweden)

1985
UK entry: 'Love Is', Vikki Watson (5)
Grand Prix winner: 'La Det Swinge', Bobby Socks (Norway)

1986 Bergen, Norway
UK entry: 'Runner in the Night', Ryder (7)
Grand Prix winner: 'J'Aime la Vie', Sandra Kim (Belgium)

1987 Brussels, Belgium
UK entry: 'Only the Light', Rikki (13)
Grand Prix winner: 'Hold Me Now', Johnny Logan (Eire)

1988 Dublin, Eire
UK entry: 'Go', Scott Fitzgerald (2)
Grand Prix winner: 'Ne Partez pas sans Moi', Celine Dior (Switzerland)

In 1987 Johnny Logan became the first artist to win the Eurovision Song Contest twice: 1980 and 1987. He also wrote 'Terminal 3', Ireland's 1984 entry, which came second.

Portugal's 1974 entry was used as the signal for the army to begin the overthrow of a forty-eight-year-old right-wing dictatorship.

Britain's 1978 act, CoCo, included Cheryl Baker, who would later turn up in Bucks Fizz, the UK's 1981 Grand Prix-winning act. Ryder, the UK's 1986 act, included actor Bill Maynard's son, later a star of BBC's *Truckers*.

Jaqueline Boyer's 'Tom Pillibi' was the first foreign entry to enter the UK charts.

In 1987 Plastic Bertrand, who had a 1978 Euro-punk hit with 'Ça Plane pour Moi', came twenty-first of twenty-two entries with 'Amour Amour' for Luxembourg. He scored four points. This event clearly affected him, as he was next heard of making a record with the Pope.

The 1969 contest was the first to be broadcast in colour.

In its first year (1956) only seven countries competed. Each submitted two songs.

Britain's 1974 entry, 'Long Live Love', was written by Val Avon, formerly of the pop group the Avons. The 1988 entry was written by Julie Forsyth, formerly of Guys and Dolls.

Stock, Aitken and Waterman provided an entry for Cyprus; it came eighteenth.

Boxer Barry McGuigan's dad, Pat, performed Ireland's 1967 entry.

■ Four acts who have failed to score any points at all

Jan Teigen (Norway), 'All Kinds of Everything', 1978
Aldril Livel (Norway), 'Finn Kalvick', 1980

Seyyal Taner and Grup Locomotif (Turkey–how apt!), 'Sarkim Sevgi Ustune', 1987
Wilfred (Austria), 'Lisa Mona Lisa', 1988

■ Best placed UK entries

First	'Save Your Kisses for Me', Brotherhood of Man
	'Making Your Mind Up', Bucks Fizz
	'Puppet on a String', Sandie Shaw
Joint First	'Boom Bang A Bang', Lulu
Second	'Are You Sure?', Allisons
	'Sing Little Birdie', Pearl Carr and Teddy Johnson
	'Rock Bottom', Lynsey De Paul and Mike Moran
	'Go', Scott Fitzgerald
	'Knock, Knock, Who's There?', Mary Hopkins
	'Looking High High High', Bryan Johnson
	'I Belong', Kathy Kirby
	'I Love the Little Things', Matt Monro
	'Beg, Steal or Borrow', New Seekers
	'Congratulations', Cliff Richard
	'Let Me Be the One', Shadows

The UK's worst placed entry to date was Rikki's 'Only the Light' in 1987, which came thirteenth, scoring only 47 points out of a possible 264.

■ Most successful countries

France	5 Grand Prix (including one shared)
Luxembourg	5 Grand Prix
Netherlands	4 Grand Prix (including one shared)
United Kingdom	4 Grand Prix (including one shared)
Eire	3 Grand Prix

Anyone who really wants to know more about the Eurovision Song Contest should write to the fan club. It can be reached at Eurovision Network, Alan Murrell, 48 Boscobel House, Royal Oak Road, London E8 1BU. And may you 'Eeene Beetje', 'Non Ho l'Eta per Amarti', 'La La La La, A Ba Ni Bi' and 'Diggi Loo Diggi Ley' happily ever after.

■ DISCO BEATLEMANIA

Herewith a small selection from the hundreds of records about the Beatles: some genuine tributes; most just cheap cash-ins.

1. 'Peppermint Beatles', Standells
2. 'All I Want for Christmas Is a Beatle', Dora Bryan
3. 'I Wanna Be a Beatle', Gene Cornish and the Unbeetables
4. 'Letter to the Beatles', Four Preps
5. 'Get Back Beatles', Gerrard Kenny and the New York Band
6. 'Ringo I Love You', Bonny Jo Mason
7. 'Saint Paul', Terry Knight
8. 'Ringo for President', Rolf Harris
9. 'We Love the Beatles', Vernon Girls
10. 'I Hate the Beatles', Allan Sherman
11. 'Saga of the Beatles', Johnny and the Hurricanes
12. 'Beatle Be Bop', Frenchy and the Chessmen
13. 'Boy with the Beatle Hair', Swans
14. 'I'll Let You Hold My Hand', Bootles
15. 'The Beatles' Barber', Scott Douglas
16. 'Frankenstein Meets the Beatles', Jekyll and Hyde
17. 'The Beatle Story', Real Original Beatles
18. 'Beatle Song', Japanese Beatles
19. 'We're Better than the Beatles', Brad Berwick
20. 'We're All Paul Bearers', Zacherias and the Beatles

The Standells were an American garage band famous for songs like 'Dirty Water', 'Sometimes Good Guys Don't Wear White' and 'Riot On Sunset Strip'; Dora Bryan is a British comedy actress; Gene Cornish was formerly in Joey Dee and the Starlighters and later in the (Young) Rascals; the Four Preps were a vocal quartet who had a big hit with 'Big Man' and included a certain Ed Cobb, who, apart from writing 'Tainted Love', wrote for and produced the aforementioned Standells; Gerrard Kenny is the well-known singer/songwriter ('New York New York', etc.); Bonny Jo Mason is better known as Cher; Terry Knight led his own band, Terry Knight and the Pack, in San Francisco in the late Sixties and then went on to manage Grand Funk Railroad; Rolf Harris is the inspirational antipodean artist and singer ('Sun Arise', 'Two Little Boys', etc.); the Vernon Girls provided backing vocals on many of the earlier UK pop TV shows; Allan Sherman was the American comedian best known for his 'Hello Muddah Hello Faddah' hit record; Johnny and the Hurricanes were probably the top rock instrumental group before the Shadows; as for the rest, you tell me.

In 1964 Bing Crosby, Sammy Davis Jr, Dean Martin and Frank Sinatra formed a group called the Bumblers and recorded a Beatles parody.

The four vultures in the Walt Disney film *Jungle Book* were called John, Paul, George and Ringo.

There are five Beatles on the cover of the *Abbey Road* LP: the Fab Four and a VW Beetle parked on the left.

According to the prestigious *Guinness Book of British Hit Singles*, the first Beatles' record to reach Number One in the British charts was 'From Me to You', their third single. This has brought consternation from many people, including George Martin, who claim that the group's second single, 'Please Please Me', topped the charts. In fact they are all correct. The *Guinness* book used the *Record Retailer* chart for the Sixties and in this chart 'Please Please Me' peaked at Number Two, held off the top spot first by Frank Ifield's 'Wayward Wind' and then by Cliff Richard's 'Summer Holiday'. The *Record Retailer* chart has become the most important chart in recent years thanks to its adoption in 1969 by the BBC and its use by the *Guinness* team. In the Sixties, however, the influential *New Musical Express* (*NME*) ran its own chart, which was widely regarded as the most important at the time, and in this chart 'Please Please Me' led the pack.

'Back in the USSR' was originally written for Twiggy to record.

Eric Segal, who wrote *Love Story*, the million-selling book and box office smash, co-wrote the screenplay for the *Yellow Submarine* animated film.

When the Beatles turned up at Abbey Road Studios to record their first single, it was with their new drummer Ringo Starr, who had recently replaced Pete Best amid great controversy and anger from many fans. Like the Beatles, George Martin had not been over-confident about Best's ability and (not knowing that he had been ousted) had booked session drummer Andy White for the recordings. When the band turned up with a new drummer, Martin saw no reason to change his plans and started recording with White on drums and Ringo on tambourine. However, Ringo was most upset about this and in the end Martin let Ringo sit in for a few takes of 'Love Me Do', promising to release the best one as a single. The takes were so similar that Beatle historians argued for years over which version was released, and in the end it has been decided that Ringo's drumming features on the single while Andy White's is on the LP version of the track.

The Beatles' second film, *Help!*, was dedicated to Elias Howe, inventor of the sewing machine.

The most recorded Lennon/McCartney composition is 'Yesterday', with over 1000 covers.

In 1976 Capitol Records' mystery group, Klattu, released their first US LP and speculation quickly grew that the band were in fact a re-formed Beatles. The music was described as similar to material on the *Sgt Pepper's Lonely Hearts Club Band* LP. Another supposed clue was that the word Klattu had appeared on the cover of Ringo's *Goodnight Vienna* LP. This 'evidence' along with clever marketing by Capitol and certain press reports (notably one in the *Providence Journal* by one Steve Smith – not me!) sent the LP into the US Top Forty. In fact, the band were four Canadian musicians and by 1978 their brief stint of fame was over. The only memorial to their work is the Carpenters' cover of 'Calling Occupants of Interplanetary Craft (The Recognized Anthem of World Contact Day)' which first appeared on Klattu's début LP.

A late Sixties single, 'We Are the Moles', by the Moles, was also rumoured to be the Beatles but in fact turned out to be Simon Dupree and the Big Sound.

Despite many varying dates from several sources, Paul McCartney and John Lennon first met at Woolton Church Fête on 6 July 1957. Some books, including Hunter Davies' official biography, put the date as 1955 and others as 1956 but almost all agree on one point: John Lennon was impressed with Paul McCartney because Paul knew all the words to Eddie Cochran's 'Twenty Flight Rock'. As Cochran didn't record the song until August 1956, it would have been impossible for Paul to have heard it in the summer of 1956, let alone 1955. This leaves 1957 as the only possible date from the popular selections and a quick glance at the local paper's write-up of the 1957 church fête will confirm that John's group, the Quarrymen, did indeed perform that day.

One of the characters in the *Magical Mystery Tour* film was called Buster Bloodvessel, a name later adopted by the lead singer of Bad Manners.

US record companies had to pay higher royalties if more than ten tracks were put on an album; this is why many Beatles tracks were cut from LPs and put out as singles in the States.

While in Hamburg the Beatles had a bet with Rory Storme as to who could break the stage first. The Beatles lost and had to buy a case of champagne for the victor.

Among those to have interviewed the Beatles in the early Sixties are: Gay Byrne, now the presenter of the Dublin-based chat show *The Late Late Show*, who was the first person to introduce the band on television; David Coleman, now best known as a sports commentator; Gordon Kaye, star of *'Allo 'Allo*, who interviewed them for Huddersfield Hospital Radio in 1963; and news-reader Peter Woods, who interviewed them in 1964.

The only Beatles' song to credit a fifth member is 'Get Back', which was billed 'the Beatles with Billy Preston'.

The *Sgt Pepper . . .* cover shows several famous people including: each of the Beatles twice, Bob Dylan, W. C. Fields, Aleister Crowley, Edgar Allan Poe, William Burroughs, Sir Robert Peel, Oliver Hardy, Karl Marx, George Bernard Shaw and Lewis Carroll.

John Lennon won the Foyle's Literary Prize for his book *In His Own Write*.

Some pillow cases used by the Beatles in a Kansas City hotel were cut into 160,000 1-inch squares and sold at $1 (55p) each.

Screams from the film *A Hard Day's Night* were used by John's Children on their mock live LP *Orgasm*.

Paul produced the Bonzo Dog Doodah Band's 'I'm the Urban Spaceman' single under the pseudonym Apollo C. Vermouth.

Booker T and the MGs' LP *McLemore Avenue* consists entirely of instrumental versions of the Beatles' *Abbey Road* set.

■ Fifteen LPs featuring guest appearances by former Beatles

1. *Young Americans*, David Bowie (Lennon)
2. *Freeze Frame*, Godley and Creme (McCartney)
3. *Stills*, Stephen Stills (Starr)
4. *Songs for a Tailor*, Jack Bruce (Harrison)
5. *One of These Days in England*, Roy Harper (McCartney)
6. *The Last Waltz*, The Band (Starr)
7. *Son of Schmilsson*, Harry Nilsson (Harrison)
8. *B. B. King in London*, B. B. King (Starr)
9. *Footprint*, Gary Wright (Harrison)
10. *Is This What You Want?*, Jackie Lomax (Harrison and Starr)
11. *Pussycats*, Harry Nilsson (Lennon)
12. *Postcard*, Mary Hopkins (McCartney)
13. *Coming Out*, Manhattan Transfer (Starr)
14. *It's Like You Never Left*, Dave Mason (Harrison)
15. *I Survive*, Adam Faith (McCartney)

■ FACTS AND FIGURES

'As a pop seismograph the charts may not be sensitive to every micro-tremor, but they never miss a world eruption!' John Pidgeon, rock writer and historian.

The charts, the hit parade, the Top Forty or whatever else you choose to call the weekly listings of the best-selling records in set categories in certain territories are the barometer of a record's success, which, in turn, shows how popular a group is at the time. The charts have always been the focus of the music industry, with the ultimate aim of most record companies to get their product into the charts by fair means or foul. In recent years many rock writers have sought to manipulate the charts into as many statistics as possible. This chapter reiterates some of these astounding arithmetical acrobatics and chucks in a few fascinating facts about the charts and record sales as well.

The first American chart was published in the trade magazine *Billboard* in the issue dated 20 July 1940. The top-selling single of the time was listed as Tommy Dorsey's 'I'll Never Smile Again'. The first UK chart based on sales of records as opposed to sales of sheet music (thus registering the artist's popularity as much as the song's) was published in the *New Musical Express* dated 14 November 1952. Al Martino was Number One with 'Here In My Heart'.

Pete and Annie Fowler were the first to log the British charts, in *Rock File* in 1973. Pete was a recording artist for Oval Records, which was run by Charlie Gillett, broadcaster, writer and editor of *Rock File*. In 1977 the first edition of *The Guinness Book of British Hit Singles* was published. This biennial 'chart-ology', compiled originally by brothers Tim and Jo Rice with broadcasters Paul Gambaccini and Mike Read, has established itself as the industry bible. When I refer to the British charts in this book I use the same sources as the *Guinness* book unless otherwise stated: the *NME* chart from November 1952 to March 1960 and British trade magazine *Record Retailer* chart hence, though the latter has undergone several name changes and is now the *Music Week* chart compiled by Gallup for *Music Week* and the BBC. Despite recent attempts by the MRIB and independent radio to topple this chart from power, it remains top of the charts.

In America Joel Whitburn is the undisputed champion chart-tracker. He bases his research on *Billboard*'s long running 'Hot 100'. The only serious contender to the *Billboard* chart was the one compiled by *Cashbox*.

No record has ever surpassed the eighteen weeks spent at the top of the UK singles chart by Frankie Laine's 'I Believe', nor, in any one year, has any band or artist spent more than Frankie's twenty-seven weeks atop the charts in 1953.

Frank Sinatra's 'My Way' has spent a total of 122 weeks in the British charts in 9 separate runs, way ahead of its closest rival, Judy Collins' 'Amazing Grace' – a mere 67 weeks from 8 runs.

As of 1987, to qualify for the UK charts a record must have 5 or less tracks, run for less than 25 minutes in total, have a wholesale price not exceeding £1.81 and be one of the 75 best-selling records in the country.

Jackie Wilson's 'Reet Petite' reached Number One in the UK chart on 27 December 1986–an incredible 29 years and 6 weeks after it made its first appearance in the chart. However, it does not hold the record for the longest period between chart appearances of a record: Nat 'King' Cole's rendition of 'When I Fall in Love' originally entered the UK charts on 19 April 1957. After a twenty-week run, it did not show up again until 12 December 1987.

Nowadays the average Number One record shifts about 150,000 copies per week for about two peak weeks.

Most records are sold on a Saturday.

Lionel Richie wrote or co-wrote a US Number One record every year from 1978 to 1985 inclusive.

■ Richie compositions

'Three Times a Lady', Commodores, 1978
'Still', Commodores, 1979

'Lady', Kenny Rogers, 1980
'Endless Love', Diana Ross and Lionel Richie, 1981
'Truly', Lionel Richie, 1982
'All Night Long (All Night)', Lionel Richie, 1983
'Hello', Lionel Richie, 1984
'We Are the World', written with Michael Jackson, USA For Africa, 1985

Grand Funk Railroad's 'Inside Looking Out' (their only UK hit) is, at 9 minutes 27 seconds, the longest 7-inch single A side to make the British charts.

At the time of writing, eighteen records had made their début in the UK chart at Number One. Here they are listed in order.

'Here in My Heart' (which débuted at the top only because it had built up its peak sales at the time the first chart was published), Al Martino
'Jailhouse Rock', Elvis Presley
'It's Now or Never', Elvis Presley
'The Young Ones', Cliff Richard
'Get Back', Beatles
'Cum on Feel the Noize', Slade
'Merry Xmas Everybody', Slade
'Going Underground', Jam
'Don't Stand So Close to Me', Police
'Stand and Deliver', Adam and the Ants
'A Town Called Malice', Jam
'Beat Surrender', Jam
'Is There Something I Should Know?', Duran Duran
'Two Tribes', Frankie Goes To Hollywood
'Do They Know It's Christmas?', Band Aid
'Dancing in the Street', David Bowie and Mick Jagger

■ BEER DRINKERS AND HELL RAISERS

The world of rock 'n' roll has thrown up more than its fair share of dedicated dipsomaniacs, drunken droners and singing soaks. If the pre-rock scene had Dean Martin as its champion boozer, then the rock era's top tipplers are Southern Comfort-swigging Janis Joplin, brandy-and-ginger glugging Keith Moon, the Guinness-guzzling Pogues, and a host of giggin' liggin' champagne Charlies. There have been casualties too; both Bon Scott and John Bonham died after heavy all-night drinking sessions, and drink was a contributing factor to many other rock stars' deaths.

Below are just a few of the multitude of songs written in praise (or occasionally not) of the demon drink. The list is far from complete: it finds no room for either Slim Dusty's lament 'A Pub With No Beer' nor for the Dead Kennedies' unmentionable tale of the problems of over-indulgence. No matter! Kindly raise your glasses high and toast the following drinking ditties.

1. '2000 Light Ales from Home', Pop Will Eat Itself
2. 'Streams of Whiskey', Pogues
3. 'Little Ole Wine Drinker Me', Lurkers
4. 'Alabama Song (Whisky Bar)', Doors
5. 'I Am a Cider Drinker', Wurzels
6. 'Whiskey in the Jar', Thin Lizzy
7. 'Two Pints of Lager and a Packet of Crisps Please', Splodgenessabounds
8. 'Tequila', Champs
9. 'The Nips Are Getting Bigger', Mental As Anything
10. 'Milk and Alcohol', Dr Feelgood
11. 'Malt and Barley Blues', McGuinness Flint
12. 'Drinking Wine Spo Dee O Dee', Jerry Lee Lewis
13. 'Red Red Wine', Jimmy James and the Vagabonds

14. 'White Lightning', Gene Vincent
15. 'One Scotch One Bourbon One Beer', Alfred Brown
16. 'Someone Put Something in My Drink', Ramones
17. 'One Drink Too Many', Sailor
18. 'Seven Drunken Nights', Dubliners
19. 'Wide Eyed and Legless', Andy Fairweather Low
20. 'I Can't Stand Up for Falling Down', Elvis Costello

We should also thank Greg Winkfield for exposing 'The Man Who Waters the Workers Beer'.

Ron Watts – booker at the 100 Club in Oxford Street, organizer of the infamous 1976 punk festival there and early manager of the Damned – was in a Seventies RCA group called Brewer's Droop.

In the early Eighties successful rockney purveyors Chas and Dave bought a North London pub, kicked out the juke-boxes, fruit machines and pizza bar snacks, and brought in the piano, pies and mash, and jellied eels. The pub, in Highbury, was formerly known as the Pegasus and it was in its car park in 1977 that Johnny Rotten was attacked and injured by knife-wielding thugs.

Southern Comfort were so pleased by the constant free advertisement Janis Joplin provided for them, they sent her a fur coat as a present.

■ THE GROOVER

Surprisingly for such an esteemed artist, I can recall only one tribute record to (and this is where the cliché is never more deserving) *the late, great* Marc Bolan. That record is Del Aaron Shears' 'Keep a Little Marc in Your Heart'. I welcome information concerning any other tribute records.

As a child Marc was apparently in a skiffle group called Susie and the Hoola Hoops. The Susie in question was said to be a certain Helen Shapiro. However, it should be remembered that Marc was a great story-teller and such claims should not be construed as the gospel truth.

As a teenager Marc appeared on the cover of the magazine *Town* as an 'ace face' Mod.

On the last edition of *Supersonic* Marc joined an all-star band to perform a version of Chuck Berry's 'Sweet Little Rock 'n' Roller'. Other members included Dave Edmunds, Ray Davies, Alvin Stardust and Elkie Brooks, with Steve Currie and Dino Dines from Marc's band.

Marc recorded a demo of Betty Everett's 'You're No Good' under his pseudonym, Toby Tyler.

Marc made his first TV appearance on *Ready Steady Go.*

Marc called the music room in his Notting Hill flat Toadstool Studios.

His song 'Baby Boomerang' allegedly is about Patti Smith.

Gloria Jones, Marc's companion and fiancée at the time of his death, wrote 'I Haven't Stopped Dancing Yet', a 1979 hit for Gonzalez.

■ Five songs that mention T Rex in their lyrics

1. 'All the Young Dudes', Mott The Hoople
2. 'Do You Remember Rock 'n' Roll Radio?', Ramones
3. 'You Better You Bet', Who
4. 'Kool in the Kaftan', B. A. Robertson
5. 'Prime Mover', Zodiac Mindwarp and the Love Reaction

■ DON'T PLAY YOUR ROCK 'N' ROLL TO ME

There are people, particularly among those working in the media, who consider themselves moral guardians of society and impose censorship. Below are some records that have been banned – or effectively banned by being removed from play-lists or having restrictions put on them – either permanently or for a short period by broadcasting authorities.

'Relax', Frankie Goes to Hollywood
After Radio 1 had been playing the record for several weeks in 1984, Breakfast Time DJ Mike Read announced that he was no longer going to play it because the lyrics referred to gay sex. Other DJs followed his lead: the record stopped getting Radio 1 air-play – and screamed to Number One.

'Eight Miles High', Byrds; 'Along Comes Mary', Association; 'A Day in the Life', Beatles; and 'My Friend Jack', Smoke
All banned in the Sixties because of alleged drug references.

'They're Coming to Take Me Away HA-HAAA!', Napoleon XIV
Some US radio stations considered it offensive to the mentally ill.

'Spasticus Autisticus', Ian Dury
Widely banned by programmers who totally misunderstood this poignant Dury song released in the Year of the Disabled.

'Dominique', Singing Nun
Banned by station WHYN in Springfield, Massachusetts, which found it 'degrading to Catholicism'.

'I Can't Control Myself', Troggs
Radio bosses found the line 'Your slacks are low and your hips are showing' too suggestive.

'Speedy Gonzales', Pat Boone
Amazingly, even Mr Bland himself could upset the programmers. This song was found to be racially offensive by several Mexican and Latin stations.

'Da Doo Ron Ron', Ian Matthews
Banned by the Beeb because Matthews left the lyric as it was when originally sung by the Crystals, thus upsetting the homophobes of Broadcasting House.

'Give Ireland Back to the Irish', Wings
Too political.

'Love to Love You Baby', Donna Summer
Too sexy.

'Je T'Aime . . . Moi Non Plus', Jane Birkin and Serge Gainsborough
Too suggestive.

'A Hundred Pounds of Clay', Craig Douglas
Irreligious.

'Celebrate (The Day After You)', Blow Monkeys
This anti-Thatcher anthem was kept off the airwaves until after the June 1987 election.

'The Boiler', Rhoda Dakar
A rather harrowing song about rape that the BBC preferred to sweep under the carpet.

Cliff Richard has perhaps the most unique of all banned records. He recorded a song called 'Honky Tonk Angels' in the Seventies. After its release he found out that Honky Tonk Angels are, in fact, prostitutes, so he demanded the record company withdraw the disc, thus banning his own record.

Seven minutes was cut from the pre-recorded *Juke Box Jury* on 7 January 1967 because the Games' 'The Addicted Man' (about cigarettes) was considered unsuitable for transmission.

In 1987 Pete St John's 'The Hole Song' was officially banned by Radio Telefis Eireann, which considered the lyrics 'open to ambiguous interpretation'. The song was actually about the plague of roadworks in the fair city of Dublin at that time.

The Rockin' Vicars – who at one time included future Hawkwind and Motorhead bassist Lemmy – were banned from playing at their local Blackpool Pleasure Beach Casino in the late Sixties. A spokesman for the company said 'It is just the name and the general appearance we object to. The members have been arriving in a van bearing a gilded crucifix, covered with lipstick. There is a cross on the drums. We do not feel this is in keeping with family entertainment.'

■ TAKIN' CARE OF BUSINESS

A look at the industry that turns songs into records.

□ Sound Systems

Man has long known how to produce sound mechanically but it was not until 1877 that a device was patented capable of reproducing stored sound. That device was the phonograph and the inventor registering the patent was Thomas Edison. Sound was recorded on to a cylinder coated with tin foil. The vibration of the air created by the voice or instrument caused a metal point to undulate against the revolving cylinder, cutting a patterned groove of the sound in the foil. Later the process could be reversed: the pattern in the foil would move a needle, which would vibrate a diaphragm that would create sound waves. These sound waves, which were a reproduction of the original sound, could be amplified through a large horn and so be heard by the listener.

There were many others working in the same field as Edison and the medium began to develop quickly. Wax cylinders soon replaced tin foil. Ten years after Edison's ground-breaking patent, a German immigrant in America, Emile Berliner, made the next important step in sound reproduction by patenting the flat, lateral cut disc. Over the next twenty-five years the disc gradually replaced the cylinder. The original discs were made of zinc coated with a thin layer of fat. During recording the stylus cut away the fat depending on the pitch of the sound. Then the disc was immersed in an acid bath, which dissolved the zinc in the places where no fat remained, so preserving the sound recording. Later it was realized that a negative could be made, and from this master disc almost unlimited copies of the original recording could be produced.

The next developments were in the materials used for discs and the speeds at which they were recorded and replayed. These standardized at 78 revolutions per minute (rpm) for music, and 16 rpm for the spoken word. The discs at this time varied in diameter, but most were ten inches across.

In 1920 the development of the microphone made it possible to record electrically rather than acoustically. In 1933 the first experimental stereo discs were made, though it was not until 1958 that the first commercial stereo recordings were commercially available. Stereo gave the listener more realistic reproductions.

In 1948 vinyl became the new material for discs, replacing the shellac of which most 78s were made. The following year the familiar 7-inch 45 rpm records appeared for the first time, and a year later Decca released the first 12-inch 33 rpm multi-track long players in Britain.

In the mid-Sixties a new and totally different form of capturing sound was introduced to the public. Magnetic tape stored sound in the pattern of microscopic pieces of metal arranged magnetically on a thin tape. This led to the development of the popular cassette.

In ensuing years, although the quality of recording, storing and reproducing sound improved, there were few major developments until 1976, when Philips developed the laser-vision disc. It was a 12-inch disc containing an hour of stereo sound and colour vision that was read by a laser beam and fed through a television. Some films were released on laser disc, but the system was soon made obsolete by the dramatic growth of domestic video, which had the major advantage of enabling you to record for yourself and not rely on pre-recorded material.

Not wishing to waste their research, Philips developed the compact disc (CD), a five-inch disc that can contain an hour or so of stereo music on its one playing side. The sound is again read by a laser and played through a CD system that hooks up to a hi-fi. With the advent of digital recording (which stores sound as an electrical signal and not on tape, thus reducing noise) at much the same time, the ability of CDs to play without hiss or distortion gave the listener near-perfect reproductions of the original sound. Unlike vinyl records, CDs are virtually undamageable and the laser beam will happily ignore scratches on the clear cover that protects the groove. When CD was launched in 1982, classical music accounted for about 75 per cent of the market but within four years pop music had taken the lion's share.

The most recent development in music reproduction is digital audio tape (DAT), which offers CD quality sound reproduction from a cassette (and a very expensive player).

☐ I Love My Label

Twenty influential, important, or just plain interesting record labels

■ A&M

An American company formed by Herb *A*lpert and Jerry *M*oss in 1962. Originally called Carnival. In its early years its only real success came with part owner Alpert and his Tijuana Brass. In the Seventies, however, A&M began to strengthen its roster, signing successful acts like the Carpenters.

Major artists: Herb Alpert and his Tijuana Brass, Police, Carpenters, Supertramp, Squeeze, Joan Armatrading, Chris De Burgh

■ APPLE

The Beatles formed their own label in 1968. Although the group's own records were still released on Parlophone, they did carry the Apple logo. The operation was first run from Wigmore Street in London and later moved to the more famous building at 3 Savile Row. The idea behind it was to launch new pop talent, which it did most successfully with Mary Hopkins. Although the label had several hits, it was doomed because of the lax way in which it was run.

Major artists: Mary Hopkins, Badfinger

■ ATLANTIC

Founded in New York in 1947 by Ahmet and Neshui Ertegun and Herb Abramson to market R&B records. It established itself in the pop charts with mid-Fifties cross-overs like 'Sh-Boom' by the Chords. Its first white hit was Bobby Darin's 'Splish Splash'. During the Sixties it had an impressive roster of soul stars and later in the decade began to sign rock bands as well. In Britain it became part of the Warner Elektra Atlantic (WEA) conglomerate.

Major artists: Ray Charles, Drifters, Aretha Franklin, Ben E. King, Wilson Pickett, Led Zeppelin, Yes

■ Beggars Banquet

In 1974 DJs and record dealers Nick Austin and Martin Mills opened the Beggars Banquet record shop in Earls Court, London. It was the first record shop in England selling both new and second-hand records side by side. After moving into concert promotion, Austin and Mills went into management, signing the punk band the Lurkers. No other record company would sign the band and so the Beggars Banquet Records label was born. Indie label 4AD started as a BB label, but when it was strong enough it severed its umbilical cord to the mother company.

Major artists: Lurkers, Gary Numan, Bauhaus, Freeez, Icicle Works, Fall, Cult, Flesh For Lulu

■ Capitol

Formed in America in 1942 (as Liberty) by Buddy De Sylva of Paramount Pictures, Johnny Mercer the song-writer and Glen E. Wallicus, an influential Hollywood record store boss. In June of the same year they became Capitol. They established themselves in America over the next decade and in 1955 EMI took them over as they wanted an American outlet. In 1956 the Capitol Tower in Hollywood, a building supposedly resembling a stack of records, became their main headquarters and studios.

Major artists: Nat King Cole, Peggy Lee, Tennessee Ernie Ford, Gene Vincent, Beach Boys, Glen Campbell, Grand Funk, Bob Seger, Steve Miller Band, the Beatles (in the US)

■ CBS

Columbia Broadcasting Systems started in 1965. Its catalogue over the years has tended to stick with easy listening or middle of the road artists. Occasionally it makes forays into more aggressive rock (for example, the Clash), but it seems more at home with singer/songwriters or West Coast type laid-back rock. Epic is a CBS label. CBS is now known as CBS/Sony.

Major artists: Bob Dylan, Simon and Garfunkel, Johnny Mathis, Michael Jackson, Wham!, Clash, Barbra Streisand, Julio Iglesias

■ Charly

Founded in 1974 by Joop Visser, Charly specializes in re-issuing previously released material. In its early days it specialized almost entirely in country, blues, rockabilly and rock 'n' roll, and established its reputation with the cult fans of these styles. The catalogue has now expanded to cover a wider range of material, varying from the progressive rock band Gong to the Yardbirds. It has also signed the Bollock Brothers (including John Lydon's brother Jimmy) to make new recordings.

■ Chess

Leonard and Phil Chess arrived in America from Poland in the late Twenties. In the Forties they started running clubs on Chicago's South Side, booking mostly black acts. In 1947 they formed their first label, Aristocrat. When they came across Muddy Waters playing guitar for Sunnyland Slim, they decided to concentrate on recording the blues. The label became Chess in 1950 and over the next decade or so recorded the finest blues and R&B around. The label was sold off soon after Leonard Chess died in 1969. The Rolling Stones recorded a tribute to the label, '2120 South Michigan Avenue', titled after the studio's address.

Major artists: Muddy Waters, Chuck Berry, Bo Diddley, Howlin' Wolf, the Moonglows

■ Decca

In 1928 Decca began to make its own records, having previously made the instruments played on them and the gramophones on which they were played. The label rapidly established itself as a major UK label. US Decca was formed in 1934. Decca's best-known studio complex, in West Hampstead, was purchased from the Crystalte Company in 1937. Decca was the first company to issue LPs in Britain (1950). It is always remembered as the label that turned down the Beatles (though several others made that mistake as well). In 1980 the ailing label was taken over by PolyGram.

Major artists: Rolling Stones, Tommy Steele, Billy Fury, Zombies, Tom Jones

■ Def Jam

Started by Rick Rubin and Russell Simmons in New York in 1981, inspired by the growing hip-hop scene in the city, Def (for definitive, meaning best) Jam's first releases were 12-inch discs by people like LL Cool J. As the label developed, it produced a variety of linked but differing styles from the metal hip-hop hybrid of the Beastie Boys and the demonic thrash of Slayer to the sweet soul of Tashan. Def Jam is the most potent label to emerge in the Eighties.

Major artists: Beastie Boys, LL Cool J, Oran 'Juice' Jones, Run DMC, Slayer, Tashan

■ EMI

The *E*lectrical and *M*usical *I*ndustries Company was formed in April 1931 when Gramophone, Columbia Gramophone, Parlophone, Regal and Zonophone all merged, creating the largest recording organization in the world at that time. The famous Abbey Road Studios opened later that year. Since then EMI has remained the most important British (and, possibly, international) label thanks to its diversity (it has arms in all areas of the business) and a wide range of artists.

Major artists: Beatles, Cliff Richard, Duran Duran, Pink Floyd, and many more

■ Factory

TV presenter Tony Wilson, who had hosted the new wave pop show *So It Goes*, started Factory Communications in 1977 in Manchester. It built its reputation on the back of the cult success of Joy Division. The label blossomed in the early Eighties, ironically with the death of Ian Curtis and Joy Division, and the birth of New Order.

Major artists: Joy Division, New Order, A Certain Ratio, Durutti Column, the Railway Children, James

■ Island

Island was founded in Jamaica in 1959 by Chris Blackwell. Its first success in Jamaica was with Laurel Aitken's 'Little Sheila'. In 1962 it moved operations to Britain, where its first release was Owen Gray's 'Twist Baby'. Although it started as a black music label, it quickly diversified into rock. In the late Sixties Island signed numerous progressive British bands. Success has continued into the Eighties thanks to acts like U2.

Major artists: Bob Marley, U2, Traffic, Grace Jones, Robert Palmer, John Martyn, Courtney Pine

■ Motown

Founded in 1958 by Berry Gordy in Detroit, Michigan, a major car-producing area often known as Motor Town, hence the label's name. It consists of several subsidiary labels, such as Tamla and Anna, but they were all known as Tamla Motown in the UK. Motown described itself as 'the sound of young America'. In its Sixties heyday it had a house band that consisted of Eli Fountain (sax),

Earl Van Dyke (keyboards), Robert White (guitar), James Jamerson (bass), Joe Messina (guitar) and Benny Benjamin (drums).

Major artists: Supremes, Four Tops, Temptations, Smokey Robinson and the Miracles, Stevie Wonder

■ PYE/PRT

Pye established itself as a major label in the late Fifties thanks mainly to the success of Lonnie Donegan. In the early Sixties Pye International became the British outlet for numerous American labels, including Red Bird, Chess and Kama Sutra. Pye (UK) had its own success with British acts, most notably the Kinks. In the early Eighties Pye became PRT (Precision Records and Tapes).

Major artists: Kinks, Real Thing, Lonnie Donegan

■ Radar

Founded in late 1977 by Andrew Lauder and Martin Davis (formerly of United Artists) and Jake Riviera (formerly Stiff). Jake brought Elvis Costello, Nick Lowe and the Yachts with him from Stiff, and Lowe's 'I Love the Sound of Breaking Glass' launched the label in 1978. As well as issuing new product, Radar also made available old material, such as Iggy Pop's unreleased 1974 LP *Kill City*. It also arranged a licensing deal with Lelan Rogers (elder brother of Kenny) to release product originally issued in the Sixties and early Seventies on his International Artists label. In November 1979 Radar's distributors, WEA, bought the label and the following year Lauder and Costello formed F. Beat.

Major artists: Elvis Costello, Nick Lowe, Yachts, Inmates, Bram Tchaikovsky

■ Rak

Formed in 1969 by Mickie Most, an established producer and minimally successful singer. During the early Seventies he built a successful roster of pop and teenybopper groups, relying heavily on the production line writing and production techniques he could give them. Although the hits are less forthcoming, the label still exists.

Major artists: Hot Chocolate, Mud, Suzi Quatro, Smokie, Kim Wilde

■ Stiff

Formed in July 1976 by Dave Robinson and Jake Riviera. Dave ran the studio at the Hope and Anchor pub while Jake had just returned from being a tour manager on Dr Feelgood's US tour. Everything about the label was tongue-in-cheek, except the music. Even the name was taken from the record business expression for a flop! Nick Lowe launched the label with his 'So It Goes' and although it wasn't a hit, it got the label noticed. Many people predicted the label would fold when Costello, Lowe and the Yachts left for Radar with Rivierra, but Robinson proved them wrong and got even bigger success with Madness. The label has been absorbed by the Island/ZTT organization.

Major artists: Elvis Costello, Nick Lowe, Ian Dury, Wreckless Eric, Madness, Belle Stars, the Pogues

■ 2-Tone

Started in Coventry in 1979 by a group of like-minded musicians, the label was dedicated to promoting the cause of Ska music. It was also a label that decried racism, hence its title, logo and multi-racial bands. Success at first was phenomenal but after the 1979/80 Ska boom the hits dropped away and so did the acts. Closely linked to Chrysalis, today only the Special AKA keep the label alive.

Major artists: Specials, Special AKA, the Selector

■ Virgin

Started out as a mail order record shop run by Richard Branson and distant cousin Simon Draper. When a postal strike held up the mail orders, they opened a shop in Tottenham Court Road and started Virgin Records. They started the record label as a means of releasing records by experimental British musicians not otherwise being released. Mike Oldfield gave them their first hit LP, but they had to wait for old 'New Wavers' the Motors for singles success.

Major artists: Mike Oldfield, Hatfield and the North, Sex Pistols, Motors, Culture Club

A group called Warner Bros. recorded for a host of Chicago labels in the Sixties.

Motown Records product was originally released in the UK by (in order): London–American, Fontana, Oriole and Stateside before attaining its own Tamla Motown identity.

It is highly unlikely that any collector, no matter how dedicated, will be able to complete his collection of releases on the Factory label. The reason is that Factory don't release only records in their catalogue sequence, but other items as well. For example FAC 1 is a poster, FAC 2 is a badge, but what makes it hardest of all for the collector is FAC 51 – the Hacienda Club in Manchester.

Rough Trade, the independent stalwart, got a slagging off from Stiff Little Fingers in the song 'Rough Trade', while Graham Parker had things to say about his American label, Mercury, in the song 'Mercury Poisoning'.

Chrysalis' name comes from an amalgam of the names of its two founding fathers *Chris* Wright and Terry *Ellis*: Chris-Ellis.

Island took its name from the 1957 movie *Island in the Sun*.

Bang Records was founded by *B*ert Berns, *A*hmet Ertegun, *N*eshui Ertegun and *G*erald (Jerry) Wexler.

John Peel's Dandelion label was named after Marc Bolan's pet hampster.

Solar Records is an acronym for the *S*ound *o*f *L*os *A*ngeles *R*ecords.

When Virgin came to signing its first contract (with Mike Oldfield), it had to borrow Sandy Denny's recording contract, as no one had a clue what to write.

Zarjazz, the label owned by ex-members of Madness, takes its name from *2000 AD* comic-speak. It means fab, brill, etc.

The honour of having the Decca catalogue number F 12345 went to Noel Harrison with his cover of Dylan's 'It's All Over Now Baby Blue' in February 1966.

The Eurythmics almost signed to Radar.

'Let's Dance' (Chris Montez) was written by Jim Lee, chief of Monogram Records.

■ Ten artists who own their own labels

1. Elton John, Rocket
2. Madness, Zarjazz
3. Beatles, Apple
4. Paul Weller, Respond
5. Starship, Grunt
6. Rolling Stones, Rolling Stones
7. Gary Numan, Numa
8. Gene Chandler, Bamboo
9. Beach Boys, Brother
10. Hoyt Axton, Jeremiah

□ IN THE STUDIO

Many bands, both past and present, owe much of their success to their producer and consequently some producers become well known and much sought after. Here are a few of the top producers and some of the recordings they have produced.

■ Phil Spector

1. 'To Know Him Is to Love Him', Teddy Bears (1959)
2. 'He's A Rebel', Crystals (1962)
3. 'You've Lost That Lovin' Feeling', Righteous Brothers (1963)
4. 'Baby I Love You', Ronettes (1964)
5. 'River Deep Mountain High', Ike and Tina Turner (1966)

6. 'Instant Karma', John Lennon (1970)
7. 'My Sweet Lord', George Harrison (1970)
8. 'Make the Woman Love Me', Dion (1975)
9. 'Do You Remember Rock 'n' Roll Radio', Ramones (1980)
10. 'Walking on Thin Ice', Yoko Ono (1981)

■ Joe Meek

1. 'Green Jeans', Fabulous Flee Rekkers (1960)
2. 'Angela Jones', Michael Cox (1960)
3. 'Swinging Low', Outlaws (1961)
4. 'You've Got What I Like', Cliff Bennett and the Rebel Rousers (1961)
5. 'Night of the Vampire', Moontrekkers (1961)
6. 'Johnny Remember Me', John Leyton (1961)
7. 'Telstar', Tornados (1962)
8. 'Jack the Ripper', Screaming Lord Sutch (1963)
9. 'Just Like Eddie', Heinz (1963)
10. 'Have I the Right', Honeycombs (1964)

■ George Martin

1. *The Best of Sellers*, Peter Sellers (1959)
2. *Milligan Preserved*, Spike Milligan (1961)
3. 'You're Driving Me Crazy', Temperance Seven (1961)
4. 'From Me to You', Beatles (1963)
5. 'How Do You Do It', Gerry and the Pacemakers (1963)
6. 'Little Children', Billy J. Kramer and the Dakotas (1964)
7. 'Anyone Who Had A Heart', Cilla Black (1964)
8. *Wired*, Jeff Beck (1976)
9. 'High Priests of Rhythmic Noise', Cheap Trick (1980)
10. *Nowhere To Run*, UFO (1980)

■ Chris Thomas

1. *Tightly Knit*, Climax Blues Band (1970)
2. 'Pandora's Box', Procul Harum (1973)

3. 'Apple of My Eye', Badfinger (1974)
4. 'Love Is the Drug', Roxy Music (1975)
5. 'Rough Kids', Kilburn and the High Roads (1974)
6. 'God Save the Queen', Sex Pistols (1977)
7. 'Glad to Be Gay', Tom Robinson Band (1978)
8. 'Kid', Pretenders (1979)
9. 'Old Siam Sir', Wings (1979)
10. 'Rough Boys', Pete Townshend (1980)

■ Dave Edmunds

1. 'Down on the Farm', Shakin' Stevens (1970)
2. 'Shake Some Action', Flamin' Groovies (1972)
3. '(What's So Funny 'Bout) Peace, Love & Understanding', Brinsley Schwarz (1974)
4. 'I Fought the Law', Ducks Deluxe (1975)
5. 'Let's Go to the Disco', Disco Brothers (1976)
6. 'England's Glory', Max Wall (1977)
7. *And the Music Played On*, Del Shannon (1978)
8. 'John I'm Only Dancing', Polecats (1981)
9. 'Destination Zululand', King Kurt (1983)
10. 'Rollin' Home', Status Quo (1986)

■ Nick Lowe

1. 'So It Goes', Nick Lowe (1976)
2. 'New Rose', Damned (1976)
3. 'Jump for Joy', Stones Masonry (1976)
4. 'Alison (My Aim Is True)', Elvis Costello (1977)
5. 'Whole Wide World', Wreckless Eric (1977)
6. 'New York Shuffle', Graham Parker (1977)
7. 'Old Rock 'n' Roller', Mickey Jupp (1978)
8. 'Ring of Fire', Carlene Carter (1980)
9. 'Violent Love', Dr Feelgood (1980)
10. 'Keep On Keepin' On', Redskins (1984)

■ Jerry Leiber and Mike Stoller

1. 'Hound Dog', Big Mama Thornton (1952)
2. 'Searchin'', Coasters (1957)
3. 'Lavender Blue', Sammy Turner (1959)
4. 'Only in America', Jay and the Americans (1963)
5. 'There Goes My Baby', Drifters (1959)
6. 'Iko Iko', Dixie Cups (1964)
7. 'Is That All There Is', Peggy Lee (1969)
8. 'Stuck in the Middle with You', Stealer's Wheel (1973)
9. 'Pandora's Box', Procul Harum (1975)
10. 'Pearl's A Singer', Elkie Brooks (1977)

■ Mickie Most

1. 'House of the Rising Sun', Animals (1964)
2. 'Tobacco Road', Nashville Teens (1964)
3. 'Is It True', Brenda Lee (1964)
4. 'I'm into Something Good', Herman's Hermits (1964)
5. 'To Sir with Love', Lulu (1967)
6. 'Hi Ho Silver Lining', Jeff Beck (1967)
7. 'Sunshine Superman', Donovan (1966)
8. 'Knock Knock Who's There', Mary Hopkins (1970)
9. 'Motor Biking', Chris Spedding (1975)
10. 'Lay Your Love on Me', Racey (1978)

■ Trevor Horn

1. 'Video Killed the Radio Star', Buggles (1979)
2. 'Poison Arrow', ABC (1982)
3. 'Give Me Back My Heart', Dollar (1982)
4. 'Back of My Hand'*, Jags (1979)
5. 'Cry', Godley and Creme (1985)
6. 'Dr Mabuse', Propaganda (1984)
7. 'Owner of a Lonely Heart', Yes (1983)
8. 'Relax', Frankie Goes To Hollywood (1984)
9. 'Do They Know It's Christmas', Band Aid (1984)
10. 'Girl to the Power of 6', Mint Juleps (1987)

* with several co-producers

■ Mike Stock, Matt Aitken and Peter Waterman

1. 'The Upstroke', Agents Aren't Aeroplanes (1984)
2. 'So You Think You're a Man', Divine (1984)
3. 'Whatever I Do (Wherever I Go)', Hazell Dean (1984)
4. 'You Spin Me Round (Like a Record)', Dead or Alive (1984)
5. 'Say I'm Your Number One', Princess (1985)
6. 'It's a Man's Man's World', Brilliant (1985)
7. 'Respectable', Mel and Kim (1987)
8. 'Let It Be', Ferry Aid (1987)
9. 'Toy Boy', Sinitta (1987)
10. 'Whenever I Need Somebody', Rick Astley (1987)

Producer Steve Lillywhite (Simple Minds, etc.) is married to singer Kirsty McColl.

EMI engineer and producer Norman Smith worked with many top groups during his time at Abbey Road Studios, including the Beatles, Pink Floyd, and the Pretty Things. In 1971 the former jazz trumpeter made the charts under the name Hurricane Smith, singing 'Don't Let It Die', the first of three Top Thirty hits.

Anita Ward was the second choice to record the Frederick Knight song 'Ring My Bell'. He had written it for Stacy Lattisaw (then 11 years old) but she signed to a different label.

In 1969 Rod Stewart sang a guide vocal on a song called 'In a Broken Dream' for the Australian group Python Lee Jackson. In the end everyone was so pleased with the demo that Rod's voice was left in. The song was eventually released as a British single in 1971 and became a hit the following year.

Little Richard's 'Keep A Knockin'' was only a 57-second demo, edited into a 2 minute 10 second song. Conversely, Simon and Garfunkel's 'The Boxer' was culled from 100 hours of studio tape.

Mister Mister's massive hit 'Kyrie' was recorded in just one and a half hours.

The Fastest Group Alive's 1967 B side '5–15' is just 40 seconds long, and Martin Mull's 'Duelling Tubas' (a US hit) clocks in at just 86 seconds, but the Electro-Hippies' 'Mega-Armageddon Death' beats all-comers clocking in at just 1 second.

Several records have utilized a studio trick of cutting bits of their songs backwards. The most famous to do so are the Beatles, who have a backward bit at the end of 'Rain' (1966). The flip of Napoleon XIV's 'They're Coming To Take Me Away HA-HAAA!' (1966) is 'Aaah-Ah Yawa Em Ekat Ot Gnimoc Er'yeht', which is the A side played backwards. Be Bop Deluxe's 'Rocket Cathedrals' (from *Axe Victim*) incorporates the cryptic backwards message 'Automatic destruction will commence on the mother planet'. Weirdest of all: in 1986 the moral watchdogs of Ironton, Ohio, publicly burned copies of the theme song to the Sixties TV show *Mr Ed* (about a talking horse) because they claimed that played backwards the record contained satanic messages.

The day Mickie Most flew to America to produce Sam Cooke was sadly the same day that the soul star was shot dead.

In 1974, with the streaking craze bared to the public, Hank Ballard released a song called 'Let's Go Streaking', which he recorded in the nude. Former Teardrop Explodes leader Julian Cope recorded his LP *Fried* in a similiar state of undress, while former Buzzcock Steve Diggle recorded a track on Flag of Convenience's *Northern Skyline* LP naked in order to 'get the right ambience'. John Lennon recorded 'Revolution' flat on his back but at least he had clothes on.

■ Ten groups or artists who have owned studios

1. Beatles: Apple
2. Jimi Hendrix: Ladyland
3. Trevor Horn: SARM
4. Marty Wilde: Select Sound Studios
5. Bob Lamb (ex-Locomotive and Steve Gibbons): Bob Lamb's Recording Studio (Birmingham)
6. Kinks: Konk Studios
7. Barry Blue: Aosis Audio Visual
8. Rick Buckler: Arkantide Studios
9. Pete Townshend: Eel Pie Recording Studios
10. John Foxx: The Garden Recording Studios

In the mid-Eighties the charts were flooded with remixed versions of old hits (particularly disco and dance music), which were given a new lease of life by producers and engineers. Records to benefit from such treatment include Donna Summer's 'I Feel Love', the Real Thing's 'You To Me Are Everything' and the Cure's 'Boys Don't Cry'.

Lots of groups included different mixes of their current single on the 12-inch version or LP. They often gave these remixes ridiculous names as the following list shows:

1. 'The Fly on the Wall Mix': 'Madam Butterfly' (Malcolm McLaren)
2. 'The Splashdown Remix': 'Apollo 9' (Adam Ant)
3. 'The Beat on the Drum Mix': 'Mother's Talk' (Tears For Fears)
4. 'I Mean, After All It's Only Deadman's Curve Mix': 'Driving Away from Home' (It's Immaterial)
5. 'Below the Belt Mix': 'Flesh for Fantasy' (Billy Idol)
6. 'Spic 'n' Span Mix': 'Grimly Fiendish' (Damned)
7. 'Alternative Mix Known to Friends as Tom': 'Spies Like Us' (Paul McCartney)
8. 'Torch Song Mix': 'If You Love Somebody Set Them Free' (Sting)
9. 'Cake Mix': 'I Feel Love' (Bronski Beat)
10. 'The Extended Bleep Mix': 'Toy Boy' (Sinitta)

□ Silence Is Golden

Composer John Cage wrote a piece called '4'33"'. It consisted of a single note of the performer's choice to signify the commencement of the piece followed by four minutes and thirty-three seconds of complete silence. During the piece the performer, usually a pianist, is expected to use his fingers to show the audience which of the song's three parts they are listening to.

In 1953 CBS issued '3 Minutes of Silence' – a blank record for juke-boxes so that people fed up with the music could buy three minutes of peace and quiet. Hush records released a similar disc in 1959.

The last note of 'She's Leaving Home' on the Beatles' *Sgt Pepper . . .* LP lasts forty-three and a half seconds – the final bit being at a high frequency audible to dogs but not to most human beings.

John Lennon's *Mind Games* LP featured a short track called 'The Nutopian International Anthem'. It was three seconds of complete silence. In 1986 Shaved Fish released a cover of another John Lennon track called 'Two Minutes Silence', which also consisted of absolutely nothing.

The title track of Afrika Bambaataa's 1986 LP *Beware (The Funk Is Everywhere)* is a band of silence.

Magic Records (Stiff in disguise) released an LP credited to Ronald Reagan, titled *The Wit and Wisdom of Ronald Reagan.* It consisted of two blank sides.

In 1986 Sigue Sigue Sputnik announced that they were to sell the bands of silence between tracks on their LP *Flaunt It* as advertising space. It was not a totally original idea: the Who did something similar on *The Who Sell Out* LP. However Sigue Sigue Sputnik were the first to do it for financial gain. Incidentally, after entering the chart at Number Ten *Flaunt It* bombed and disappeared off the chart within a few weeks.

■ Silent Top Ten

1. 'Sounds of Silence', Simon and Garfunkel
2. 'Leave in Silence', Depeche Mode
3. 'Silence Follows', Victorian Parents
4. 'Quiet Life', Japan
5. 'The Silent Sun', Genesis
6. 'Shut Up', Stranglers
7. 'Noise Annoys', Buzzcocks
8. 'Hush', Deep Purple
9. 'Quietly and Softly Now', Catherine Howe
10. 'Silent Night', Dickies

□ Be My Guest

The rock 'n' roll world seems to be one big happy family, with musicians turning up on other people's records all the time. Below is a list of some interesting guest appearances (some credited, others not), which includes some cases of people appearing on a well-known person's record before they themselves were famous.

The Crickets backed Eddie Cochran on his last recording session, including the posthumous Number One 'Three Steps to Heaven'.

Sounds Incorporated played on the Beatles' track 'Good Morning Good Morning'.

The Crusaders backed Joan Baez on her 1975 LP *Diamonds and Rust*.

Peter Gabriel played flute on Cat Stevens' 'Lady D'Arbanville'.

Eric Clapton played on 'While My Guitar Gently Weeps' for the Beatles.

Elvis Presley's original backing vocalists, the Jordonaires, sang on the Judds' version of 'Don't Be Cruel'.

Luther Vandross sang backing vocals on David Bowie's *Young Americans* (and co-wrote 'Fascination') as well as being the lead vocal on Chic's 'Dance Dance Dance' and Change's 'Searchin''.

James Burton, the legendary guitarist, cropped up on Elvis Costello's *King of America*.

Linda Ronstadt, Los Lobos, Good Rockin' Dopsie and the Twisters, and Ladysmith Black Mombazo are among the many guests on Paul Simon's *Gracelands*.

Rockpile (Nick Lowe, Dave Edmunds, Billy Bremner and Terry Williams) backed Carlene Carter on *Musical Shapes*, while Bette Bright and Glenn Tilbrook were among the backing vocalists on the follow-up *Blue Nun*.

Bruce Springsteen sang back-up on Graham Parker's 'Endless Night' off *The Up Escalator* LP and on Lou Reed's 'Street Hassle' from the LP of the same name.

Ellie Greenwich and Mikki Harris (the song-writer and former Shirelle, respectively) sang behind Debbie Harry on 'In the Flesh' and 'Man Overboard' from Blondie's first LP.

John Lennon and Paul McCartney lent their voices to the Rolling Stones on 'We Love You' while Mick Jagger returned the favour on

'All You Need Is Love'. Jagger also sang on Peter Tosh's 'You Gotta Walk (Don't Look Back)' and Carly Simon's 'You're So Vain'.

Rolling Stones founder Brian Jones played oboe on the Beatles' 'Baby You're a Rich Man' and 'You Know My Name Look Up My Number'.

Martha and the Vandellas helped out John Lee Hooker on his track 'San Francisco' while it was the Shirelles aiding and abetting Jimi Hendrix on 'Earth Blues'.

Curtis Mayfield cropped up on the Blow Monkeys' 'Celebrate (The Day After You)'.

Three-quarters of the Nice (namely Keith Emerson, Blinky Davidson and Lee Jackson) were on Roy Harper's 'Hells Angels', while the eccentric Harper appeared on Pink Floyd's 'Have a Cigar'.

Flo and Eddie (alias Mark Volman and Howard Kaylam) were on T. Rex's 'Hot Love'.

Jan and Dean were among the many voices on the Beach Boys' version of the Regents' 'Barbara Ann'.

Rod Stewart, Gary Glitter and Bobby Womack all provided backing vocals on Ted Woods' 1975 single 'Am I Blue'. Stewart is, of course, credited as being the harmonica player on Millie's 'My Boy Lollipop' though the passage of time has left everyone uncertain about this.

Marc Bolan played guitar on David Bowie's 'The Prettiest Star', and on Ike and Tina Turner's 'Nutbush City Limits'.

Mickey Thomas provided the uncredited vocal on the 1976 Elvin Bishop hit 'Fooled Around and Fell in Love'.

Paul Young and Elvis Costello sang on Squeeze's 'Black Coffee in Bed'.

Sandy Posey sang backing vocals on Percy Sledge's 'When a Man Loves a Woman'.

Jerry Lee Lewis played on Billy Lee Riley's rockabilly classic 'Flying Saucers Rock 'n' Roll'.

Famed Sixties organist Jimmy Smith played on Michael Jackson's 'Bad'.

The Ivy League sang backing vocals on the Who's 'I Can't Explain'.

Cliff Richard played bongos on the Shadows' 'Apache'.

Elton John played piano for Marc Bolan doing 'Get It On' on *Top of the Pops*.

David Bowie is on Tyrannosaurus Rex's 'Demon Queen'.

☐ Short Cut to Somewhere

Some industry abbreviations

© is the international copyright symbol. It designates the owner of an original literary, dramatic, musical or artistic work, who usually is the creator of the material or his agent.

℗ designates the performance owner, which in the case of records is the record company.

A&R	Artists and Repertoire
ASCAP	American Society of Composers, Authors and Publishers
ACGB	Arts Council of Great Britain
AM	amplitude modulation
APRS	Association of Professional Recording Studios
BBC	British Broadcasting Corporation
BIRLA	Black Independent Record Labels' Association
B/W	backed with
BPI	British Phonographic Industry
C/W	coupled with
DJ	disc jockey
DJA	Disc Jockey Association
EP	extended play
FM	frequency modulation
IMA	International Music Association
IPI	Independent Phonographic Industry
ISA	International Songwriters' Association
GRRA	Gramophone Record Retailers' Association
LP	long play

LW long wave
MCPS Mechanical-Copyright Protection Society
MPA Music Publishers' Association
MRP manufacturer's recommended price
MRS Mechanical Rights Society
MU Musicians' Union
MW medium wave
PA public address (system)
personal appearance
PRS Performing Right Society
RIAA Recording Industry of American Artists
RPM revolutions per minute
RRP recommended retail price
SO symphony orchestra
SW short wave
TV television
UHF ultra high frequency
VHF very high frequency
VJ video jockey

■ LIKE A ROLLING STONE

First, a couple of songs about the Rolling Stones:

'There Are But Five Rolling Stones', Andrew Oldham Orchestra
'365 Rolling Stones (One for Every Day of the Year)', Andrew Oldham Orchestra

On 5 July 1969 the Stones played a concert in London's Hyde Park, which was turned into a tribute to former Stone Brian Jones, who had died two days earlier. Jagger read from Shelley's 'Adonais', and thousands of white butterflies were released from boxes around the stage. Unfortunately, the insufficiently ventilated boxes had succeeded in suffocating most of the insects; those that were still alive were too weak to fly far and fell to the ground like albino leaves.

Ian Stewart wins the accolade of sixth Rolling Stone, as he spent over two decades augmenting their sound with his keyboard playing. He died suddenly in 1985.

In 1967 the Stones were reported to be on the verge of making their first film, to be called *Only Lovers Left Alive.*

The first person, apart from the band, to record a Jagger/Richards song was George Bean, who recorded 'Will You Be My Lover Tonight' in January 1964.

The first Stones LP to contain solely Jagger/Richards compositions was *Aftermath* released in 1966.

Doug Sanders of the Lambrettas sometimes wears a stage suit originally owned by Charlie Watts.

At the time of his death Brian Jones was contemplating forming a group with Alexis Korner.

When they played *The Ed Sullivan Show* they were forced to change the title and lyrics of 'Let's Spend the Night Together' to 'Let's Spend Some Time Together'.

The play *The Trials of Oz* featured a Stones song called 'Schoolboy Blues'. Its more controversial title is 'Cocksucker Blues'.

Among the unreleased Stones rarities are some tracks recorded by ex-Mamas and Papas leader John Phillips, produced by Jagger.

The Rolling Stones were the first band to receive record royalties from the USSR (June 1975).

On 21 April 1963 the Stones met the Beatles for the first time, at the Crawdaddy Club in Richmond.

Cleo Sylvester, who recorded 'To Know Him Is To Love Him' backed by the Rolling Stones, appeared in the famous TV programme *Cathy Come Home*.

The band played on the *New Musical Express* stand at the opening of the Battersea Fun Fair in 1963.

In 1961 Charlie Watts wrote 'Ode to a High Flying Bird', a tribute to jazzman Charlie 'Bird' Parker.

Keith Richards was once knocked cold for seven minutes after receiving an electric shock from his microphone.

During a Canadian tour in 1972 the band's equipment van was dynamited.

■ Five groups that have contained at least one Rolling Stone

1. Ian Stewart and the Railroaders: *Bill Wyman, Keith Richard*, Ian Stewart and Tony Meehan
2. New Barbarians: *Keith Richard, Ron Wood,* Ziggy Modeliste, Stanley Clarke, Ian McLagen and Bobby Keys
3. Creation: *Ron Wood*, Kenny Pickett, Kim Gardner and Jack Jones
4. John Mayall's Bluesbreakers: *Mick Taylor*, John Mayall, Steve Thompson and Colin Allen
5. Byrds: *Ron Wood*, Ali McKenzie, Tony Munroe, Kim Gardner and Peter McDaniels

■ GIVE A LITTLE LOVE

It was Bob Geldof's passionate efforts to get the world to respond to the problems of Ethiopia, with the Band Aid! single and Live Aid! concert, that put the spotlight on charity fund-raising by the entertainment industry, particularly the music business. In fact Geldof's efforts started an avalanche of copycat attempts both for Ethiopia and other causes.

Band Aid! was something special: it was spontaneous, started by Geldof after he and future wife Paula Yates watched Michael Buerk's BBC news report on famine-stricken Ethiopia; it was credible, a good, timely song written by Geldof and Midge Ure; and it was genuine, pop stars' eyes opened by Geldof to the fact that they could and should help the less fortunate. What it wasn't, however, was original. Below are some of the ways pop music has worked for charity and good causes both before and after Band Aid!

In the Sixties several top artists donated tracks to compilation LPs whose royalties were donated to the Save The Children Fund.

In 1962 Frank Sinatra paid the costs of a world tour out of his own pocket and donated the proceeds of that tour to a children's charity.

In the early Sixties a *Double Your Money* quiz show special featured Lord Sutch answering questions on pop, Caravelles on modern jazz, and Mike Sarne on Shakespeare. The prize money went to charity.

In 1966 Welsh group the Llan donated royalties from a single to the victims of the Aberfan disaster, where a giant slag heap slid and buried a primary school, killing 116 children and 28 adults.

In 1971 George Harrison hosted two all-star benefit concerts at Madison Square Garden for the people of Bangladesh. Spin-offs included a three-LP box set and a film featuring Harrison, Bob Dylan, Eric Clapton and Leon Russell.

Bob Dylan has affiliated himself to many good causes including the plight of boxer Rubin Carter, wrongly gaoled for manslaughter.

In 1979 Wings, the Pretenders, Rockpile and Ian Dury were among those playing a series of benefit shows known as the Concerts for Kampuchea.

Then in December 1984 Bob Geldof assembled a multitude of stars into SARM studios and recorded 'Do They Know It's Christmas?'. Everybody (including the record company and record shops) relinquished their royalties and all the money was channelled to the Band Aid! fund, which provided food and other supplies to the starving people of Ethiopia. Follow-ups and inspired events include USA For Africa's 'We Are the World'; Ar Log's 'Dwyld Cros Y Mer (Hands across the Sea)', a single by fifty or so Welsh acts; Starvation's 'Tam Tam Pour L'Ethiope'; Austria for Africa; Chateuse San Frontieres; efforts by three German groups; Carol Aid (pop stars in a December carol sing-a-long at Heaven, Charing Cross); Live Aid!; British Reggae Artists for Africa Appeal Team's 'Let's Make Africa Green Again'; Jersey Artists for Mankind with 'We Got the Love'; Disco Aid and 'Give Give Give'; Hear 'N' Aid's 'Stars'; 'Everybody Wants to Run the World', a re-recorded version of Tears For Fears' 'Everybody Wants to Rule the World' (used as the anthem to Sport Aid), and the Young Ones' remake of Cliff Richard's 'The Young Ones', which spearheaded Comic Relief's efforts.

In the wake of Ethiopia came:

'Doctor in Distress', Who Cares; a protest at the BBC's decision to suspend *Dr Who*, with proceeds to cancer research
'You'll Never Walk Alone', The Crowd; for victims of the Bradford FC fire disaster
'That's What Friends Are For', Dionne Warwick and friends; for AIDS research
'Soul Deep', Council Collective; for striking miners
Pete Townshend's Double O project for heroin addicts
The Phoenix House drug rehabilitation centre's *Live in World* LP and concerts
Farm Aid
'Shout It Out', Childwatch; for victims of child abuse
'Let It Be', Ferry Aid; for victims of the Zeebrugge ferry disaster
The list really does seem endless.

■ WE ARE FAMILY

'It's a family affair . . .' sang Sly Stone, and how true that is of rock 'n' roll. There are those groups whose members are all from one family: The Osmonds, the Jacksons, the Pointer Sisters and the Nolans. Those that aren't include the Righteous Brothers and the Ramones.

Less well known are pairs of siblings within groups: the Campbells in UB40, Mike and Jay of Gene Loves Jezebel, Craig and Charlie Reid of the Proclaimers.

There are also husband and wife teams in rock 'n' roll who either work together or have separate careers: John Lennon and Yoko Ono, Carly Simon and James Taylor, Mark E. Smith and Brix, Sonny and Cher, Cher and Gregg Allman, Stevie Wonder and Syreeta, Ike and Tina Turner, Kris Kristofferson and Rita Coolidge, Lulu and Maurice Gibb, Paul and Linda McCartney, Johnathon and Tane Cain, Suzi Quatro and Len Tucker, Tommy Sands and Nancy Sinatra, Clarence Carter and Candi Staton, Nick Lowe and Carlene Carter.

There are relationships that involve relatives being famous in different fields: Larry Tamblyn of the Standells is the brother of actor Russ Tamblyn, song-writer Chip Taylor is the brother of actor Jon Voight, Joan Armatrading's brother Tony has appeared in several British TV programmes (most notably *Angels*), Peter Asher (of Peter and Gordon) is the brother of actress Jane Asher.

And there are assorted points of interest about other relatives of the famous:

Luther Vandross' sister was in the Crests.

Blondie drummer Clem Burke's uncle drummed for Joey Dee and the Starliters.

John Denver's dad was a USAF pilot who held three world aviation records. Sammy Hagar's dad was a boxer.

Jeremy Clyde (Chad and Jeremy) is a direct descendant of the Duke of Wellington, while singer/song-writer Tim Hardin has more dubious origins going back to the outlaw John Wesley Hardin.

Mike Nesmith's mum invented Liquid Paper, the original correcting fluid.

Clark Datchler's (Johnny Hates Jazz) dad was in Fifties vocal groups the Polka Dots and the Stargazers.

Andrew Gold's dad wrote the score for *Exodus* and several other films.

Local Boy Makes Good are led by Jeff Allen, brother of Ultravox's Chris Cross.

Valerie Simpson's (Ashford and Simpson) brother Ray is lead vocalist with Village People.

Lol Creme and Eric Stewart of 10CC married sisters Anne and Gloria.

Ricky Slaughter, former drummer with the Motors, is the cousin of Knox, singer with the Vibrators.

Owen Paul's brother Brian McGee was the original Johnny and the Self Abusers/Simple Minds drummer.

Jerry Lee Lewis may have got into trouble for marrying his 13-year-old third cousin but Loretta Lynn also married at 13 and had four children by the time she was 18.

■ ALL AROUND THE WORLD

While rock 'n' roll is a truly international movement, from time to time the spotlight focuses on a particular area or city. Let's look at eight cities that have played an important role in the history of rock.

□ San Francisco

Situated on the west coast of America in the state of California, San Francisco's golden age as far as rock 'n' roll is concerned was 1965–8. It was the home of 'flower power' and a hotbed for the American progressive music then known as acid rock.

■ Some key groups that have emerged from, or established themselves in, the San Francisco area

Beau Brummels
Big Brother and the Holding Company
Charlatans
Country Joe and the Fish
Creedence Clearwater Revival
Family Dogg
Flamin' Groovies
Gentleman's Band
Golliwogs
Grateful Dead
Jefferson Airplane
Terry Knight and the Pack

Loose Gravel
Steve Miller Band (emigrés from Chicago)
Moby Grape
Mystery Trend
Quicksilver Messenger Service
Syndicate of Sound
VIPs
Warlocks

■ Some key venues

The Fillmore Auditorium
The Avalon Ballroom
Longshoreman's Hall
Red Dog Saloon
Matrix

■ Key figures

Promoter Bill Graham
FM radio pioneer Tom Donahue
LSD experimenter Ken Kesey
DJ, A&R man, performer Sly Stewart

■ Some songs about San Francisco

1. 'San Francisco (Be Sure to Wear Some Flowers in Your Hair)', Scott McKenzie
2. 'Let's Go to San Francisco', Flowerpot Men
3. 'San Francisco', John Lee Hooker
4. 'I Left My Heart in San Francisco', Tony Bennett
5. 'San Francisco (You've Got Me)', Village People
6. 'San Franciscan Nights', Eric Burdon and the Animals
7. 'San Francisco Girls', Fever Tree
8. 'San Francisco China Town', Daisy Clan
9. 'San Francisco Bay', Lee Oskar
10. 'The Bells of San Francisco', Carnegie Hall

11. 'I'm Always Drunk in San Francisco', Carmen McRae
12. 'San Francisco Woman', Bob Lind
13. 'The Streets of San Francisco', Barclay James Harvest
14. 'Frisco Band', Loose Gravel

In the mid-Sixties many Texan bands and many Los Angeles bands moved into SF.

□ London

England's capital city, London, lies about thirty miles inland from the east coast. It has long been the music capital of the country as well, at least as far as the industry is concerned. In the Fifties London was where Britain's rock 'n' roll contenders came from or to; in the early Sixties London's R&B scene ran parallel to the Mersey explosion, and the Swinging Sixties were epitomized in London, particularly in places like Carnaby Street; in 1976 punk transformed London, crawling out of areas like the once bustling (then decaying, now touristic) Covent Garden. Love it or loathe it, London Is The Biz!

■ Some key groups to emerge from the London area or establish themselves there

The Bluesbreakers (founded by Macclesfield expatriate John Mayall)
David Bowie
Clash
Generation X
Manfred Mann
Brian Poole and the Tremeloes
Pretty Things
Cliff Richard
Rolling Stones
Sex Pistols
Siouxsie and the Banshees

Spandau Ballet
Stranglers
The Who

■ Key venues

Marquee
100 Club
Rainbow
Roxy
UFO Club
Vortex
Town and Country
Dingwalls
Astoria
Hope and Anchor
Red Cow
Nashville

■ Key figures

Larry Parnes
Malcolm McLaren
Steve Dagger

■ Some songs about London

1. 'London's Burning', Clash
2. 'Swinging London', Barbara Windsor
3. 'Last Train to London', ELO
4. '(I Don't Want to Go to) Chelsea', Elvis Costello
5. 'London Girl', Pogues
6. 'London Town', Bucks Fizz
7. 'Solo in Soho', Phil Lynott
8. 'Shut 'Em Down in London Town', Majority
9. 'Streets of London', Ralph McTell
10. 'Euston Station', Barbara Ruskin

11. 'London Rock', Hank Mizell
12. 'London My Home Town', Chantelles
13. 'North London Boy', Incognito
14. 'Waterloo Sunset', Kinks
15. 'Souvenir of London', Procul Harum
16. 'London Boys', T. Rex
17. 'Singer's Hampstead Home', Microdisney
18. 'London Leather Boys', Accept
19. 'London Lady', Stranglers
20. 'The Boy from Chelsea', Truly Smith
21. 'Next Plane to London', Rose Garden
22. 'Hey Young London', Bananarama
23. 'Bench Number 3 at Waterloo Station', Tony Booth
24. 'New Thing from London Town', Sharpe and Numan
25. 'London Posse', London Posse
26. 'London Town', Wings
27. 'Sightsee MC (Souvenir of London)', BAD
28. 'London Boy', Johnny Thunders
29. 'London Calling', Clash
30. 'London is the Biz', Firm

The Nashville was opened in 1969 by special guest Chet Atkins. Previously a pub called The Three Kings, it became London's prime country and western venue, with the Nashville Rooms hosting live music every night. Several British New Wave acts played there in the mid-Seventies, such as Lowe and Costello.

□ New York City

Like London, New York City has long been associated with rock 'n' roll: from the Italian doo-wop groups out of the Bronx to the folk of Greenwich Village. Its golden age began in the mid-Seventies, when American punk bands born on the Bowery (and in Queens, Brooklyn and elsewhere) led to the British and world punk explosion. Shortly afterwards hip-hop began to seep out of its Bronx breeding ground and spawn the most innovative musical style of the Eighties. New York City lies on the east coast of the USA and encompasses the boroughs of Brooklyn, Bronx, Queens, Manhattan and Staten Island.

■ Some key groups to emerge from, or establish themselves in New York

Blondie
David Blue
Wayne County
Dead Boys
Mink Deville
Bob Dylan
Cass Elliot
The Fast
Tim Hardin
Heartbreakers
Richard Hell
Hollywood Brats
Last Poets
Jim McGuinn
New York Dolls
Felix Pappalardi
Tom Paxton
Phil Ochs
Ramones
John Sebastien
Shirts (pronounced Shoits)
Patti Smith
Television

■ Key venues

Max's Kansas City
CBGBs*

* CBGBs stands for Country, Blue Grass, Blues and other music for urban gourmets. Originally owned by Hilly Kristal, it was a Hell's Angels hangout on Bowery Street that became an influential New Wave club.

Apollo Theatre
Fillmore East
Peppermint Lounge
Gerde's Folk City
Café Au Go Go
Studio 54
Mintons

■ Key figures

Goffin and King and the other Brill Building* writers

■ Some songs about New York City

1. 'Native New Yorker', Odyssey
2. 'New York Groove', Hello
3. 'Boy from New York City', Wrens
4. 'Harlem Nocturne', Cherokees
5. 'New York on My Mind', John McLaughlin
6. 'New York's a Lonely Town When You're the Only Surfer Boy Around', Tradewinds
7. 'New York New York', Gerard Kenny
8. 'New York Shuffle', Graham Parker
9. 'The Bronx', Kurtis Blow
10. 'New York Connection', Sweet
11. 'I Guess the Lord Must Be in New York', Eternal Triangle
12. 'Brooklyn Roads', Neil Diamond
13. 'New York State of Mind', Bill Joel
14. 'New York Afternoon', Yasuko Aguwa
15. 'The Only Living Boy in New York', Simon and Garfunkel
16. 'First We Take Manhattan', Jennifer Warnes
17. 'New York City Rhythm', Barry Manilow
18. 'Manhattan Skyline', A-ha
19. 'South Bronx', DJ Scott La Rock
20. 'New York Mining Disaster 1941', Bee Gees

* The Brill Building was where songwriters like Carole King turned out production line pop songs in the early Sixties.

21. 'From New York to L A', Patsy Gallant
22. 'Up on the Streets of Harlem', Drifters
23. 'New York Eyes', Nicole
24. 'Brooklyn Blew Up the Bridge', M C Mitchski
25. 'N. Y. Times', John Pollard
26. 'I Wanna Go to New York', Blue
27. 'New York City', T. Rex
28. 'Harlem Shuffle', Bob and Earl
29. 'Manhattan Rumble', ELO
30. 'New York', Sex Pistols

□ Liverpool

In the late Fifties Liverpool, a major British port since the late eighteenth century, picked up on rock 'n' roll in a big way through the US sailors and the locals who worked for the merchant navy, particularly the Cunard and Blue Star lines to New York and New Orleans. These sailors brought in US R&B discs and triggered the subsequent Merseybeat explosion in 1963.

■ Some key Liverpool groups

Beatles
Big Three
Deaf School
Echo and the Bunnymen
Fourmost
Frankie Goes to Hollywood
Billy Fury
Gerry and the Pacemakers
Merseybeats
Orchestral Manoeuvres in the Dark
Real Thing
Searchers
Rory Storme and the Hurricanes
Wah
The Yachts

■ Key venues

Cavern
Eric's
Jacaranda
Iron Door
Blue Angel Club
Empire Theatre

■ Key figures

Brian Epstein
Allan Williams
Bill Harry

■ Some songs about Liverpool

1. 'Going Down to Liverpool', Katrina and the Waves
2. 'Liverpool Lou', Delaney Bramlett
3. 'Ferry Across the Mersey', Gerry and the Pacemakers
4. 'The Entry of God into Liverpool', Liverpool Scene
5. 'Penny Lane', Beatles
6. 'Almost Liverpool 8', Mike Hart
7. 'Liverpool', Viceroys
8. 'Liverpool Landing', Colin Whitehedge and Marmaduke Druid
9. 'Liverpool Drive', Chuck Berry
10. 'Liverpool', Gerry Marsden and Derek Nimmo

□ Los Angeles

Los Angeles is the second most populated city in the USA. It is situated almost 400 miles down the Californian coast from San Francisco, not far from the Mexican border, thus ensuring an ethnic mix that has affected its culture, including rock 'n' roll. LA has never really had a golden age as such. In the Sixties it produced its fair share of influential bands but many of them migrated north to San Francisco. What LA has done is to produce bands representing nearly every single style of music imaginable.

■ Some key Los Angeles groups

Asia
Association
Black Oak Arkansas
Brothers Johnson
Byrds
Doors
Los Lobos
Love
Tom Petty and the Heartbreakers
Shalamar
X

■ Key LA venues

The Whiskey A Go Go
Troubador
Masque

■ Some songs about LA

1. 'All LA Glory', Band
2. 'From New York to LA', Patsy Gallant
3. 'LA', Dictators
4. 'Back in LA', Peanut Butter Conspiracy
5. 'LA Run', The Carvels
6. 'Electric Los Angeles', Al Stewart
7. 'LA Nights', Yasuko Agawa
8. '99 Miles from LA', Johnny Mathis
9. 'LA Goodbye', Ides of March
10. 'LA', The Fall

Chicago

Chicago lies at the south end of Lake Michigan, which is just a few hundred miles south of the Canadian border. Chicago was one of the main jazz and blues cities – the New Orleans of the North, musically speaking. In the mid-Sixties it was also the home of garage punk. Chicago has certainly provided a few seminal rock bands and in the Eighties has provided us with the hip-hop derivative House Music.

Some key Chicago groups and artists

American Breed
Laurie Anderson
Chuck Berry
Mike Bloomfield
Paul Butterfield
Willie Dixon
Howlin' Wolf
Baby Huey and the Babysitters
Ides of March
HP Lovecraft
Minnie Riperton
Shadows of Knight
Muddy Waters

Some songs about Chicago

1. 'Chicago', Frank Sinatra
2. 'Chicago Blues', Otis Spann
3. 'The Night Chicago Died', Paper Lace
4. 'Chicago', Graham Nash
5. 'Jesus Just Left Chicago', ZZ Top

New Orleans

The Crescent City; the land of Mardi Gras; the birthplace of jazz; such are the names bestowed on the city that nestles in the folds of the Mississippi River. Indeed one of New Orleans' greatest contributions to music was the jazz that flourished in the Storyville backstreets at the turn of this century. More than that though, the state of Louisiana has many French connections and New Orleans is full of Creoles and Cajuns, who have developed their own distinctive music. Although New Orleans is rooted deeply in rural and folk music, it has contributed proudly to rock 'n' roll.

■ Some key New Orleans groups and artists

Fats Domino
Dr John
Frankie Ford
Professor Longhair
Meters
Huey Smith

■ Some songs about New Orleans

1. 'Way Down Yonder in New Orleans', Freddie Cannon
2. 'New Orleans', Gary 'U S' Bonds
3. 'Walkin' to New Orleans', Fats Domino
4. 'Battle of New Orleans', Johnny Horton
5. 'New Orleans', Wilson Pickett
6. 'Down in New Orleans', Marathons

☐ Nashville

Nashville lies in the heartland of Tennessee and is the home of country and western music. The whole city revolves around the music that is the lifeblood of American folk music. As well as well-known places like the Grand Ole Opry, there are also several wax museums crammed with the country stars and numerous other tourist traps.

Many, many country stars are associated with Nashville though lots of them migrated there from elsewhere.

■ A couple of songs about Nashville

1. 'Nashville Cats', Lovin' Spoonful
2. 'Nashville Boogie', Bert Weedon

□ Some other important cities

Berlin is the spiritual home of machine music, and the place where Bowie recorded his trilogy of sometimes gloomy, synth-heavy LPs: *Heroes, Low* and *Lodger*.

Birmingham is a strong beat city that produced the Move, ELO and the Steve Gibbons Band.

Hamburg is where so many Mersey groups learnt their trade in the seedy clubs and dives of the Reeperbahn.

Kansas City – another American home of the blues.

Manchester produced several beat groups in the Sixties, but attention centred on the city in the punk era, when it gave us the Buzzcocks, Joy Division, Crispy Ambulance, Dislocation Dance and Slaughter and the Dogs. Later this city spawned the Smiths and Simply Red.

Memphis is the home of rockabilly, Sun Studios and Elvis Presley, not to mention the Beale Street Blues scene.

Akron, Ohio, spawned a number of New Wave bands, many of whom (the Waitresses, Jane Aire, Terraplane, Tin Huey, Rachel Sweet) played on the Stiff LP *The Akron Compilation*. Chrissie Hynde of the Pretenders, the group Devo, and Howard Hewett of Shalamar also emerged from the city famous for its production of rubber, notably tyres. An earlier hit group from Akron was Ruby and the Romantics, who were previously known as the Supremes before girl singer Ruby Nash joined them.

☐ Trivia

Probably the most multi-national group ever was the Little River Band, formed in Australia in 1975. The original line-up featured Dutch-born Beeb Birtles, Australian Graham Goble, Englishmen Glenn Shorrock and Derek Pellicci, Italian Rick Formosa, and Roger McLachlan from New Zealand. A close runner-up would be the original line-up of the Mahavishnu Orchestra, which featured English-born John McLaughlin, Panamanian Billy Cobham, Rick Laird from Eire, Jan Hammer from Czechoslovakia, and American Jerry Goodman. Heatwave included four Americans, an Englishman, a Spaniard and a Czech.

Many of the following people are wrongly assumed to have been born in Britain:

Cliff Richard, born Lucknow, India
Thomas Dolby, born Cairo, Egypt
Joe Strummer, born Ankara, Turkey
Chris De Burgh, born Argentina
Annabelle Lwin, born Rangoon, Burma
Mick Karn, born Cyprus
Englebert Humperdinck, born Madras, India
Holly Johnson, born Khartoum, Sudan

David Byrne of the Talking Heads, who you may have thought was American, was born in Scotland.

■ CLASSICAL GAS

Some pop and rock songs are based on classical music, either straightforward rocked-up cover versions or songs based on a classical melody.

□ The song	□ The source
1. 'Past Present and Future', Shangri Las	'Moonlight Sonata', Beethoven
2. 'Lady Lynda', Beach Boys	'Jesu Joy of Man's Desiring', Bach
3. 'Tonight's Alright for Love', Elvis Presley	Tales from the Vienna Woods, Strauss
4. 'Sabre Dance', Love Sculpture	Sabre Dance, Khachaturian
5. 'A Lover's Concerto', Toys	Minuet in G, Bach
6. 'Piltdown Rides Again', Piltdown Men	*William Tell* Overture, Rossini
7. 'Saturday Night at the Duckpond', Cougars	*Swan Lake*, Tchaikovsky
8. 'Brandenburger', Nice	Brandenburg Concertos, Bach
9. 'Could It Be Magic', Donna Summer	Prelude in C, Chopin
10. 'Night of Fear', Move	*1812 Overture*, Tchaikovsky

11.	'Joybringer', Manfred Mann's Earth Band	'Jupiter' from *The Planets*, Holst
12.	'Pictures at an Exhibition', Emerson Lake and Palmer	*Pictures at an Exhibition*, Mussorgsky
13.	'All By Myself', Eric Carmen	Piano Concerto No. 2, Rachmaninov
14.	'If I Had You', Korgis	Symphony No. 2, Rachmaninov
15.	'Whiter Shade of Pale', Procul Harum	'Air on a G String', Bach
16.	'Bumble Boogie', B. Bumble and the Stingers	'Flight of the Bumble Bee', Rimsky-Korsakov

Some songs mentioning classical or other non-pop composers in their titles:

1. 'Rock Me Amadeus', Falco
2. 'Dinner with Gershwin', Donna Summer
3. 'Beethoven (Listen To)', Eurythmics
4. 'Mantovani's Hits', Yachts
5. 'Get off My Bach', Simon Dupree and the Big Sound
6. 'Philip Glass', Colour Box
7. 'Mantovani', Swinging Cats
8. 'Roll over Beethoven', ELO
9. 'Mozart versus the Rest', Episode Six

■ WILD WEST HERO

1. 'Western Movies', Olympics
2. 'John Wayne Is Big Leggy', Haysi Fantayzee
3. 'Jesse James', Pogues
4. 'Bo Diddley Is a Gunslinger', Bo Diddley
5. 'Ringo', Lorne Green
6. 'El Paso', Marty Robbins
7. 'Outlaw Man', Eagles
8. 'Rhinestone Cowboy', Glen Campbell
9. 'Hi Ho Silver', Jim Diamond
10. 'The Lone Ranger', Quantum Jump
11. 'They Call Me Jesse James', Dreams

■ AIN'T THAT THE TRUTH (APT TITLES)

1. 'On My Own', Michael McDonald and Patti Labelle: they recorded their parts separately.
2. 'I Can't Make It Alone', Bill Medley: unsuccessful solo single from former Righteous Brother.
3. 'What Am I Living For', Chuck Willis: he died soon after it was released.
4. 'Three Steps to Heaven', Eddie Cochran: his current single when he died.
5. 'I Need A Hit', Carlene Carter: she surely did.
6. *Mamas and Papas Deliver*, Mamas and Papas: their current LP when Mama Cass had a baby.
7. 'I Feel the Earth Move', Carole King: while it was being played on station KFSM, Calgary, Canada, in 1971 the studio collapsed.
8. 'Back Where I Started', Box of Frogs: this band saw the reunion of three of the Yardbirds.
9. *Here My Dear*, Marvin Gaye: profits from this LP go to his recently divorced wife as alimony.
10. 'I'll Never Get Out of This World Alive', Hank Williams: released shortly before his death.

■ LIES (INAPT TITLES)

1. 'Here Comes Summer', Jerry Keller: UK hit in early autumn.
2. 'It Ought to Sell a Million', Lyn Paul: it didn't.
3. 'Forget Me Not', Kalin Twins: the public did.
4. *Street Survivors*, Lynyrd Skynyrd: released a week before several band members died in a plane crash.
5. 'Celebrate Summer', Marc Bolan: released shortly before his death in 1977, which was no cause for celebration.
6. 'I Will Return', Springwater: they didn't.
7. 'I'm Doin' Fine Now', New York City: if you call one Number Seventeen US hit in 1973 'fine', then sure!
8. 'I Write the Songs', Barry Manilow: from the man whose chart career is almost entirely cover versions, including this Bruce Johnson-penned number.
9. 'Go Deh Yaka (to the Top)', Monyaka: Number Fourteen is hardly the top, darlings.
10. 'I Can't Say Goodbye to You', Helen Reddy: she did.

■ ALL-AMERICAN HERO

Bruce Springsteen trivia.

One of the most famous rock and roll (mis)quotes was written by critic Jon Landau in the *Boston Real* paper in May 1974. The full paragraph ran as follows:
'Last Thursday at Harvard Square Theatre I saw my rock and roll past flash before my eyes; I saw something else: I saw rock and roll future and its name is Bruce Springsteen. And on a night when I needed to feel young, he made me feel like I was listening to music for the first time.'

On 2 October 1975 a Springsteen concert in Milwaukee was interrupted by a bomb scare. By the time everyone was let back into the theatre at midnight a shaken Bruce had consumed a little more alcohol than normal and decided to ride back to the theatre on the roof of the car. This prompted a British journalist inside the car to remark, 'I have seen rock and roll's future and he is on my windscreen!'

On 7 March 1973 Bruce played at Max's Kansas City, in New York City. John Hammond, the man who signed him to CBS the previous June, became so excited with the performance that he had a heart attack. Happily, he survived.

Bruce once broke into Elvis's Graceland home in a bid to meet his idol. He was caught in the grounds and firmly escorted out.

Bruce was behind the early Eighties renaissance of Sixties singer Gary 'US' Bonds.

Promoter Bill Graham came close to signing Springsteen when he was in the late Sixties band Steel Mill.

In 1986 Bruce became only the third person to enter the US LP chart at Number One, with his live box set. The previous two were Elton John (*Captain Fantastic and the Brown Dirt Cowboy*) and Stevie Wonder (*Songs in the Key of Life*).

Bruce's contribution to the *We Are the World* LP was a version of Jimmy Cliff's 'Trapped'.

Former Springsteen manager Mike Appel was a member of the Sixties garage band the Balloon Farm, which released a great single called 'A Question of Temperature'.

Springsteen's UK début at the Hammersmith Odeon on 18 November 1975 was not the best of introductions: the show was generally slated in the press. Happily, he would return triumphant.

A very famous pop magazine (it rhymes with clash bits) once said that the most interesting thing about Bruce Springsteen is that he once had a canoe that broke in half. As I struggle to find interesting bits of trivia about Brooooce I must conclude they are right. Never mind Boss, keep on rockin'.

■ PRESS

A pot-pourri of trivia about music books and papers.

One of the most established British music papers is the *New Musical Express*. It started well before the rock era and changed with the times, being one of the first papers to enthuse over Bill Haley and, later, Elvis. It started the first British chart based on record sales (as opposed to sales of sheet music). In the Fifties its advertising manager was Percy Dickens, whose son Rob now runs WEA Records.

■ Ten books written by rock stars

1. *In His Own Write*, John Lennon
2. *Tarantula*, Bob Dylan
3. *Ode to a High Flying Bird*, Charlie Watts
4. *Been Down So Long It Looks Like Up to Me*, Richard Farina
5. *Diary of A Rock and Roll Star*, Ian Hunter
6. *The Lords and the New Creatures*, Jim Morrison
7. *A View from A Broad*, Bette Midler
8. *Is That It?*, Bob Geldof
9. *Daybreak*, Joan Baez
10. *I Me Mine*, George Harrison

The 'fanzine' sprang to popularity in the Seventies and by the mid-Eighties there were tens of thousands available in Britain, America and Europe. They're called fanzines because they are produced by fans of a particular group or style of music, and are mass produced on a trusty photocopying machine. The best-known fanzine is probably Mark P's famous and influential *Sniffin' Glue and Other Rock 'n'*

Roll Habits, inspired by the Ramones and first champion of punk. Some of the more peculiarly named 'zines include *Trout Fishing in Leytonstone*, *Blah Blah Blah*, *Little Things Please Littler Minds*, *Biggles Eats the Horse*, *Kill Your Pet Puppy*, *Baby Bites Back*, *Return of the Native*, *No New Rituals* and *Attack On Bzag*.

Will Birch (of the Kursaal Flyers) had his Top Ten favourite records published in the magazine *Let It Rock* in 1973 shortly before he joined the band and when he was completely unknown to the general public (OK not many people know who he is now, but *I* like the Kursaals). Among his selections were Elvis, the Doobie Brothers, Brinsley Schwarz and Clifford T. Ward.

Sounds cartoonist Edwin Pouncey (Savage Pencil) was formerly in the Art Attacks with Rob Gotobed (later in Wire) and J. D. Haney (The Monochrome Set).

NME staffer Roy Carr was in the Sixties beat and lightweight psychedelic group the Executives.

The Jim Morrison biography *No One Here Gets Out Alive* is titled after a line in the Doors' song 'Five to One' from the LP *Waiting for the Sun*.

In 1983 Tommy Steele published his début novel, a wartime thriller called *The Final Run*.

David Titlow of Blue Mercedes used to be an illustrator for *Strangled*, the Stranglers 'fanzine'.

■ Ten musicians who have worked as journalists

1. Chrissie Hynde (Pretenders), *NME*
2. Neil Tennant (Pet Shop Boys), *Smash Hits*
3. Nick Kent (Subterraneans and Sex Pistols), *NME*
4. Charles Shaar Murray (Blast Furnace), *NME* among others
5. Mark Perry (Alternative TV), *Sniffin' Glue*
6. Steve Harley (Cockney Rebel), local press
7. Roy Carr (Executives), *NME*
8. Mark Knopfler (Dire Straits), local press
9. Tony Moon (Motor Boys Motor), *Strangled*
10. Robert Bickford: in an effort to find out about life as a pop star,

this *Daily Mail* correspondent became pop singer Bicford Ford. He released a single, 'Cheat Cheat' backed with 'Sweet and Tender Romance' on Parlophone in 1963.

■ NO ONE GETS THE PRIZE

■ Short and to-the-point reviews

1. 'Forever Young', Alphaville
'Alphaville embody the frustrated egos of the massively untalented. Should have been drowned at birth.' Morrissey, *Smash Hits*, October 1984

2. 'All the Way Up', Belle and the Devotions
'Don't tempt me.' Stephen Gray, *Record Mirror*, August 1984

3. 'Let's Groove', Earth Wind and Fire
'Let's not.' Johnny Black, *Smash Hits*, November 1981

4. 'I'm Alive,' ELO
'A blatant lie. Product.' Deanne Pearson, *Smash Hits*, May 1980

5. 'Run to the Hills', Iron Maiden
'Don't think I wasn't tempted.' Red Starr, *Smash Hits*, February 1982

6. 'The Robots', Kraftwerk
'Zzzzzzzzzzzzzz.' Dean Porsche, *Zig Zag*, August 1978

7. 'Popular Music', Neon Hearts
'Don't talk wet.' Julie Porsche, *Zig Zag*, March 1979

8. 'Like a Rock', Bob Seger
'Exactly, Bob. Prehistoric.' Kevin Murphy, *Sounds*, June 1986

9. 'Away from This Town', Still Life
'And the further away the better.' Robin Smith, *Record Mirror*, September 1982

10. 'Wasting Time', Strangeways
'Yeh, mine.' Robin Banks, *Zig Zag*, April 1979

Shakespeare was the first person known to use the word critic.

Nicky Chinn and Mike Chapman were so annoyed with Charles Shaar Murray's review of a Suzie Quatro single that they sent the journalist a packet of pig's brains.

■ RADIO RADIO

The first British DJ was Christopher Stone.

Radio Caroline was the first pirate station. It kept going long after the Marine Offences Act came into force in 1967, outlawing offshore broadcasts. The station was named after Caroline Kennedy, daughter of assassinated US president John Fitzgerald Kennedy. The Fortunes thought they'd struck good fortune when Radio Caroline adopted their single 'Caroline' as a theme tune. However, constant plays on the North Sea pirate couldn't push the record into the official *Record Retailer* chart.

Other well-known pirates included Radio London, Radio City, Radio Essex and Invicta.

DJ Johnny Walker wrote and performed 'The Pirate DJ's Lament'. The Roaring Sixties released the single 'We Love the Pirates'.

It cost about £1000 for Simon Napier Bell to get 'John's Children' to Number Twenty-two in certain Sixties charts by buying plays on pirate radio, a common practice at the time.

Radio One was first broadcast on 30 September 1967.

■ Some famous Radio One themes

John Peel: 'Pickin' the Blues' (Grinderswitch)
Tommy Vance: 'Take It off the Top' (Dixie Dregs)
Rock On (*c.* 1979): 'Belgian Tom's Hat Trick' (Whitesnake)
Rock On (*c.* 1980): 'Being Boiled' (Human League)
Pick of the Pops: 'At the Sound of the Swinging Cymbal' (Brass Incorporated)

Van Der Graaf Generator recorded a progressive version of 'Theme One', the George Martin-penned tune, the original of which was used to open Radio One in September 1967, preceding Tony Blackburn's welcome and the Move's 'Flowers in the Rain', the first record to be aired on the station.

In 1986 Mike Smith, a former Capital Radio and then Radio One DJ, won the twenty-four hour endurance motor car race at Brands Hatch.

John Peel has an unwritten rule not to play any song with 'rock 'n' roll' in the title on his long running show. Incidentally, Peel qualified as a marksman during his National Service.

Peel's producer and sporadic DJ himself, John Walters, used to play trumpet in the Alan Price Set.

Radio London DJ Stuart Coleman used to play bass for Pinkerton's Assorted Colours.

Shortly after Radio One broadcast all-day stereo in the London area freak weather conditions allowed the FM transmission to be picked up in Scotland.

In 1983 Paul Simon bought the Long Island, New York radio station WHYB.

One of the biggest developments in American radio this decade has been the growth of campus radio. By 1987 there were approximately 1500 of these college stations in existence. They tend to air more contemporary, independent and cultish material than their mainstream rivals – groups like the Smiths, REM and Camper Van Beethoven.

Africa No 1, a radio station based in Libreville, Gabon, has an audience well in excess of 15 million. It has the second most powerful short-wave transmitter in the world and its broadcasts can be picked up in America.

■ STAGES

This chapter looks at all aspects of the life on the road: the clubs, the festivals, the groupies and the hotel rooms.

□ At the Club

Ten of the world's top rock venues, dance halls, and discothèques of all time (see also All Around the World, pp. 118–31).

1. The Peppermint Lounge, New York City

Situated just off Times Square, the Peppermint Lounge was the centre of several early Sixties dance crazes, most notably the Twist. It was at the Lounge that New York's then upper classes (probably yuppies today) discovered and adopted the Twist as their own. The Lounge was formerly a greaser's bar, a hangout for beehives, DAs, leather jackets and cuban heels. When the social élite moved in, its image rapidly improved. Sixties house band was Joey Dee and the Starliters (who included a couple of future Young Rascals). In recent years the Lounge turned into a New Wave club.

2. The Roxy, London

Once found at 41–43 Neal Street on the fringes of Covent Garden, the Roxy was a former gay club owned by Andrew Czezowski. At the turn of 1976/7 it became *the* punk club; not to be confused with the Harlesden Roxy. Main DJ at the Neal Street Roxy was Don Letts, now with Big Audio Dynamite. The Roxy has long since been converted in line with Covent Garden's new cultured image; the tourists admiring the specialist shops of the area have no idea how many groups were born after meeting at the Roxy.

3. The Marquee, London

Now situated in Charing Cross Road, the Marquee was formerly an Oxford Street jazz club. It moved to Wardour Street in Soho in March 1964 and began to enjoy night after night of R & B. Nowadays it is more of a mainstream rock venue – small and sweaty. In 1988 the Marquee's future looked grim, as owner Billy Gaff planned to sell it to developers, almost certainly to be turned into a shopping precinct.

4. The Whiskey A Go-Go, Los Angeles

This club on Sunset Strip came into its own in the mid-late Sixties. Like other American clubs at the time, it featured things like scantily clad go-go dancers in cages above the stage. The club is perhaps best remembered for having the Doors as its house band.

5. The Cavern Club, Liverpool

Mathew Street's subterranean Cavern Club is remembered throughout the world as being the burrow out of which the Beatles emerged. Lunch-time and evening dances were held there with groups playing or DJs spinning the latest American R&B discs brought in by the liners from the USA. Cilla Black was hat-check girl. Brian Epstein first saw the Beatles there. British Rail got there and built a ventilation shaft through it.

6. The Fillmores, New York and San Francisco

Fillmore East in New York and Fillmore West in San Francisco were Bill Graham's own venues for hosting some of the stunning psychedelic, progressive, and hard rock concerts he promoted in the late Sixties and early Seventies. Most major rock bands of the time played at one or both Fillmores. They closed down in June 1971.

7. The Rainbow, London

Finsbury Park's Rainbow Theatre acted, on and off, as a prime rock venue for many years. Formerly the Astoria, it opened as a permanent rock venue in November 1971. It closed down in March 1975, but reopened later in the decade. For a while the Rainbow 2 opened up in the foyer of the main theatre. The Rainbow closed again in the early Eighties, probably for good. Sadly missed. When it was the Astoria, Jimi Hendrix burnt his guitar on stage there for the very first time.

8. Madison Square Garden, New York

As well as hosting some of the major rock gigs of the Seventies, Madison Square Garden also doubles as a boxing arena. It is for events like George Harrison's Concerts for Bangladesh that it is best remembered in the pop world.

9. The 100 Club, London

Oxford Street's 100 Club was another club almost exclusively devoted to jazz until punk arrived in 1976. It then became a hall of residence for the Sex Pistols and their ilk. In September 1976 it had a two-day punk 'happening' ('We don't have festivals'). Sadly, a girl was blinded by a flying glass and punk was banned for a while. Nowadays all sorts of rock bands play there. It is another underground club even smaller and sweatier than most.

10. The Apollo Theatre, New York

Harlem's Apollo Theatre is remembered for hosting the best black artists of the Fifties R&B and Sixties soul eras. For many years it was an exclusive venue for black artists.

■ Some songs about venues

'Barbarellas' (a famous Birmingham club), The Prefects
'Barbarellas' (a different song about the same club), The Photos
'Max's Kansas City' (a New York club), Wayne County
'Down at the Roxy' (unrecorded number by a pre-Purple Hearts outfit), Sockets
'Down at Adam and Eve's' (a Hackney rock 'n' roll club), Flying Saucers

■ Some other venues that deserve a mention

The Hammersmith Palais, London, and its near neighbour the Odeon
Studio 54, New York, where disco dancing was cultivated
The Hacienda Club, Manchester
Max's Kansas City, New York
The Bottom Line, New York
The Bag O'Nails, London
The Star Club, Hamburg
The Speakeasy, London
The Lyceum, London
CBGBs, New York

Discothèques (literally 'record libraries') started in Paris in the Fifties, then spread via London to America about 1963. Among the best-known US discothèques were Le Club (New York), which opened on 31 December 1962; and Arthur on East 54th Street, New York, which opened in May 1965 and was owned by Sybil Burton, ex-wife of Richard Burton.

Around 1966 discothèques became 'total environment' clubs, LSD substitutes, loud music, strobes and light shows. The most famous were Andy Warhol's Exploding Plastic Inevitable, Cheetah in Manhattan (which included an integral boutique), the Electric Circus (also New York) and Rat Fink in Chicago.

Discothèques died away at the end of the Sixties as concerts and festivals became the rule of the day. The clubs re-emerged in the mid-Seventies as discos, both inspiring and being inspired by *Saturday Night Fever*.

Brothers John and Rik Gunnel have run several clubs as well as managing pop stars like Chris Farlowe. In 1987 John took over the Astoria in Charing Cross Road, London, and named the bars after clubs he has run such as the Flamingo, the Ram Jam and the Bag O'Nails.

☐ The Great Gig in the Sky

■ Ten notable live shows

1. Live Aid!, 13 July 1985, Wembley Stadium, London, and JFK Stadium, Philadelphia

The global juke-box: as a follow on to the Band Aid! and USA for Africa charity records, Bob Geldof and his cohorts arranged this spectacular concert to raise further funds for the starving in Ethiopia. The concerts took place simultaneously in Britain and America, with each country's performances being screened to the other as well as being broadcast around the world. Over £50 million was raised thanks to performances from Bryan Adams, Adam Ant, Beach Boys, Boomtown Rats, David Bowie, Phil Collins (who played live on both continents thanks to Concorde), Elvis Costello, Dire Straits, Bob Dylan, Elton John, Howard Jones, Nik Kershaw, Madonna, Paul McCartney, Alison Moyet, Pretenders, Queen, various Rolling Stones, Simple Minds, a re-formed Status Quo, Thompson Twins, U2, a re-formed Who, and a cast of thousands.

2. Woodstock, 15–17 August 1969, Max Yasgur's farm, Woodstock, New York State

Hippy Nirvana: the greatest rock festival of them all. Four hundred thousand people went to Woodstock to see Joan Baez, Paul Butterfield, Canned Heat, Creedence Clearwater Revival, Crosby Stills Nash and Young, Joe Cocker, Grateful Dead, Jimi Hendrix, Richie Havens, Jefferson Airplane, Janis Joplin, Arlo Guthrie, Tim Hardin, Santana, Sly and the Family Stone, Ten Years After, the Who and many more. Buy the record, the video and the book. Soon to be available as a computer game as well!!!

3. Monterey Pop Festival, 16–18 June 1967, Monterey, California

The first big pop festival, it was filmed by D. A. Pennebaker, who captured on celluloid fine performances by many of the artists, including the Animals, the Byrds, Buffalo Springfield, Paul Butterfield Blues Band, Blues Project, Association, Canned Heat, Jimi Hendrix, Janis Joplin, Country Joe and the Fish, Mamas and Papas,

Booker T and the MGs, Quicksilver Messenger Service, Otis Redding, Simon and Garfunkel and the Who (again).

4. The Isle of Wight Festivals, 1968, 31 August – 2 September 1969, 26 August – 1 September 1970

This small island off the south coast of England seems an unlikely setting for a major rock festival, yet at the end of the Sixties it played host to some of the biggest names in the business. The first festival included Jefferson Airplane and Tyrannosaurus Rex; the second was headlined by Bob Dylan and the Band; while the third (which was almost wrecked by trouble-makers) featured Jimi Hendrix, Free, Joni Mitchell among many others.

5. Altamont, 6 December 1969, Altamont Speedway, near San Francisco

This show will always be remembered for the wrong reasons: while headliners the Rolling Stones were on stage, the Hell's Angels they had hired as bouncers (on the advice of the Grateful Dead) stabbed to death Meredith Hunter, a young black concert-goer. This event marred what was otherwise another stunning array of talent: in order of appearance, Santana, Jefferson Airplane, Flying Burritos, Crosby Stills Nash and Young, and the Rolling Stones.

6. Elvis Presley at Las Vegas, 22 August 1969, The International Hotel, Las Vegas

This marked the return of Presley to the stage for the first time in eight years. Backed by the Sweet Inspirations (three girl singers), Elvis romped about the stage for an hour, going through several of his old classics. He continued to play Vegas for a month at a time twice a year until 1975.

7. The Beatles at Candlestick Park, 29 August 1966, Candlestick Park, San Francisco

This concert was to be the last proper live show that the Beatles would perform together; only the roof-top performance on top of the Apple building could be construed as a joint live performance after this. All the band were tired of touring and resisted hundreds of attractive offers to do 'one more' live show.

8. The Rolling Stones in Hyde Park, 5 July 1969, Hyde Park, London

The Stones played a free concert in Hyde Park with King Crimson and Family as support. The death two days earlier of former Stone Brian Jones turned the show into a memorial concert.

9. The Prince's Trust Concert, 20 June 1986, Wembley Arena, London

Charity events were to the fore in the mid-Eighties and this concert gained high profile in the media, with its takings going to the Prince of Wales Trust. Artists donating their time and talent included Paul McCartney, Phil Collins, Mark Knopfler, Elton John and Tina Turner.

10. Concert for Bangladesh, 1 August 1971, Madison Square Garden, New York

One of the earliest and most successful charity concerts was organized by George Harrison to raise money for the United Nations Children's Fund for refugee children of the newly established Bangladesh. As well as Harrison himself, performances were from Ravi Shankar, Billy Preston, Ringo Starr, Eric Clapton, Leon Russell, Bob Dylan and a host of supporting musicians.

Kaleidoscope recorded a theme tune for the 1970 Isle of Wight Festival under the pseudonym I Luv White. It was called 'Let the World Wash In'.

■ Songs about festivals and live shows

'Woodstock', Joni Mitchell
'Monterey', Eric Burdon
'Wight Is Wight' (a French song about the 1970 Isle of Wight Festival with English lyrics by Sandie Shaw), Michael Delpech
'The Tide Is Turning (After Live Aid!)', Roger Waters

□ On the Road Again

Life on the road in a rock 'n' roll band can be tedious, moving from town to town, in and out of hotel rooms with identical wallpaper and never any time to take in the sights. It's all travel–sound-check–gig, and the unwinding period that makes most tours bearable. Here's a look at how the groups make the best of the boredom and some of the other things that happen on the road.

■ Riders

A rider is a clause that a group has written into its contract with a promoter to ensure that a certain gift or service is provided at a venue when the group performs there. Obviously, the better known the group, the more they can demand in their rider. Most groups go for the obvious, like vintage champagne and caviare. Some are a little more 'exotic' in their demands:

Diana Ross insists on having cellophane wrapped loo seats.

The Psychedelic Furs required the following breakfast on an American tour: bacon and eggs, whole-wheat toast, bagels, 6 litres of milk, 6 litres of orange juice, 10 litres of spring water, 6 packs of Winston Lights cigarettes, 3 American newspapers, a British daily paper, coffee, and tea made in a pot. Their demands later in the day included much more, notably copious quantities of alcohol.

ELO demanded 2 bottles of Remy Martin cognac, 1 bottle of Glenfiddich Whisky, 1 bottle of vodka, a crate of Chablis wine, 6 bottles of red wine, 5 crates of beer, and 1 crate of Martini – all for a seven-piece band (hic).

Billy Squier demands a 10 per cent bonus if promoters spell his name wrong.

■ Groupies

A groupie is a girl (normally) who hangs around her favourite group with one aim in life – to get in bed with him/her/them. Among the most famous groupies are the Plaster Casters of Chicago. Cynthia and Diana Plaster Caster liked to keep a permanent record of their conquests by making a plaster cast of relevant anatomical areas.

Less amorous groupies were the Apple scruffs who hung around the Apple building and the Beatles' individual homes in the hopes of catching a glimpse of their idols. An orgasmic experience for them would be exchanging a few words with John, Paul, George or Ringo.

In the late Sixties Jimi Hendrix was reckoned to be the ultimate groupie conquest.

During a US tour by ELO an American roadie who called himself Rob Roy picked up a girl in Kansas City, spent the night with her and foolishly gave her his LA address. Two weeks later, when the tour was over, the girl turned up on his doorstep and stayed for a few days. While she was there a man with a shotgun burst into the apartment. Rob Roy was out, but the girl was there with two of his friends. The man, it turned out, was the girl's husband. He locked the friends in the bedroom, then took his wife into the bathroom and shot her. He then waited calmly for Rob Roy to return and shot him as well. The next day the gunman was shot dead by police.

■ Some groupie songs

1. 'Ladies of the Road', King Crimson
2. 'Star Star', Rolling Stones
3. 'Stage Door Jenny', Neil Sedaka
4. 'Groupie (Superstar)', Delaney and Bonnie and friends
5. 'We're an American Band', Grand Funk
6. 'Stray Cat Blues', Rolling Stones
7. 'Cadence and Cascade', King Crimson
8. 'Groupie Girl', Tony Joe White
9. 'Ruby Tuesday', Rolling Stones
10. 'Dirty Diana', Michael Jackson

■ Smash It Up

The Sixties gave us a new sport in rock 'n' roll: hotel wreckin'. Possibly inspired by Pete Townshend's innovative instrument destruction (certainly the Who were grandmasters of trashing hotel rooms), the new sport caught on quickly and thousands of pounds worth of damage was inflicted on hotel rooms around the world. The Who were probably the uncrowned kings of destruction, with Keith Moon as the kingpin; Led Zeppelin were right behind and the Sex Pistols (who pretended to renounce everything that the aforementioned boring old farts practised) were pretty good at it. Rumour has it that it was once considered for the Olympics.

Shortly before he left the Damned, Rat Scabies returned to his Swiss hotel room, consumed several large drinks and proceeded to take out his frustrations on his room. When the damage was discovered, instead of simply presenting Rat with a bill as was the normal procedure, several hotel flunkeys proceeded to trash poor Rat.

In 1987 the band Danny Wilson held a party to smash up their hotel room. However, they felt so silly afterwards that they tidied up.

■ General Tour Trivia

Rod Stewart used to use the Fall's 'Totally Wired' as introductory music before he appeared on stage. Thankfully, Mark E. Smith does not use 'Baby Jane' before the Fall takes to the boards.

While on an Italian tour Orchestral Manoeuvres In The Dark had their van pulled over by the police and were subjected to a lengthy interrogation because their van was similar to one used by a terrorist group.

In the Sixties double gigs were not a rare thing for up and coming bands. They'd often play a mid-evening gig at one venue, then go on to a late night show at another. The problems occurred when the two clubs were more than 100 miles apart, which often happened.

■ MATERIAL GIRL

Some trivia about Madonna, the queen of Eighties pop.

A couple of songs about Madonna (and a certain person very closely related to her):
'Madonna, Sean and Me', Sonic Youth
'Sean Penn Blues', Lloyd Cole and the Commotions

And some that name-check her:
'Mr DJ', The Concepts
'You Look Marvellous', Billy Crystal
'Have A Nice Day', Roxanne Shante

It remains to be seen whether the mega-popular Madonna will have countless tributes recorded to her in years to come.

Her full name is Madonna Louise Ciccone, and her confirmation name is Veronica.

Madonna spent several weeks in Paris performing in a revue led by Patrick Hernandez, who is best known in Britain for his 1979 hit 'Born To Be Alive'.

Her first single, 'Everybody', had to be remixed by DJ and Visage member Rusty Egan before her UK record company would release it.

'Material Girl' was available in a Chanel No. 5 scented version.

She shares manager Freddie De Mann with Michael Jackson.

Her two favourite movies are *It's a Wonderful Life* (starring James Stewart) and *A Place in the Sun* (with Elizabeth Taylor and Montgomery Clift).

In the flop film *Shanghai Surprise*, Madonna played a character called Gloria Tatlock.

Madonna's brother Christopher appeared in the video for Soft Cell's 'Tainted Love'.

Her heroine is Marilyn Monroe. The *Material Girl* video was basically a scene from the Monroe film *Diamonds Are a Girl's Best Friend*.

She sang backing vocals on Blue Zoo's 'Cry Boy Cry', but they were left off the final version.

She can play the violin.

■ I LIKE SPORT

□ Football Records Hit Single League

The records eligible for this league are British hit singles recorded in praise or celebration of an English football team by the team or a group of its supporters. It does not include attempts at pop singing by individual players. The points score is arrived at by dividing the number of weeks a record spent on the chart by its highest position, multiplying by 100 and rounding up to get a suitable figure. Any omissions are probably deliberate.

□ Team	□ Song	□ Recorded by	□ Points	□ Club total
Tottenham Hotspur	'Nice One Cyril'	Cockerel Chorus	85.9	
	'Ossie's Dream	FA Cup Final Squad 1981	160.0	
	'Tottenham Tottenham'	FA Cup Final Squad 1982	36.8	
	'Hot Shot Tottenham'	FA Cup Final Squad 1987	27.8	310.5
Chelsea	'Blue Is the Colour'	Chelsea FC	240.0	
	'Chelsea'	Stamford Bridge	2.2	242.2
Liverpool	'We Can Do It' (EP)	Liverpool FC	26.6	
	'Liverpool (We're Never . . .)'	Liverpool FC	7.4	
	'Sitting on Top of the World'	Liverpool FC	4.0	
	'Anfield Rap'	Liverpool FC	200.0	238.0
Leeds United	'Leeds United'	Leeds United FC	100.0	100.0
Manchester United	'Manchester United'	Man Utd FC	2.0	
	'Glory Glory Man United'	Man Utd FC	38.9	

Team	Song	Recorded by	Points	Club total
	'We All Follow Man United'	Man Utd FC	50.0	90.9
Arsenal	'Good Old Arsenal'	Arsenal FC First Team Squad	43.8	43.8
West Ham United	'I'm Forever Blowing Bubbles'	West Ham Utd Cup Squad	6.9	
	'I'm Forever Blowing Bubbles'	Cockney Rejects	33.3	40.2
Everton	'Here We Go'	Everton 1985	35.9	35.9
Nottingham Forest	'We've Got the Whole World in Our Hands'	Nottingham Forest & Paper Lace	25.0	25.0
Brighton & Hove Albion	'The Boys in the Old Brighton Blues'	Brighton & Hove Albion FC	3.8	3.8
Coventry	'Go For It'	Coventry City	3.8	3.8
Fulham	'Viva El Fulham'	Tony Rees and the Cottagers	2.2	2.2

Tottenham Hotspur are the only football team to chart in the *Record Retailer* EP charts (1960–7). They hit in 1967 with their 'Spurs Go Marching On' EP – a forerunner to their FA cup victory over Chelsea. Featured vocalists included Jimmy Greaves.

Heaven 17 recorded the Sheffield Wednesday tribute 'Steel City (Move On Up)' under the pseudonym the Hillsboro' Crew.

'The Boys in Blue', a 1987 anthem for Glasgow Rangers, was written by singer and comedian Bill Barclay, a confirmed *Hibernian* supporter!

Many footballing figures have attempted to make the charts. Most successful were Chris (Waddle) and Glen (Hoddle) with 'Diamond Lights', which made the charts in 1987. Kevin Keegan had a 1979 hit with 'Head over Heels', but missed the charts with several other releases. Terry Venables missed with his version of 'What Do You Want to Make Those Eyes at Me For' in 1974. QPR player Mark Lazarus also missed with 'Queen's Park Rangers Are the Greatest'. There was no joy either for Brian Clough, who prophetically cried 'You Can't Win Them All'.

■ Football-connected records by rock bands

George Best, Wedding Present
Some People Are on the Pitch They Think It's All Over.† It Is Now, Dentists
(the title is taken from the commentary on the 1966 World Cup; † marks the point where Geoff Hurst stuck away England's fourth goal)
'Pat Nevin's Eyes', Tractors
'The Game', Tackhead (includes guest vocals by Brian Moore)
'Don't Shoot the Ref', John McLeod's XI
'Why Don't Rangers Sign a Catholic', Jock McDonald
'My World Is a Football', Bruce Thompson
'All I Want for Christmas Is a Dukla Prague Away Kit', Half Man Half Biscuit

David Essex, Rod Stewart, Owen Paul and Steve Harris all played as apprentices for professional football teams.

■ Some other sport songs

□ American Football

'Backfield in Motion', Mel and Tim
'Football Season's Over', Shelley Fabres
'Super Bowl Shuffle', Chicago Bears Shufflin' Crew

□ Boxing

'In Zaire', Johnny Wakelin
'Foreman and Frazier', Big Youth
'Thank You Very Much Mr Eastwood', Dermot Morgan
'Where's Harry', Contenders
'Bruno', Johnny Wakelin
'The Ali Shuffle', Alvin Cash

☐ Cricket

'Cricket', Kinks
'When an Old Cricketer Leaves the Crease', Roy Harper
'Cricket Bloody Cricket', Violinski
'Cricket', Clifford T. Ward
'Chinese Cricket Match', Frank Holder

☐ Tennis

'Chalkdust. The Umpire Strikes Back', The Brat
'Anyone for Tennis', Cream
'Game Set and Match', PT and the Plimsouls
'Wimbledon Break Point', Bassline

☐ Snooker

'Snooker Loopy', Chas and Dave with the Matchroom Mob
'Snookeroo', Ringo Starr
'147', Alex 'Hurricane' Higgins

Cricketer Bob Willis adopted the middle name Dylan by deed poll, as he is a big fan.

Davy Jones of the Monkees was an apprentice jockey.

Terence Trent D'Arby is an experienced amateur boxer.

Ian Botham's flamboyant former manager (Lord) Tim Hudson was one-time manager of Sixties US garage rock band the Seeds.

In the Thirties Regal Zonophone released 'Back Your Fancy' records with six consecutive grooves: a horse race commentary with six possible results.

Former Hot Chocolate singer Errol Brown owns several racehorses, including the successful Gainsay.

■ THE FIRST TIME

Some claims (proven and otherwise) for music-related firsts

The first published blues song is W. C. Handy's 'Memphis Blues', written in 1909 and published in 1912.

Guitarist James Burton's first appearance on vinyl was on Dale Hawkins's 'Suzy Q'.

The first surf instrumental was Dick Dale's 'Let's Go Trippin'' (1961).

Goldy and the Gingerbreads, who formed in 1962, were the first all-girl pop group to play all their own instruments.

Chuck Berry first did his famous 'duck walk' at the Paramount Theatre, New York, in 1956. It was supposedly done to hide the creases in his suit.

The first British group to play at the Grand Ole Opry was the Hillsiders, a Liverpool country and western group who played there in 1967.

The Wailers' 'Rude Boy' was the first 'rude' record released.

The Monkees' *Pisces, Aquarius, Capricorn, and Jones* was the first pop LP to feature a Moog synthesizer (1967).

The first gold cartridge award went to Herb Alpert for the cartridge version of 'What Now My Love'.

The Beatles' 'Eight Days A Week' was the first record to feature a 'fade-in' beginning.

Dana's 'All Kinds of Everything' was the first record to be played on the GPO's Dial-a-Disc service.

The Damned were the first British punk band to play in America.

The Cars' single 'My Best Friend's Girl' was the first picture disc single.

Dire Straits' 'Brothers in Arms' was the first CD single.

The first single with a holographic sleeve was the Fall's 'Ghost in My House'.

The first LP with such a sleeve was the original sound-track to *Time*.

Morrissey Mullen's 'Love Don't Live Here Anymore' was the first UK digitally recorded single.

Elkie Brooks's *Screen Gems* LP was the first UK-pressed CD.

Blondie's *Eat To The Beat* was the first LP to have a promo film made for the whole thing. It was released in the short-lived laser disc format.

Hank Ballard made his UK live début on 11 December 1986, more than thirty years after making his first recording.

□ First Cut Is the Deepest

■ Début singles by long-established black artists

1. 'Confession Blues', Ray Charles (1948)
2. 'Please Please Please', James Brown (1956)
3. 'Kiss Me Baby', Four Tops (1956)
4. 'Reet Petite', Jackie Wilson (1957)*
5. 'Angels Cried', Isley Brothers (1957)
6. 'Let Your Conscience Be Your Guide', Marvin Gaye (1961)†
7. 'I Want a Guy', Diana Ross (as Supremes) (1961)
8. 'Thank You for Loving Me All the Way', Little Stevie Wonder (1962)

* Jackie Wilson recorded with the Dominos prior to this single release.
† Marvin Gaye had previously recorded as a member of the Marquees and the Moonglows.

9. 'Kool and the Gang', Kool and the Gang (1969)
10. 'I Want You Back', Michael Jackson (as Jackson Five) (1970)

□ In the Beginning

■ Début singles by American rock 'n' roll stars

1. 'Four Leaf Clover Blues', Bill Haley (1948)
2. 'Taxi Blues', Little Richard (1951)
3. 'That's Alright Mama', Elvis Presley (1954)
4. 'Two Blue Singing Stars', Eddie Cochran (as Cochran Brothers) (1954)
5. 'Maybellene', Chuck Berry (1955)
6. 'Crazy Arms', Jerry Lee Lewis (1956)
7. 'Blue Days Black Nights', Buddy Holly (1956)
8. 'Be Bop A Lula', Gene Vincent (1956)
9. 'Tear It Up', Johnny Burnette Rock 'n' Roll Trio (1956)
10. 'The Sun Keeps Shining', Everly Brothers (1956)

■ KING ROCKER

A small selection of the many records about Elvis; some genuine tributes, others not.

1. 'I Remember Elvis Presley', Danny Mirror
2. 'King's Call', Phil Lynott
3. 'Elvis Was Not the White Nigger, I Was', P. J. Proby
4. 'I Want Elvis for Christmas', Holly Twins
5. 'Elvis Has Just Left the Building', J. D. Sumner and the Stamps
6. 'Rock On Elvis', Tulsa McLean
7. 'Tupelo Mississippi Flash', Steve Gibbons Band
8. 'There's a Guy Works Down the Chip Shop Swears He's Elvis', Kirsty McColl
9. 'My Boy Elvis', Janis Martin
10. 'Codeword Elvis', Eberhard Schoener
11. 'Elvis Bought Dora a Cadillac', Wall of Voodoo
12. 'Elvis Presley and America', U2
13. 'Elvis We Love You', Terry Tigre
14. 'My Baby's Crazy 'bout Elvis', Billy Boyce
15. 'The Elvis I Knew Was No Junkie', Membranes
16. 'My Little Girl's Prayer for Elvis', Kelly Leroux
17. 'The King Is Gone', Ronnie McDowell
18. 'Elvis, A Legendary Angel', Melody Lloyd
19. 'That Last Encore', Jim Fagan
20. 'Why Can't They Leave Him Alone', Mark Haley
21. 'The King of Rock 'n' Roll', Dave K
22. 'Elvisly Yours', The Johnnys

'That Last Encore' is one of the sickliest, kitschest, most appalling records ever committed to vinyl.

Eddie Cochran plays guitar and sings backing vocals on the Holly Twins' tribute, which was written by Bobby Darin.

The Cramps are one of the few bands to have recorded in the original Sun Studios in recent years.

There also exists a record called 'Mum Dad Love Hate and Elvis', but for the life of me I can't remember who it's by.

Graduate's 'Elvis Should Play Ska' is directed at Mr Costello not Presley.

Approximately 20 million Presley records sold world-wide in the twenty-four hours after his death on 16 August 1977.

Miami Vice star Don Johnson played Elvis in the 1981 film *Elvis and The Beauty Queen*. Others who have played Elvis include Tim Whitnall, Shakin' Stevens, P. J. Proby, Kurt Russell and Randy Gray (who played him as a young boy in *Elvis – The Movie*).

'When blonde 15-year-old schoolgirl Jean goes to bed she turns off the light before undressing because she feels so shy. The reason: "I have 1003 photos of Elvis Presley stuck on the wall of my bedroom all smiling down on me" said Jean at her Abbey Wood home yesterday.' *Sunday Graphic*

Presley was obsessed by guns; he even used the TV for target practice. Other hobbies included boxing and karate.

The first Elvis bootleg was released in 1967. It contained tracks from the films *Jailhouse Rock* and *Loving You*. It appeared in 10-inch format and today is probably worth in excess of £10,000.

Elvis was originally scheduled to appear in *The Girl Can't Help It* and two songs were written specially for him. However, the deal fell through.

Presley's first manager was Scotty Moore, his original guitarist.

Gary Leeds (of the Walker Brothers) used to drum for Elvis.

Elvis's 1968 single 'If I Can Dream' was released as 'a plea for peace and understanding'.

'The Wonder of You' was arranged by former Cricket Glen D. Hardin.

■ Ten originals of early Elvis Presley recordings

1. 'That's Alright Mama', Arthur Crudup (1946)
2. 'Blue Moon of Kentucky', Bill Monroe (1946)
3. 'Good Rockin' Tonight', Roy Brown (1947)
4. 'My Baby Left Me', Arthur Crudup (1950)
5. 'Lawdy Miss Clawdy', Lloyd Price (1952)
6. 'Hound Dog', Willie Mae Thornton (1953)
7. 'Mystery Train', Junior Parker (1953)
8. 'Baby Let's Play House', Arthur 'Hardrock' Gunter (1954)
9. 'I Got a Woman', Ray Charles (1955)
10. 'Blue Suede Shoes', Carl Perkins (1956)

■ ROYAL EVENT

Some songs about the 1981 wedding of HRH Prince Charles and Lady Diana Spencer

'Now We Know It's Diana', Bobby and the Girls
'Diana Divine', Doris Taylor
'Diana', Mike Berry
'Lady Di', The Royals
'White Wedding', Sheila Southern
'Here's to the Couple', Spinners
'Lady D', Typically Tropical
'The Ballad of Lady D', The Hon. Nick Jones and Ian MaCrae
'Hey Diana', Heroes and Angels
'Lady Diana', Mick Gannon
'Royal Wedding Waltz', Mike Sammes Singers
'This Is My Royal Wedding Souvenir', Blurt
'Fairytale Princess', The Pearly Eights
'Charlie's Angels', Mini and the Metros
'Charlie's Getting Married at Last', Men of Harlech

The Hon. Nick Jones and Ian MaCrae were two Australian journalists who reported on the entire royal wedding ceremony from their hotel room.

■ JAIL GUITAR DOORS

Don't let them tell you rock 'n' rollers are respectable. Several have infringed the law and I don't just mean Clapton clocked doing a ton on the motorway. No, several rock musicians have actually been put away.

Chuck Berry spent two years inside in the early Sixties for violating the Mann Act in bringing a 14-year-old prostitute over the Mexican border to the US. In 1979 he spent another 100 days inside for tax evasion.

Hugh Cornwell of the Stranglers spent two months at Her Majesty's pleasure in 1980 for possession of drugs and later that year spent a week inside a French gaol with Jet Black and Jean Jacques Burnel, accused of inciting a riot at a Nice gig.

Paul and Linda McCartney were arrested and stuck away for several days in Tokyo for possessing marijuana.

Mick Jones and Joe Strummer of the Clash were jailed overnight in Newcastle for nicking hotel towels. Former Clash drummer Topper Headon got far more serious treatment in 1987 for supplying heroin and was stuck away for fifteen months. Another rock star turned drugs dealer was the MC5's Wayne Kramer, who got two years in 1980 for his crimes.

R&B mouth organist Lew Lewis got seven years for armed robbery in 1987 after holding up a post office. Former ABC trumpeter Stephen Chappel also robbed a PO, but, as he was unarmed, got away with only five years.

James Brown was stuck inside as a youngster for grand theft auto, and many years later (in 1987) Patrick Waite of Musical Youth got four months for car theft.

The Who were held overnight for trashing a hotel room in Montreal.

Rick Stevens of Tower of Power was gaoled for the murder of three drugs dealers.

Ted Hawkins, the blues singer who waited donkey's years to be discovered, was gaoled for three years when he was 15 for burglary. Another young thief was Roy Harper, who spent a year inside Walton Gaol, Liverpool, for his sins.

David Crosby was stuck away in the mid-Eighties for possession of drugs and keeping a concealed gun.

Ian Astbury of the Cult was held overnight in Vancouver after assaulting a security man at a show. He spent the night in a cell with Arthur Lee's (of Love) brother.

Nazi Dog of the Vicetones is currently doing time for armed robbery.

Kevin Wright of Always was in gaol for embezzlement when he learnt to play guitar. He was signed to El Records on release. This real life event almost mirrored the Elvis character in *Jailhouse Rock*.

Apparently (much scepticism here) an up and coming pop singer was sent to San Quentin for life after severing the hand of a record company employee who asked him to remix his music.

Kevin Coyne has composed a series of songs about the Kray Twins under the collective title 'England England'.

Spandau Ballet's Kemp brothers are to play the Krays in a film. Roger Daltrey did play the criminal McVicar, while Phil Collins played Great Train Robber Buster Edwards.

■ Some gaol songs

1. 'Have You Ever Spent the Night in Jail', Standells
2. 'Jailhouse Rock', Elvis Presley
3. 'Borstal Breakout', Sham 69
4. 'Life in Prison', Merle Haggard
5. 'Cell 151', Steve Hackett
6. 'Riot in Cell Block No. 9', Robins
7. 'I'm Here to Get My Baby out of Jail', Everly Brothers
8. 'Fulsom Prison Blues', Slim Harpo

9. 'Rubber Bullets', 10CC
10. 'Jailhouse Rap', Fat Boys
11. 'The Prisoner's Song', Joe Barry
12. 'Care of Cell 44', Zombies
13. 'In the Jailhouse Now', Sonny James
14. 'Cell Number 7', John Entwhistle's Ox

■ THEY'RE COMING TO TAKE ME AWAY HA HAAA!

The pressures of rock 'n' roll have affected the minds of many rock stars. Several have gone as far as being committed (or committing themselves) into asylums (or whatever polite name they're given these days).

Archetypal British eccentric and former Pink Floyd guitarist Syd Barrett was committed for drug-induced personality problems.

Roky Erikson (13th Floor Elevator) was committed on 8 October 1969 to the Rush State Hospital for the Criminally Insane. He was released in 1972 and has since made some manic records.

Billy Joel admitted himself to hospital for depression when he was 21.

Don Drummond of the Skatelites was committed to an asylum after killing his common-law wife; he died there in 1971.

Fleetwood Mac's Peter Green was put away in January 1977 after threatening his accountant with a rifle.

Terry Dene was invalided out of the army on the grounds of mental health, thus dispersing any hopes that the army would be as good for his career as it was for Presley's.

■ Some mad songs

1. 'Madness', Madness
2. 'Lunacy's Back', Marc Bolan
3. 'The Idiot', Iggy Pop
4. 'Crazy for You', Madonna
5. 'Mad Eyed Screamer', Creatures
6. 'Fool for Your Lovin'', Whitesnake

7. 'The Lunatics Have Taken over the Asylum', Fun Boy Three
8. 'Fools Rush In', Rick Nelson
9. 'Crackin' Up', Nick Lowe
10. 'You're Driving Me Crazy', Temperance Seven

■ THE NAME OF THE GAME

□ The Name Game

A selection of songs that feature pop stars' names in the title

'You're Alright Ray Charles', Joe Tex
'Jackie Wilson Said (I'm in Heaven)', Van Morrison
'I Wish Marvin Gaye's Father Had Shot Me Instead', Chrysanthemums
'Wood Beez (Pray Like Aretha Franklin)', Scritti Politti
'The Revenge of Al Green', Hook and Pull
'Denny Laine's Valet', Jona Lewie
'Iggy Pop's Jacket', Those Naughty Lumps
'Joe Strummer's Wallet', Stingrays
'Billy Eckstein's Shirt Collar', Rip Rig and Panic
'Brian Wilson's Bed', Bob
'This Is Your Life Patti Smith (So Why Did You Jump off the Stage)', The Cads
'The Lonesome Death of Thurston Moore' (of Sonic Youth), Slaughter Joe
'I've Got the Fleetwood Mac Chicken Shack John Mayall Can't Fail Blues', Liverpool Scene
'The Bastard Son of Dean Friedman', Half Man Half Biscuit
'Jim Croce', Jerry Reed
'Alex Chilton', Replacements
'I Know Where Syd Barrett Lives', Television Personalities
'The Story of Bo Diddley', Animals
'Bo Diddley', Bo Diddley
'Bo Diddley Is a Gunslinger', Bo Diddley
'Hey Bo Diddley', Bo Diddley

'Bo Diddley Is a Communist', Eugene Chadbourne
'Bo Diddley Rides the Wild Surf', Beachniks
'The Rise and Fall of Laurel Aitken', Laurel Aitken
'Remember Hon. Robert Nesta Marley', Freddie Chambers
'They Died with Their Willie Nelson T-Shirts On', Sewer Rats
'The Night Hank Williams Came to Town', Johnny Cash
'I'll Change Your Flat Tyre Merle' (Haggard), Big Brother and the Holding Company
'I Love You Because You Look Like Jim Reeves', Half Man Half Biscuit
'Dolli Parten's Tits' (their spelling!), McLean and McLean
'If I Could Sing a Country Song (Exactly Like George Jones)', James O' Gwynne
'Please Play More Kenny Rogers', Steve Lee Cook
'There's a Little Bit of Hank Williams in Me', Charlie Pride
'The Real Buddy Holly Story', Sonny Curtis
'Goodbye and Thanks Buddy Holly', The Pilot*
'Oh Buddy Holly', The Pilot
'A Tribute to Buddy Holly', Beat Buddies
'My Buddy Holly Days', Rubettes
'The Story of Buddy Holly', The Familee
'Tribute to Buddy Holly', Mike Berry
'I Feel Like Buddy Holly', Alvin Stardust
'Sweet Gene Vincent', Ian Dury and the Blockheads
'The Ballad of Rick Nelson', Imus In The Morning
'Hooray for Chuck Berry', Jerry Reed
'Tribute to Eddie Cochran', Heinz
'Like Frankie Lymon', Weather Prophets
'I'm Sorry (But So Is Brenda Lee)', Marshall Crenshaw
'Mary Hopkins Never Had Days Like These', P. J. Proby
'Dick Dale Is Alive and Well and Living in Palm Springs F.C.A.', Beachniks
'Salutes the Magic of Freddie Mercury and Queen', Frank Sidebottom
'John Barry', The Godfathers
'The Ballad of Ron Grainer', Exhibit B
'The Birth of Captain Beefheart', Frank Zappa and the Mothers of Invention

* What sick mind made a tribute to Holly under the group name The Pilot?

'Paul Simon in the Park with Canticle', Game Theory
'Please Phil Spector', Attack
'Afternoon Tea with Dave Greenfield', Gaye Bikers On Acid
'Desperately Seeking Alan McGhee' (ex-H_2O), Tractors
'We Love Jimmy Young', Bill Oddie and the Average Mothers
'Ballad of John and Yoko', Beatles
'Lady Day and John Coltrane', Gil Scott Heron
'John Coltrane Stereo Blues', Droogs
'Sweet Georgie Fame', Blossom Dearie
'Glenn Miller Is Missing', Rock Follies
'I Washed My Hands in Muddy Waters' (that's pushing it a bit far!), Stonewall Jackson

☐ Heroes

A selection of songs that feature sportsmen's names in the title (and an explanation for the uninformed)

'Pat Nevin's Eyes' (footballer), Tractors
'Jackie Charlton Said' (ex-footballer), Jung Analysts
'Frankly Mr Shankly' (former football manager), Smiths
'Do the Earl Campbell' (US football star), Joe Tex
'Fuckin' Hell It's Fred Titmus' (cricketer), Half Man Half Biscuit
'Cassius Clay' (boxer), Prince Buster
'George Foreman' (boxer), Big Youth
'Foreman and Frazier' (boxers), Big Youth
'Salute to Sir Francis Chichester' (yachtsman), Roland Shaw and his Orchestra
'Frank Bough' (former sports programme presenter), Baby Sitters
'Dickie Davis' Eyes' (sports programme presenter), Half Man Half Biscuit

☐ Painter Man

A selection of songs with an artist's or writer's name in the title

'Vincent', Don McLean
'Another Vincent Van Gogh', Jimmy Campbell
'Jean Cocteau', Be Bop Deluxe
'Picasso's Last Words, Drink to Me', Wings
'Pablo Picasso', Modern Lovers
'A Portrait of V. I. Lenin in the Style of Jackson Pollack', The Red Crayola with Art and Language
'Christ versus Warhol', Teardrop Explodes
'Andy Warhol', David Bowie
'Michelangelo', 23rd Turnoff
'Shakespeare's Sister', Smiths
'Graham Greene', John Cale
'Hey Jack Kerouac', 10,000 Maniacs
'Mark Twain', The Amazing George Finksten

☐ Stand up and Say That

Songs about politicians, political and other activists

'Malcolm X (No Sell Out)', Keith Le Blanc
'George Jackson', Bob Dylan
'Sean Flynn', Clash
'Winnie Mandela', Carlene Davis
'Jim Callaghan', Mr John Dowie
'Gaddafi', Ebenezer
'Willie Whitelaw's Willie', Attila the Stockbroker
'Haf Found Bormann', Fall
'Goebbels, Mosley, God and Ingrams', JJ Burnel
'Joe Stalin's Cadillac', Camper Van Beethoven

'Stalin Wasn't Stallin'', Robert Wyatt
'Jeremy* Is Innocent', Rex Barker and the Ricochets
'P. W. Botha's Funeral', Nigel Rolfe
'Margaret Thatcher', Lion
'I'm in Love with Margaret Thatcher', Not Sensibles
'Thatcher's Dead', Don Valley and the Rotherhides
'I Was Kaiser Bill's Batman', Whistling Jack Smith
'Do the Mussolini', Cabaret Voltaire
'The Day John Kennedy Died', Lou Reed
'Song to Abe Lincoln', Roky Erikson
'God Bless Robert E. Lee', Johnny Cash

□ I've Got Lots of Famous People Living under the Floorboards of My Humble Abode

. . . and an explanation of the title in case they aren't as famous as they thought.

'Oh Bosanquet' (news-reader Reginald), Not The Nine O'Clock News
'I'm in Love with Angela Rippon' (news-reader), Bernard Wrigley
'Ronnie Biggs Was Only the Tea Boy' (train robber), Train Robbers
'King Selassie' (figurehead of Rastafarian religion), Black Uhuru
'Paul Revere' (U S War of Independence hero), Beastie Boys
'I Was Queen Victoria's Chambermaid' (a queen), Mrs Mills
'Don't Dig Twiggy' (Sixties model), Barbara Windsor
'Jackie O' (rich lady), John Kennedy
'Janie Jones' (prostitute involved in 'sex for air-play' scandal), Clash
'Christine Keeler' (prostitute in the Profumo affair), Glaxo Babies
'99% of Gargoyles Look Like Bob Todd' (Benny Hill's stooge), Half Man Half Biscuit

* Thorpe

'Where's Bill Grundy Now' (television host), Television Personalities
'Me and Howard Hughes' (eccentric millionaire), Boomtown Rats
'Freddie Laker (Concorde and Eurobus)' (businessman), Jean Jacques Burnel
'We're All Behind You Freddie' (Laker again), Gatwick People
'Rod Hull Is Still Alive! Why?' (man who earns a living by sticking his hand up an emu's bum), Half Man Half Biscuit
'Lady Godiva's Operation' (the original streaker), Velvet Underground
'Einstein A Go Go' (a clever person), Landscape
'Mr Crowley' (Aleister, the black magic chappie), Blizzard of Oz
'Rasputin' (mad monk), Boney M
'Joan of Arc' (lady at the stake), Orchestral Manoeuvres in the Dark
'Ask Johnny Dee' (famed fanzine writer), Chesterfields
'Ballad of Bonnie and Clyde' (gangsters), Georgie Fame
'This Nelson Rockefeller' (politician), McCarthy
'Sean Penn Blues' (hooligan), Lloyd Cole and the Commotions
'D'Ya Ken Ted Moult' (farmer who advertised windows), Half Man Half Biscuit
'I Never Loved Eva Braun' (Hitler's girl-friend), Boomtown Rats
'Billy Graham' (spokesman for God), Larks
'Basil Dalton' (chap who wrote lots of books about the card game Patience), Living in a Box

□ We Love You

A selection of genuine (heart-felt?) tributes to real people that don't fully name the person in the title.

'Janis', Country Joe (Janis Joplin)
'Queen of the Blues', Blood Sweat and Tears (Janis Joplin)
'Janis This One's for You', The Band of Holy Joy (Janis Joplin)
'Under A Ragin' Moon', Roger Daltrey (Keith Moon)
'Pride (In the Name of Love)', U2 (Martin Luther King)

'Hats Off to Harper', Led Zeppelin (Roy Harper)
'Belfast Boy', Don Farden (George Best)
'Godstar', Psychic TV (Brian Jones)
'The End', Leo Sayer (Sid Vicious)
'O Caroline', Matching Mole (Caroline Coon, rock journalist)
'Happy Birthday', Stevie Wonder (Martin Luther King)
'Shine On You Crazy Diamond', Pink Floyd (Syd Barrett)
'Tribute to A King', William Bell (Otis Redding)
'A Young Man Is Gone', Beach Boys (James Dean)
'Candle in the Wind', Elton John (Marilyn Monroe)
'Now That You're Gone', Donna (Richie Valens)
'Song to Woody', Bob Dylan (Woody Guthrie)
'Matchstick Men and Matchstick Cats and Dogs', Brian and Michael (L. S. Lowrie)
'Geno', Dexy's Midnight Runners (Geno Washington)
'Why? (The King of Love Is Dead)', Nina Simone (Martin Luther King)
'It Was A Normal Day for Brian, the Man Who Dies Everyday', Pete Townshend (unreleased demo about Brian Jones)
'When Smokey Sings', ABC (Smokey Robinson)
'Little Johnny Jewel', Television (James Jewel Osterburg aka Iggy Pop)
'Donny', Mandy Ann (Donny Osmond)
'King Holiday', Kurtis Blow (Martin Luther King)
'Berry Rides Again', Steppenwolf (Chuck Berry)
'House of Jansch', Donovan (Bert Jansch)
'Suite: Judy Blue Eyes', Crosby Stills and Nash (Judy Collins)
'Lonely Joe', Rob Shenton (Joe Meek)
'Three Young Men', Lee Davis (Holly, Valens and the Big Bopper)
'Three Stars', Eddie Cochran (Holly, Valens and the Big Bopper)
'The Ballad of Donna and Peggy Sue', Ray Campi (Valens and Holly)
'Just Like Eddie', Heinz (Eddie Cochran)
'Cole, Cooke and Redding', Wilson Pickett (Nat, Sam and Otis)
'Johnny and Dee Dee', The Eastern Dark (Two Ramones)
'Sir Duke', Stevie Wonder (Duke Ellington)
'Roman P', Psychic TV (Roman Polanski)
'Bopper 486609', Donna Dameron (the Big Bopper)
'Buddy, Big Bopper and Ritchie', Loretta Thompson (Holly, the Big Bopper and Valens)
'Maid of Orleans', Orchestral Manoeuvres in the Dark (Joan of Arc)

'King Rocker', Generation X (Elvis Presley and John Lennon)
'Black Superman', Johnny Wakelin (Muhammad Ali)
'Two Blue Singing Stars', Cochran Brothers (Hank Williams and Jimmy Rodgers)
'We Love Malcolm', The O'Levels (Malcolm McLaren)
'Tribute to the Prince', Dandy Livingstone (Prince Buster)
'Dagenham Dave', Stranglers (a 'fan' who 'hit the water high')
'Toe Knee Black Burn', Binky Baker (a DJ. Binky is Anne Nightingale's hubby)
'Lou', Adam and the Ants (Lou Reed)
'My Girl Janis', Rockateens (Janis Martin, 'the female Elvis')
'A Day Without Me', U2 (Ian Curtis)
'Abraham, Martin and John', Marvin Gaye (Lincoln, Luther King and Kennedy)
'My Man', Eagles (Gram Parsons)
'Artists and Poets', Johnny Rivers (Gram Parsons)
'Crazy Eyes', Poco (Gram Parsons)
'The Memory of You', Janis Martin (James Dean)
'Black Leather Rebel', Johnny Carroll (Gene Vincent)
'Little Caesar', Go West (Edward G. Robinson)
'Nightshift', Commodores (Marvin Gaye and Jackie Wilson)
'Missing You', Diana Ross (Marvin Gaye)
'Empty Garden', Elton John (John Lennon)
'For John', Yoko Ono (John Lennon)
'Thanks John', Flamin' Groovies (John Lennon)
'For A Rocker', Jackson Browne (John Lennon)
'Much Missed Man', Phil Boardman (John Lennon)
'Ole Pal', Brush Shiels (Phil Lynott)
'Jody', Jermaine Stewart (Jody Watley, ex-Shalamar)
'We'll Be Together', Sharon Sheeley (an unreleased tribute to her fiancé, Eddie Cochran, written *c.* 1961 by Sheeley and Jackie De Shannon)
'You Got Your Baby Back', Mystic Knights of the Dingo Boingo (about Patti Hearst)
'All Those Years Ago', George Harrison (John Lennon)
'Song for Jimmy', Thin Lizzy (Jimi Hendrix – their spelling)
'Song for Convict Charlie', Birdmen of Alcatraz (Charles Manson)

☐ Calling Your Name

How or why groups chose their name.

Abba An acronym derived from the group members' forenames: *A*gnetha, *B*enny, *B*jorn and *A*nnifred
A Flock of Seagulls A line from the Stranglers' song 'Toiler on the Sea'
Alphaville A 1965 Jean Luc Godard-directed sci-fi film
Amen Corner A section of the Negro spiritual church where a group of women sat and hollered the 'Amens'
Arcadia After the central region of the Greek Peloponnese, home of the god Pan
Bad Company After a Robert Benton Western
Bangles After the Electric Prunes' song of that name
Barracudas After the Standells' song 'Barracuda'
Bauhaus After a group of pre-war designers in Germany
BB&Q Band *B*rooklyn, *B*ronx and *Q*ueens Band
Bee Gees From B.G.s for Brothers Gibb – their surname
B-52s After a famous bouffant hair-style of the Sixties
Blow Monkeys Jazz slang for saxophone players
Blue Rondo a la Turk After a jazz song, best known in its version by Dave Brubeck
Boney M After an Australian TV detective
Boomtown Rats A gang of kids in Oklahoma who were the children of the casual oil-well labourers. Geldof learned of them through Woody Guthrie's autobiography, *Bound for Glory*.
Brilliant So DJs would announce, 'That was Brilliant'
Bucks Fizz A cocktail of champagne and orange juice
Buffalo Springfield After a make of steamroller
Buzzcocks From the catch-phrase of a character in the TV series *Rock Follies*, who would say 'Give me a buzz, cock!'
Chicken Shack After a blues song, 'Chicken Shack Blues'
Clannad Gaelic for 'family'
Communards After a French Socialist group who revolted in 1871
Creedence Clearwater Revival A combination from a friend called Creedence, a beer advert for Clearwater, and because they considered themselves revivalists

Deep Purple After a Joe South song of that name
Depeche Mode After a French fashion magazine
Dire Straits From the financial state the band were in when they formed
Doobie Brothers A doobie is slang for a joint
Doors From a William Blake poem quoted in Aldous Huxley's drug-related book *The Doors of Perception*
Dr Feelgood After a much covered blues song
Duran Duran After a character in the sci-fi film *Barbarella*
Eurythmics After a form of rhythmic body movement (actually spelt eurhythmics) popular in the early twentieth century
Fiat Lux Latin for 'Let there be light'
Fleetwood Mac Arrived at from the names of its two founding members, Mick Fleetwood and John McVie
Frankie Goes to Hollywood From a newspaper headline about Frank Sinatra about to make a movie
Gang of Four After the Chinese politicians responsible for the Cultural Revolution
Gap Band From the initial letters of the three main streets (*G*reenwood, *A*rcher and *P*ine) in the band's home town of Tulsa, Oklahoma
Gaye Bykers on Acid After a Ray Lowrie cartoon
Generation X After a Sixties paperback about Mod style and fashion
Grateful Dead From an Egyptian prayer
Harpers Bizarre After a fashion magazine
Heaven 17 After a band in the film *Clockwork Orange*
Herman's Hermits Peter Noone misheard another band member, who told him he resembled the cartoon character Sherman from *The Adventures of Bullwinkle and Rocky*
Human League One of the sides in a science fiction board game
Iron Maiden After a medieval torture device
Jefferson Airplane After a device used for holding marijuana cigarettes
Jethro Tull After an eighteenth-century agriculturist
Jo Jo Gunne After a character in a Chuck Berry song
Josef K From the book *The Trial* by Franz Kafka
Joy Division After a band of prostitutes 'commandeered' for German troops' use during the Second World War

Judas Priest From a Bob Dylan song, 'The Ballad of Frankie Lee and Judas Priest'
Kissing the Pink A term used in snooker
Kraftwerk The German for 'power plant'
Kursaal Fliers After the train that paraded along the front at Southend advertising the Kursaal Pleasure Park
Lambrettas After a motor scooter popular with Mods
Led Zeppelin After Keith Moon commented that the band would go down like a lead Zeppelin
Level 42 In the BBC TV series *The Hitchikers' Guide to the Galaxy*, the answer to 'Life, the Universe and everything' is 42, so this seemed a suitable level for the band to aim at
Lindisfarne After an island off the Northumberland coast
Los Lobos Spanish for 'the wolves'
Lynyrd Skynyrd After a certain Leonard Skinner, a gym teacher renowned for punishing boys with long hair
Madness After a Prince Buster song of that name
Marillion From *The Silmarillion*, a Tolkien novel
Marshall Tucker Band After the piano tuner who owned their rehearsal hall
Matchbox After a Carl Perkins track
MFSB Stands for *M*other, *F*ather, *S*ister, *B*rother
Molly Hatchet After Hatchet Molly, an infamous US whore who castrated her clients
Motorhead After a Hawkwind track, in turn named after a US term for a speed freak
Mott the Hoople From a William Manus novel
Mud They wanted a name that would stick
Mungo Jerry From T. S. Eliot's *Old Possum's Book of Practical Cats*
Naked Lunch From the William Burroughs novel of that name
New Model Army After the name given to Oliver Cromwell's troops
New Riders of the Purple Sage After a famous Western novel (*Riders of the Purple Sage*) by Zane Grey
Nine below Zero After a Sonny Boy Williamson blues track
Nirvana Hindu term for 'beatific state'
NRBQ *New Rhythm and Blues Quintet*
101ers After the torture room (Room 101) in Orwell's *1984*
Pere Ubu After a character in a play by Alfred Jarry
Pink Floyd From two bluesmen, Pink Anderson and Floyd Council

Pogues Originally Pogue Mahone, Gaelic for 'kiss my arse'
Procul Harum Latin for 'beyond these things'
Quantum Jump A term used in physics
Ramones After the pseudonym Paul Ramon, which Paul McCartney adopted on a tour by the Silver Beatles
Redbone A derogatory Cajun term for a half-breed
Revillos After a Marvel comics creation, Café Dr Revillo
Rich Kids After a Jean Cocteau book
Righteous Brothers After their audience shouting out 'Hey that's really righteous, brothers!'
Rolling Stones After a Muddy Waters song
Sad Café After the book *The Ballad of the Sad Café* by Carson McCullers
Scritti Politti Italian for 'political writing'
Searchers After a John Wayne film of that name
Shangri Las Shangri La is another name for paradise in a novel by James Hilton
Shirelles From lead singer Shirley Alston (née Owen)
Simple Minds From a line in the David Bowie song 'Jean Genie'
Soft Machine From a William Burroughs novel
Standells After a make of amplifier
Starry-eyed and Laughing From a line in the Bob Dylan song 'Chimes of Freedom'
Stars of Heaven From a biblical quotation: 'I will multiply thy seed as the stars of heaven/And as the sand which is upon the sea shore', Gen. 22:17
Status Quo Latin for the 'existing position of or in society'
Steeleye Span A character from an old English ballad
Steely Dan After the metal dildo in William Burroughs' *Naked Lunch*
Steppenwolf From a Herman Hesse novel
Stiff Little Fingers After a Vibrators track
Strawberry Switchblade After an Orange Juice song
Styx After the river in the Greek underworld of Hades
Supertramp From the W. H. Davies book *The Autobiography of a Supertramp*
Talking Heads A TV term for a head-and-shoulders-only shot of a presenter
Teardrop Explodes A picture caption from the Marvel comic *Daredevil*

Tears for Fears   Derived from Roland Orzabel's interest in primal therapy
Thompson Twins   From two detective characters in *Herge's Adventures of Tin Tin*
Three Dog Night   An Australian term for a very cold night, which comes from the thinking that a man on the outback would need to sleep with one dog to keep him warm on a mild night, two on a colder night and three when it's freezing
Throbbing Gristle   After a Pork Dukes' track
Tom Tom Club   After the hall where they rehearsed
Toto   After Dorothy's dog in *The Wizard of Oz*
Troggs   Short for troglodyte man
UB40   After the reference number of the Unemployment Benefit card
Ultravox   Latin for 'many voices'
Unit 4 + 2   In the Sixties the chart rundown was divided into units (1–4). The group called themselves Unit 4 and later when two more people joined they became Unit 4 + 2.
Uriah Heep   A character from a Dickens novel
Velvet Underground   After a Sixties soft porn paperback
Ventures   Because they considered themselves 'venturing' into a new style of music, rock instrumentals
Wang Chung   Previously Huang Chung, which is Chinese for 'perfection in music'
W.A.S.P.   Stands for *W*e *A*re *S*exual *P*erverts
Woodentops   After a children's TV puppet show
XTC   A phonetic interpretation of 'ecstasy'
ZZ Top   They wanted to be last in record shop bins

Blue Oyster Cult's name comes from an anagram of Cully Stout Beer, an American brew that future manager Sandy Pearlman and future producer Richard Meltzer were drinking while thinking up a band name. Other names they came up with included Trolleybus Cute, Stout Belly Cure, and Trycolute Blues. They could easily have been True Coy Bullets, Truly Close Tube, Cut Lobster Yule, Tellycue Or Bust, or Cute L T Boys Rule!

☐ To Cut a Long Story Short

Some groups got so fed up with their lengthy names that they abbreviated them. At other times it's their fans and music journalists who unofficially shorten the names for convenience. Such unofficial abbreviations are marked *.

ELO* Electric Light Orchestra
Devo Devolution
BAD Big Audio Dynamite
Bauhaus Bauhaus 1919
Gen X Generation X
GTOs Girls Together Outrageously
Stranglers Guildford Stranglers
Starship Jefferson Starship
Kaja Kajagoogoo
KTP Kissing The Pink
OMD* Orchestral Manoeuvres in the Dark
Pogues Pogue Mahone
Punilux Punishment of Luxury
M+M Martha and the Muffins
Quicksilver Quicksilver Messenger Service
Cult Southern Death Cult
Spirit Spirits Rebellious
Vicious Pink Vicious Pink Phenomena
Wah Wah Heat
Fuzzbox* We've Got A Fuzzbox and We're Gonna Use It
Giant Sand The Giant Sandworms

☐ Who Can It Be Now

■ Some artists' nicknames

The Empress of the Blues Bessie Smith
The Queen of the Blues Billie Holiday
Satchmo (Satchel Mouth) Louis Armstrong

The First Lady of Jazz Ella Fitzgerald
The Gospel Queen Mahalia Jackson
The Sweethearts of the Blues Shirley and Lee
The Iceman Jerry Butler
The Wicked Mr Pickett Wilson Pickett
The Fat Man Fats Domino
The King Elvis Presley
The Killer Jerry Lee Lewis
The Man in Black Johnny Cash
The Screaming End Gene Vincent
King of the Surf Guitar Dick Dale
The Godfather of Soul James Brown
The Queen of Soul Aretha Franklin
The Thin White Duke David Bowie
The Legend That Is George Michael
The Air Raid Siren Bruce Dickinson
The Upsetter Lee Perry
The Night Tripper Dr John
The Bacofoil Bulk Gary Glitter

○ Pseudonyms

Sometimes groups, for various reasons, need to use an alternative name either for a live show, a guest appearance or a clandestine release:

Apollo C. Vermouth – Paul McCartney
Rikki Nadir – Peter Hamill
Winston O' Boogie – John Lennon
Klark Kent – Stewart Copeland
Wynder K. Frog – Mick Weaver
The Imposter – Elvis Costello
Ariel Bender – Luther Grosvener
La Place De La Concorde – Julian Cope and Dave Balfe
The Spots – Sex Pistols

Dove – Devo
Cyclone – Matchbox
Fish City Five – Housemartins
3 Roman Gods – Fleshtones
Gargoyles – Housemartins
Leppo and the Jooves – Soft Boys
Spinning Wighats – Long Ryders
Bombadil – Barclay James Harvest
Blanket of Secrecy – Attractions
Dukes of the Stratosphere – XTC
The Young Ones – XTC
Too Many Cooks – XTC
Three Wise Men – XTC
Chuddy Nuddies – Yachts
Moles – Simon Dupree and the Big Sound

A few groups have had to change their name for another territory because there is an indigenous group of that name or the name could be misconstrued. Here are what some UK groups are known as in the US.

Yazoo – Yaz
Squeeze – UK Squeeze
the Beat – the English Beat
Matchbox – Major Matchbox

□ Call up the Groups

As well as solo artists, some songs name-check entire groups in their titles. Often it is a song of the same name as the group performing it. At other times it is a tribute, a spoof or a dig by another group

'Chic Cheer', Chic
'Kool and the Gang', Kool and the Gang
'Living in A Box', Living in A Box

'Give It To the Soft Boys', Soft Boys
'Beastie Boys', Beastie Boys
'Rich Kids', Rich Kids
'The Colourfield', Colourfield
'The Story of Them', Them
'Talk Talk', Talk Talk
'Motorhead', Motorhead
'Madness', Madness
'Johnny Says Yeah', Johnny Says Yeah
'Sympathy for the Mekons', Mekons
'More Ning', Ning
'The Story of Bogshed', Bogshed
'Wild Angels Rock 'n' Roll', Wild Angels
'I Hate the Simple Minds, Success, Game, Big Hits Etc', Chrysanthemums
'ZZ Top Goes to Egypt', Camper Van Beethoven
'Rockin' Crickets', Hot Toddy's
'I Can't Get Bouncing Babies by the Teardrop Explodes', Freshies
'Tribute to Queen', Frank Sidebottom
'I Lost My Love (To A UK Sub)', Gonads
'Stranglers', Rude Kids

□ Something Stupid

Some weird group names, every one a 100 per cent genuine group.

Grab Grab the Haddock
Impaired Penile Throttle Condition
The New York Pig Funkers
Stitched Back Foot Airman
 (Freur)
Die Electric Eels
Fra Lippo Lippi
Nurse with Wound
Sigue Sigue Sputnik

I Spit on Your Gravy
Splodgenessabounds

Some groups like to keep a freshness about them by changing their name regularly. Jim Thirlwell has been the leader of Foetus Under Glass, You've Got Foetus On Your Breath, Philip and his Foetus Vibrations, Foetus Über Frisco and Scraping Foetus Off The Wheel, among others. Spizz 77 became Spizz Oil, Spizz Energi, Athletico Spizz '80, Spizzles, Spizzenergi 2, Spizzorwell, Spizz and the Astronauts, Spizz's Big Business and Spizzsexual.

☐ Hard to Say I'm Sorry

Some difficult to pronounce rock 'n' roll related names

1. Bill Szymczyk – producer
2. Mark Brezezicki – Big Country
3. Reebop Kwakubaak – Traffic
4. Wolfgang Dziony – Scorpions
5. Andrew Czezowski – owner of various rock clubs
6. Larry Steinbechak – Bronski Beat
7. Alex Dmochkowski – Bluesbreakers and Animals
8. Benjamin Drzechowski – Ben Orr of the Cars
9. Norman Kuhlke – Swinging Blue Jeans
10. Patricia Andrezejewski – Pat Benatar's real name

☐ Who Are We?

One of the commonest rock 'n' roll names would appear to be Mike Smith. Here are seven of him.

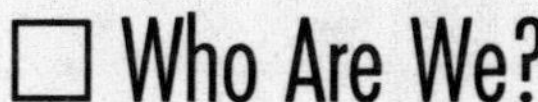

1. The former Radio One jock
2. The Dave Clark 5 vocalist and organist
3. The Amen Corner saxophonist
4. Paul Revere and the Raiders' drummer
5. The CBS producer
6. The Decca A & R man who auditioned the Beatles
7. A Duran Duran merchandising agent

☐ What's Your Name

A selection of artists' real names and stage names. Some names have changed simply through marriage and not for effect. Generally the real name listed is that given at birth.

Real name	Stage name
Marvin Lee Aday	Meatloaf
Leonard Ainsworth	Dobie Gray
Gary Anderson	Gary 'US' Bonds
Roberta Joan Anderson	Joni Mitchell
William Ashton	Billy J. Kramer
Myant Myant Aye Dunn-Lwin	Annabelle Lwin
Billy Baldwin	Bruce Johnson
John Baldwin	John Paul Jones
Susan Ballion	Siouxsie Sioux
Michael Barrett	Shakin' Stevens
Roger Barrett	Syd Barrett
David Batt	David Sylvian
Mark Bell	Marky Ramone
Robert Bell	Kool (and the Gang)
John Beverly	Sid Vicious aka John Ritchie
Salvatore Bono	Sonny (and Cher)
Elaine Bookbinder	Elkie Brooks
Eric Boucher	Jello Biafro
William Broad	Billy Idol

Thomas August Darnell Browder	Kid Creole
Rosemary Brown	Dana
Fanny Mae Bullock	Tina Turner
Frederick Bulsara	Freddie Mercury
Ray Burns	Captain Sensible
Buster Campbell	Prince Buster
Harry Casey	KC (and the Sunshine Band)
Walton Robert Cassotto	Bobby Darin
Francis Casteluccio	Frankie Valli
James Chambers	Jimmy Cliff
Madonna Ciccone	Madonna
Eric Patrick Clapp	Eric Clapton
Douglas Colvin	Dee Dee Ramone
Cecil Connor	Gram Parsons
David Cook	David Essex
Eugene Vincent Craddock	Gene Vincent
John Cummings	Johnny Ramone
Desmond Dacres	Desmond Dekker
John Henry Deighton	Chris Farlowe
Antoine Domino	Fats Domino
Jerry Dorsey	Englebert Humperdinck
Daryl Dragon	Captain (and Tennille)
Reg Dwight	Elton John
Robert Ellidge	Robert Wyatt
Glynn Ellis	Wayne Fontana
Scott Engel	Scott Walker
Tom Erdelyi	Tommy Ramone
Dave Evans	The Edge
Ernest Evans	Chubby Checker
Mark Feld	Marc Bolan
Janis Eddy Fink	Janis Ian
Louis Firbank	Lou Reed
Concetta Franconero	Connie Francis
Vince Furnier	Alice Cooper
Paul Gadd	Gary Glitter (a.k.a. Paul Raven)
Donna Gaines	Donna Summer
Steven Georgiou	Cat Stevens
Stuart Goddard	Adam Ant
Sandra Goodrich	Sandie Shaw
Barry Green	Barry Blue

Dave Harman	Dave Dee
Steve Harrington	Steve Strange
Charles Hatcher	Edwin Starr
Bobby Hatfield	Righteous Brother
Frederick Heath	Johnny Kidd
Paul Hewson	Bono
Brian Hines	Denny Laine
Charles Hardin Holley	Buddy Holly
Patricia Holt	Patti Labelle
Alex Hughes	Judge Dread
Harold Jenkins	Conway Twitty
Bernard Jewry	Alvin Stardust (a.k.a. Shane Fenton)
David Jones	David Bowie
Steveland Judkins	Stevie Wonder (a.k.a. Steveland Morris)
Herbert Khaury	Tiny Tim
Carole Klein	Carole King
Cherilyn LaPier	Cher
Joan Larkin	Joan Jett
Marie Lawrie	Lulu
Gary Leeds	Gary Walker
Dennis Leigh	John Foxx
Donovan Leitch	Donovan
Manfred Lubowitz	Manfred Mann
John Lydon	Johnny Rotten
Mark Manning	Zodiac Mindwarp
Pauline Matthews	Kiki Dee
John Maus	John Walker
Dan McArthur	Jah Wobble (a.k.a. John Wordle)
Elias McDaniel	Bo Diddley
Declan McManus	Elvis Costello
Bill Medley	Righteous Brother
John Mellencamp	John Cougar
John Mellor	Joe Strummer
Sam Moore	Sam (and Dave)
Steveland Morris	Stevie Wonder (a.k.a. Steveland Judkins)
George Ivon Morrison	Van Morrison
Terry Nelhams	Adam Faith
Prince Rogers Nelson	Prince
Mary O'Brien	Dusty Springfield

George O'Dowd	Boy George
James Jewel Osterburg	Iggy Pop
Raymond O'Sullivan	Gilbert O'Sullivan
Christophen Päffgen	Nico
Yorgos Kyriakou Panayioutu	George Michael
Vangelis Papathanassiou	Vangelis
Ian Patterson	Ian Hunter
Richard Penniman	Little Richard
William Perks	Bill Wyman
Paul Pond	Paul Jones
Clive Powell	Georgie Fame
Dave Prater	(Sam and) Dave
J. P. Richardson	The Big Bopper
Thomas Robertson	Thomas Dolby
Ray Charles Robinson	Ray Charles
Melanie Safka	Melanie
Clive Sarstedt	Robin Sarstedt
Rick Sarstedt	Eden Kane
Martha Sharpe	Sandy Posey
James Marcus Smith	P. J. Proby
James Todd Smith	L. L. Cool J.
Kim Smith	Kim Wilde
Reg Smith	Marty Wilde
Benjamin Earl Solomon	Ben E. King
Richard Starkey	Ringo Starr
Yvette Stevens	Chaka Khan
Sylvester Stewart	Sly Stone
Gordon Sumner	Sting
Brenda Mae Tarpley	Brenda Lee
Peter Thorkelson	Peter Tork
Don Vliet	Captain Beefheart
Gary Webb	Gary Numan
Harry Webb	Cliff Richard
Charles Westover	Del Shannon
Priscilla White	Cilla Black
Grace Wing	Grace Slick
Ulysses Adrian Wood	Roy Wood
Thomas Woodward	Tom Jones
Ronald Wycherly	Billy Fury
Robert Zimmerman	Bob Dylan

Two artists have gone for straight colour changes when picking their stage names: Cavern hat-check girl Priscilla White became Brian Epstein's star Cilla Black, while Barry Blue ('Dancing On A Saturday Night', etc.) was christened a more pastoral Barry Green.

Ernest Evans decided to pay tribute to his idol Fats Domino when selecting his new name, and so, taking Chubby instead of Fat, and Checkers instead of Dominos, he became Chubby Checker! Johnny Paycheck selected his stage name in a similar homage to Johnny Cash.

Contrary to popular opinion, Robert Zimmerman adopted his new surname after a family name of Dillon and not after the Welsh poet Dylan Thomas, though this may have been why he chose the spelling (source: *Bob Dylan in His Own Words*).

Some stars have adopted religious names during the course of their career, including Cat Stevens (Yusef Islam), Joe Tex (Yusef Hazziez), John McLaughlin (Mahavishnu) and Carlos Santana (Devadip).

■ THE SONG OF MY LIFE

A look at the staple product of the music business – the songs – and at the people who write them.

□ I Write the Songs

○ The songs of Paul McCartney and John Lennon

A selection of songs credited to the song-writing partnership of John Lennon and Paul McCartney (although it is well documented that many of the songs were written almost solely by one or other of the pair), plus a small selection of the myriad of cover versions of these songs. All these songs were originally recorded by the Beatles.

'A Day in the Life': Brian Auger, Eric Burdon and War, Fall, Barry Gibb and the Bee Gees, Ken Thorne, Frankie Valli

'Can't Buy Me Love': Chet Atkins, Terry Baxter, George Brooks, Chipmunks, Dave 'Baby' Cortez, Eliminators, Brenda Lee, Johnny Rivers, Santo and Johnny, Keely Smith, the Supremes

'Come Together': Aerosmith, George Benson, Booker T and the MGs, Chairman of the Board, Ben E. King, Gladys Knight and the Pips, La De Da Band, Diana Ross, Ike and Tina Turner, Tina Turner

'Daytripper': Cheap Trick, Electric Light Orchestra, José Feliciano, Steve Gibbons Band, Jimi Hendrix, Ramsey Lewis, Lulu, McCoys, Sandy Nelson, Billy Preston, Otis Redding, Vanilla Fudge, Geno Washington, the Yellow Magic Orchestra

'Eleanor Rigby': Paul Anka, P. P. Arnold, Booker T and the MGs, John Denver, Aretha Franklin, Bobbie Gentry, Ides of March, Bernie Lyon, Rare Earth, Standells, Temptations, Kim Weston

'Got to Get You into My Life': Bagatelle, Cliff Bennett, Blood Sweat and Tears, Dino Desi and Billy, Earth Wind and Fire, John Fred and his Playboy Band, Thelma Houston, Carmen McRae, Sonny and Cher, the Surprise Sisters

'Help': Count Basie, Damned, Deep Purple, John Farnham, Henry Gross, Newbeats, Dolly Parton, Peter Sellers, Ray Stevens, Tina Turner, Mary Wells

'Here There and Everywhere': Count Basie, Episode Six, Fourmost, Bobbie Gentry, Astrud Gilberto, Jay and the Americans, Lettermen, Rod McKuen, Carmen McRae, the Mustang, Doc Severinson, Three Good Reasons

'Hey Jude': Area Code 615, Mike Bloomfield and Al Kooper, Brothers Johnson, Wayne Cochran and the C. C. Riders, Everly Brothers, Jimmy Helms, Gerry Lockran, Wilson Pickett, Elvis Presley, Smokey Robinson and the Miracles, Diana Ross and the Supremes, Sonny and Cher, Tottenham Hotspur Football Club

'Lady Madonna': Area Code 615, Chet Atkins, Booker T and the MGs, José Feliciano, Four Freshmen, Richie Havens, Ramsey Lewis, Junior Parker, Gary Puckett and the Union Gap, Wings

'Let It Be': Joan Baez, Clarence Carter, Ray Charles, Chevy Chase, King Curtis, Chris De Burgh, Ferry Aid, Aretha Franklin, Bobby Hatfield, Bill Medley, Leo Sayer, Earl and Randy Scruggs, Ike and Tina Turner, Bill Withers

'Norwegian Wood': Bachelor Pad, Colosseum, Frugal Sound, Hour Glass, Brian Hyland, Jan and Dean, Frank Marino and Mahogany Rush, Hugh Masekela, Buddy Rich

'Ob La Di Ob La Da': Bedrocks, Joyce Bond, Arthur Conley, Floyd Cramer, Four Freshmen, Marmalade, Bobby Vinton, Jack Wild

'Penny Lane': Baskerville Hounds, 18th Century Concepts, Good Vibrations, Anita Harris, David McCallum, the Sinners

'She's Leaving Home': Bee Gees, Billy Bragg with Cara Tivey, David and Johnathon, David Essex, Bryan Ferry, Richie Havens, Al Jarreau, Esther and Abi Ofarim, Big Jim Sullivan, Syreeta, Mel Tormé

'Strawberry Fields Forever': Peter Gabriel, Noel Harrison, Richie Havens, David McCallum, Todd Rundgren, Tomorrow, the Ventures

'Ticket to Ride': Glen Campbell, Carpenters, Hüsker Dü, The In Sect, New Seekers, Sly and Robbie, Vanilla Fudge, Mary Wells, White Sister

'We Can Work It Out': Maxine Brown, George Burns, Petula Clark, Deep Purple, Four Seasons, Humble Pie, Kasenetz Katz Super Cirkus, Melanie, Naked Truth, Johnny Nash, Stevie Wonder

'With A Little Help from My Friends': Bee Gees, Joe Brown, Joe Cocker, Mickie Finn Group, Peter Frampton, Jaggers, Jeff Lynne, Ike and Tina Turner, Wet Wet Wet, the Young Idea

'Yesterday': P. P. Arnold, Beau Brummels, Cilla Black, Blues Magoos, James Brown, Ray Charles, Dillards, Dr John, David Essex, Marianne Faithfull, Bill Medley, Matt Monro, the Ventures

Of the 1000-plus covers of 'Yesterday', 446 were recorded by February 1967.

Elvis Costello's dad, Ross McManus, recorded a cover of 'The Long and Winding Road' under the pseudonym Day Costello.

Del Shannon was the first person to enter the US charts with a Lennon/McCartney song, beating even the Beatles themselves. He heard 'From Me to You' while on a UK tour in 1963 and recorded a version of his own.

○ The songs of Mick Jagger and Keith Richards

A selection of songs written by Mick Jagger and Keith Richards, with some covers. All these songs were originally recorded by the Rolling Stones.

'Backstreet Girl': Nicky Scott, the Frugal Sound

'Blue Turns to Grey': Flamin' Groovies, Mighty Avengers, Cliff Richard

'(I Can't Get No) Satisfaction': Bubblerock, Devo, Chris Farlowe, Aretha Franklin, Herbie Goins, R. Stevie Moore, Otis Redding, the Residents

'Jumpin' Jack Flash': Aretha Franklin, Wynder K. Frog, Thelma Houston

'The Last Time': Electric Chairs, Clive Langer and the Boxes, Arlon Roth, the Who

'19th Nervous Breakdown': Brent Ford and the Nylons, Jason and the Scorchers, Nash the Slash, the Standells

'Paint it Black': Anvil, Echo and the Bunnymen, Modettes, Smack, Standells, Yew

'So Much in Love': Charles Dickens, the Herd, the Mighty Avengers

'Under My Thumb': Chubby Checker, Wayne Gibson, Del Shannon, the Who

Blood Sweat and Tears recorded a version of 'Sympathy for the Devil' that utilized the Stones' original words set to a different tune.

Nanker and Phelge was a pseudonym for band compositions, not just an alias for Jagger and Richards, as has been stated (source: Bill Wyman on a 1986 BBC documentary). The name Phelge was borrowed from a flatmate of Mick, Keith and Brian.

Gene Pitney was the first person to make the US charts with a Jagger/Richards song. He charted with his version of 'That Girl Belongs to Yesterday'.

○ The songs of Bob Dylan

A selection of songs written by Bob Dylan, with a few of the many cover versions made of them. All these songs were originally recorded by Bob Dylan.

'All Along the Watchtower': Randy California, Jimi Hendrix, Barbara Keshta, Nashville Teens, Spirit, XTC

'Blowin' in the Wind': Marianne Faithfull, Walter Jackson, Peter Paul and Mary, Stevie Wonder

'Don't Think Twice It's Alright': Joan Baez, Fairies, Ivy League, Wonder Who

'I Shall Be Released': the Band, De Forest, Tom Robinson Band, Tremeloes, Jesse Winchester

'It Ain't Me Babe': Johnny Cash, Cruisers, Bryan Ferry, the Iguana Foundation, Davy Jones, the Turtles

'It's All Over Now Baby Blue': Joan Baez, Cops 'n' Robbers, Falco, Chris Farlowe, Noel Harrison, Manfred Mann's Earth Band, Them, Link Wray

'Like A Rolling Stone': Mouse and the Traps, the Soup Greens (as Like A Dribbling Fram)

'Maggie's Farm': Blues Band, Solomon Burke, the Specials

'Mr Tambourine Man': Barbarians, John D. Bryant, Byrds, Gene Clark, Judy Collins, Joe Gilstrap Band, Stevie Wonder

'This Wheel's on Fire'*: Byrds, Julie Driscoll, Brian Auger and the Trinity, Siouxsie and the Banshees

* co-written by Rick Danko of the Band

○ The songs of Ray Davies

A selection of songs written by Ray Davies, with a few of the cover versions of them. All were originally recorded by the Kinks.

'All Day and All of the Night': Beverly Byrd, Ian and the Zodiacs, Jaybirds, Jolt, Kenny and the Kasuals, Gary Lewis and the Playboys, Los Rockin' Devils, Prayin' Mantis, Speed, the Stranglers, Bernie Torme

'Dandy': Nigel Denver Four, Clinton Ford, David Garrick, Haricot's Rouge, Herman's Hermits, James Last, Johnny Lion, Rockin' Vicars, Michelle Torr

'Dedicated Follower of Fashion': Boris, Petula Clark, David Garrick, the Ravers

'I'm Not Like Everybody Else': Chocolate Watch Band, Droogs, Sacred Mushrooms, Chris Spedding

'I Need You': Count Bishops, Rational Skins, Rezillos, Zakary Thaks

'Lola': CCS, Don Farden, Nina and Michael, Raincoats, Sweet Power, Nicky Thomas

'So Mystifying': Candidates, Hep Stars, Jay Jays, Petrified Forest, Scorpion

'Sunny Afternoon': Dino Desi and Billy, Haricot's Rouge, Vince Hill, Dave Kelly, the Standells

'Till the End of the Day': Afrika Korps, Count Bishops, Hounds, Swamp Rats, Angelic Upstarts

'Tired of Waiting for You': Frank Alama, Cotton Socks, Flock, Larry Page Orchestra, Suzi Quatro

'Waterloo Sunset': Affair of the Heart, Peter Convent, Norman Percival, Soho Gamblers, Catarina Valente

'Where Have All the Good Times Gone': David Bowie, Shapes, Van Halen, Zoo

'Who'll Be Next in Line': Françoise Hardy, Gary Myrick and the Figures, the Sir Douglas Quintet

'You Really Got Me': Boss Guitars, Al Capola, Dalek I, 801, Hammersmith Gorillas, Heavy Cruiser, Hot Squirrels, Johnny and the Hurricanes, Steve Marriot's Moments, Buddy Miles, Mott The Hoople, Robert Palmer, Johnny Smash, Rosetta Stone, 13th Floor Elevators, Van Halen, the Wackers

The first cover of a Ray Davies composition was 'I've Got That Feeling' by the Orchids, a Liverpool school-girl trio.

Davies wrote the theme to the BBC comedy *Till Death Us Do Part*. It was sung by actor Tony Booth. Davies also wrote music for the film *The Virgin Soldiers*.

Jimmy Page rewrote Davies' 'Revenge' as 'She Just Satisfies'.

□ Tainted Love

'Tainted Love', a world-wide hit for Soft Cell in 1981, is an interesting song because of the many different styles in which it has been recorded. It was written by Ed Cobb, former member of the Four Preps and, later, the instrumental combo the Piltdown Men. He also wrote for, and produced two of, America's finest garage bands, the Standells and the Chocolate Watch Band. Other Cobb songs include 'I'll Always Love You' (Michael Cox) and 'Heartbeat' (Gloria Jones, and the Hour Glass).

■ Some covers of 'Tainted Love'

1. Gloria Jones (1965): a northern soul classic; the inspirational version.
2. Jezebelles (1975): see 3.
3. Ruth Swann (1975): two simultaneously released covers fighting for the honours on the mid-Seventies dance floor.

4. Sandy Wynns (1979): no, she loses.
5. Soft Cell (1981): the full electro-disco treatment that gave Soft Cell the hard sell.
6. David Phillips and the Hot Rod Gang (1983): a rockabilly shake-up proves the versatility of the song.
7. P. J. Proby (1985): Paul Newman's former chauffeur went cover-mad in the Eighties, everything from 'Anarchy in the UK' to 'Heroes'. 'Tainted Love' didn't escape a tainting by his tonsils.
8. The Remayns (1986): garage revivalists revive a soul song from the original garage era.
9. Coil (1987): the indies get in on the act.

□ Your Song

Song-writing is as much of a craft as carpentry or bricklaying; words and notes can't just be thrown into a pile or tacked together haphazardly, or they won't become a song. The song-writer shapes the words and the music into a structure so they make sense and, he hopes, appeal to the ear. Some people are natural song-writers, others work hard to achieve the finished product. First we look at ten covers of songs written and originally performed by six of my favourite song-writers and then at ten songs crafted by some of the top song-writing teams of the rock era along with some of their cover versions.

■ Ten covers of David Bowie songs

1. Oscar Beuselinck: 'Over the Garden Wall'
2. Billy Fury: 'Silly Boy Blue'
3. Lulu: 'The Man Who Sold the World'
4. Associates: 'Boys Keep Swinging'
5. Mott the Hoople: 'All the Young Dudes'
6. Simon Turner: 'The Prettiest Star'
7. Bauhaus: 'Ziggy Stardust'
8. Frankie Goes to Hollywood: 'John I'm Only Dancing'
9. Blondie: 'Heroes'
10. Peter Noone: 'Oh You Pretty Things'

Oscar Beuselinck was, in fact, Paul Nicholas, now best known for his acting roles, such as Vince in *Just Good Friends*.

David has never recorded his own studio version of 'All the Young Dudes'. The Scottish punk band the Skids have also covered it.

The first cover of a David Bowie song was Kenny Miller's version of 'Take My Tip' (on which the writing credit was David Jones).

■ Ten covers of Marc Bolan songs

1. Polecats: 'Jeepster'
2. Power Station: 'Get It On'
3. Department S: 'Solid Gold Easy Action'
4. Nikki Sudden: 'Sailors of the Highway'
5. Times: 'The Slider'
6. Siouxsie and the Banshees: '20th Century Boy'
7. Necessitarians: 'The Groover'
8. Protex: 'Jeepster'
9. Frankie Goes to Hollywood: 'Get It On'
10. Girlsschool: '20th Century Boy'

When Marc heard Siouxsie Sioux's version of '20th Century Boy' at a Banshees gig, he was unaware it was one of his songs until a companion told him.

The Barracuda Blue label specializes in releasing covers of Marc Bolan songs by contemporary artists.

■ Ten covers of Elvis Costello songs

1. Dave Edmunds: 'Girls Talk'
2. Guana Batz: 'Radio Sweetheart'
3. Robert Wyatt: 'Shipbuilding'
4. Barry Christian: 'Alison (My Aim Is True)'
5. Nick Lowe: 'Indoor Fireworks'
6. Dusty Springfield: 'Shabby Doll'
7. Linda Ronstadt: 'Party Girl'

8. Paul McCartney: 'Back on My Feet'*
9. Winston Reedy: 'Everyday I Write the Book'
10. Dyan Diamond: 'Mystery Dance'

One of the more obscure Costello covers is the Shakin' Pyramids' 'Just A Memory'.

'Less Than Zero' is about fascist leader Oswald Mosley.

■ Ten covers of Lou Reed songs

1. Joy Division: 'Sister Ray'
2. Japan: 'All Tomorrow's Parties'
3. Paul Quinn and Edwyn Collins: 'Pale Blue Eyes'
4. Paul Gardiner: 'Venus in Furs'
5. Roky Erikson: 'Heroin'
6. Duffo: 'Walk on the Wild Side'
7. David Bowie: 'White Light White Heat'
8. REM: 'Femme Fatale'
9. Real Moral Fibre: 'Venus in Furs'
10. Nick Cave: 'All Tomorrow's Parties'

'Sister Ray' was co-written with the rest of the Velvet Underground.

■ Ten covers of Bruce Springsteen songs

1. Robert Gordon: 'Fire'
2. Big Daddy: 'Dancing in the Dark'
3. Frankie Goes To Hollywood: 'Born To Run'
4. Dave Edmunds: 'From Small Things (Big Things One Day Come)'
5. Natalie Cole: 'Pink Cadillac'
6. Warren Zevon: 'Jeannie Needs A Shooter'
7. Manfred Mann's Earth Band: 'Blinded by the Light'
8. Beat Farmers: 'Reason To Believe'
9. Mojo Dixon and Skid Roper: 'Big Payback'
10. Zeitgeist: 'Atlantic City'

* co-written by McCartney

One of Bruce's first big hits as a song-writer came in 1978 when Patti Smith recorded 'Because the Night'. She earned a co-writing credit on her version of the song.

Springsteen wrote 'Fire' specially for Gordon, but it was the Pointer Sisters who had the big hit with it.

■ Ten covers of Neil Young songs

1. The Mission: 'Like A Hurricane'
2. Prelude: 'After the Goldrush'
3. Beat Farmers: 'Powder Finger'
4. Pete Wylie and the Icicle Works: 'The Needle and the Damage Done'
5. Mint Juleps: 'Only Love Can Break Your Heart'
6. Curtis Mayfield: 'Tonight's the Night'
7. Blacky Ranchette: 'Revolution Blues'
8. Died Pretty: 'When You Dance I Can Really Love'
9. Dave Edmunds: 'Dance Dance Dance'
10. Roxy Music: 'Like A Hurricane'

Both Prelude and the Mint Juleps render a cappella versions of their chosen Neil Young songs.

■ Ten of Burt Bacharach's and Hal David's best songs, with a selection of covers

1. 'Anyone Who Had A Heart': Cilla Black, Mary May, Sandie Shaw, Smith and Mighty, Dusty Springfield, Dionne Warwick
2. 'Do You Know the Way to San José': Frankie Goes to Hollywood, Gilbert O'Sullivan, Dionne Warwick
3. 'I Just Don't Know What to Do with Myself': Brook Benton, Elvis Costello, Joni Lyman, Dusty Springfield, Dionne Warwick
4. 'Make It Easy on Yourself': Long John Baldry, Jerry Butler, Bern Eliot, Walker Brothers, Dionne Warwick
5. 'My Little Red Book': Burt Bacharach Orchestra, Love, Manfred Mann, Rockin' Berries, Rumour, Sounds Incorporated, the Standells

6. 'The Story of My Life': Alma Cogan, Michael Holliday, Dave King, Marty Robbins
7. '(They Long To Be) Close To You': Carpenters, Gwen Guthrie, Dusty Springfield, Dionne Warwick
8. 'This Guy's in Love with You': Herb Alpert, Dionne Warwick (as 'This Girl's in Love with You')
9. 'Trains and Boats and Planes': Burt Bacharach Orchestra, Billy J. Kramer, Dionne Warwick
10. 'Walk On By': Average White Band, Carnival, D-Train, Isaac Hayes, Stranglers, Dionne Warwick

Burt Bacharach wrote the music, Hal David provided the lyrics.

Bacharach wrote 'Baby It's You' with Hal's brother Mack, a song-writer in his own right, and Barney Williams. It's been recorded by Dave Berry, the Beatles, Nick Lowe and Elvis Costello, Smith, and the Shirelles.

Bacharach married song-writer Carole Bayer Sager and they later co-wrote 'That's What Friends Are For' for Dionne Warwick and friends (Stevie Wonder, Elton John and Gladys Knight).

■ Ten of Ellie Greenwich's and Jeff Barry's best songs, with a selection of covers

1. 'Baby I Love You'*: Dave Edmunds, Andy Kim, Ramones, the Ronettes
2. 'Be My Baby'*: Andy Kim, the Ronettes
3. 'Chapel of Love'*: Dixie Cups, Holly and the Italians, Ronettes, Shirley and Johnny
4. 'Da Doo Ron Ron'*: Shaun Cassidy, Crystals, Four Pennies, Billy J. Kramer, Ian Matthews, Andrew Loog Oldham Orchestra (Mick Jagger on lead vocals), Raindrops, Searchers, Spitting Image (with altered lyrics)
5. 'Doo Wah Diddy Diddy': Beau Jangle, Exciters, Manfred Mann
6. 'Hanky Panky': Tommy James and the Shondells, the Raindrops
7. 'Leader of the Pack'†: Detergents (as 'Leader of the Laundromat'), Downliner's Sect (as 'Leader of the Sect'), Bette

* with Phil Spector † with George Goldner

Midler, Roadies (as 'Packer of the Leads'), Shangri Las, Twisted Sister

8. 'River Deep Mountain High'*: Eric Burdon and the Animals, Jennie Darren and the Second City Sound, Easy Beats, Saints, Supremes and the Four Tops, Ike and Tina Turner
9. 'Tell Laura I Love Her': Ray Peterson, Ricky Valence
10. 'Then He Kissed Me'*: Beach Boys (as 'Then I Kissed Her'), Crystals, Hard Ons, Hollywood Brats, the Lurkers (as 'Then I Kicked Her')

Greenwich and Barry married in October 1962 and were later divorced.

The Raindrops ('Hanky Panky', 'Da Doo Ron Ron') were Greenwich and Barry. To make them look more like a group Ellie's younger sister was pictured on the LP cover and publicity shots.

In January 1984 a show called *Leader of the Pack* opened at the Bottom Line in Greenwich Village. The show, which later made Broadway, was written around several Greenwich/Barry songs. It starred Patrick Cassidy, younger brother of Shaun, who had a US Number One with 'Da Doo Ron Ron'.

■ Ten of Barry Mann's and Cynthia Weill's best songs, with a selection of covers

1. 'Bless You': Bonnie and Rita, Demons, Gary Mills, Tony Orlando
2. 'Home of the Brave': Bonnie and the Treasures, Jody Miller, Peanut
3. 'Kicks': Paul Revere and the Raiders
4. 'On Broadway'*: George Benson, Eric Carmen, Crystals, Drifters, Mike Melvoin, the Purple Underground.
5. 'Saturday Night at the Movies': Drifters
6. 'Walking in the Rain': Ronettes
7. 'Uptown': Crystals, Little Eva, the Marvellettes
8. 'We've Gotta Get Out of this Place': Angelic Upstarts, Animals, Blue Öyster Cult, Gilla, Kit Kats, Partridge Family, Leslie West

* with Phil Spector

9. '(You're My) Soul and Inspiration': Blossoms, Chad Everitt, Donny and Marie Osmond, Righteous Brothers, Steve and Edyie
10. 'You've Lost That Lovin' Feeling'*: Barbara Ann, Long John Baldry, Berlin, Cilla Black, Blossoms, Hall and Oates, Heptones, Human League, Su Pollard, Righteous Brothers, Telly Savalas, Spring Fever, Unit 4 + 2, Dionne Warwick.

Mann and Weill married in 1961. Mann had previously written several hits with other writers, and he had his own hit with the novelty rocker 'Who Put the Bomp'.

When Barry Mann first heard the completed Righteous Brothers' original of 'You've Lost That Lovin' Feeling', he was convinced it was playing too slow, so deep was Bill Medley's baritone.

■ Ten of Gerry Goffin's and Carole King's best songs, with a selection of covers

1. 'Chains': Beatles, Cookies, Late Show, Little Esther
2. 'Go Away Little Girl': Ray Bennett, Happenings, Steve Lawrence, Osmonds, Mark Wynter
3. 'Goin' Back': Byrds, Dusty Springfield
4. 'Halfway to Paradise': Billy Fury, Nick Lowe, Tony Orlando, Bobby Vinton
5. 'The Locomotion': Grand Funk, Little Eva, Kylie Minogue, Brian Poole and the Tremeloes, Dave Stewart and Barbara Gaskin, the Vernon Girls
6. 'Remember (Walkin' in the Sand)': Louise Goffin, the Shangri Las
7. 'Take Good Care of My Baby': Dion, Smokie, Bobby Vee, Bobby Vinton
8. 'Up on the Roof': Drifters, Julie Grant, Little Eva, Kenny Lynch, James Taylor
9. 'When My Little Girl Is Smiling': Craig Douglas, Drifters, Paul Jones, Jimmy Justice

* with Phil Spector

10. 'Will You Love Me Tomorrow': Pat Boone, Laura Branigan, Chiffons, Jackie De Shannon, Barbara Dickson, Four Seasons, King Everall, Ben E. King, Carole King, Little Eva, Dave Mason, Melanie, Tony Orlando, Helen Shapiro, Shirelles, Bobby Vee, Dionne Warwick

Normally Carole writes the music, Gerry writes the lyrics.

Goffin and King were formerly married. Louise Goffin ('Remember (Walkin' in the Sand)') is their daughter; the same daughter who had Little Eva ('The Locomotion') as a babysitter.

Carole used to record demos with Paul Simon.

As seen above, Dusty Springfield recorded Goffin and King's 'Goin' Back'. In return Carole recorded Dusty's 'Some of Your Lovin''.

'Go Away Little Girl' was the first song of the rock era to be taken to the top of the US charts by two different acts (Lawrence 1963, Osmonds 1971). The second record to achieve this was 'The Locomotion' (Little Eva 1962, Grand Funk 1974).

The Cookies ('Chains') were Little Eva's backing group.

■ Ten of Jerry Leiber's and Mike Stoller's best songs, with a selection of covers

1. 'Hound Dog': Freddie Bell and the Bellboys, Pat Boone, Duffy's Nucleus, Easybeats, Chris Farlowe, Elvis Presley, Big Mama Thornton
2. 'Kansas City': Herb Alpert, Applejacks, Hank Ballard and the Midnighters, Beatles, James Brown, Dave 'Baby' Cortez, Champion Jack Dupree, Everly Brothers, Freddie and the Dreamers, Wilbert Harrison, Peter Jay and the Jaywalkers, Spike Jones, Little Richard, Little Willy Littlefield (under its original title 'K.C. Lovin''), Trini Lopez, Graham Parker, Ten Years After
3. 'I (Who Have Nothing)'*: Shirley Bassey, Tom Jones, Ben E. King, Manfred Mann's Earth Band, Sylvester

* with Donida and Mogul

4. 'Love Potion No. 9': Clovers, Coasters, Mike Cotton Sound, Tony Jackson, Searchers, the Tygers of Pan Tang
5. 'Poison Ivy': Coasters, Lambrettas, Paramounts, the Rolling Stones
6. 'Riot in Cell Block No. 9': Beach Boys (as 'Student Demonstration Time'), Robins, Shakin' Stevens, Johnny Winter
7. 'Ruby Baby': Billy 'Crash' Craddock, Dion, the Drifters
8. 'Stand by me'*: Cassius Clay, Mickey Gilley, Ben E. King, John Lennon, Little Eva, Kenny Lynch, Spyder Turner
9. 'Young Blood'†: Bad Company, Coasters, Bunk Dogger, Ricky Lee Jones
10. '(You're So Square) Baby I Don't Care': Kiki Dee, Bryan Ferry, Buddy Holly, Joni Mitchell, Elvis Presley, Cliff Richard

Elvis recorded 'Hound Dog' after hearing Freddie and the Bellboys' (somewhat humorous) version of the song.

On 25 July 1956 the Italian liner *Andre Doria* was steaming back to America from Europe when it was rammed by the liner *Stockholm*. Mike Stoller was on board and thankful not to be among the fifty-two killed. However, when he arrived safely in the States all his partner Jerry Leiber could say was 'Elvis Presley has recorded "Hound Dog".'

The Beatles' version of 'Kansas City' was actually a medley with Little Richard's 'Hey Hey Hey', a fact overlooked for several years, which caused the rocker to receive a belated $30,000 (£16,500) royalty cheque.

■ Ten of the best songs by Eddie Holland, Lamont Dozier and Brian Holland, with covers

1. 'Baby Love': Honey Bane, the Supremes
2. 'Come See About Me': Nella Dodds, Shakin' Stevens, Supremes, Junior Walker and the All Stars
3. 'Heatwave': Jam, Martha Reeves and the Vandellas, Linda Ronstadt
4. 'I Can't Help Myself (Sugar Pie Honey Bunch)': Donnie Elbert, Four Tops, Bonnie Pointer, the Real Thing

* with Ben E. King
† with Doc Pomus

5. 'Stop! in the Name of Love': Roni Hill, Hollies, Margie Johnson, the Supremes
6. 'There's A Ghost in My House': Fall, Paul Jones, R. Dean Taylor, the Yachts
7. 'Reach Out (I'll Be There)': Chris Farlowe, the Four Tops
8. 'You Can't Hurry Love': Phil Collins, the Supremes
9. 'You Keep Me Hanging On': Ken Booth, Jackie De Shannon, Roni Hill, Tom Jones, Wilson Pickett, the Supremes, Vanilla Fudge, Kim Wilde
10. 'Where Did Our Love Go': Jackie De Shannon, Donnie Elbert, J. Geils Band, Manhattan Transfer, Soft Cell, the Supremes

When H/D/H left Motown in 1968 they formed their own Invictus/ Hot Wax label.

☐ Do It Do It Again

There are a number of songs that, during the past three decades, have worked their way into the repertoire of countless pub combos, bar bands and club groups in their formative years, sometimes remaining in the band's live set or even being committed to vinyl after the lucky ones have found fame. Below are ten such rock 'n' roll standards, along with their writers, followed by the original recording artists, the year of release and some of the many acts who have since recorded them.

1. 'Louie Louie', Richard Berry, Richard Berry and the Pharoes, 1958

Blondie, Bryan and the Brunelles, Black Flag, Cramps, George Duke, Flamin' Groovies, Charlie Harper, John the Postman, Kingsmen, Kinks, Julie London, David McCallum, Motorhead, Iggy Pop and the Stooges, Pretenders, Paul Revere and the Raiders, Otis Redding, Rhythm and Blues Inc., Sandpipers, Time Code, Toots and the Maytals, Troggs, Turtles, Barry White, the Wailers

2. 'Hey Joe', William Roberts a.k.a. Chester Powers,* The Leaves,† 1965

Roy Buchanan, Byrds, Nick Cave, Cher, King Curtis, Deep Purple, Jimi Hendrix, Love, Music Machine, Wilson Pickett, Tim Rose, Saker, Shadows of Knight, Patti Smith, Soft Cell, Soul Benders, Spirit, the Standells

3. 'St James Infirmary', Irving Mills under pseudonym Joe Primrose

Animals, Dave Berry and the Cruisers, Bobby Bland, Graham Bond Organization, Bobby Dean, Standells, the Triffids

4. 'Twist and Shout', Bert Russel and Phil Medley, Topnotes, 1960

Beatles, Blockheads, Curiosities, Isley Brothers, Mamas and Papas, Brian Poole and the Tremeloes, Rezillos, Searchers, Shangri Las, the Who

5. 'I Put A Spell On You', Jay Hawkins, Screaming Jay Hawkins, 1959

Animals, Alice Cooper, Crazy World of Arthur Brown, Creedence Clearwater Revival, the Five Americans, Alan Price, Nina Simone, Them, the Trekkas

6. 'Summertime', George and Ira Gershwin (from the musical *Porgy and Bess*)

Barons, Buckinghams, Sam Cooke, Chris Farlowe, Fun Boy Three, Marcels, Al Martino, Rick Nelson, Janis Joplin, Kingsmen, Billy Stewart, Tommy Vance, Gene Vincent, Walker Brothers, the Zombies

7. 'Money', Berry Gordy and Janie Bradford, Barrett Strong, 1959

Beatles, Buddy Britten and the Regents, Bern Elliot and the Fenmen,

* Both of these are pseudonyms for Dino Valenti, a writer, singer and guitarist from New York City. He was to have been one of the founding members of the group Quicksilver Messenger Service, but he was gaoled on a drugs rap before the group could be launched. They went ahead without him and he joined them on his eventual release.

† It is unclear just who recorded the song first, but the Leaves had an early US hit with it and this inspired many of the other bands to put it in their repertoire.

Flamin' Groovies, Freddie and the Dreamers, Flying Lizards, Kingsmen, Renee Geyer, Rolling Stones, Searchers, Shakers, the Undertakers

8. 'I Heard It through the Grapevine', Norman Whitfield and Barrett Strong, Smokey Robinson and the Miracles,* 1967

Albino Gorillas, Brian Bennett, Joe Cocker, Creedence Clearwater Revival, King Curtis, Marvin Gaye, Elton John, Gladys Knight and the Pips, Paul Mauriat, Ike and Tina Turner

9. 'Gloria', Van Morrison, Them, 1965

Blue Magoos, Doors, Jimi Hendrix, Shadows of Knight, Patti Smith

10. 'Shake', Sam Cooke, Sam Cooke, 1963

Eddie and the Hot Rods, Kasenetz Katz Super Cirkus, Otis Redding, Small Faces, Rod Stewart, Roulettes, Shadows of Knight

Other songs that might have made the list include: 'A Shot of Rhythm and Blues', 'Route 66', 'Kansas City', 'Suzy Q', 'Slow Down', 'Wild Thing', 'My Little Red Book', '99½ Just Won't Do', 'Woolly Bully' and 'Summertime Blues'.

□ De Do Do Do De Da Da Da

Now we take a look at some very silly and some very long song titles First some very serious and meaningful titles.

1. 'Don't Worry Kyoko, Mummy's Only Looking for Her Hand in the Snow', Yoko Ono and John Lennon
2. 'My Head Is My Only House Unless It Rains', Captain Beefheart
3. 'Love Goes to a Building on Fire', Talking Heads
4. 'Liquid Acrobat as Regards the Air', Incredible String Band

* Gladys Knight's version was *recorded* after Smokey's version, though it was *released* first.

5. 'Earache My Eye Featuring Alice Bowie', Cheech and Chong
6. 'May the Bird of Paradise Fly up Your Nose', Little Jimmy Dickens
7. 'Earschplittenloudeboomen', Steppenwolf
8. 'Take Up Thy Stethoscope and Walk', Pink Floyd
9. 'A Plague of Lighthouse Keepers', Van Der Graaf Generator
10. 'I Was the Stable Boy Who Grew Up To Be a Most Unstable Man', St Vitus Dance

Not to mention country and western classics like 'Dropkick Me Jesus through the Goalposts of Life' and 'We're Gonna Hire a Wino to Decorate Our Home'.

Now some very long song titles.

1. 'The Strange Circumstances Which Led to Vladimar and Olga requesting Rehabilitation in a Siberian Health Resort as a Result of Stress in Furthering the People's Policies', The Stranglers
2. 'Sir B. McKenzie's Daughter's Lament for the 77th Mounted Lancers Retreat from the Straits of Loch Knombe in the Year of Our Lord 1727 on the Occasion of Her Marriage to the Lord of Kinleakie', Fairport Convention
3. 'The Young Electric Psychedelic Hippy Flippy Folk and Funky Philosophic Turned On Groovy Twelve String Band', Barry Mann
4. 'When the Apple Blossoms Bloom in the Windmills of Your Mind I'll Be Your Valentine', Emerson Lake and Palmer
5. 'You Can Make Me Dance Sing or Anything (Even Take the Dog for a Walk, Mend a Fuse, Fold Away the Ironing Board, or Any Other Domestic Short Comings)', Faces
6. 'The Men from Banana Island Whose Stupid Ideas Never Caught On in the Western World As We Know It'*, Freshies
7. 'I'm Looking for A Saxophonist Doubling French Horn Wearing Size 37 Boots', Artwoods
8. 'Chance Meeting on a Dissecting Table of a Sewing Machine and an Umbrella', Nurse With Wound

* Actually the title of an EP that didn't contain a track of that name at all.

9. 'This Is Where the Hurdie Gurdie Heebie Geebie Greenie Meenie Man Came In', Bubbles
10. 'The Man Who Took the Valise off the Floor of Grand Central Station at Noon,' Siw Malmkuist

☐ Answer Me

In the sixties it was quite common for a group or artist to record a reply to a recent hit record. Below are some 'answer' records followed by the record to which they were replying.

☐ Answer	☐ To
'Hey Neil', Carole King	'Hey Carol', Neil Sedaka
'Got a Job', Miracles	'Get a Job', Silhouettes
'We Put the Bomp', Bob and Jerry	'Who Put the Bomp', Barry Mann
'Tell Tommy I Miss Him', Laura Lee	'Tell Laura I Love Her', Ray Peterson
'Dawn of Correction', Spokesmen	'Eve of Destruction', Barry McGuire
'When a Woman Loves a Man', Esther Phillips	'When a Man Loves a Woman', Percy Sledge
'Poor Begonia', Jerri Lynn Fraser	'Itsy Bitsy Teensy Weeny Yellow Polka Dot Bikini', Brian Hyland
'I'll Save the Last Dance for You', Damita Jo	'Save the Last Dance for Me', Drifters
'You're Having the Last Dance with Me', Billy Fury	
'Not Just Tomorrow But Always', Bertelle Danere	'Will You Love Me Tomorrow', Shirelles
'Come Back Little Girl', Ronnie Rice	'Go Away Little Girl', Steve Lawrence
'Superstar', Lydia Murdock	'Billie Jean', Michael Jackson
'Devils and Angels', The Passage	'Heart and Soul', Joy Division
'Papa Only Wants the Best', Daniel Aiello	'Papa Don't Preach', Madonna

'I wish I Had a Job to Shove', Rodney Lay	'Take This Job and Shove It', Johnny Paycheck
'My Pussycat', Miss Chuckleberry	'My Ding A Ling', Chuck Berry
'Billy I've Got to Go to Town', Geraldine Stevens	'Ruby Don't Take Your Love to Town', Kenny Rogers
'Bear Cat', Rufus Thomas	'Hound Dog', Big Mama Thornton
'Ringo's Revenge', Robin Garrett	'Ringo', Lorne Greene
'Daddy's Home', Shep and the Limeliters	'A 1,000 Miles Away', Heartbeats

As well as answer records there have been records that continue the saga of a hero or character in a previous song. These follow-ups are often recorded by the same artist who recorded the original.

Judy Gore followed her 'It's My Party' with 'Judy's Turn to Cry', which continued the story.

Ernie K. Doe returned to the theme of his big hit 'Mother in Law' with 'My Mother in Law (Is in My Hair Again)'.

The Delicatessens gave us the 'Red Baron's Revenge' as a sequel to the Royal Guardsmen's 'Snoopy versus the Red Baron'.

Bob Geldof's 'Love Like a Rocket' takes Terry and Julie from Ray Davies' song 'Waterloo Sunset' into the space age.

Both 'Ashes to Ashes' (David Bowie) and 'Major Tom (Coming Home)' (Peter Shilling) shed further light on the central character to Bowie's 1969 hit 'Space Oddity'.

■ Other chain records

'Johnny B. Goode' (Chuck Berry), 'Bye Bye Johnny' (Berry), 'The Last Gig of Johnny B. Goode' (Leo Sayer)
'Peggy Sue' (Buddy Holly), 'Peggy Sue Got Married' (Holly)
'Vladimar and Olga' (Stranglers), 'Vladimar and Sergei' (Dave Greenfield and J. J. Burnel), 'Vladimar and the Beast Part III' (Stranglers), 'The Strange Circumstances . . . '* (Stranglers), 'Viva Vlad!' (Stranglers)

* See long titles, page 216, for full title.

☐ Laugh at Me

One form of cover version with a distinctly tongue-in-cheek attitude is the parody or spoof record in which an artist changes the lyrics of a song to make it humorous or writes a new song mocking the lyrics or style of a previous song. Below are some such spoofs followed by the record they are parodying.

☐ Spoof	☐ Of
'Leader of the Laundromat', Detergents	'Leader of the Pack', Shangri Las
'Eat It', Weird Al Yankovic	'Beat It', Michael Jackson
'Like a Dribbling Fram', Race Marble	'Like a Rolling Stone', Bob Dylan
'N-n-nineteen Not Out', Commentators	'19', Paul Hardcastle
'Boozy Nights', Barron Knights	'Boogie Nights', Heatwave
'Purple Aeroplane', Spike Milligan	'Yellow Submarine', Beatles
'A13, Trunk Road to the Sea' Billy Bragg	'Route 66', various
'Another One Rides the Bus', Weird Al Yankovic	'Another One Bites the Dust', Queen
'Packer of the Leads', Roadies	'Leader of the Pack', Shangri Las
'In the Brownies', Billy Connolly	'In the Navy', Village People
'Letter B', Sesame Street Gang	'Let It Be', Beatles
'Marty Feldman's Eyes', Weird Al Yankovic	'Bette Davis Eyes', Kim Carnes
'Start Wreckin'', B-Boys	'Star Trekkin'', Firm
'All Stuck Up', Hoorah and the Henrys	'All Shook Up', Elvis Presley
'The Devil Went Down to Brixton', Jim Davidson	'The Devil Went Down to Georgia', Charlie Daniels Band

☐ Titles

Some songs never appear on vinyl with the same title that they started out with.

When Paul McCartney was writing 'Yesterday' he used the dummy lyrics and title 'Scrambled Eggs'.

Micky Dolenz wrote the song 'Randy Scouse Git' because he heard the phrase (on *Till Death Us Do Part*) and loved it. When someone (presumably Davy Jones) told him how rude it was (for the times) he changed the title to . . . 'Alternate Title'.

Mr Acker Bilk's big hit 'Stranger on the Shore' was originally called 'Jenny' while Herb Alpert's 'The Lonely Bull' started out as 'Twinkle Star'.

Dr Hook's 'The Cover of the *Rolling Stone*' became 'The Cover of the *Radio Times*' in the UK.

The Smiths' 'Money Changes Everything' metamorphosed into Bryan Ferry's 'The Right Stuff'.

'Ashes to Ashes' by David Bowie was originally titled 'People Are Turning to Gold'.

In 1976 the music press announced that David Bowie's new LP was to be called *New Music: Night and Day*. Eventually it came out as *Low*. Incidentally, Nick Lowe was so chuffed about Bowie calling his LP *Low* that he put out an EP called *Bowi*. The Rumour followed suit by releasing an LP called *Max* in return for Fleetwood Mac issuing *Rumours*.

The Black Sabbath LP *Paranoid* was to have been called *War Pigs* until the success of the single 'Paranoid'.

The Stranglers' début LP *Rattus Norvegicus* was scheduled to be called *Dead on Arrival*.

'Street Fighting Man' by the Rolling Stones was originally called 'Everybody Pays Their Dues'.

Ray Davies originally intended to call 'Waterloo Sunset', 'Liverpool Sunset', but as the Beatles were singing about 'Penny Lane' and 'Strawberry Fields' at the time he decided to come south.

Mott the Hoople's eponymous début LP was to have been called *Talking Bear Mountain Picnic Massacre Disaster Dylan Blues*.

Billy Ocean released three different versions of one of his songs: for the American market it was 'Caribbean Queen'; for Europe, 'European Queen', and for Africa, 'African Queen'. The record flopped in the UK at first but when the 'Caribbean Queen' version was released it became a big hit.

'Wipeout' (Surfaris) was originally called 'Stiletto'.

Chuck Berry originally recorded 'My Ding A Ling' in 1958 as 'My Tambourine'.

When Pink Floyd first performed 'See Emily Play' at a concert at the Queen Elizabeth Hall in London, it was called 'Games for May'.

When Crazyhead covered Ruts DC's 'West One (Shine On Me)' they retitled it 'Shine On You'.

When the Damned did the Stooges' 'Fan Club' on their début LP, they retitled it 'I Feel Alright'.

□ SYSLJFM (The Letter Song)

■ Some abbreviations in song titles and their meaning

'A.A.C.S.B.T.A.' (Anaheim, Azuza and Cucamonga Sewing Circle Book review and Timing Association), Jan and Dean
'D.M.S.R.' (Dance, Music, Sex, Romance), Prince
'F.L.M.' (Fun, Love and Money), Mel and Kim
'L.A.F.S.' (Love At First Sight), Nick Lowe
'L.A.M.F.' (Los Angeles Mother Fuckers), Heartbreakers
'L.O.D.' (Love On Delivery), Billy Ocean
'S.O.S.' (Stop Her On Sight), Edwin Starr
'M.F.S.B.' (Mother, Father, Sister, Brother), T.S.O.P. (The Sound of Philadelphia)
'W.P.L.J.' (White Port and Lemon Juice), Four Deuces
'Y.M.C.A.' (Young Men's Christian Association), Village People

☐ Cover me

The next section contains general information, trivia and astounding facts about cover versions and trivia about songs in general.

'Palisades Park', first recorded by Freddy Cannon, was written by Chuck Barris, then manager of ABC TV's daytime programmes, to commemorate the opening of a new American fun fair. The song was later covered by UK rockabilly revivalists Matchbox, under the name Cyclone.

'There's Always Something There to Remind Me', written by Bacharach and David, was originally recorded in the US by Lou Johnson. Mickie Most wanted to record a cover with Tony Sheridan. When this fell through he considered Brenda Lee, but in the end settled for Sandie Shaw, who didn't let him down. However, 'It's Not Unusual', which was written by Gordon Mills and Les Reed for Sandie to record, was first sung on disc by Tom Jones.

Bobby Darin recorded Tim Hardin's 'If I Were a Carpenter'. Hardin recorded Darin's 'Simple Songs of Freedom'. Similarly, John Lennon recorded Ben E. King's 'Stand By Me' while King recorded Lennon's 'Imagine'.

'Layla' and 'Wonderful Tonight', both by Eric Clapton, and 'Something', sung by the Beatles and written by George Harrison, were all written about Patti Boyd.

Gadfly are a weird Texan outfit who have recorded covers of songs as diverse as 'Thriller' (Michael Jackson), 'Move Over Darling' (Doris Day) and Frankie Goes to Hollywood's 'Relax', which they did as 'A Tax'. Their 1986 single, 'Peace', contained twenty-three languages within the one lyric, and one of their LPs contained fourteen different lyrics set to the tune of 'Stars and Stripes'.

In 1986 Iggy Pop had his first UK hit with 'Real Wild Child', a song originally performed in 1958 by Australian rock star Johnny O'Keefe (who co-wrote the song with Johnny Greenan and Dave Owen). It was also covered in 1958 by Cricket Jerry Allison under a pseudonym. His version was produced by Buddy Holly. Albert Lee also covered the song in 1982.

Only three people have dared commit to vinyl a cover of Joy Division's classic 'Love Will Tear Us Apart': both Paul Young and P. J. Proby failed to treat the song with the respect it deserves, though the Swans treated it a little kinder in 1988. Grace Jones did a little better with her version of the group's 'She's Lost Control'. Frank Sidebottom did use 'Love Will Tear Us Apart' in an indies medley he recorded, which also included the Fall's 'How I Wrote Elastic Man', and Camper Van Beethoven's 'Take The Skinheads Bowling'. Frank is a real hero!

Audrey Hall kicked off her recording career with a lover's rock version of Foreigner's 'I Want To Know What Love Is'.

Bad News (the comic strip heavy metal group) and We've Got a Fuzzbox And We're Gonna Use It have both recorded their own interpretations of Queen's epic 'Bohemian Rhapsody'.

The Lords of the New Church put the sleaze back into Madonna's poppy 'Like A Virgin'.

Mick Ronson played on the Manchester punk band Slaughter and the Dogs' version of the Bubblegum classic 'Quick Joey Small (Run Joey Run)'.

Pop Will Eat Itself's 1987 EP contained covers of Sigue Sigue Sputnik's 'Love Missile F1-11' (which made the original seem worse than ever), Hawkwind's 'Orgone Accumulator' (Hawkwind LPs are essential Grebo wear), Mighty Lemon Drops' understated pop anthem 'Like an Angel' and Shriekback's 'Everything That Rises'.

Simon Dupree and the Big Sound were offered 'He Ain't Heavy He's My Brother' but turned it down, allowing the Hollies to have a massive hit with it. The Housemartins are one of many groups to have recorded this emotive song.

One of the all-time feminist anthems – Helen Reddy's 'I Am Woman' – was co-written by a man. Another – Julie Covington's 'Only Women Bleed' – was written by the all-American male Alice Cooper and a male co-writer.

The Soup Dragons, Dion and Roto Rooter have all covered Jimi Hendrix' 'Purple Haze', while American lunatics Devo tackled 'Are You Experienced?'.

In 1987 Black recorded a double cover single that featured Kraftwerk's 'The Model' on the A side, and Cheap Trick's 'He's a Whore' on the flip. The pic sleeves were good imitations too.

The much maligned Barry Manilow has attempted to gain more credibility by recording Shakin' Stevens' 'Julie' and Meatloaf's 'Read 'Em and Weep'.

The American band the Nerves did the original version of the Blondie hit 'Hanging on the Telephone' in 1976. It was written by band member Jack Lee. Fellow member Paul Collins went on to form Paul Collins' Beat while Peter Case went solo. Jack Lee also wrote 'Come Back and Stay', which was a hit for Paul Young. Blondie have also covered Randy and the Rainbows' 'Denis(e)', Buddy Holly's 'I'm A Gonna Love You Too' and the Paragons' 'The Tide Is High' (written by John Holt, who also wrote 'Help Me Make It through the Night', a hit for Kris Kristofferson).

Joey Ramone with Holly Vincent (ex Holly and the Italians), UB40 with Chrissie Hynde, and the Dictators have all recorded covers of Sonny and Cher's 'I Got You Babe'.

The Savoy Hitler Youth Band (including P. J. Proby) have recorded New Order's 'Blue Monday' tune with the lyrics from Bruce Springsteen's 'Cadillac Ranch'.

Both Leif Garrett and Child have butchered the Who's 'I Can't Explain'.

Cissy Houston (Whitney's mum) did the original version of 'Midnight Train to Georgia', a big hit for Gladys Knight.

Bobby Troup, who wrote 'Route 66', also wrote 'The Girl Can't Help It' for Little Richard. In 1988 Depeche Mode made an excellent cover of 'Route 66'.

'Running Bear', a hit for Johnny Preston in 1960, a sometime encore by Stiff Little Fingers and covered by British Summertime Ends, was written by DJ and novelty singer The Big Bopper.

'It's All in the Game', a hit for Tommy Edwards, Cliff Richard, and the Four Tops, was written in 1912 by Charles Gates Dawes, a US Vice-President.

Darrell Glen wrote 'Indescribably Blue' for Elvis Presley. Darrell's father, Artie, wrote 'Crying in the Chapel', originally recorded by Darrell and later covered by Elvis.

Both Charlie Chaplin and Harpo Marx have written 'serious' songs. One of Chaplin's, 'This Is My Song', was a UK Number One for Petula Clark.

The Randells' 'Martian Hop' was written by Jeff Wayne. This was obviously the starting point for his concept album *War of the Worlds*, about invaders from Mars, which he produced many years later.

'Dance On' by the Shadows was written by three members of the Avons.

Among some of the more amusing song-writing collaborations have been Nick Lowe's imaginary partners Mr Ceiling and Mr Profile while at least one XTC song was co-written by Messrs Bunsen and Burner.

'Come Back When You Grow Up', a hit for Bobby Vee, was written by Martha Sharpe, which is the real name of singer Sandy Posey. She also wrote her own hits 'Born A Woman' (excellently covered by Nick Lowe) and 'Single Girl'. 'Sunglasses', however (later covered by Tracey Ullman), was written for Sandy by American song-writer John D. Loudermilk, whose other writing credits include 'Three Stars' and 'Sitting in the Balcony' (both covered by Eddie Cochran) and 'Ebony Eyes' (Everly Brothers).

Abba's role in the glam rock movement has always been underrated, though in recent years this has changed. Among the acts to pay homage by recording their songs are: The Favourites ('SOS'), Blancmange ('The Day Before You Came'), Dr and The Medics ('Waterloo') and both Erasure and the Leather Nun ('Gimme Gimme Gimme A Man After Midnight').

The following lists are covers of songs by particular groups. Generally, the songs were originally recorded by the group in question and often written by one or more group members.

■ Sex Pistols

1. Kingswoods, 'Perty Vacant'*
2. Frank Sidebottom, 'Anarchy in the UK'
3. Bollock Brothers, *Never Mind the Bollocks*†
4. Neil, 'God Save the Queen'
5. Bananarama, 'No Feelings'
6. P. J. Proby, 'Anarchy in the UK'
7. Frank Sidebottom, 'God Save the Queen'
8. P. J. Proby, 'God Save the Queen'
9. Paul Jones, 'Pretty Vacant'
10. Megadeth, 'Anarchy in the UK'

■ Led Zeppelin

1. CCS, 'Whole Lotta Love'
2. Voice of the Beehive, 'D'yer Maker'
3. Blonde on Blonde, 'Whole Lotta Love'
4. Great White, 'The Immigrant Song'
5. Doppelganger, 'Communication Breakdown'
6. Temple City Kazoo Orchestra, 'Whole Lotta Love'
7. Far Corporation, 'Stairway to Heaven'
8. Vicious Rumour Club, 'Whole Lotta Love'
9. King Curtis, 'Whole Lotta Love'
10. Bollock Brothers, 'Heartbreaker'

■ Prince

1. Chaka Khan, 'I Feel for You'
2. Bette Bright, 'When You Were Mine'
3. Sheena Easton, 'Sugar Walls'
4. Age of Chance, 'Kiss'
5. Millie Jackson, 'I Wanna Be Your Lover'
6. Melissa Morgan, 'Do Me Baby'
7. Jill Jones, 'With You'
8. Tom Jones, 'Kiss'

* A country punk version of 'Pretty Vacant'
† A cover of the entire début LP

9. Cyndi Lauper, 'When You Were Mine'
10. Pointer Sisters, 'I Feel for You'

■ Gary Glitter

1. Human League, 'Rock 'n' Roll'
2. Joan Jett and the Blackhearts, 'Do You Wanna Touch Me'
3. Rock Goddess, 'I Didn't Know I Loved You Till I Saw You Rock 'n' Roll'
4. Davidsons, 'I Didn't Know I Loved You Till I Saw You Rock 'n' Roll'
5. Young Gods, 'Did You Miss Me'
6. Shakin' Stevens, 'A Little Boogie Woogie in the Back of My Mind'

Some people have recorded LPs consisting entirely of cover versions of other people's songs. This is usually done as a kind of tribute.

1. *Pin Ups*, David Bowie
2. *Kicking Against the Pricks*, Nick Cave and the Bad Seeds
3. *Music for Parties*, Silicon Teens
4. *Rock and Roll*, John Lennon
5. *Through the Looking Glass*, Siouxsie and the Banshees
6. *Sentimental Journeys*, Ringo Starr
7. *Wall of Sound*, Dr Mix and the Remix
8. *Royal Bastard*, The King of Luxembourg
9. *The Silkie Sing the Songs of Bob Dylan*, Silkie
10. *The Temptations Sing Smokey*, Temptations

Finally, some more unusual and unpredictable covers

1. Aztec Camera, 'Jump' (Van Halen)
2. Wilson Pickett, 'Born To Be Wild' (Steppenwolf)
3. Manfred Mann's Earth Band, 'Going Underground' (Jam)
4. Fools, 'Psycho Chicken' (Talking Heads-Psycho Killer)
5. Sort Sol, 'Ode to Billy Joe' (Bobbie Gentry)

6. Shakin' Stevens, 'Evil-Hearted Ada' (Flamin' Groovies)
7. The Brickwall Band, 'Distant Drums' (Jim Reeves)
8. We've Got a Fuzzbox and We're Gonna Use It, 'Spirit in the Sky' (Norman Greenbaum)
9. Flying Lizards, 'Summertime Blues' (Eddie Cochran)
10. The Fall, 'Victoria' (Kinks)

■ BAND PLAYED THE BOOGIE

Instrument trivia.

The most basic instrumentation for a rock band is guitar, bass and drums, the latter two being commonly known as the rhythm section. Common additions are second guitar and/or keyboards.

Donovan's guitar was embossed with the slogan 'This Machine Kills', which was copied from a plaque on Dylan's guitar. Dylan had nicked the idea from Woody Guthrie, whose slogan read 'This Machine Kills Fascists'.

■ Mr Guitar: ten guitarists with John Mayall's band

1. Alan Ditchburn
2. Davy Graham
3. Sammy Prosser
4. John Gilbey
5. Bernie Watson
6. Roger Dean
7. Eric Clapton
8. Peter Green
9. Mick Taylor
10. Jon Mark

During the six-year recording of Boston's third LP, group member Tom Scholz designed the Rockman, a paperback-sized guitar practice amp made to be used with headphones.

The double-necked guitar was not an innovation of the progressive rock era; the guitarist in Bob Willis' Texas Playboys used one back in the Forties.

In 1961 400,000 guitars were sold in the US.

One of the contributing reasons to the growth of British guitar bands in the late Fifties and early Sixties was the introduction of the hire purchase system, which enabled many youngsters to buy guitars which had previously been too expensive.

Bands with two or more drummers include: Adam and the Ants, Big Pig, CCS, the Glitter Band, the Grateful Dead, and Pere Ubu.

Larry Ludwig (Farmers Boys) and Pete De Freitas (Echo and the Bunnymen) both replaced drum machines.

The violin solo on 'Bridge over Troubled Water' was actually a synthesizer.

Rolf Harris's contribution to rock instrumentation was the wobble-board. Classic wobbleboard solos include . . . er . . . um . . .

■ WAR

Some songs about the war in South-east Asia.

1. '19', Paul Hardcastle
2. 'The Ballad of the Green Beret', Staff Sergeant Barry Sadler
3. 'Camouflage', Stan Ridgeway
4. 'Beach Party Vietnam', The Dead Milkman
5. 'Cambodia', Kim Wilde
6. 'Matchstick Flotilla', Thrashing Doves
7. 'Vietnam Blues', Lightning Hopkins
8. 'Back to Vietnam', Television Personalities
9. 'Vietnamerica', Stranglers
10. 'Love Vietnam', 14th July
11. 'Let's Send Batman to Vietnam', Seeds of Euphoria
12. 'Ruby Don't Take Your Love to Town', Kenny Rogers and the First Edition
13. 'Singing Vietnam Talking Blues', Johnny Cash
14. 'Frontline', Stevie Wonder
15. 'Letter from Vietnam', Staff Sergeant Barry Sadler

Frank Zappa got draft exemption because he produced a porno tape and received a short jail sentence.

Jesse Winchester, the first to record Bob Dylan's 'I Shall Be Released', was a draft dodger. Diana Ross's brother went, though.

■ CHANGES

David Bowie trivia.

David went to the same school as Peter Frampton.

David Bowie apparently chose his surname after the famous Bowie knife because of his idol, Mick Jagger, a jagger being an old English knife.

In 1963 David formed a band called the Kon Rads using the pseudonym David Jay.

Mick Ronson, Bowie's guitarist in the early Seventies, is totally deaf in one ear.

■ Ten songs David Bowie has covered

1. 'Sorry' (Merseys)
2. 'Across the Universe' (Beatles)
3. 'Here Comes the Night' (Them)
4. 'Knock on Wood' (Eddie Floyd)
5. 'I Pity the Fool' (Bobby Bland)
6. 'I Can't Explain' (Who)
7. 'White Light White Heat' (Velvet Underground)
8. 'Round and Round' (Chuck Berry)
9. 'Friday on My Mind' (Easybeats)
10. 'Alabama Song' (From the 1930 opera *The Rise and Fall of the City of Mahagony* by Kurt Weill and Bertolt Brecht.)

The *Space Oddity* LP was originally going to be called *Man of Words, Man of Music* but the success of the 'Space Oddity' single put paid to that.

In 1973 Bowie wrote a song called 'Laser' for a group called the Astronettes, which he did not record himself until 1981, when it became 'Scream Like A Baby'. 'Fashion' started life as a song called 'Jamaica'.

In 1968 Bowie appeared in adverts for the stylophone pocket electric organ, which was all the rage at the time.

During the *Young American* sessions Bowie started to record Bruce Springsteen's 'It's Hard to Be a Saint in the City', but it was never completed.

The Italian version of 'Space Oddity' is called 'Ragazzo Solo Ragazza Sola', which means 'lonely boy lonely girl', and has totally different lyrics to the English original.

'The Prettiest Star' was written about David's then-to-be wife Angie.

David plays saxophone on Steeleye Span's version of the old Teddy Bears' tearjerker 'To Know Him Is to Love Him'.

David's attempt to turn Orwell's *1984* into a musical was blocked by Orwell's widow, Sonia.

The original *Diamond Dogs* LP cover was considered obscene by RCA so they painted out the Bowie-dog creature's knick-knacks.

■ BITS AND PIECES

And now some trivia about areas of rock 'n' roll not yet covered.

□ Some songs about specific events

Deep Purple's 'Smoke on the Water' is about the razing of Montreux Casino, which overlooks Lake Geneva. The fire was started by a flare gun during a Frank Zappa concert at which Deep Purple were playing support.

The MC5's 'Motor City Is Burning' is about the Detroit riots on the night of 24 July 1967. The riots started after a 'routine' police raid; when they finished 43 people were dead, 7,000 had been arrested and 1,200 homes and businesses were destroyed, mostly by fire.

The Men They Couldn't Hang's 'The Ghosts of Cable Street' refers to the 4 October 1936 stand against Oswald Mosley's fascist Black Shirts, which culminated in a street battle on Cable Street in the East End of London.

Orchestral Manoeuvres in the Dark's 'Enola Gay' is about the bombing of Hiroshima with a nuclear device. *Enola Gay* was the name of the American plane that dropped the bomb.

Roy Orbison wrote 'It's Too Soon to Know' after his wife Claudette (about whom he wrote 'Claudette', covered by the Everly Brothers) was killed in a motorcycle accident.

The Smiths' 'Heaven Knows I'm Miserable Now' bears a remarkable similarity of title to a 1969 single by Morrissey's idol Sandie Shaw: her single was 'Heaven Knows I'm Missing Him Now'.

The lyrics that open Billy Bragg's 'A New England' – 'I was twenty-one years when I wrote this song. I'm twenty-two now but I won't be for long' – were originally used to open 'The Leaves That Are Green' from Simon and Garfunkel's *Sounds of Silence*.

Richard Berry, who wrote and originally performed 'Louie Louie' in the late Fifties, also did a lot of session work. His is the voice on the Robins' 'Riot in Cell Block No. 9', and the Flairs' 'Footstompin''.

Eccentric millionaire Howard Hughes was infatuated with singer Bobbie Gentry, so much so that he paid her £1 million to perform three years running in Las Vegas.

In February 1986 Feargal Sharkey's mother, Sybil, and sister, Ursula, were held at gunpoint by terrorists for four hours while visiting friends in Londonderry. It was thought to be an ambush on security forces, but the gunmen left without a shot being fired. Feargal was in Sheffield on tour at the time.

In 1985 terrorists hijacked an American civil airliner and flew to Beirut, where a number of passengers were held hostage. Among the prisoners were Greek singer Demis Roussos and the elder brother of Cheap Trick drummer Bun E. Carlos.

In 1967 Brian Epstein announced plans (ultimately unfulfilled) to star the Who in a weekly show *à la* Monkees.

Melanie's LP *Garden in the City* had a scratch-and-sniff cover, as did Stiff's *Akron Compilation* and the Damned's *Strawberries*.

Moby Grape simultaneously released all ten tracks of their eponymous début LP as singles in 1967.

In 1987 UK aviation historian Roy Nesbitt claimed to have unearthed evidence that suggested the RAF shot down the plane that Glenn Miller was travelling on.

The Real Thing's Chris Amoo is a top Afghan breeder. In 1986 one of his dogs won Pup of the Year at Crufts. At the next year's show his dog won the Champion of the Show award.

Eccentric country and western star Hank Wangford was Gram Parsons's doctor *circa* 1970.

Frank Sinatra loathes 'My Way'.

Both Bing Crosby and Marc Bolan died within weeks of recording TV shows with David Bowie; both before the shows were aired.

Stiff Records co-founder Jake Riviera is a bicycle fanatic. In 1986 he stepped in (financially) to save the tiny Hetchlings of Southend, the Rolls Royce of bicycles.

Roy Harper is said once to have been stricken with a rare disease after giving the kiss of life to a sheep.

Walter Carlos, composer of 'Switched on Bach', became Wendy Carlos after a sex-change operation. US punk star Wayne County became Jayne County.

Janis Joplin almost joined the 13th Floor Elevators.

The longest running group in the world are the New Christy Minstrels, who were originally formed in 1842 by Edwin 'Pops' Christy as the Christy Minstrels and included at various times Eddie Cantor and Al Jolson. They disbanded in 1921 but re-formed as the New Christy Minstrels in 1961. Amongst those to pass through their ranks during the Sixties were Kenny Rogers, Roger McGuinn, John Denver, Kim Carnes and Barry McGuire.

In 1964 Ronnie Dio and the Prophets (yes *that* Ronnie Dio) released a version of 'Love Potion No. 9'. The flip side was . . . the same song. They did it as a gimmick, the precursor to the Eighties craze for putting remixed, dubbed or instrumental versions of the top side on the flip.

☐ Fans

Grateful Dead fans are known as Dead Heads. The term originally applied to people given free tickets for a play or concert.

Duran Duran fans are known as Durannies.

Adam and the Ant fans were Ant People.

Fans of cult band the Hoodoo Gurus are known as Guru-vers.

Bets

Steve Earle fan Bruce Springsteen challenged an executive at Earle's record company to a game of racquetball, staking money against a crate of Steve's LP *Guitar Town*. Springsteen won and handed his prize around personally.

The Beatles and Rory Storme had a bet in Hamburg as to which band could break the stage first. Rory and co. stomped their way through to victory and supped champagne at the Beatles' expense.

□ Before they were famous

David Coverdale and Chris Rea played in a group called the Beautiful Losers together.

Kris Kristofferson was a US football star.

Brian Poole was a butcher.

Lowell George played briefly in the Seeds and the Standells before joining the Mothers of Invention, then forming Little Feat.

Cilla Black was the hat-check girl at the Cavern.

Sandy Nelson played drums on Gene Vincent's *Crazy Times* album.

Leonard Cohen was a leading Canadian poet.

Hugh Cornwell (Stranglers) and Richard Thompson (Fairport Convention) were in a school group called Emile and the Detectives together.

Gary Glitter was a warm-up man on *Ready Steady Go*.

Larry Blackmon (Cameo) and Gwen Guthrie were in the band East Coast together.

Sting and Bryan Ferry were teachers.

Beck and Fagin (Steely Dan) played in Jay and the Americans for a while.

Elvis Costello was a computer programmer.

Al Kooper (Blood Sweat and Tears) was in the Royal Teens, of 'Short Shorts' fame.

Craig Douglas and Freddie Garrity were milkmen.

Steve Strange and Chrissie Hynde were in the Moors Murderers together.

Desmond Dekker was a welder.

Minnie Riperton was in a psychedelic soul group called the Rotary Connection.

Solomon Burke was a mortician (amongst countless other things).

Carly Simon sang briefly with Elephant's Memory, renowned for their work with John and Yoko.

Alex Harvey claimed to be a lion tamer.

Justin Hayward played bass for Marty Wilde.

Christopher Cross was a roadie for the Doobie Brothers.

□ D-a-a-ance

The waltz – ha! The tango – child's play. The foxtrot – piece of cake. Get on the dance floor and dance the . . . Barracuda, Beng Beng, Bird, Birdie Dance, Block, Bluebeat, Boogaloo, Boomerang, Bop, Bossa Nova, Bounce, Break, Bristol Stomp, British Hustle, Bump, Bunny Hop, Bus Stop, Calypso, Chicken, Chicken Hop, Chicken Strut, Cissy Strut, Clam, Class, Climb, Continental, Creep, Crocodile Rock, Crocodile Walk, Crusher, Deadfly, Dog, Duck, European, Footstomp, Freak, Freddie, Freestyle, Freeze, Frug, Funky Chicken, Go Go, Hand Jive, Hanky Panky, Hitchhiker, Hooka Tooka, Horse, Hucklebuck, Hula Hoop, Hully Gully, Hustle, Idiot Dancing, Jerk, Jitterbug, Jive, Latin Hustle, Limbo, Lindy Hop, Locomotion, Loop-Di-Loop, Madison, Magilla, Majestic, Martian Hop, Mashed Potato, Mess Around, Monkey, Monster Mash, Peppermint Twist, Philly Freeze, Pogo,

Pony, Rambo Rhumba, Rat, Reggae, Robot, Rock Steady, Rowing Song, Rub-A-Dub, Screw, See Saw, Shag, Shake, Shimmy, Shing-A-Ling, Shortstop, Shotgun, Shuffle, Simple Simon, Ska, Skank, Skip, Slam, Slide, Slop, Sophisticated Boom Boom, Soul Twist, Southern Freeze, Spanish Hustle, Spank, Standing Still, Stranglehold, Stroll, Strut, Suzy Q, Swim, Switcheroo, Texas Hop, Twine, Twist, Ubangi Stomp, Waddle, Walk or the Worm!

In 1987 the Shag became the latest dance craze with songs like the Tams' 'There Ain't Nothin' Like Shaggin'' and 'My Baby Sure Can Shag', and Chairmen of the Board's 'Shag Your Brains Out'. However, there was nothing particularly new about the dance. Sidney Bechet recorded 'Shag' in 1932 and Nate Leslie recorded 'Shaggin' at the Shore' five years later.

The famous Lindy Hop was named after Lindberg's transatlantic flight.

In an episode of the TV series *Quincy* the pathologist had to investigate the death of a punk rocker who died because he'd been Slam Dancing, a particularly violent hard-core form of Pogoing, which involves throwing oneself at other people, the stage and solid walls.

□ Listen to What the Man Said

Among the songs written about Dylan are David Bowie's 'Song to Bob Dylan', and McLean and McLeans' 'Bob Dylan Goes Punk'.

Bob Dylan has never had a British Number One himself (his highest position was Number Four with 'Like A Rolling Stone'), but two of his songs have reached the summit. They are 'Mr Tambourine Man' (for the Byrds) and 'Mighty Quinn' (for Manfred Mann).

On his first visit to Britain Dylan appeared in the BBC drama *Madhouse on Castle Street*.

'Sad-eyed Lady of the Lowlands' was written by Dylan about his wife, Sarah.

On his first album Dylan fretted his guitar with a lipstick holder belonging to his girl-friend Susie Rotolo, who appeared with him on the cover of *The Freewheelin' Bob Dylan*.

Singer/song-writer Phil Ochs once upset Dylan by saying he 'liked, but not loved' a Dylan single.

(Dennis) Coulson, (Dixie) Dean, (Tom) McGuinness and (Hughie) Flint recorded an LP of unissued Bob Dylan songs. It was called *Lo and Behold*.

'Catfish', a song that Dylan wrote but never recorded himself, is about baseball pitcher Jim Hunter. 'Hurricane' was co-written by Dylan in support of boxer Rubin Carter, who was wrongly convicted of manslaughter in the Sixties and whose sentence was quashed in 1986.

Al Kooper, formerly of the Royal Teens and later of Blood Sweat and Tears, played organ on many of Dylan's songs, including those on *Highway 61 Revisited*.

Bob Dylan's first Grammy was awarded for Best Rock Vocal Performance on 'You Gotta Serve Someone' in 1979.

Dylan appeared on the Tom Rush LP *Take A Little Walk With Me* under the pseudonym Roosevelt Gook.

Bob Dylan apparently wrote a number of songs with Gene Clark of the Byrds. Unfortunately, they were thrown away by a hotel maid and no record of them remains.

☐ Sharing You

■ Fifteen pairs of LPs sharing a title

1. *Dark Side of the Moon:* Medicine Head, Pink Floyd
2. *Tapestry:* Carole King, Don McLean
3. *One Step Beyond:* Chocolate Watch Band, Madness
4. *Thriller:* Eddie and the Hot Rods, Michael Jackson
5. *L:* Steve Hillage, Godley and Creme

6. *The Gift:* Jam, Midge Ure
7. *Saints and Sinners:* Steve Gibbons Band, Whitesnake
8. *First Offence:* Bunk Dogger, Inmates
9. *Grave New World:* Strawbs, Discharge
10. *Live at Leeds:* John Martyn, the Who
11. *Once Upon A Time:* Siouxsie and the Banshees, Simple Minds
12. *Wish You Were Here:* Badfinger, Pink Floyd
13. *Dragon Fly:* Strawbs, Jefferson Starship
14. *Parade:* Spandau Ballet, Prince and the Revolution
15. *Stormbringer:* John Martyn, Deep Purple

☐ Year of Decision

1. 'New York Mining Disaster 1941', Bee Gees
2. 'December '63', Four Seasons
3. 'Soul Clap '69', Booker T and the MGs
4. 'Spirit of '76', Alarm
5. '1977', Clash
6. '1983 . . . A Merman I Shall Be', Jimi Hendrix
7. 'Sex Crime (Nineteen Eighty-Four)', Eurythmics
8. '1999', Prince
9. '2001 A Space Odyssey', Deodato
10. 'In the Year 2525 (Exordium and Terminus)', Zager and Evans

☐ What's Another Year

1. 'January', Pilot
2. 'January February', Barbara Dickson
3. 'March of the Mods', Joe Loss
4. 'April Love', Pat Boone
5. 'First of May', Bee Gees
6. 'June Night', Jimmy Dorsey

7. '4th of July', John Christie
8. 'August', Love
9. 'September Song', Ian McCulloch
10. 'October', U2
11. 'November 22nd 1963', Destroy All Monsters
12. 'December Will Be Magic Again', Kate Bush

☐ This Is England

1. 'Village Green', Kinks
2. 'When An Old Cricketer Leaves the Crease', Roy Harper
3. 'English Country Garden', Jimmie Rodgers
4. 'Anyone for Tennis', Cream
5. 'The English Rose', Jam
6. 'Adventures in a Yorkshire Landscape', Be Bop Deluxe
7. 'Streets of London', Ralph McTell
8. 'This Is Still England', Nikki Sudden
9. 'Life in a Northern Town', Dream Academy
10. 'England Swings', Roger Miller

☐ Mr Success

■ Ten rock 'n' rollers on Larry Parnes' books

1. Tommy Steele
2. Marty Wilde
3. Billy Fury
4. Georgie Fame
5. Duffy Power
6. Dickie Pride
7. Vince Eager
8. Johnny Gentle
9. Nelson Keene
10. Johnny Goode

☐ Power in the Darkness

■ Ten blind artists

1. Stevie Wonder
2. Ray Charles
3. José Feliciano
4. Lennie Peters
5. Clarence Carter
6. Al Hibbler
7. Blind Lemon Jefferson
8. Ray Burns
9. Ronnie Milsap
10. Rev. Gary Davies

The sleevenotes to Stevie Wonder's *Talking Book* LP are in braille.

Many people assumed Roy Orbison was blind because he always wore dark glasses; in fact, he had nearly perfect vision.

☐ Drugs

'If you can remember the Sixties, then you weren't really there!' Paul Kantner, Jefferson Airplane

1. 'Lucifer in Powder Form', Bally
2. 'King Heroin', James Brown
3. 'White Lines (Don't Do It)', Grandmaster Flash and Melle Mel
4. 'The Needle and the Damage Done', Neil Young
5. 'White Rabbit', Jefferson Airplane
6. 'Opium', Bill Nelson
7. 'Needle of Death', Bert Jansch
8. 'Heroin', Velvet Underground

9. 'Cocaine', John Cale
10. 'I'm Waiting for the Man', Velvet Underground

□ Smoke Gets in Your Eyes

1. 'Smoke Smoke Smoke That Cigarette', Tex Williams
2. 'The Long Cigarette', Roulettes
3. 'The Addicted Man', The Game
4. 'Tar', Visage
5. 'Lipstick Traces on Cigarettes', O'Jays
6. 'A Beer and a Cigarette', Terraplane
7. 'Smokin' in the Boys' Room', Brownsville Station
8. 'Smokey Places', Corsairs
9. 'A Kind of Drag', Buckinghams
10. 'Smoke on the Water', Deep Purple

□ Sing Little Birdie

■ Fourteen 'bird' doo-wop groups

1. Flamingos
2. Penguins
3. Robins
4. Crows
5. Meadowlarks
6. Swallows
7. Sparrows
8. Cardinals
9. Ravens
10. Hollywood Blue Jays
11. Swans
12. Drioles

13. Larks
14. Wrens

Other common themes for doo-wop groups included cars (Edsels, Corsairs, etc.) and royalty (Five Kings, Earls, and so on).

□ Ghosts

1. 'Ghost Dancing', Adrissi Brothers
2. 'There's A Ghost in My House', Yachts
3. 'Haunted', Pogues
4. 'Haunted House', Johnny Fuller
5. 'Spooky', Classics IV
6. 'Ghost of Love', Fiction Factory
7. 'Ghost Satellite', Bob and Jerry
8. 'Little Ghost', Boy George
9. 'Doin' It in a Haunted House', Yvonne Gage
10. 'Ghostbusters', Ray Parker Jr

Frank Marino, of Mahogany Rush, insists that the spirit of Jimi Hendrix came to him in the night and told him to play guitar.

□ Tiptoe through the Tulips

1. 'Flower Punk', Frank Zappa and the Mothers of Invention
2. 'San Francisco (Be Sure to Wear Some Flowers in Your Hair)', Scott McKenzie
3. 'Flowers of Manchester', Bakerloo Junction
4. 'Prairie Rose', Roxy Music
5. 'Beware the Flowers ('Cause I'm Sure They're Gonna Get You)', Otway and Barrett

6. 'Paper Roses', Marie Osmond
7. 'The Floral Dance', Terry Wogan
8. 'I'm Allergic to Flowers', Jefferson Handkerchiefs
9. 'Flowers in the Rain', Move
10. 'Build Me Up Buttercup', Foundations

The Dandelion label was co-owned by DJ John Peel.

Floral musicians include Tim Rose and Herbie Flowers.

☐ Electricity

1. 'Everything's Electric', Dazz
2. 'Electric Avenue', Eddy Grant
3. 'Electric Boogaloo', Ollie and Jerry
4. 'Electric Guitar', Talking Heads
5. 'Bring Back the Spark', Be Bop Deluxe
6. 'I Like 'Lectric Motors', Patrick D. Martin
7. 'Are "Friends" Electric', Tubeway Army
8. 'Together in Electric Dreams', Georgio Moroder and Phil Oakey
9. 'Lucy 'Lectric', Patrick D. Martin
10. 'You Light Up My Life', Debbie Boone

The Blue Magoos wore $700 (£400)-leather, electric jackets that lit up. They were designed by Diana Dews, creator of the famous Sixties electric dress.

☐ Cruel to Be Kind

1. 'Oh Bondage Up Yours', X-Ray Spex
2. 'Beat on the Brat', Ramones

3. 'Hit Me with Your Rhythm Stick', Ian Dury and the Blockheads
4. 'Beat My Guest', Adam and the Ants
5. 'Chains', Cookies
6. 'Hurt So Good', Susan Cadogan
7. 'Tie Your Mother Down', Queen
8. 'Whip in My Valise', Adam and the Ants
9. 'Violent Love', Dr Feelgood
10. 'Tie Me Kangaroo Down Sport', Rolf Harris

■ DEAD POP STARS

Rock 'n' roll has probably got one of the highest casualty rates in any industry outside the armed forces. Of course, many of rock's deaths are self-inflicted by drug and drink abuse, but the stars' high profiles can also cause problems.

□ Bang Bang

■ Gunshot fatalities in the rock world

1. John Lennon: shot dead by Mark Chapman, in New York City.
2. Mal Evans: former Beatles roadie (and close friend), was shot dead by the Los Angeles Police Department while brandishing a gun during a rare fit of anger.
3. Larry Williams: self-inflicted or murder? The police are unsure how this Fifties rocker was shot.
4. Felix Pappalardi: Cream's producer was shot dead by his wife.
5. Al Jackson: another killed by his spouse.
6. Marvin Gaye: killed by his father.
7. Carlton Barrett: the former Wailer was murdered in JA.
8. Jimmy Widener: Hank Snow's guitarist was shot dead.
9. Sam Cooke: shot dead while allegedly assaulting a woman.
10. Lee Morgan: the jazz trumpeter was shot dead by his girl-friend.
11. Peter Tosh: shot dead by burglars in his JA mansion only five months after Wailer colleague Carlton Barrett was killed.
12. Scott La Rock: the New York DJ and rapper was shot dead in Bronx gangland.
13. Phil King: Blue Öyster Cult's manager was shot three times in the head over a gambling argument.

14. Rob Roy: an American roadie, he had just finished an ELO tour when he was caught with his trousers down and killed by an angry husband.
15. Reg Calvert: Lord Sutch's manager and the owner of the pirate radio station Radio City was shot dead in the Sixties. A rival pirate station owner (and Liberal MP) was charged with his murder.

□ Gun Law

Those who survived gunshot wounds

1. Bob Marley: wounded in a 1976 assassination attempt.
2. Jackie Wilson: wounded by a deranged fan in the early Sixties.
3. Mick Jagger: accidentally shot in the leg during the filming of *Ned Kelly*.
4. Andy Warhol: shot in his office in 1968.
5. Eddie Cochran: wounded in a hunting accident.
6. Archie Bell: shot in the leg in Vietnam.
7. Garfield Morgan: Run DMC's sound engineer was shot in the head by a gang of youths after the group pulled out of a gig late in 1987. The bullet was successfully removed.
8. Dusty Hill: the ZZ Top guitarist accidentally shot himself in the stomach but recovered after three and half hours of surgery.

□ Rock and Roll Suicide

1. Pete Ham of Badfinger, and co-writer on the Nilsson hit 'Without You'.
2. Joe Meek, the legendary producer, shot himself on the eighth anniversary of Buddy Holly's death.
3. Ron 'Pigpen' McKernan of the aptly named Grateful Dead.

4. Paul Williams of the Temptations was in poor health and had heavy tax debts when he shot himself a few streets away from the Motown offices.
5. Soeur Sourire, better known as the Singing Nun.
6. Ian Curtis of Joy Division.
7. Phil Ochs, the talented singer and song-writer.
8. Dagenham Dave, a fanatical Stranglers follower who jumped into the Thames. Hear the song on the *No More Heroes* LP.
9. Rory Storme, the Mersey beat star, entered a suicide pact with his mother.
10. Richard Manuel of the Band hanged himself during a reunion tour.
11. Yogi Horton, Luther Vandross's drummer.
12. Michael Holliday, the British pop singer, unable to cope with his success, shot himself in 1963.
13. Bobby Bloom, who recorded 'Montego Bay', shot himself.
14. Jimmy Donley, the US swamp-rock star.
15. Pete Meadon, the Who's former publicist and manager of the Steve Gibbons Band.
16. Danny Rapp, the former leader of Danny and the Juniors.
17. Billy Stewart, the radio pioneer who introduced the Top Forty format.
18. Dennis Hughes, of cult band the Deviants, jumped off Caernarvon Castle.
19. Johnny Ace lost at Russian roulette.
20. Terry Kath, the Chicago guitarist, apparently planned to amuse party guests when he pointed what he thought was an empty gun at his head.

Randy California of Spirit tried to commit suicide by jumping off Chelsea Bridge. He survived. Other survivors include Jackie Fox of the Runaways, who slashed her wrists, and Sid Vicious, who survived a suicide attempt while in police detention (for the murder of Nancy Spungen), but died of an overdose after he was released on bail.

Rigor Mortis (aka John Entwhistle) recorded a little ditty called 'Do the Dangle', while the Fabulous Poodles gave us 'Suicide Bridge'. Barclay James Harvest sang simply 'Suicide', and *M.A.S.H.* said 'Suicide Is Painless'. Buddy Knox told us rather frankly 'I Think I'm Gonna Kill Myself'.

In 1984 an American youth committed suicide apparently after listening to Ozzy Osbourne's track 'Suicide Solution'. Thankfully, Ozzy was absolved of any blame or responsibility.

Legend has it that two records in the Thirties caused people to commit suicide when they heard them: the first is 'Gloomy Sunday', written by Hungarian poet Lazzlo Javer and recorded by Billie Holiday; the other is Bessie Smith's version of 'Strange Fruit', which apparently was responsible for seven people taking their own lives.

Paul Simon was quite happy to kill off characters in his songs, or rather, he let them do it themselves: 'Richard Cory' shot himself while 'A Most Peculiar Man' gassed himself.

Animals lead singer Eric Burdon is convinced that Jimi Hendrix was actually trying to commit suicide when he took the drugs that caused him to vomit in his sleep and choke to death. Burdon claims there was a suicide note that mysteriously vanished.

The early Sixties saw a spate of so-called 'death discs', which dealt with the deaths of (mostly) loved ones. Nearly all of them were somewhat sick and morose, and most were banned by the BBC because of the subject matter. Check out the following (including some more recent ones) when you feel like a cringe.

'I Want My Baby Back', Jimmy Cross
'Endless Sleep', Jody Reynolds
'Running Bear', Johnny Preston
'Leader of the Pack', Shangri Las
'Terry', Twinkle
'New Angel Tonight', David McEnery
'Last Kiss', J. Frank Wilson and the Cavaliers
'El Paso', Marty Robbins
'Tell Laura I Love Her', Ray Peterson
'Ebony Eyes', Everly Brothers
'Drunken Driver', Ferlon Huskey
'Patches', Dicky Lee
'Old Shep', Elvis Presley
'Teen Angel', Mark Dinning
'Laura (Strange Things Happen in this World)', Dicky Lee
'Deadman's Curve', Jan and Dean

'Give Us Your Blessings', Shangri Las (originally recorded by Ray Peterson)
'Jeannie's Afraid of the Dark' (100 on the cringeometer!), Dolly Parton
'Big Bad John', Jimmy Dean
'The Bells', Dominoes
'Johnny Don't Do It', 10CC
'Hello This Is Joannie', Paul Evans
'Ode To Billy Joe', Bobby Gentry
'Camouflage', Stan Ridgeway

According to reports, on the evening of 16 April 1960 Eddie Cochran, who was about to play the last gig on the first half of a UK tour before flying home to America to marry his fiancée, played some of his old friend Buddy Holly's records. This was apparently the first time that Eddie had played them since the Texan singer was killed in a plane crash more than a year earlier. If this story is true, then it is with some irony that the next day the taxi carrying Eddie from Bristol to London Airport crashed, killing Eddie and injuring Gene Vincent.

In 1986 Le Cam records of Fort Worth released King and Kelli's 'I Love A Rainy Night'. The male singer, King, was purported to be Elvis Presley . . . recorded *after* his death.

The pallbearers at Otis Redding's funeral were Joe Tex, Percy Sledge, Joe Simon, Johnny Taylor, Solomon Burke, Sam Moore and Don Conway.

In October 1967 hippies in San Francisco staged a 'death of hippy' funeral procession in protest over the commercialization of the love and peace brigade.

In a tragic coincidence both Duane Allman and Berry Oakley of the Allman Brothers were killed in motor-bike accidents. They happened almost a year apart and within a few blocks of each other.

Hank Williams died on New Year's Day 1953 from heart failure brought on by drink and drug abuse. His widow, Audrey, married another singer, Johnny Horton, who was killed in a car crash in November 1960.

According to rock folklore, the only two people who saw Jim Morrison's body were his wife, Pam, and the doctor who signed the death certificate. Both died within a few years of Morrison, helping fuel speculation that Morrison is in fact alive and well, and living in exile. If you are Jim, the taxman wants a word.

In 1970, two months before her own death, Janis Joplin bought a headstone for the grave of Bessie Smith, thirty-three years after the blues and jazz singer died.

When Gram Parsons died in 1973, his body was to be taken to New Orleans for burial. However, Gram had expressed a desire to be cremated, so his manager Phil Kaufman and a friend hijacked the coffin and took it to Joshua Tree (where Gram had died) and set it ablaze.

'Bandleaders come and go but the perennial Duke Ellington, like Tennyson's brook, seems to go on forever.' *Bath and West Chronicle*, 23 May 1974. The Duke died the following day.

The late Sixties were full of rumours that Paul McCartney had made an early exit from this world and his place in the Beatles was taken by a look-alike (a young Mike Yarwood perhaps). The rumours were started in America, of course, and below are some of the things that the 'Paul is dead' camp came up with to support their theory.

1. Paul is the only Beatle on the cover of the *Abbey Road* LP not wearing shoes.
2. The cover of the *Sgt Pepper's Lonely Hearts Club Band* LP is clearly meant to be a funeral scene and it's Paul's instrument, the bass, that is shaped out of yellow hyacinths. Also John, Ringo and George all hold gold instruments but Paul's is black – the colour of death. Finally, from certain angles the flowers shaped like a bass guitar look like the name Paul.
3. On the back cover of *Sgt Pepper* . . . is a photo of the band. John, George and Ringo all face the camera but a fourth person has his back to it. Paul-is-deaders say this is because Paul wasn't available to pose, which is true, but he was out of the country – not dead. The fourth figure is, in fact, Mal Evans.
4. On the inside cover of *Sgt Pepper* . . . Paul wears a badge on his arm that carries the letters OPD, which doctors sometimes use to abbreviate Officially Pronounced Dead.
5. In the *Magical Mystery Tour* booklet all the Beatles wear red carnations, except Paul, who wears a black one.

Paul answered the above (and other theories) with the comment, 'I'm dead am I? Why does nobody ever tell me anything?'

■ ANYTHING THAT'S ROCK 'N' ROLL

This chapter looks at the many varied styles of pop and rock music over the ages and, briefly, at the styles that pre-date them. The section falls short of perfection because music cannot easily be pigeon-holed; after all, why should restraints of style be stamped upon it? Nevertheless it does serve as a useful guide to how, and even why, rock music developed. I've included a Top Twenty of tracks I consider representative of, or milestones in, each style and though I've tried to be totally objective, it was inevitable that my personal prejudices would affect the selection. Most tracks in the Top Twenties are singles, though some are LP tracks. Each artist is represented only once in any one category.

□ In the Beginning: (a rapid waltz through early music)

We can only assume that music was discovered by people when they started banging two bits of rock together rhythmically and liked the sound. Well, they could hardly have come across a Stratocaster lying idly at the back of the cave! The voice was the first true instrument and probably the first songs were work chants used to help folk carry out manual tasks more efficiently. Religion cottoned on fairly early and the church and monastery were among the great homes of music. Each area of the world developed its own styles. America, being a hotch-potch of various peoples (some of whom went willingly, others who didn't), was where many of these musical styles blended and spawned the music that would eventually lead to the many varied styles of rock 'n' roll. Read on and see just what different strains of music there have been.

□ Before the Revolution: (easy listening from when 'pop' was lemonade)

In the years before the Fifties there was no gentle graduation from childhood to adulthood. Until a certain age one was considered a child, and at that magical age he or she would become an adult. Equally, there was no music between crass juvenile offerings and the sophisticated singing of mum and dad's favourites. The singing stars of the time were nearly all crooners and emotive balladeers. There were other styles of music of course: the big bands, jazz musicians and even blues singers, though you were unlikely to hear the latter on British radio. While there is much to be said for many of the fine voices of the era (such as those listed below), it is no surprise that when the Fifties acknowledged the teen years as a magical period between childhood and maturity, teenagers were quick to seek a musical identity of their own; rock 'n' roll would give them that opportunity.

We have to remember though that as well as the soon-to-be rock 'n' roll fans, the soon-to-be rock 'n' roll stars were growing up with this rather staid music and everyone from Elvis Presley to Gene Vincent was quite prepared to slip the odd 'Mona Lisa' or 'Unchained Melody' into his repertoire.

Many of the artists below failed to survive the onslaught of rock 'n' roll – at least as far as the charts were concerned. They were the last bastion of the pre-rock era.

1. Nat 'King' Cole, 'When I Fall in Love'
2. Eddie Fisher, 'Outside of Heaven'
3. Vera Lynn, 'My Son My Son'
4. Al Martino, 'Here in My Heart'
5. Don Cornell, 'Hold My Hand'

6. Alma Cogan, 'Dreamboat'
7. Dickie Valentine, 'Mr Sandman'
8. Jimmy Young, 'Unchained Melody'
9. Kay Starr, 'Comes a Long a Love'
10. Mario Lanza, 'Because You're Mine'
11. David Whitfield, 'Answer Me'
12. Rosemary Clooney, 'Half As Much'
13. Ronnie Hilton, 'I Still Believe'
14. Perry Como, 'Wanted'
15. Ruby Murray, 'Softly Softly'
16. Frank Sinatra, 'Three Coins in the Fountain'
17. Guy Mitchell, 'Look at That Girl'
18. Frankie Laine, 'I Believe'
19. Doris Day, 'Secret Love'
20. Slim Whitman, 'Rose Marie'

☐ Breakin' the Chains: the blues

The blues, as emotions, are so called because possibly the worst job African slaves could be given was to unload the cargoes of indigo dye from the trading ships, which left them with indigo-stained bodies. It is also the origin of the term 'mood indigo'. The blues, as a musical style, was developed by those same slaves on the American plantations and homesteads where they worked. The (usually) sad songs started in the eighteenth century as field hollers, or call-and-response songs, and developed into songs typically performed by just voice and guitar. The call-and-response style was retained in the AAB lyric pattern common to many blues songs.

Any area of America with a high percentage of blacks was sure to have blues musicians, but certain areas, like the Mississippi Delta, turned out more than their fair share of classic blues. In the first few decades of the twentieth century blues were spread throughout the United States by the advent of radio and recording. The interest of John and Alan Lomax in cataloguing American folk music also helped.

There have been several 'blues revivals', notably in the late Sixties, when many bands played a rock-blues fusion.

1. Robert Johnson, 'Terraplane Blues'
2. Elmore James, 'Dust My Broom'
3. John Lee Hooker, 'Boogie Chillun No. 2'
4. Howlin' Wolf, 'Howlin' for My Baby'
5. Little Walter, 'Juke'
6. Screaming Jay Hawkins, 'I Put a Spell on You'
7. Muddy Waters, 'I'm a Man'
8. Son House, 'Death Letter'
9. Big Joe Williams, 'Baby Please Don't Go'
10. Otis Rush, 'Three Times a Fool'
11. Lightning Hopkins, 'Big Mama Jump'
12. Mississippi Jook Band, 'Dangerous Woman'
13. Willie Dixon, 'Little Red Rooster'
14. Bobby Bland, 'Ain't No Love in the Heart of the City'
15. Little Milton, 'Blind Man'
16. Sonny Boy Williamson, 'Bring It On Home'
17. Jimmy Reed, 'Big Legged Woman'
18. Cream, 'Crossroads'
19. Savoy Brown, 'Train to Nowhere'
20. Robert Cray, 'The Grinder'

☐ Blowin' up a Storm: jazz

While the blues were emerging in America a very close cousin was also stirring, particularly in areas like New Orleans and Chicago. Jazz was a more syncopated music than the blues, the lyrics were less important and the instrumentation was more reliant on woodwind and piano. The word jazz is from the Creole French *chasse beaux* (beau chaser), a dandy who chased away all the other prospective suitors (beaus). This became jassbo, then jass, and finally jazz. One of the hotbeds for jazz in the early part of the twentieth century was the Storeyville district of New Orleans. Traditionally the city's red light area, Storeyville would taint jazz with the same seedy image and it was some time before it gained any respectability with whites – and even then it was in the much watered down form of 'swing'.

There were several major styles of jazz. Dixieland, aka Dixie, was the style that developed in the southern states in general and in New Orleans in particular around 1900. Some say the area is known as Dixieland because it lies south of the Mason-Dixon line, which divided the slave and free states during the Civil War. Boogie Woogie, aka Boogie, was the style best suited to piano and the most closely related to the blues. A constant bass riff is pounded out with the left hand while the right provides the melody. It was popular in the Twenties and its leading exponent was Clarence 'Pinetop' Smith, who is often credited with coining the term, though other sources say it developed from Booger Rooger, a term used by Blind Lemon Jefferson in 'Booger Rooger Blues'. Bebop, aka Bop, aka Rebop, developed in the mid-to late-Forties as a reaction to the rather staid and rigid structure of swing, which was then popular. Bebop is by far the most free-form jazz style and its masters include jazz greats like Charlie 'Bird' Parker, Dizzy Gillespie and Miles Davis.

1. Original Dixieland Jass Band, 'Darktown Strutters Ball'
2. Billie Holiday, 'Strange Fruit'
3. Charlie Parker, 'Hootie's Blues'
4. Coleman Hawkins, 'In a Mellow Tone'
5. Bix Beiderbecke, 'I'm Coming Virginia'
6. Dave Brubeck, 'Take Five'
7. Louis Armstrong, 'Tiger Rag'
8. Woody Herman, 'Cousins'
9. Cab Calloway, 'The Jumpin' Jive'
10. Benny Goodman, 'King Porter Stomp'
11. Art Pepper, 'Round Midnight'
12. Count Basie, 'The King'
13. Ella Fitzgerald, 'Cabin in the Sky'
14. Thelonious Monk, 'Straight No Chaser'
15. Gil Evans, 'Sketches of Spain'
16. John Coltrane, 'Giant Steps'
17. Duke Ellington, 'Take the "A" Train'
18. Cannonball Adderly, 'Mercy Mercy Mercy'
19. Stan Getz and Charlie Byrd, 'Desafinado'
20. Courtney Pine, 'Big Nick'

□ Shape of Things to Come: rhythm and blues

Somewhere along the line the blues got touched by the more percussive and faster jazz rhythms and became, naturally enough, rhythm and blues. Like the blues and, to a certain extent, jazz, R&B was essentially black or race music and it was decried by the self-appointed guardians of America's WASP (White Anglo Saxon Protestant) society. Fortunately, there were plenty of radio stations in the early Fifties that were prepared to play R&B records.

Though almost all the original performers were black, their audience was very mixed and by the mid-Fifties numerous white acts were covering R&B songs. R&B sparked the rock 'n' roll explosion and then promptly shot off at a completely different tangent, developing in the Sixties into soul and the root of all black dance music.

Another spin-off of R&B in the Fifties was what we now know as doo wop (after a common vocal phrase used in such songs). This was a style of harmonized singing (often unaccompanied by instruments) from a small group of singers using their voices for rhythm as well as melody. The original doo wop groups were black, but they spawned their white imitators particularly from American cities' Italian communities.

1. Big Joe Turner, 'Shake Rattle and Roll'
2. Jackie Brenston, 'Rocket 88'
3. Merille Moore, 'House of Blue Lights'
4. Bo Diddley, 'Hey Bo Diddley'
5. Bobby Charles, 'See You Later Alligator'
6. Fats Domino, 'Walkin' to New Orleans'
7. Robins, 'Riot in Cell Block No. 9'
8. Ray Charles, 'Hit the Road Jack'
9. Roy Brown, 'Good Rockin' Tonite'
10. Moonglows, 'Sincerely'
11. Clovers, 'One Mint Julep'
12. Amos Milburn, 'One Scotch One Bourbon One Beer'
13. Jodimars, 'Well Now Dig This'

14. Treniers, 'Rockin' Is Our Business'
15. Dominos, 'Sixty Minute Man'
16. Arthur Crudup, 'That's Alright Mama'
17. Platters, 'Only You'
18. Big Mama Thornton, 'Hound Dog'
19. Penguins, 'Earth Angel'
20. Dion, 'The Wanderer'

Jackie Brenston's 'Rocket 88' is widely regarded as the first rock 'n' roll record. Brenston is the featured vocalist, though the band was in fact Ike Turner's Rhythm Kings, for which Brenston normally played saxophone.

☐ The Other Side of the Tracks: country and western

While American blacks were bringing us the blues and dancing the Lindy Hop, their white counterparts were dancing at their hoe-downs to the sound of country and western music. The music, often known just as country, or as hillbilly, developed out of the traditional ballads and folk songs that the British took to America when they settled there in the seventeenth century. The music relies heavily on stringed instruments such as the fiddle, steel guitar and banjo, and, like most forms of popular music, borrows from the blues. It emerged in the south-eastern states and while many areas developed their own brand of C&W, such as honky tonk and bluegrass, Nashville became the country music centre of America and eventually the world. Country music rose to national popularity in the US in the Twenties thanks to radio and the growth of record markets plus the artists who toured the country.

Rock 'n' roll drew on many country influences but never overwhelmed the style. Many rock 'n' rollers, including Jerry Lee Lewis, have returned to their original style and are playing C&W again. In the Sixties rock flirted with country and started a relationship that continues to this day with people like Steve Earle and Dwight Yoakam.

1. Hank Williams, 'Your Cheating Heart'
2. Carter Family, 'Wildwood Flower'
3. Jimmie Rodgers, 'Blue Yodel'
4. Johnny Cash, 'I Walk the Line'
5. Merle Haggard, 'All My Friends (Are Gonna Be Strangers)'
6. Loretta Lynn, 'Coal Miner's Daughter'
7. Kenny Rogers, 'The Gambler'
8. Bill Monroe, 'Blue Moon of Kentucky'
9. Jim Reeves, 'He'll Have to Go'
10. Patsy Cline, 'Crazy'
11. Willie Nelson, 'On the Road Again'
12. Carlene Carter, 'Ring of Fire'
13. George Jones, 'Stranger in the House'
14. Marty Robbins, 'El Paso'
15. Billy Jo Spears, ''57 Chevrolet'
16. Roy Acuff, 'Wabash Cannonball'
17. Jerry Lee Lewis, 'Chantilly Lace'
18. Waylon Jennings, 'Amanda'
19. Steve Earle, 'I Ain't Ever Satisfied'
20. Elvis Costello, 'Good Year for the Roses'

☐ South's Gonna Rise Again: rockabilly

Sun Studios in Memphis, Tennessee, were the birthplace of practically all the prime rockabilly to emerge in the Fifties. Memphis had a large black community and there were ample opportunities to hear the blues and R&B on local radio stations and, as Tennessee was one of the strong country and western states, it was the ideal spawning ground for the hillbilly/R&B fusion that was rockabilly.

Rockabilly was, by a matter of months, a forerunner of rock 'n' roll, similar in style, but with the country influence showing. It featured acoustic rhythm guitars, slap basses, lots of echo and yelping, gulping, stuttering, hiccuping vocals.

Many of the original rockabilly artists drifted into more mainstream rock 'n' roll, others moved into conventional country. Rockabilly became a very low-key affair after the end of the Fifties, though it enjoyed great popularity in the north of England in the early Sixties, actually helping start what would become the famed northern soul scene. Then, in the wake of punk, a rockabilly revival raised its quiff again in England.

1. Elvis Presley, 'That's Alright Mama'
2. Carl Perkins, 'Matchbox'
3. Johnny Burnette Trio, 'Tear It Up'
4. Peanuts Wilson, 'Cast Iron Arm'
5. Jerry Byrne, 'Lights Out'
6. Eddie Cochran, 'Skinny Jim'
7. Joe Turner, 'Honey Hush'
8. Buddy Holly, 'Rock Around with Ollie Vee'
9. Roy Orbison, 'Devil Doll'
10. Ronnie Hawkins, 'Forty Days'
11. Sleepy LaBeef, 'Too Much Monkey Business'
12. Mac Curtis, 'Ducktail'
13. Buddy Knox, 'Party Doll'
14. Billy Lee Riley, 'Red Hot'
15. Warren Smith, 'Ubangi Stomp'
16. Jimmy Elliss, 'Blue Moon of Kentucky'
17. Hank Mizell, 'Jungle Rock'
18. Wanda Jackson, 'Party'
19. Dave Edmunds, 'Baby Let's Play House'
20. Stray Cats, 'Rock This Town'

□ The World Explodes: the birth of rock 'n' roll

To American blacks in the early Fifties rock 'n' roll was just a euphemism for sex. Several R&B records had used the term to this end and it was through hearing these songs that Bill Haley innocently used the lines 'Rock, rock, rock everybody, Roll, roll, roll everybody' to open his song 'Rock-A-Beatin' Boogie'. The Treniers recorded the song and DJ Alan Freed played it and eventually adopted the words rock and roll to describe the new music that Haley and others were now playing. Of course, to those playing this hybrid of R&B and hillbilly it probably didn't sound all that new, but to America's teenagers, closely followed by others all around the world, it was unlike anything they knew.

It developed simultaneously in several areas, notably Memphis (Presley, Lewis) and Texas (Holly). For three to four years it took the music world between its teeth and shook hard. However, once the business moguls had come to terms with it, rock and roll (or rock 'n' roll) became bland and sanitized. The spontaneous excitement of 1955 and 1956 was soon just a memory but a new era of popular music had just begun; rock 'n' roll really was here to stay.

1. Elvis Presley, 'Jailhouse Rock'
2. Gene Vincent, 'Bluejean Bop'
3. Jerry Lee Lewis, 'Great Balls of Fire'
4. Buddy Holly, 'Rave On'
5. Little Richard, 'Tutti Frutti'
6. Bill Haley and his Comets, 'Rock around the Clock'
7. Eddie Cochran, 'Somethin' Else'
8. Rick Nelson, 'It's Late'
9. Chuck Berry, 'Johnny B. Goode'
10. Larry Williams, 'Slow Down'
11. Danny and the Juniors, 'At the Hop'
12. Everly Brothers, 'Bird Dog'
13. Cliff Richard, 'Move It'
14. Johnny Restivo, 'The Shape I'm In'
15. Johnny Burnette Trio, 'Honey Hush'
16. Johnny Kidd and the Pirates, 'Shakin' All Over'
17. Lloyd Price, 'Stagger Lee'
18. Eddie Fontaine, 'Nothing Shakin' but the Leaves on the Trees'
19. Gary 'US' Bonds, 'New Orleans'
20. Tommy Steele, 'Rock with the Caveman'

☐ Washboard Folk: skiffle and the US folk revival

While rock 'n' roll was establishing itself around the world two strains of another type of music were enjoying a purple patch on opposite sides of the Atlantic. In America folk music, the social history of the country in song, was enjoying a revival by some of the more socially and politically aware musicians. Songs about the working man were traditionally performed by the so-called jug bands (who did use a jug, as well as anything else that came to hand, as part of their instrumentation).

In the UK a similar strain of music, though more closely related to hillbilly and rock 'n' roll, was inducing hundreds of kids to form their own bands. Skiffle was performed using the acoustic guitar, a tea chest bass (basically a piece of string stretched between a broom handle and an upturned tea chest on which the handle stood) and a washboard played with thimbles. Any other instrument was a luxury. Skiffle was first performed in the UK by certain jazz musicians (for example, Lonnie Donegan from Chris Barber's Jazz Band) playing blues and American folk music; soon the nation was alive to the sound of skiffle. Many future UK pop stars started out as skifflers: John Lennon, Paul McCartney and George Harrison were all in the skiffle group the Quarrymen; Adam Faith was in the Worried Men, and Helen Shapiro and Marc Bolan supposedly played together in Suzy and the Hula Hoops.

1. Huddie Leadbetter, 'Rock Island Line'
2. Lonnie Donegan, 'Lost John'
3. Johnny Duncan and his Bluegrass Boys, 'Last Train to San Fernando'
4. Vipers, 'Don't You Rock Me Daddy O'
5. Woody Guthrie, 'This Land Is Your Land'
6. Nancy Whisky and Chas McDevitt, 'Freight Train'
7. Kingston Trio, 'Tom Dooley'
8. Ken Colyer's Skiffle Group, 'The Grey Goose'
9. Morris and Mitch, 'What Is a Skiffler'
10. Don Lang and his Frantic Five, '6'5 Special'

11. Beryl Bryden's Backroom Skiffle, 'Kansas City'
12. Bob Cort Skiffle, 'Schooldays (Ring Ring Goes the Bell)'
13. Weavers, 'Goodnight Irene'
14. Ramblin' Jack Elliot, 'Black Snake Moan'
15. Alan Lomax, 'Dirty Old Town'
16. Pete Seeger, 'If I had a Hammer'
17. Alexis Korner's Skiffle, 'Death Letter'
18. Brothers Four, 'Greenfields'
19. Blue Jeans Skiffle, 'Lonesome Traveller'
20. Shakin' Pyramids, 'Take a Trip'

☐ Teenage Dreaming: pop between Elvis and the Beatles

By the end of the Fifties rock 'n' roll had established itself as the undisputed music of the young. The music business had quickly cottoned on and pop music was now being tailored to suit many varied demands. Rock 'n' roll was a very fast, sometimes aggressive music, and lighter styles were needed. What we got, mostly from America though Europe did follow suit, was a plethora of pop that ranged from classic three-minute pop songs (for example, Del Shannon's 'Runaway') to bland white covers of rock 'n' roll and R&B (such as Pat Boone's 'Ain't That A Shame'). In some areas it was a continuation of the vocal style of doo wop that gave us harmony groups like the Four Seasons and Phil Spector's entourage. Spector's production genius made him the master of the whole 'girl group' sound. Then there were dance crazes like the Twist, Brill Building song-writers like Goffin and King, death discs and much more.

Though there were several good, great and classic songs from the era (see twenty of the better ones below), much of the music was insipid and uninspiring (who ever cites Bobby Vinton as an influence?). It was to be the way the music scene remained until late 1962, when Liverpool had something to say.

1. Del Shannon, 'Runaway'
2. Shangri Las, 'Leader of the Pack'
3. Little Eva, 'The Locomotion'
4. Neil Sedaka, 'Breakin' Up Is Hard to Do'
5. Bonnie and the Treasures, 'Home of the Brave'
6. Johnny Tillotson, 'Poetry in Motion'
7. Kalin Twins, 'When'
8. Four Seasons, 'Big Girls Don't Cry'
9. Dixie Cups, 'Chapel of Love'
10. Chubby Checker, 'The Twist'
11. Helen Shapiro, 'Walking Back to Happiness'
12. Barrett Strong, 'Money'
13. Dee Dee Sharp, 'Ride'
14. Cliff Richard, 'Please Don't Tease'
15. Ray Peterson, 'Tell Laura I Love Her'
16. Crystals, 'Da Doo Ron Ron'
17. Bobby Vee, 'Take Good Care of My Baby'
18. Jarmels, 'A Little Bit of Soap'
19. Kathy Young and the Innocents, 'A Thousand Stars'
20. Little Peggy March, 'I Will Follow Him'

□ And the Word Is Shazam: rock instrumentals from the Fifties and early Sixties

As the Sixties dawned, a new breed of rock group emerged, often stepping out from behind a singer to become a band in its own right. These bands (perhaps because none of them could sing) relied on their instrumental virtuosity and simple riffs, rhythms and melodies to produce a new sound – the rock instrumental.

The sound, common to the UK and US, was typically guitar orientated, usually twangy or trebly, clearly plucked notes rather than fuzzy chords. Other instruments, such as the sax, organ and piano, played major roles on certain records. All the top groups adopted their own style and were instantly recognized. A common trick was to 'rock-up' a classical or traditional piece.

Even today there are the occasional rock instrumentals, but they are usually film and TV themes, boring instrumental B sides of vocal A sides or showcases for the prowess of a particular musician – a ten-minute guitar solo on a heavy metal LP. The instrumental we mean was all but dead by 1966 (surf instrumentals excluded; they are dealt with on p. 268). Only Lieutenant Pigeon's 'Mouldy Ole Dough', Terry Dactyl's 'Seaside Shuffle' and Popcorn's 'Hot Butter' spring to mind as being in the spirit of this Sixties style.

1. Shadows, 'Shazam'
2. Ventures, 'Walk Don't Run'
3. Duane Eddy, 'Forty Miles of Bad Road'
4. Johnny & the Hurricanes, 'Beatnik Fly'
5. Tornados, 'Telstar'
6. Bill Justis, 'Raunchy'
7. Sandy Nelson, 'Let There Be Drums'
8. Piltdown Men, 'Piltdown Rides Again'
9. Cougars, 'Saturday Night at the Duckpond'
10. Floyd Cramer, 'On the Rebound'
11. Outlaws, 'Ambush'
12. Duals, 'Stick Shift'
13. Nero and the Gladiators, 'Entry of the Gladiators'
14. Flee Rekkers, 'Green Jeans'
15. Rockateens, 'Woo Hoo'
16. Dave 'Baby' Cortez, 'Happy Organ'
17. Phil Upchurch Combo, 'You Can't Sit Down'
18. Bill Black's Combo, 'Don't Be Cruel'
19. 'Boots' Randolph, 'Yakety Sax'
20. Eddie Cochran, 'Strollin' Guitar'

The Outlaws included both Chas Hodges (Chas and Dave), and Richie Blackmore (Deep Purple and Rainbow).

☐ Surfin' through the Pipeline to Success: surf music

Surfing is the sport of riding incoming waves on a board. It's popular in Australia and has become big in Cornwall, but the spiritual home of surfing is in southern California. A whole culture and life-style grew around surfing in the Fifties. It developed its own language, full of wonderful phrases like 'hang five', 'goofy foot' and 'wipe out'. The stereotyped surfer was the sun-bleached blond beach bum who surfed all day and hung out at beach parties all night. He would have a woody (car) and no doubt be surrounded by several bikini-clad girls.

In the early Sixties surfing also developed its own music. In the first place it was racing instrumentals of rapid fire guitar and staccato drumming with titles full of surf jargon. Later, another type of surf music was that performed by the Beach Boys and their cohorts: harmonized vocals with lyrics about surfing. Both strains of the music ran happily side by side for a few short years in the early Sixties.

The early Eighties saw something of a minor surf revival in the US and UK. The instrumental side was revisited by bands like Jon and the Nightriders, while the Barracudas put a harsher edge on the vocals.

1. Dick Dale, 'Let's Go Trippin''
2. Beach Boys, 'Surfin' Safari'
3. Surfaris, 'Wipe Out'
4. Jan and Dean, 'Ride Ride Ride the Wild Surf'
5. Catalinas, 'Banzai Washout'
6. Fantastic Baggies, 'Tell 'Em I'm Surfin''
7. Marketts, 'Surfer's Stomp'
8. Honeys, 'Surfin' Down the Swanee River'
9. Sunrays, 'I Live for the Sun'
10. Survivors, 'Pamela Jean'
11. Bel Airs, 'Mr Moto'
12. Busters, 'Bust Out'
13. Chantays, 'Pipeline'
14. Trashmen, 'Surfin' Bird'
15. Jon and the Nightriders, 'Rumble at Waikiki'

16. Barracudas, 'I Want My Woody Back'
17. Astronauts, 'Baja'
18. Likely Ones, 'Walkin' the Board'
19. Surfmen, 'Paradise Cove'
20. Rip Chords, 'Three Window Coupe'

☐ All Eyes on Liverpool: Merseybeat

Britain was fast to catch on to rock 'n' roll in the late Fifties and many groups sprang up around the country. Liverpool had more than its fair share because it was a major port with direct links to places such as New Orleans, so Liverpudlians had easier access to R&B and other discs from these American cities. Thanks to local entrepreneur Allan Williams, many of the young rock 'n' roll groups in Liverpool were able to go and play in the night-clubs of Hamburg, where a distinctive Merseybeat sound developed. The bands returned from Hamburg to the 'Pool amidst great receptions at clubs like the Cavern and the Iron Door, and then . . . Well it wasn't quite the overnight success history seems to make it. Many singles were released by Mersey bands before the upper realms of the chart were ever conquered. Even the Beatles' first single for Parlophone in 1962 stopped short at Number Seventeen. By mid-1963 however Merseybeat and Beatlemania headlines were splashed all over the music and national press. A year later America, its defences already undermined from within by the likes of Bobby Vinton, yielded. The second age of rock 'n' roll had begun.

1. Beatles, 'She Loves You'
2. Gerry and the Pacemakers, 'How Do You Do It'
3. Searchers, 'Don't Throw Your Love Away'
4. Swinging Blue Jeans, 'Hippy Hippy Shake'
5. Big Three, 'Some Other Guy'
6. Fourmost, 'Hello Little Girl'
7. Billy J. Kramer and the Dakotas, 'Bad To Me'
8. Merseybeats, 'I Think of You'
9. Mojos, 'Everything's Alright'

10. Rory Storme and the Hurricanes, 'America'
11. Dennisons, 'Walking the Dog'
12. Escorts, 'The One to Cry'
13. Faron's Flamingos, 'Let's Stomp'
14. Kubas, 'I Love Her'
15. Undertakers, 'Just A Little Bit'
16. Howie Casie and the Seniors, 'Bonie Maronie'
17. Freddie Starr and the Midnighters, 'It's Shakin' Time'
18. Pete Best Four, 'I'm Gonna Knock On Your Door'
19. Nomads, 'My Whole Life Through'
20. Casey Jones and the Governors, 'Lucille'

Rory Storme's 'America' is the only record produced by Brian Epstein, the man who managed the Beatles and many other Mersey stars.

□ Blues Rumblings in the Smoke: the R&B revival

Three main factors could be held responsible for the blues and R&B revival that spawned bands like the Rolling Stones and the Yardbirds: firstly, the close affinity between jazz and blues led to a number of jazz bandleaders and club owners bringing American blues stars over to the UK; secondly, a number of former jazz musicians – such as Cyril Davies and Alexis Korner – began playing the blues; finally, a number of young fans of R&B records by the likes of Chuck Berry and Bo Diddley began watching the visiting US stars and their UK counterparts and set about forming their own bands.

While Liverpool was developing its distinct Merseybeat style, London became the focal point for the R&B renaissance. Clubs like the Flamingo and the Marquee showcased the visiting US singers, and the British house bands were the training ground for several UK musicians. The new bands became popular with London Mods (along with original R&B and, later, soul) and gained fervent followings. Perhaps the most important band was John Mayall's Bluesbreakers, who stayed faithful to the blues while the other bands strayed into more commercial territories. Among the musicians who passed through the ranks of Mayall's bands were Eric Clapton, Peter Green, Mick Fleetwood, Keef Hartley, Andy Fraser and Jack Bruce.

The R&B revival was an important stepping stone in the path of rock 'n' roll, as it helped start the US garage band scene and laid the foundations of progressive rock and heavy metal.

1. Cyril Davies All Stars, 'Preachin' the Blues'
2. Rolling Stones, '(Get Your Kicks on) Route 66'
3. John Mayall's Bluesbreakers, 'I'm Your Witch Doctor'
4. Yardbirds, 'Smokestack Lightning'
5. Manfred Mann, 'Got My Mojo Working'
6. Animals, 'Bring It On Home'
7. Alexis Korner's Blues Incorporated, 'Stormy Monday'
8. Kinks, 'You Really Got Me'
9. Georgie Fame, 'Yeh Yeh'
10. Pretty Things, 'Rosalyn'
11. Chris Farlowe and the Thunderbirds, 'Buzz with the Fuzz'
12. Small Faces, 'What 'cha Gonna Do about It'
13. Steampacket, 'Can I Get a Witness'
14. Who, 'My Generation'
15. Graham Bond Organization, 'Wade in the Water'
16. Long John Baldry, 'Goodbye Baby'
17. The Zoot Money Big Roll Band, 'Something Is Worrying Me'
18. Spencer Davis Group, 'Every Little Bit Hurts'
19. Shotgun Express, 'I Could Feel the Whole World Turn Around'
20. Gary Farr and the T Bones, 'C. C. Rider'

Chris Farlowe, whose biggest chart success came with a cover of Jagger and Richards' 'Out of Time', is now a keen collector and dealer of Nazi memorabilia.

Gary Farr's father, Tommy, was a well-known boxer and once fought Joe Louis.

☐ Return of the Balladeer: the big voices

Although the Sixties was the decade in which rock music found its feet and started to run in several new directions, it was also the era that saw the big voices of the balladeers return to power. Theirs was a music that could appeal to people right across the board from mum to son, gran to grandson; sentimental songs sung with gusto and emotion by cabaret type artists (with some exceptions). Few of the balladeers had survived from the pre-rock era – only Sinatra came through with all guns blazing. The new breed came from a variety of sources: Jones was ex-beat group, Reeves was out of country and western, Baldry was British blues, Black was from the Mersey scene, Orbison was a Sun rocker, and so on.

Many of them crossed over to television and got their own 'family entertainment' shows. Others blazed the Las Vegas trail and earned mega-bucks for a handful of sequin and sweat concerts. Some are still doing it today and if Tom Jones and Dusty Springfield can appeal to the youth of the Eighties, who can knock them?

1. Frank Sinatra, 'Strangers in the Night'
2. Dusty Springfield, 'You Don't Have to Say You Love Me'
3. Tom Jones, 'Green Green Grass of Home'
4. Tony Bennett, 'I Left My Heart in San Francisco'
5. Shirley Bassey, 'Goldfinger'
6. Cilla Black, 'Alfie'
7. Dionne Warwick, 'Anyone Who Had a Heart'
8. Engelbert Humperdinck, 'Please Release Me'
9. Louis Armstrong, 'Wonderful World'
10. Lulu, 'To Sir with Love'
11. Roy Orbison, 'Only the Lonely'
12. Jim Reeves, 'Distant Drums'
13. Gene Pitney, 'Twenty-four Hours from Tulsa'
14. Long John Baldry, 'Let the Heartaches Begin'
15. Petula Clark, 'Downtown'
16. Val Doonican, 'Elusive Butterfly'
17. Julie Rogers, 'The Wedding'
18. Roger Whittaker, 'Durham Town'
19. Matt Monro, 'From Russia with Love'
20. Elvis Presley, 'It's Now or Never'

□ Motor City Music: the growth of soul and Motown

Soul, as a classification of music, was first used by jazz fans and musicians in the mid-Fifties to describe a movement to make jazz more 'black'. By the Sixties, however, it was in use to describe the gospel/R&B hybrid that was coming out of all of America's black areas. Most of the soul acts (nearly all black in those earliest days) had cut their teeth in R&B and doo wop bands. Many had had a strict religious upbringing that introduced them to the joys of gospel singing at an early age.

The music was emotive, and perfect dance music whether for slow smooching or fast boppin'. Soul was epitomized by the Motown label based in Detroit. Berry Gordy started the label in the late Fifties, releasing R&B records, but by the Sixties Motown and Gordy's other associated labels had developed their own distinctive sound thanks to a somewhat production-line style of creating a record. Teams of song-writers (notably Holland, Dozier and Holland) and producers tried to create a record that would sound its best coming through the tiny tinny speakers of a transistor radio. Motown had smash hit after smash hit, particularly in the States, but also across the world. The organization is still going strong today. The other major soul label of the era was Stax Records in Memphis.

1. James Brown and his Famous Flames, 'Papa's Got a Brand New Bag'
2. Supremes, 'Back in My Arms Again'
3. Martha Reeves and the Vandellas, 'Nowhere to Run'
4. Otis Redding, 'Respect'
5. Booker T and the MGs, 'Green Onions'
6. Marvin Gaye, 'How Sweet It Is to Be Loved by You'
7. Joe Tex, 'Hold What You've Got'
8. Smokey Robinson and the Miracles, 'Tears of a Clown'
9. Four Tops, 'Walk Away Renée'
10. Little Stevie Wonder, 'Fingertips Part 2'
11. Aretha Franklin, 'Chain of Fools'
12. Junior Walker and the All Stars, '(I'm a) Roadrunner'

13. Robert Parker, 'Barefootin''
14. Sam and Dave, 'Hold On I'm Comin''
15. Sam Cooke, 'You Send Me'
16. Fontella Bass, 'Rescue Me'
17. Wilson Pickett, 'Mustang Sally'
18. Edwin Starr, 'War'
19. Temptations, 'My Girl'
20. Eddie Floyd, 'Knock on Wood'

☐ America Bites Back: American Sixties pop

In 1964 the Beatles broke America and were followed by countless other bands in what became known as the British invasion. The Americans loved bands like the Dave Clark 5 and Herman's Hermits. They were inspired to form their own groups, while established groups found renewed enthusiasm, and the American kickback began. It took two paths: some groups stepped out of the garages where they rehearsed and (obviously affected by carbon monoxide poisoning) began pounding out their Farfisa-fired freakbeat garage punk (see pp. 276–7) – more Rolling Stones than Beatles; and the other bands took what would prove a more commercial path. There were many diversities in the sound but all were basically Beatles-influenced guitar groups singing with lots of harmonies. There were exceptions, of course, such as the soulful Righteous Brothers, responsible for one of the greatest pop singles ever.

1. Monkees, 'Last Train to Clarksville'
2. Righteous Brothers, 'You've Lost That Lovin' Feeling'
3. Bobby Fuller Four, 'I Fought the Law'
4. Paul Revere and the Raiders, 'Kicks'
5. Turtles, 'Elenore'
6. Lovin' Spoonful, 'Do You Believe in Magic'
7. Sir Douglas Quintet, 'She's about a Mover'
8. Beau Brummels, 'Laugh Laugh'
9. Association, 'Along Comes Mary'

10. Walker Brothers, 'The Sun Ain't Gonna Shine Anymore'
11. Box Tops, 'The Letter'
12. Byrds, 'Mr Tambourine Man'
13. McCoys, 'Hang On Sloopy'
14. Tommy James and the Shondells, 'Mony Mony'
15. Strawberry Alarm Clock, 'Incense And Peppermints'
16. Knickerbockers, 'Lies'
17. Gary Puckett and the Union Gap, 'Young Girl'
18. Jay and the Americans, 'Come a Little Bit Closer'
19. Jackie DeShannon, 'When You Walk in the Room'
20. Sonny and Cher, 'I Got You Babe'

☐ In the Wake of the Mop Tops: British pop post-Merseybeat

The Mersey explosion and the R&B scene emanating predominantly from London brought a new age to British pop. Soon bands were springing up all over the country, not just the established centres like Liverpool and London. Suddenly places like Kent, Hampshire and Norfolk became hotbeds of beat groups (Norwich probably had more bands than it had pubs and churches combined in the mid-Sixties). The sound was fairly standard – guitars, bass and drums, catchy verse-chorus-verse three-minute pop songs.

Many of the new groups marched on America in the footsteps of the Beatles. Many of them were predicted as being the group who would topple the Beatles from the pop throne. The Dave Clark 5 were hot favourites, promoting banner headlines like 'Tottenham sound to crush Mersey sound'. Although the bands listed below mostly managed prolonged success, for each of them there were dozens of one-hit wonders, hundreds of bands who made records but never made the charts and thousands of bands who didn't even record. It was probably the most active time ever in British pop.

1. Zombies, 'She's Not There'
2. Hollies, 'I'm Alive'

3. Dave Clark 5, 'Glad All Over'
4. Move, 'Blackberry Way'
5. Dave, Dee, Dozy, Beaky, Mick and Tich, 'Legend of Xanadu'
6. Troggs, 'I Can't Control Myself'
7. Wayne Fontana and the Mindbenders, 'Game of Love'
8. Unit 4 + 2, 'Concrete and Clay'
9. Bern Elliot and the Fenmen, 'Money'
10. Honeycombs, 'Have I the Right'
11. Herman's Hermits, 'Silhouettes'
12. Cliff Bennett and the Rebel Rousers, 'One Way Love'
13. Status Quo, 'Pictures of Matchstick Men'
14. Mindbenders, 'A Groovy Kind of Love'
15. Amen Corner, '(If Paradise Is) Half As Nice'
16. Moody Blues, 'Go Now'
17. Them, 'Here Comes the Night'
18. Equals, 'Baby Come Back'
19. Freddie and the Dreamers, 'If You Gotta Make a Fool of Somebody'
20. Fortunes, 'Caroline'

☐ Garage Guys Go Groovin': American mid-Sixties garage punk

Garage punk was part of the US kickback against the British invasion. The garage tag derives from the fact that it was normally the garage (large double and treble sized garages in suburban America) where the bands rehearsed; the punk bit comes from the American use of the word to mean a young ruffian or hoodlum. Presumably the long-haired, jean-clad purveyors of Rolling Stones songs resembled every parent's vision of a lout. The expression would later be used to describe an even more loutish music of course.

The standard hardware of the garage band was a guitar or two, a Farfisa organ, bass and drums, and a Jaggeresque vocalist. The songs were often covers of British beat songs or other pop standards played by groups all over the country. There was a cross-over with psychedelic music later in the decade, with many of the groups playing a lightweight pop-psych music. Many of these groups' performances can be seen today thanks to countless cameo appearances in American B movies of the period. There was also a plethora of recorded music from the era, as can be gauged from the numerous re-issue series like Pebbles and Nuggets.

1. Shadows of Knight, 'Gloria'
2. Seeds, 'Pushin' Too Hard'
3. Standells, 'Dirty Water'
4. Count 5, 'Psychotic Reaction'
5. Music Machine, 'Talk Talk'
6. Kingsmen, 'Louie Louie'
7. Leaves, 'Hey Joe'
8. Mouse and the Traps, 'A Public Execution'
9. Brogues, '(I'm Not a) Miracle Worker'
10. ? & the Mysterians, '96 Tears'
11. Syndicate of Sound, 'Little Girl'
12. Remains, 'Don't Look Back'
13. Cryan Shames, 'It Could Be We're in Love'
14. Terry Knight and the Pack, 'You're a Better Man Than I'
15. Outsiders, 'Time Won't Let Me'
16. Novas, 'The Crusher'
17. Cannibal and the Headhunters, 'Land of 1,000 Dances'
18. Swinging Medallions, 'Double Shot of My Baby's Love'
19. Castaways, 'Liar Liar'
20. Hombres, 'Let It All Hang Out'

☐ Living inside Your Brain: psychedelic music

The word 'psychedelic' is Greek for 'making the soul clear', but it came to mean 'mind expanding'. The psychedelic age came about because of the development of lysergic acid diethylamide, more commonly LSD, a powerful hallucinogenic drug. It sent the taker into another world, often with wild hallucinations. Though LSD may have been hedonistically addictive, it didn't create the physical dependency that heroin and other drugs do. Until it was outlawed in October 1966 many writers and artists used it for pleasure and inspiration. Musicians, too, began to experiment with LSD, swiftly followed by their audience.

Psychedelic music and its accompanying light shows were, depending on whom you ask, either an attempt to aurally and visually emulate an 'acid' trip or simply a method of enhancing one. Psychedelia ranged from lightweight pop psychedelia (more closely related to garage punk or ordinary pop) to the progressive, heavy sound that would help shape the hard rock of the late Sixties. The sound was typified by fuzz-tone guitars, swirling musical phrases, esoteric lyrics (nonsense lyrics to many) and often certain Asian musical influences, such as the sitar. Groups like Pink Floyd also used many electronic effects. The majority of American psychedelic music came out of the Haight-Ashbury area of San Francisco. Spin-offs included psychedelic soul.

1. Jefferson Airplane, 'White Rabbit'
2. Beatles, 'Glass Onion'
3. Pink Floyd, 'Astronomy Domine'
4. Love, '7 and 7 Is'
5. Byrds, 'Eight Miles High'
6. Paul Kantner, 'Have You Seen the Stars Tonight'
7. 13th Floor Elevators, 'She Lives'
8. Grateful Dead, 'Dark Star'
9. Ambrose Dukes, 'Journey to the Center of My Mind'
10. Jimi Hendrix, 'Are You Experienced?'
11. Cream, 'Tales of Brave Ulysses'
12. Doors, 'Light My Fire'
13. Kaleidoscope, 'Flight from Ashiya'
14. Traffic, 'Paper Sun'
15. Crazy World of Arthur Brown, 'Fire'
16. Simon Dupree and the Big Sound, 'Kites'
17. Temptations, 'Psychedelic Shack'
18. Vanilla Fudge, 'Season of the Witch'
19. Lothar and the Hand People, 'Looking at the World through Rose-coloured Glasses'
20. Stranglers, 'Golden Brown'

☐ Music to Hang in the National Gallery: progressive rock

Progressive rock is practically the bridge between psychedelic and acid rock and early heavy metal, often overlapping with both. It was at its peak towards the end of the Sixties, and though many of the groups survived into the Seventies they often became more stylized and less innovative. Many took the jazz fusion root. Progressive rock was the first type of music to be seriously considered as an art form and this tended to lead to a lot of pompous concept LPs and suites of music with distinct classical pretensions. It was a long way from pop.

This was also the era that showed the first signs of stadium rock, with the groups playing at huge open-air concerts to thousands of fans enthralled by lengthy keyboard runs and guitar solos.

Although the bands did release singles, the album was the medium that best displayed their style – after all, twenty-minute singles are a pretty rare commodity.

1. Pink Floyd, 'Money'
2. Velvet Underground, 'Venus in Furs'
3. Van Der Graaf Generator, 'White Hammer'
4. Genesis, 'I Know What I Like in Your Wardrobe'
5. Doors, 'L. A. Woman'
6. Spirit, 'Uncle Jack'
7. Soft Machine, 'Moon in June'
8. Emerson, Lake and Palmer, 'Lucky Man'
9. King Crimson, '21st Century Schizoid Man'
10. Man, 'Scotch Corner'
11. Yes, 'Close to the Edge'
12. Gentle Giant, 'The Power and the Glory'
13. Jethro Tull, 'Living in the Past'
14. Blind Faith, 'Presence of the Lord'
15. Quicksilver Messenger Service, 'Who Do You Love'
16. Steve Miller Band, 'Living in the USA'
17. Gong, 'Flying Teapot'
18. Hatfield and the North, 'Let's Eat (Real Soon)'
19. Henry Cow, 'Bitter Storm Over Ulm'
20. Spooky Tooth, 'What's That Sound'

□ The Guitar Speaks Out: folk rock and protest singers

Amidst the turmoil of the Sixties – Beatlemania, Monkee-madness, etc. – a crowd of like-minded musicians, mostly based in Greenwich Village in New York City, had been listening to a more traditional American music, the folk music of Woody Guthrie and his ilk. These musicians began to emulate their heroes by writing their own songs and performing them in the clubs and coffee houses in the Village. However, as a generation that grew up with Elvis Presley and witnessed the British Invasion, it was inevitable that their own writing would be significantly different from that of their predecessors. Vietnam, of course, made a lot of difference to the spirit of the age.

The songs became known as protest songs, as they were anti-war and anti-establishment. The music was folk rock. In its early days it was often just a singer accompanied by his own acoustic guitar playing, but in the mid-Sixties a lot of folkies went electric, led of course by Dylan. Dylan, it is said, first picked up the electric guitar after hearing the Animals' version of 'House of the Rising Sun', a song the Animals recorded after hearing Dylan's version on his début LP.

By the mid-Seventies the differences between the folkies and the bedsit singer-song-writers were minimal. Bands like Steeleye Span continued to play their own rocked up version of traditional folk and the protest singer all but disappeared. Only in more recent years has the protest singer returned, with the rise of people like Billy Bragg and Phranc.

1. Bob Dylan, 'A Hard Rain's Gonna Fall'
2. Joan Baez, 'Diamonds and Rust'
3. Phil Ochs, 'Chords of Fame'
4. Tom Paxton, 'Talkin' Vietnam Pot Luck Blues'
5. Simon and Garfunkel, 'The Sound of Silence'
6. Barry McGuire, 'Eve of Destruction'
7. Fairport Convention, 'Now Be Thankful'
8. The Band, 'The Weight'
9. Richard and Linda Thompson, 'Walking on a Wire'
10. Buffalo Springfield, 'For What It's Worth'

11. Steeleye Span, 'Gaudette'
12. Donovan, 'Universal Soldier'
13. Peter, Paul and Mary, 'Blowin' in the Wind'
14. Strawbs, 'Part of the Union'
15. Proclaimers, 'Letter from America'
16. Billy Bragg, 'Between the Wars'
17. Redskins, 'Go Get Organized'
18. Andy White, 'Religious Persuasion'
19. Country Joe and the Fish, 'Feel Like I'm A Fixin' to Die Rag'
20. Mac Davis, 'In the Ghetto'

□ The Marriage of the Electric and the Steel Guitar: country rock

In the same way that American folk music had been rediscovered and reworked on a rock backcloth, it was perhaps inevitable that country music would undergo the same treatment. Country was (and is) the most popular music in terms of its total world audience, but had been looked at with contempt by most rock musicians, who were more attuned to the blues. However, in the late Sixties people like Bob Dylan and then the Byrds began to recognize country as one of the roots of rock, and began to move their own music in that direction.

Although country music had used electric guitars before, the rock bands played them in a way that gave country-rock a highly distinctive sound. The first wave of country-rockers were all established musicians who just altered their style of playing. However, many groups formed especially to play country-rock.

In the Seventies, although Dylan and some others drifted away from country into other areas, country-rock had established its niche in American music at least. One particular strain of country-rock in that decade was outlaw rock where established country musicians (like Willie Nelson and Waylon Jennings) worked with established rock musos.

1. Gram Parsons, 'In My Hour of Darkness'
2. Byrds, 'Hickory Wind'
3. Bob Dylan, 'Girl from the North Country'
4. Poco, 'Hoe Down'
5. Nitty Gritty Dirt Band, 'Will the Circle Be Unbroken'
6. Flying Burrito Brothers, 'Sin City'
7. Eagles, 'Take It Easy'
8. Dillards, 'Duellin' Banjos'
9. Linda Ronstadt, 'Rock Me on the Water'
10. Rick Nelson and the Stone Canyon Band, 'Garden Party'
11. Charlie Daniels Band, 'The Devil Went Down To Georgia'
12. Asleep at the Wheel, 'Bump Bounce Boogie'
13. Band, 'All L. A. Glory'
14. Wayne Cochran, 'Sleepless Nights'
15. Alabama, 'Tennessee River'
16. Brinsley Schwarz, 'Country Girl'
17. Creedence Clearwater Revival, 'Who'll Stop the Rain'
18. Long Ryders, 'Lights of Downtown'
19. Albert Lee, 'Country Boy'
20. Dave Edmunds, 'Ju Ju Man'

☐ Be Bop Guitars and the Electric Samba: jazz and Latin rock

As rock reached its teens it began, like all teenagers, to experiment. Among the music that rock flirted with were jazz and the Latin style from South America. Many rock musicians found, to their surprise, that electric guitars and the high amplification of rock went very well with these syncopated styles and thus jazz-rock (aka jazz-fusion) and Latin-rock were born. The former was played both by rock stars who had made their name with more conventional blues-based music and jazz players who were enthralled by the new dimension that could be added to their sound. Latin-rock, however, tended to be played by musicians who had grown up to the infectious rhythms of South America.

Most jazz- and Latin-rock relies on instrumental virtuosity, especially exemplary guitar work. Its heyday was between about 1968 and 1974 and though there are still a few groups prepared to work in the jazz and Latin fields, their popularity is with jazz and Latin fans rather than rock fans.

1. Miles Davis, 'Bitches Brew'
2. John McLaughlin, 'Love Supreme'
3. Santana, 'Jingo'
4. Weather Report, 'Birdland'
5. Chick Corea's Return to Forever, 'Light as a Feather'
6. Chicago, '25 or 6 to 4'
7. Graham Bond Organization, 'Wade in the Water'
8. Herbie Hancock, 'Chameleon'
9. Colosseum II, 'Scorch'
10. Tony William's Lifetime, 'Emergency'
11. Billy Cobham, 'Shabazz'
12. Blues Image, 'Ride Captain Ride'
13. José Feliciano, 'Samba Pa Ti'
14. Shakti, 'Handful of Beauty'
15. Mahavishnu Orchestra, 'The Inner Mounting Flame'
16. Chase, 'Get It On'
17. Ornette Coleman, 'Dancing in Your Head'
18. Brian Auger's Oblivion Express, 'Second Wind'
19. Soft Machine, 'Hot Biscuit Slim'
20. Tempest, 'Living in Fear'

☐ The Guitars Grind On: the early years of heavy metal

Many musicians who started life in beat and pop groups in the early Sixties, both in the US and the UK, came together later in the decade to form rock bands. These new, gutsier bands played some wicked amplified blues, dosed liberally with screaming voices and guitars, flailing drums and pulsing, throbbing basses. The bands ranged from the more controlled hard rock, to the excesses of heavy metal – a term, incidentally, coined by author William Burroughs in his book. *The Naked Lunch*.

The imagery of these groups was very macho – leather jackets, motorbikes and studs. The single was more or less a redundant medium, the LP and, more importantly, the live show were the best ways of expressing this music. Pyrotechnics, long solos, machismo-strutting and on-stage acrobatics greeted the audiences at live shows. In the late Sixties open-air festivals became an annual event and in the beginning they were almost exclusively for HM bands. Even today festivals such as those at Knebworth, Castle Donington and Reading are normally headed by hard rock or heavy metal bands.

1. Led Zeppelin, 'The Immigrant Song'
2. Jimi Hendrix, 'Voodoo Chile'
3. Steppenwolf, 'Born to Be Wild'
4. Deep Purple, 'Smoke on the Water'
5. MC5, 'Motor City is Burning'
6. Hawkwind, 'Silver Machine'
7. Grand Funk Railroad, 'We're an American Band'
8. Wishbone Ash, 'Persephone'
9. Blue Cheer, 'Summertime Blues'
10. Black Sabbath, 'Paranoid'
11. Iron Butterfly, 'In a Gadda Da Vida'
12. Nazareth, 'Bad Bad Boy'
13. Ted Nugent, 'Cat Scratch Fever'
14. Queen, 'Seven Seas of Rhye'
15. Be Bop Deluxe, 'Maid in Heaven'
16. Alice Cooper, 'Elected'
17. Uriah Heep, 'Blind Eye'
18. Edgar Winter Group, 'Frankenstein'
19. Derek and the Dominos, 'Layla'
20. Motorhead, 'Motorhead'

☐ FM Radio – No Static on the West Coast: West Coast rock and its contemporaries

California was noted for its sunshine and its hippies, and at the end of the Sixties it had become the spiritual home of a laid-back, almost MOR, brand of rock. The music was harmonic not harsh, it had some country influence but with light bluesy overtones. It was being played on the FM stations of the West Coast and sent California drifting dreamily into the next decade. Although most of the original groups started in California, other bands from across America, and even from the UK, followed suit. Some were established bands like Fleetwood Mac and Chicken Shack, who toned down their blues for a much mellower sound.

On the negative side, this dreamy Californian crooning was one of the starting points for the bland rock music that would clog the arteries of the music scene by the mid-Seventies and necessitated the by-pass operation of punk. West Coast rock should be listened to only on a hot, balmy day under a blue sky. Have your own private love-in!

1. Beach Boys, 'Do It Again'
2. Mamas and Papas, 'California Dreaming'
3. Tim Buckley, 'Sweet Surrender'
4. Love, 'Alone Again or . . .'
5. Eagles, 'Hotel California'
6. Spanky and Our Gang, 'Sunday Will Never Be the Same'
7. Neil Young, 'Heart of Gold'
8. Crosby, Stills and Nash, 'Déjà Vu'
9. Matthew's Southern Comfort, 'Woodstock'
10. Fleetwood Mac, 'Albatross'
11. Mama Cass, 'It's Getting Better'
12. Stephen Stills, 'Love the One You're With'
13. Brinsley Schwarz, 'Shining Brightly'
14. Steely Dan, 'Haitian Divorce'
15. Doobie Brothers, 'What a Fool Believes'
16. Chicken Shack, 'I'd Rather Go Blind'
17. Mike Nesmith, 'Rio'

18. Dobie Gray, 'Drift Away'
19. America, 'Horse with No Name'
20. Medicine Head, 'One and One Is'

☐ Jah Rockin': the rise of reggae

Jamaica is a smallish island some 600 miles south–south-east of Florida. Its original inhabitants were Arawak Indians but slaves were imported from Africa after British forces occupied the island in 1665. Since that time there have been strong British connections with the island, which was granted independence in 1962. The original music of black Jamaica was a strange calypso variation called 'mento', but in the Fifties J A became as taken with R&B as the rest of the world. As R&B records were quite difficult to obtain there in the early Sixties, many Jamaicans began playing their own version. Although their music used similar instrumentation to R&B, it was played – thanks to their own mento – with a different rhythm, which had the accent on the off beat. The first of this new music was known as ska, bluebeat, rock steady and – by the late Sixties – reggae. The name is probably derived from ragga, short for ragamuffin.

Chris Blackwell's Island Records label was almost solely responsible for bringing reggae to Britain, where it catered for the demands of many Jamaican expatriates who had come in search of work. The first heyday of reggae was around 1969, when British skinheads adopted the music as their own and labels like Trojan provided them with as much ska and reggae as they could handle. Since then it has continued to grow and adapt, enjoying notable purple patches such as the 2-Tone ska revival about 1979. Rock has also been quick to borrow the rhythms of reggae.

1. Bob Marley, 'Exodus'
2. Wailing Wailers, 'Simmer Down'
3. Desmond Dekker, '007 (Shanty Town)'
4. Prince Buster, 'Al Capone'
5. Keith McCarthy, 'Everybody Rude Now'

6. Augustus Pablo, 'Up Warrika Hill'
7. Maytals, 'Do the Reggay'
8. Alton Ellis, 'Rock Steady'
9. Greyhound, 'Black and White'
10. Audrey Hall, 'Smile'
11. Harry J. Allstars, 'The Liquidator'
12. Mighty Diamonds, 'Pass the Kouchie'
13. Skatalites, 'Guns of Navarone'
14. Uniques, 'Too Proud To Beg'
15. Dave and Ansell Collins, 'Double Barrel'
16. Smiley Culture, 'Cockney Translation'
17. Max Romeo, 'Wet Dream'
18. Black Uhuru, 'Sponji Reggae'
19. Clash, 'Police and Thieves'
20. Specials, 'Rudy A Message To You'

☐ Catering for the Teenyboppers: tin-pan alley's formula pop

For many people making music is done for pure joy; of course it's very nice to be able to earn a living from it, but the most important thing is to play. For others, however, the only motivation is profit and they see the music industry like any other business – a market demanding a product, a product that can be designed and mass produced to suit current taste. It probably started to get out of hand with the Brill Building song-writing technique in the early Sixties, when teams of song-writers would sit in their allocated office at their allocated piano and churn out songs on a production line basis for whichever artist was in the market for a song. At least the songs of teams like Goffin and King, and Mann and Weill had some meat on them. Later in the decade the bubble gum production companies and labels like Buddah, Kirshner and the Kasenetz-Katz team started to turn out records created by staff writers and producers and performed by the same faceless bunch of studio musicians. If a record looked like becoming a hit, a group had to be hastily assembled to go on the road to promote it. In the early Seventies production-line pop crossed the Atlantic and people like Nicky Chinn and Mike Chapman, Jonathan King and Mickie Most became adept at writing the same song seventy different times. The Americans then exacted their revenge for the British invasion of 1964 by sending over a stream of teen-idols. While these teenyboppers may have had a better class of song, they delivered them all in the same bland, cutesy way, thus giving them the tin-pan alley effect!

1. Archies, 'Sugar Sugar'
2. Kasenetz-Katz Super Circus, 'Quick Joey Small (Run Joey Run)'
3. Ohio Express, 'Yummy Yummy Yummy'
4. Osmonds, 'Crazy Horses'
5. 1910 Fruitgum Company, 'Simon Says'
6. Flowerpot Men, 'Let's Go to San Francisco'
7. Sweet, 'Little Willy'
8. Slik, 'Forever and Ever'
9. White Plains, 'When You Are a King'
10. Racey, 'Lay Your Love on Me'
11. Music Explosion, 'Little Bit o' Soul'
12. Tommy James and the Shondells, 'Crimson and Clover'
13. David Cassidy, 'The Puppy Song'
14. Bay City Rollers, 'Shang A Lang'
15. Little Jimmy Osmond, 'I'll Be Your Long-haired Lover from Liverpool'
16. Piglets, 'Johnny Reggae'
17. Mud, 'Tiger Feet'
18. Rick Astley, 'Never Gonna Give You Up'
19. First Class, 'Beach Baby'
20. Kenny, 'The Bump'

□ Bedsit Blues: the singer/song-writer generation

The rise of the singer/song-writer in the Seventies was probably a continuation of the folk-rock boom of the Sixties. This time though it was back to basics with just one person singing his or her own songs, accompanying him/herself on guitar or piano. The subject matter of the lyrics was less worldly now and harked back to the teen-*angst* days of singer/song-writers like Eddie Cochran and Chuck Berry. Bed-sit music (so called because it was typically performed by students and arty types who lived in seedy one-room accommodation in the city where they sought their education or fortune) was normally an outlet for personal and emotional problems or, occasionally, for an individual's views. They were seldom 'calls to arms' like many of the protest singers had written.

The bed-sit artists were as renowned for their songs as for their performances. Often a version of the song by another artist would fare better than the artist's own version. More often still, the writer would gain great acclaim, particularly from other artists, but without reaping great financial or commercial reward. The music sometimes verges towards MOR but at other times reflects rock's emotive side.

1. Paul Simon, 'Fifty Ways To Leave Your Lover'
2. Al Stewart, 'Year of the Cat'
3. Carole King, 'You've Got A Friend'
4. Leonard Cohen, 'Suzanne'
5. Elton John, 'Your Song'
6. Cat Stevens, 'First Cut Is The Deepest'
7. Carly Simon, 'You're So Vain'
8. Don McLean, 'American Pie'
9. James Taylor, 'Fire and Rain'
10. Joni Mitchell, 'Big Yellow Taxi'
11. Jim Croce, 'Time in A Bottle'
12. Janis Ian, 'At Seventeen'
13. Bobby Goldsboro, 'Summer the First Time'
14. Laura Nyro, 'And When I Die'

15. Randy Newman, 'Gone Dead Train'
16. Tim Hardin, 'Reason To Believe'
17. Leslie Duncan, 'Love Song'
18. Tom Waits, 'Downtown Train'
19. Neil Diamond, 'Beautiful Noise'
20. Suzanne Vega, 'Marlene on the Wall'

□ Bubblegum Grows Up: glitter and glam

After the inspiration of the Sixties, the Seventies looked set to remain very unimpressive. The underground and cult markets (such as heavy metal) lumbered on uninterrupted but the more mainstream market of the charts seemed somewhat stagnant. One of the few memorable chart trends from the first half of the decade emerged around 1972: the flashy, trashy, visually striking glam rock and glitter.

Musically the songs were (in the main) little more than an adolescent version of tin-pan alley formula pop. The groups, however, were something else: long-haired youths tottering about on six-inch platform shoes, bedecked in garish sparkling and sequinned costumes and wearing multi-coloured make-up. Many had an air of bisexuality about them, and several admitted this to be the case. *Top of the Pops* would be saturated with these groups every week, each trying to be more outrageous than the last (though, with hindsight, it was generally a fairly subdued outrage). It was a short-lived fad, though many groups outlasted it and moved on to pastures new, but its influence has cropped up in groups as diverse as the Rezillos and Motley Crue.

1. Sweet, 'Ballroom Blitz'
2. Alice Cooper, 'School's Out'
3. T. Rex, 'Children of the Revolution'
4. Sparks, 'This Town Ain't Big Enough for the Both of Us'
5. Roxy Music, 'Virginia Plain'
6. New York Dolls, 'Looking for A Kiss'
7. Slade, 'Cum On Feel the Noize'
8. Hello, 'New York Groove'

9. Rolling Stones, 'It's Only Rock 'n' Roll'
10. Nick Gilder, 'Roxy Roller'
11. Arrows, 'I Love Rock 'n' Roll'
12. Kenny, 'Fancy Pants'
13. Suzi Quatro, '48 Crash'
14. Gary Glitter, 'Rock and Roll Part 2'
15. Mott the Hoople, 'Roll Away the Stone'
16. Glitter Band, 'Goodbye My Love'
17. Wizzard, 'See My Baby Jive'
18. Kiss, 'Rock and Roll All Nite'
19. Rubettes, 'Sugar Baby Love'
20. Lou Reed, 'Vicious'

□ Philadelphia Freedom: soul and Motown into the Seventies

Whatever fads rock music went through in the Sixties and Seventies, the growth of soul music was steady. In the early Seventies the epicentre of the soul movement switched from Detroit to Philadelphia, PA. The influential Philadelphia International label was started in 1972 by Kenny Gamble and Leon Huff, a pair of former performers (the Romeos), producers, and song-writers, who had previously run the Gamble label (US hits with the Intruders) and the Neptune label (hits with the O'Jays). Other writers and producers on the Philly label included Thom Bell and McFadden and Whitehead.

Motown had far from faded away, though. Its various labels were bringing hits from Diana Ross (now out of the Supremes), Stevie Wonder and the Jackson Five, while other labels, like Invicta, Hi and Stax, were making their own contributions to the soul scene. *Soul Train*, the TV programme dedicated to the cause of black dance music, was helping all these records into the charts.

The American nation was dancing harder than the rest of the world, but everyone was just a few fleet-footed dance steps away from the dance craze that would see the entire globe gyrating: disco was only just around the corner.

1. Al Green, 'Let's Stay Together'
2. O'Jays, 'Love Train'
3. Jackson Five, 'ABC'
4. Temptations, 'Just My Imagination'
5. Gloria Gaynor, 'Never Can Say Goodbye'
6. Diana Ross, 'I'm Still Waiting'
7. Stevie Wonder, 'My Cherie Amour'
8. MFSB, 'The Sound of Philadelphia'
9. Stylistics, 'Star on A TV Show'
10. Billy Paul, 'Me and Mrs Jones'
11. Chi Lites, 'Homely Girl'
12. Sly and the Family Stone, 'Dance to the Music'
13. Harold Melvin and the Bluenotes, 'Don't Leave Me This Way'
14. Ann Peebles, 'I Can't Stand the Rain'
15. Billy Ocean, 'Love Really Hurts'
16. Freda Payne, 'Band of Gold'
17. Tams, 'Hey Girl Don't Bother Me'
18. Love Unlimited Orchestra, 'Love's Theme'
19. Limmie and the Family Cooking, 'You Can Do Magic'
20. Commodores, 'The Zoo (The Human Zoo)'

☐ A Pint of the Best: pub rock and the new R & B revival

Britain always held the rougher, rockier side of R&B to its heart, and in the early Seventies several British bands began to perform their own brand of it in different areas of the country, notably the Southend/Canvey Island neck of the woods. Britain's record-buying public was more interested in the latest pop fad or in the big dinosaur bands, so the R&B scene remained very cliquey. For these bands big venues were out of their league, so they played the smaller clubs and that great British institution, the pub, hence the term pub-rock.

Dr Feelgood was the first guitar-grinding, harmonica-wailing R&B band to gain any national attention and in its wake came people like Eddie and the Hot Rods, and Graham Parker, who, due to a matter of timing, got lumped in with the punk and new wave movements, which at least afforded them some publicity they might otherwise have foregone. Other long-standing pub rock bands (such as Brinsley Schwarz) also got some attention in the late Seventies when various members got involved on the New Wave scene. Although essentially a British phenomenon, there were a handful of American bands involved on the pub circuit (for example, Eggs Over Easy).

The popularity of R&B escalated in 1978–9 in line with the mod revival. The original mods of the Sixties had always had a taste for R&B and so revivalist bands like Nine Below Zero gained much support. In the Eighties R&B seemed to disappear from the public view but there are still plenty of bands to be found on the pub and small club circuit sweating out their meaty blues in smoke-filled rooms full of half-cut fans.

1. Dr Feelgood, 'Back in the Night'
2. Ducks Deluxe, 'Fireball'
3. Brinsley Schwarz, '(What's So Funny 'Bout) Peace, Love and Understanding'
4. Chilli Willi and the Red Hot Peppers, 'Bongos over Balham'
5. Kilburn and the High Roads, 'Rough Kids'
6. Tyla Gang, 'Styrofoam'
7. Eddie and the Hot Rods, 'Quit This Town'
8. Graham Parker & the Rumour, 'Soul Shoes'
9. Rockpile, 'Teacher Teacher'
10. Fabulous Thunderbirds, 'You Ain't Nothing But Fine'
11. Blast Furnace, 'You Can't Stop the Boy'
12. Q Tips, 'SYSLJFM (The Letter Song)'
13. Little Roosters, 'She Cat Sister Floozie'
14. Red Beans And Rice, 'That Driving Beat'
15. Pirates, 'Dr Feelgood'
16. Bees Make Honey, 'Boogie Queen'
17. Dance Band, 'Stacks of Tracks'
18. Blues Band, 'Maggie's Farm'
19. Kursaal Flyers, 'Speedway'
20. Snakes, 'Teenage Head'

□ Tribal Rites of a Saturday Night: first generation disco 1974–80

Someone, somewhere, sometime in the mid-Seventies figured out that if you vamped up the back-beat on certain soul and Motown records, perhaps enhanced them with electronic effects, certainly increased the tempo and then thundered them out of big bass speakers in a dance hall, you had an almost irresistible form of dance music. Around this time vast numbers of American whites started to rediscover the benefits of black music and wanted to dance to it. Consequently all over the States, though particularly in the big cities like New York City and LA, discothèques and dance halls began to cater for this new interest, and thus the boom in discothèque dancing (aka disco) was started.

In 1976 English writer Nik Cohn, living in America, wrote a feature on the growing phenomenon, which he called 'The Tribal Rites of a Saturday Night'. Record company boss and general music biz mogul Robert Stigwood read the article and asked Cohn to turn it into a screenplay. Cohn duly did this while Stigwood knocked together a sound-track using a group he had long managed but who had enjoyed little success in recent years. The group were the Bee Gees and, along with performances from the Tavares and Yvonne Elliman, they provided the sound-track to *Saturday Night Fever*, which became a world-wide success, breaking box-office records everywhere. Suddenly disco dancing was the big craze. Night-clubs, boutiques and restaurants were pulsating to the sound of black, then white, disco artists. Though the initial furore soon died down, the music remains one of the most popular forms about, albeit in an ever more sophisticated form.

1. George McRae, 'Rock Your Baby'
2. Ritchie Family, 'The Best Disco in Town'
3. Bee Gees, 'Night Fever'
4. Tramps, 'Hold Back the Night'
5. Hues Corporation, 'Rock the Boat'
6. Sylvester, 'You Make Me Feel Mighty Real'
7. Donna Summer, 'Love To Love You Baby'

8. Sister Sledge, 'We Are Family'
9. Evelyn 'Champagne' King, 'Shame'
10. Real Thing, 'Can You Feel the Force'
11. Chic, 'Le Freak'
12. Rose Royce, 'Car Wash'
13. Blondie, 'Heart of Glass'
14. Odyssey, 'Native New Yorker'
15. Kool and the Gang, 'Celebrate'
16. Heatwave, 'Boogie Nights'
17. Gloria Gaynor, 'I Will Survive'
18. Edwin Starr, 'Contact'
19. Earth Wind and Fire, 'September'
20. Anita Ward, 'Ring My Bell'

□ Dancing the Night Away: northern soul

Northern soul is probably the most prominent musical 'craze' that America never saw. Mind you, most of the south of England is blissfully unaware of it as well, yet in the north of the country it is a fervent, heavily supported scene. It doesn't refer to a distinct style of music but to all the music popular on the 'circuit'. Records are mostly drawn from the Sixties soul and R&B scene, though this was not always the case. When this cult scene started in the mid-Sixties, it was R&B and rockabilly that were the favoured styles of music. Gradually the success of Stax and Motown made soul the order of the day. The term 'northern soul' was coined by *Rhythm and Soul* magazine.

The clubs – places like the Wigan Casino and Stoke-on-Trent's Torch – hold what are called 'All-Nighters' at which the dancing starts late at night and carries on until early the next morning, when dancers may even move on to another venue and another session of dancing. The typical dress of these soul fans is designed to accommodate the vigorous dancing they enjoy so much; the boys typically wear loose-fitting trousers called baggies and sport leather-soled shoes.

The soul they favour is generally less funky than that favoured on the London scene, though in the mid-Eighties the Chicagoan house sound was championed by the northern soul brigade.

1. Gloria Jones, 'Tainted Love'
2. Jackie Wilson, '(I Get the) Sweetest Feeling'
3. Lowell Fulsom, 'Tramp'
4. Mohawks, 'The Champ'
5. Betty Everett, 'Getting Mighty Crowded'
6. Homer Banks, 'Hooked By Love'
7. Dobie Gray, 'Out on the Floor'
8. Al Wilson, 'The Snake'
9. Tams, 'Be Young Be Foolish Be Happy'
10. Headliners, 'You're Bad News'
11. Sapphires, 'Slow Fizz'
12. Parliament, 'Time'
13. Millie Jackson, 'A House for Sale'
14. J. J. Barnes, 'Competition Ain't Nothing'
15. Doris Troy, 'I'll Do Anything He Wants Me To Do'
16. Ramsey Lewis, 'Wade in the Water'
17. Wigan's Chosen Few, 'Footsie'
18. Marvels, 'Stop'
19. Maxine Nightingale, 'Right Back Where We Started From'
20. Lee Williams, 'Lost Love'

□ The Guitar Bites Back: late Seventies US and Canadian rock

Rock took on a new life east of the Atlantic in the closing years of the Seventies. It lightened up slightly from the heavy intense rock sound favoured by British and American heavy metal bands. Instead, they played an altogether more melodic brand of rock that owed more to Neil Young and the Byrds than it did to Led Zeppelin or Deep Purple. It was pretty much confined to the States – Britain was undergoing a double assault of punk and disco at the time – though some records did cross over in the course of time. By the Eighties this particular strain of rock had lost its freshness and was sounding tired and clichéd. It would soon be replaced by an altogether more sophisticated sound.

1. Blue Oyster Cult, 'Don't Fear the Reaper'
2. Boston, 'More Than A Feeling'
3. Foreigner, 'Juke Box Hero'
4. Journey, 'Anyway You Want It'
5. Iron Horse, 'Sweet Lui Louise'
6. Tom Petty, 'American Girl'
7. Kansas, 'Carry On Wayward Son'
8. Lynyrd Skynyrd, 'Free Bird'
9. Cheap Trick, 'Surrender'
10. Prism, 'See Forever Eyes'
11. Steve Miller Band, 'Fly Like An Eagle'
12. Styx, 'Come Sail Away'
13. Pablo Cruise, 'Love Will Find A Way'
14. Aerosmith, 'Walk This Way'
15. Heart, 'Barracuda'
16. J. Geils Band, 'One Last Kiss'
17. Rossington Collins Band, 'Don't Misunderstand Me'
18. Nils Lofgren, 'Shine Silently'
19. REO Speedwagon, 'Take It On The Run'
20. Little Feat, 'Oh Atlanta'

☐ Spitting in the Wind of Change: punk rock

To many people the pop scene in 1975 was a stagnant pool. They were sick of the 'Boring Old Farts' and their dinosaur rock bands like Yes, Genesis and ELP playing 200-date world tours at major venues; they were sick of ten-a-penny teen-idols and formula pop bands playing for little girls. They wanted something else.

Those lucky enough to be in the know (mostly art students) were passing around records by American bands like the New York Dolls,

Iggy Pop and the MC5. Those moved enough by these rather raw and aggressive bands set out to form their own groups. The first influential groups started on the London scene and were Bazooka Joe, the London SS and the Swankers. Musically they were not outstanding; Sixties covers played with a Rolling Stones-ish aggression. It was their attitude that set them apart – a desire to be different. From these first bands were born the Clash, Chelsea, Generation X, the Damned and most importantly of all, the Sex Pistols.

During 1976 punk developed its own culture: an image (ripped off from US band Television's Richard Hell) of spiky hair and torn clothes held together with safety pins and an anti-establishment stance and a desire to shock, even offend, their own clubs and hangouts. The media were not slow to pick up on the burgeoning movement and soon our moral guardians were ranting and raving over the punks (a term applied to them by journalist Caroline Coon) and their swearing and gobbing. They were, however, here to stay.

A similar movement ran concurrently in the US, though the bands there (Television, Talking Heads, etc.) tended to be a little more arty and less simple than their British counterparts (the Ramones always excluded of course).

1. Sex Pistols, 'Anarchy in the UK'
2. Ramones, 'Blitzkrieg Bop'
3. Clash, 'Complete Control'
4. Television, 'Marquee Moon'
5. Damned, 'New Rose'
6. Richard Hell, 'Blank Generation'
7. Buzzcocks, 'What Do I Get'
8. Ruts, 'In a Rut'
9. Stiff Little Fingers, 'Alternative Ulster'
10. Stranglers, 'Go Buddy Go'
11. X-Ray Spex, 'Oh Bondage Up Yours'
12. Adverts, 'Gary Gilmore's Eyes'
13. Lurkers, 'I Don't Need to Tell Her'
14. Generation X, 'Ready Steady Go'
15. Dead Boys, 'Sonic Reducer'
16. Siouxsie and the Banshees, 'Love in a Void'
17. Wayne County and the Electric Chairs, 'If You Don't Want to Fuck Me Baby, Baby Fuck Off'

18. Heartbreakers, 'Chinese Rocks'
19. Saints, 'This Perfect Day'
20. Skids, 'Into the Valley'

☐ Pure Pop for Now People: the new wave

The 'new wave' has become a catch-all term for all pop music that emerged alongside punk, or in its immediate wake, that was too melodic or poppy to be punk. Undoubtedly, many of the new wave bands were inspired by punk but wanted to play something less angry. Others would almost certainly have emerged whether or not punk ever happened. And not all the new-wavers were as young and fresh as their punk counterparts anyway – in 1976 Nick Lowe and Debbie Harry had already spent nearly ten years each in the business.

Nevertheless, the new wave heralded a golden era for pop music: pop music in the good old-fashioned three-minute single form. For about three years (1978–80) the new chart revealed every Tuesday lunch-time was worth listening to; and for every good new wave band that made the chart there were a dozen goodies that didn't.

There were tangents from the straight pop of the new wave as well. The so-called power pop movement encapsulated everyone from the Rich Kids to bands like the Pleasers, whose energetic R&Besque sound crossed over with the mod and R&B revival. Many of the bands who rose to fame as new wave bands would go on to be successful as mainstream rock bands: U2, the Police and the Cars, for example.

I honestly expect the period to be covered one day on a series of LPs in the same way Nuggets, Boulders and Pebbles have covered the mid-Sixties garage scene. Twenty new wave records, every one a classic.

1. Blondie, 'Rip Her to Shreds'
2. Only Ones, 'Another Girl Another Planet'
3. Elvis Costello, '(I Don't Want to Go to) Chelsea'
4. Jam, 'Down in the Tube Station at Midnight'
5. Undertones, 'Teenage Kicks'

6. Boomtown Rats, 'Rat Trap'
7. XTC, 'Making Plans for Nigel'
8. Nick Lowe, 'So It Goes'
9. Devo, 'Come Back Jonee'
10. Police, 'Can't Stand Losing You'
11. Cars, 'My Best Friend's Girl'
12. B 52s, 'Rock Lobster'
13. U2, 'I Will Follow'
14. Squeeze, 'Goodbye Girl'
15. Magazine, 'Shot By Both Sides'
16. Yachts, 'Love You Love You'
17. Graham Parker, 'Hold Back the Night'
18. Rich Kids, 'Rich Kids'
19. Pretenders, 'Kid'
20. TV Smith's Explorers, 'Tomahawk Cruise'

□ Spine Shiftin' Syncopation: funk

One strain of Sixties soul and R&B that came into its own in the following decade was funk. The word comes from 'funky', which originally meant 'sexy' in black slang. Funk is a very bass heavy dance music that cuts closer to rock than does any other black dance style. It is, to be more technical, a percussive, polyrhythmic dance music with minimal melody and maximum syncopation; in other words, it shakes your spine so much your feet just have to move.

James Brown probably started playing funky music early in the Sixties, and later in the decade the torch was carried by Sly and the Family Stone, thanks largely to bass player Larry Graham. In the Seventies it became dominated by the Parliament/Funkadelic family overseen by 'Bootsy' Collins and George Clinton. Some rock bands from this era played a brand of rock music so damned funky that it was funk!

Lately funk has been somewhat overawed by the hip-hop movement, but every now and again a band like Cameo will come out with something funky enough to tear your spine out.

1. Funkadelic, 'Who Says a Funk Band Can't Play Rock'
2. James Brown, 'Stone Cold Drag'
3. Cameo, 'Word Up'
4. Kool and the Gang, 'Hollywood Swinging'
5. Dyke and the Blazers, 'Funky Broadway'
6. Sly and the Family Stone, 'Family Affair'
7. Parliament, 'Tear the Roof Off the Sucker'
8. Earth Wind and Fire, 'Keep Your Head to the Sky'
9. Charles Wright and the Watts 103rd Street Rhythm Band, 'Do Your Thing'
10. War, 'Cisco Kid'
11. Screaming Tony Baxter, 'Get Up Ofta'
12. Ohio Players, 'Who'd She Coo'
13. Equals, 'Black-skinned Blue-eyed Boys'
14. Tower of Power, 'Don't Change Horses in the Middle of the Stream'
15. Black Britain, 'Ain't No Rockin' in a Police State'
16. Wild Cherry, 'Play That Funky Music'
17. Jimmy Castor, 'It's Just Begun'
18. Chakachas, 'Jungle Fever'
19. Herman Kelly, 'Dance to the Drummer's Beat'
20. Clash, 'Overpowered by Funk'

□ The Sounds of Silicone: two sides of synthesizer music

In the years immediately after the Second World War the science of electronics broke new ground in almost every field. In the Sixties Dr Robert Moog unveiled his Moog Synthesizer, an electronic keyboard capable of producing synthesized notes and effects not possible on an ordinary piano or organ. From there on the progress was rapid. In 1971 the Mini Moog, probably the most used synthesizer in the world, was introduced.

Two strains of music evolved from the use of the ever more sophisticated synthesizer. Firstly, in the Seventies, there were the arty bands (mostly European, especially German) who played a semi-classical synthesizer-generated machine music. The music consisted of lengthy instrumental passages often making use of the synth's ability to play unaided loops and rhythms.

On the lighter side many pop musicians began to use the synth on their recordings. Roxy Music's non-musician Brian Eno was one of the most notable. Chicory Tip became the first band to reach Number One in the UK with a single featuring a synth ('Son of My Father'). By the late Seventies many pop bands had emerged using synthesizers as the prominent (if not the only) instrument on their records. The very early Eighties saw a purple patch for the synth, which was now being used by almost every type of band from HM stalwarts to disco prima donnas.

■ Machine music

1. Kraftwerk, 'Autobahn'
2. Can, 'I Want More'
3. Mike Oldfield, 'Tubular Bells'
4. Suicide, 'Dream Baby Dream'
5. Tangerine Dream, 'Encore'
6. Brian Eno, 'The King's Lead Hat'
7. Neu, 'Hallogallo'
8. David Bowie, 'Warsawza'
9. Cabaret Voltaire, 'Seconds Too Late'
10. Thomas Leer, 'Letter from America'

■ Synth pop

1. Soft Cell, 'Tainted Love'
2. New Order, 'Blue Monday'
3. (Freur), 'Doot Doot'
4. Visage, 'Fade to Grey'
5. Human League, 'Being Boiled'
6. Bill Nelson, 'Banal'
7. Gary Numan, 'Cars'
8. Heaven 17, 'Crushed by the Wheels of Industry'
9. Orchestral Manoeuvres in the Dark, 'Enola Gay'
10. The Normal, 'Warm Leatherette'

☐ Metallic KO: the New Wave of British Heavy Metal and its contemporaries

Punk was responsible for a return to popularity of fast, high-energy music in the UK. It also created an atmosphere similiar to the Sixties in which loads of people believed they could go out and form a group and make their own records. This led to a succession of new heavy metal bands springing forth throughout the country. *Sounds*, probably *the* pop music paper of the time, picked up the trend and brazenly labelled it the 'New Wave of British Heavy Metal'; several European and American bands followed in its wake.

For perhaps two years its popularity crossed over to the Radio 1 audience and several records made the charts. It soon slipped back into cult status, but it had a very loyal following. In the mid-Eighties it spawned Thrash. It was HM taken to its extreme: fast, loud and raucous, more akin to punk than anything else. Shortly afterwards the so-called grebo bands like Zodiac Mindwarp began to churn out their own version of metal. Again it was as close to the Pistols as it was to Zeppelin. The grebo bands were everything stereotyped rockers should be: ugly, dirty, offensive and exciting. HM marches on.

1. AC/DC, 'Whole Lotta Rosie'
2. Def Leppard, 'Getcha Rocks Off'
3. Saxon, '747 (Strangers in the Night)'
4. Iron Maiden, 'Can I Play with Madness'
5. Krokus, 'Easy Rocker'
6. Van Halen, 'Runnin' with the Devil'
7. Scorpions, 'Love Drive'
8. Michael Schenker Group, 'Cry for the Nations'
9. W.A.S.P., 'Shoot from the Hip'
10. Rose Tattoo, 'Rock 'n' Roll Outlaw'
11. Waysted, 'Black and Blue'
12. April Wine, 'I Like To Rock'
13. Great White, 'Face the Day'
14. Metallica, 'Damage Inc.'

15. Anthrax, 'I Am the Law'
16. Gaye Bykers on Acid, 'Everythang's Groovy'
17. Quiet Riot, 'Metal Health'
18. Whitesnake, 'Here I Go Again'
19. Girlschool, 'Hit and Run'
20. Zodiac Mindwarp and the Love Reaction, 'Prime Mover'

□ Dancerama: disco, the second wave, 1980 onwards

Once the dust had settled on *Saturday Night Fever*, disco music settled into its own little groove and boogied along at a steady pace. In the Eighties it became more and more sophisticated, with productions becoming tighter all the time. It also became more credible with the rock audience who had previously been somewhat alienated from it. This was probably best illustrated by Eddie Van Halen's guitar contributions to Michael Jackson's *Thriller* LP.

A variety of disco-based spin-offs came from this period: firstly, there was the dreadful medley craze in which short snippets of well-known songs were segued together over a syn drum disco beat; then there was Hi NRG, a fast dance music that gained great popularity on the gay scene.

Much of the pop music of the last decade has been dance music, as it seems to have a wide appeal. Michael Jackson's *Thriller* LP is the all-time best selling album in the world.

1. Michael Jackson, 'Thriller'
2. Madonna, 'Into the Groove'
3. Third World, 'Dancing on the Floor (Hooked on Love)'
4. Prince, '1999'
5. Boystown Gang, 'Can't Take My Eyes Off of You'
6. Spandau Ballet, 'Chant No. 1 (I Don't Need This Pressure On)'
7. Oran 'Juice' Jones, 'The Rain'
8. Lionel Richie, 'All Night Long (All Night)'

9. Freeez, 'Southern Freeez'
10. Five Star, 'Rain or Shine'
11. Imagination, 'Music and Lights'
12. Chaka Khan, 'I Feel For You'
13. Linx, 'Intuition'
14. Weather Girls, 'It's Raining Men'
15. Mel and Kim, 'Respectable'
16. Eartha Kitt, 'Where Is My Man'
17. Lipps Inc, 'Funky Town'
18. Shalamar, 'A Night to Remember'
19. Shannon, 'Let the Music Play'
20. Eddy Grant, 'I Don't Wanna Dance'

☐ Video Killed the Pop Star: pop of the Eighties

Rock and pop music, to these ears at least, reached one of its rare zeniths in the last three years of the Seventies, and by the Eighties was tumbling back down to a level dictated by record company marketing techniques rather than talent. Record company marketing offices were given a new toy to play with – the promotional video. Although short films had previously been made for some groups for *Top of the Pops*, the age of cheap video equipment made these promotional tools a much better investment. It followed then that a group's image became more important than ever before and, sadly, it seemed that it became more important than the music itself. A whole new pop scene emerged. It was mostly British – America was busy with its bland rock bands and dance music. Many of the acts had started out after being inspired by punk and new wave, though this would rarely show through in their music. A group's life became almost predictable: they would spring to success after being picked up by Radio 1 or gaining a dance-floor hit; have several hits in a similar vein with maybe the odd ballad or slightly out-of-style tune to break the monotony; group members would be tabloid headliners for their secret sex lives and alleged drug taking; music papers would overflow with rumours of an imminent rift that management would strictly deny; and then the lead singer would zoom off on a solo career. Sounds familiar, doesn't it?

1. ABC, 'The Look of Love'
2. Wham!, 'Wake Me Up Before You Go-Go'
3. Duran Duran, 'Is There Something I Should Know'
4. Frankie Goes to Hollywood, 'Relax'
5. Culture Club, 'Church of the Poison Mind'
6. Madness, 'Our House'
7. Dexy's Midnight Runners, 'Come On Eileen'
8. Adam and the Ants, 'Stand and Deliver'
9. Simple Minds, 'Don't You Forget About Me'
10. Thompson Twins, 'Hold Me Now'
11. Eurythmics, 'Love Is a Stranger'
12. Madonna, 'Like a Virgin'
13. Go West, 'We Close Our Eyes'
14. A-ha, 'Take on Me'
15. Howard Jones, 'New Song'
16. Stephen 'Tin Tin' Duffy, 'Kiss Me'
17. Pet Shop Boys, 'Opportunities (Let's Make Lots of Money)'
18. Tears For Fears, 'Everybody Wants to Rule the World'
19. Prince, 'Raspberry Beret'
20. Nik Kershaw, 'I Won't Let the Sun Go Down on Me'

☐ A Certain Kind of Madness: experimental, avante garde and out of the ordinary

While most rock and pop music follows fairly similar basic structures – such as verse-chorus-verse or twelve-bar boogie – or uses the same sort of instrumentation (guitar, bass, drums, keyboards, etc.) or writes about the same old things (love, politics, money), there are those who are willing to experiment. The records selected below are mostly very different from one another and mostly very different from mainstream pop and rock records.

Experimental rock really started in the Sixties. It was vaguely related to progressive rock but drew more on jazz and classical ideas and structures. It is often esoteric music, sometimes so much so that it comes across as pompous and one wonders if the artist was trying to entertain anyone but his ego. Most experimental musicians consider themselves more than just pop performers; they consider themselves artistes and often produce a stage show that stimulates all the senses.

Few of the acts have found more than cult success, which has even led to the break-up of some acts before their potential was realized. The world still mourns the dissolution of Half Man Half Biscuit.

1. Talking Heads, 'Psycho Killer'
2. Patti Smith, 'Hey Joe'
3. Laurie Anderson, 'Language Is A Virus'
4. Throbbing Gristle, 'Zyclon B Zombie'
5. Philip Glass, 'North Star'
6. Pere Ubu, '30 Seconds Over Tokyo'
7. Fall, 'Totally Wired'
8. Captain Beefheart, 'Yellow Brick Road'
9. Devo, 'Mongoloid'
10. Robyn Hitchcock, 'The Man with the Lightbulb Head'
11. PiL, 'Death Disco'
12. Will Powers, 'Kissing with Confidence'
13. Thomas Dolby, 'She Blinded Me With Science'
14. Soft Boys, '(I Wanna Be An) Anglepoise Lamp'
15. Half Man Half Biscuit, '99% of Gargoyles Look Like Bob Todd'
16. Deep Freeze Mice, 'Minstrel Radio Yoghurt'
17. Gadfly, 'A Tax'
18. Was (Not Was), 'Out Come the Freaks'
19. Frank Zappa, 'Don't Eat the Yellow Snow'
20. Chrysanthemums, 'Gloucestershire Is Just An Illusion'

□ The Bronx Beat Boogie: rap, hip-hop and house

Rap is the rhythmic use of spoken or semi-spoken/semi-sung lyrics usually over some form of backing track. It was first used by black DJs in the Bronx area of New York in the early Seventies. The first rap group was the Last Poets but the style was brought to world attention by the Sugarhill Gang and later by Grandmaster Flash. It was followed out of the Bronx by hip-hop, which was a catch-all term for a new style of black music developed by those blacks who were discontent with the lightweight cross-over disco of the late Seventies and wanted something more hard-core and funky. Hip-hop developed by DJs taking the instrumental passages from records (any sort of music from James Brown to the Rolling Stones, but mostly funk records) and mixing in other records and their own voices to extend them so the B-boys (break boys) could dance.

House music developed in Chicago and was also known as the garage sound after Larry Levan's Paradise Garage Club, where it was popularized. House strips dance music down to its basics, eliminating many of the electronic effects that were starting to overwhelm hip-hop. The most dominant strain of house has been jack music.

The three styles are quite happy to interact and between them they have provided the most significant development in pop music in general since punk.

1. Trouble Funk, 'Drop the Bomb'
2. MARRS, 'Pump Up the Volume'
3. Kurtis Blow, 'The Breaks'
4. Run DMC, 'Rock Box'
5. Steve 'Silk' Hurley, 'Jack Your Body'
6. Grandmaster Flash, 'The Message'
7. Beastie Boys, 'Fight for Your Right to Party'
8. Man Parrish, 'Hip Hop Be Bop (Don't Stop)'
9. Afrika Bambaattaa, 'Planet Rock'
10. Doug E. Fresh, 'The Show'
11. Farley 'Jackmaster' Funk, 'Love Can't Turn Around'
12. Davy DMX, 'One for the Treble'

13. Whodini, 'Freaks Come Out at Night'
14. Sugarhill Gang, 'Rapper's Delight'
15. Marshall Jefferson, '(The House Music Anthem) Move Your Body'
16. Real Roxanne, 'Bang Zoom Let's Go'
17. Blondie, 'Rapture'
18. T Ski Valley, 'Catch the Beat'
19. LL Cool J, 'Rock the Bells'
20. Double D and Steinski, 'Lesson Three'

☐ New Guitars in Town: the mid-Eighties 'indies' scene

Perhaps it's wrong for me to lump all these bands together, but as I have, what shall we call them? The most popular term applied to the likes of the Smiths and the Woodentops has been the indies because they mostly appear(ed) on independent record labels. However, some of the bands in this category appear on major labels, and there are plenty of bands on indie labels who wouldn't qualify for this category (if we ever define it).

So what is the common link of these bands (and their cohorts)? Well, there's a predilection for the good old guitar that makes sweet music to these ears, but otherwise they vary from the melodic pop of the Pastels, the psychedelia of the Shamen and the sub HM of the Cult to the thrash of Stump. They are, at least, an antidote to the prepackaged, preproduced, preposterous pop of the Eighties. They were (as is often the case with good music) not totally acceptable to the masses, but there were several chart breakthroughs from the genre.

Finally some other words that have been bestowed on this cult with no name; judge for yourself if any ring true: shambling, anoraks, gothic, students, wimps . . .

1. Smiths, 'How Soon Is Now'
2. Echo and the Bunnymen, 'Heaven Up Here'

3. Mighty Lemon Drops, 'Like an Angel'
4. Bodines, 'Therese'
5. Billy Bragg, 'Walk Away Renee'
6. Age Of Chance, 'Kiss'
7. Cure, 'Charlotte Sometimes'
8. Cult, 'Rain'
9. Jesus and Mary Chain, 'Never Understand'
10. Pop Will Eat Itself, 'Candydiosis'
11. We've Got A Fuzzbox and We're Gonna Use It, 'XX Sex'
12. Lloyd Cole and the Commotions, 'Perfect Skin'
13. Soup Dragons, 'Hang Ten'
14. Woodentops, 'Why'
15. Stump, 'Quirk Out'
16. Housemartins, 'Happy Hour'
17. Shop Assistants, 'Train to Kansas City'
18. Mission, 'Like A Hurricane'
19. Bogshed, 'Good Morning Sir'
20. Primitives, 'Stop Killing Me'

□ Rock Comes of Age: rock's new sophistication

Rock music has rarely dominated the singles chart – lightweight, mainstream pop has generally had that wrapped up. In the Eighties, however, this has not always been the case. Rock music has had its rough edges chopped and become an altogether more sophisticated, cleanly produced (bland and sanitized) sound. Aided and abetted by stunning videos (with bigger budgets than most British films), many of these rock records have become big hits. Suddenly the names that half a decade ago were 'Boring Old Farts', are now pop stars and, joined by newer imitators, have made massive gains of chart ground. The bands and artists are American, British, Australian . . . you name it. Unlike some of the styles of music discussed earlier, this new sophisticated rock is popular right across the world.

The purveyors of this music tend to traipse around the world on gruelling tours, playing huge stadiums in major cities. Giant video screens and webs of lasers embellish their stage act. Their records sell in millions and Radio 2 often plays them. Ah well . . . even Eric Clapton gets older.

1. Bruce Springsteen, 'Born in the USA'
2. Dire Straits, 'Money for Nothing'
3. ZZ Top, 'Legs'
4. Big Country, 'Where the Rose Is Sown'
5. Phil Collins, 'One More Night'
6. Eric Clapton, 'Behind the Mask'
7. Mister Mister, 'Kyrie'
8. Starship, 'We Built This City'
9. Paul Simon, 'Graceland'
10. Europe, 'The Final Countdown'
11. Queen, 'Hammer to Fall'
12. Bryan Adams, 'Run to You'
13. Marillion, 'Incommunicado'
14. Tom Petty and the Heartbreakers, 'Don't Come Around Here No More'
15. Robert Palmer, 'Addicted to Love'
16. Bon Jovi, 'Wanted Dead or Alive'
17. Eurythmics, 'Who's That Girl'
18. INXS, 'Devil Inside'
19. Berlin, 'You Take My Breath Away'
20. Van Halen, 'Jump'

■ WAVES

As you have already seen (p. 268), the Californian surfing scene of the early Sixties had its own musical accompaniment. Here are several more records that are associated with, or owe allegiance to, the surfin' scene.

'Surfin'', Beach Boys
'Surfin' Safari', Jan and Dean
'Surf Hootin' Annie', Al Casey
'King of the Surf Guitar', Dick Dale and the Deltones
'Tuff Surf', Likely Ones
'Your Baby's Gone Surfin'', Duane Eddy
'Surfin' Down the Swanee River', Honeys
'Surfer Girl', Beach Boys
'Ride the Wild Surf', Jan and Dean
'Tell 'Em I'm Surfin'', Fantastic Baggies
'Surf Beat', Dick Dale and the Deltones
'Surfing SW 12', Monochrome Set
'Old English Surfer', Ray Stevens
'Surfin' USA', Beach Boys
'Sidewalk Surfin'', Jan and Dean
'Little Surfer Girl', Kenny and Denny
'The Rise of the Brighton Surf', Bo and Beep
'Surf Drums', Likely Ones
'Surfer Street', Gary Knight's Chess Men
'Surf's Up', Beach Boys
'Surf City', Jan and Dean
'Surfer Boogie', Likely Ones
'Surfer's Stomp', Marketts
'Valley Surf Stomp', The Stomach Mouths

'New York's a Lonely Town When You're the Only Surfer Boy Around', Tradewinds
'Surfer's Lament', Likely Ones
'Subway Surfing', Barracudas
'Surfside', Digger Revell's Denver Men
'Bustin' Surfboard', Likely Ones
'Surfer's Nitemare', Surf Punks
'Night Surfin'', Teenbeats
'Blood Surfin'', Skeletons
'Surfin' Senorita', Herb Alpert
'Loin of the Surf', Swell Maps
'Surfing with a Spoon', Midnight Oil
'The Surfer Moon', Beach Boys
'Hillbilly Surf', Likely Ones
'Kill Surf City', Jesus and Mary Chain
'Lonely Surfer', Jack Nitzshe
'Surfer's Christmas List', Surfaris
'The Rockin' Surfer', Beach Boys
'Surfin' Drums', Dick Dale
'Surfin' Santa', Ramblers
'Surf Riding', Reaction
'Surfer Dan', Turtles
and surf orth (but whatever happened to 'Grandma Got Run Down By Surfboard'?)

Dennis Wilson was the only member of the Beach Boys who could surf.

■ THE TWIST

It wasn't the first dance craze and it certainly wasn't the last, but the twist was undoubtedly the biggest dance craze of the Sixties. The original record was recorded as a B side by Hank Ballard; when Chubby Checker recorded it and demonstrated the dance on American television, the kids were hooked and, what's more, it caught on with the cocktail set as well. Soon everybody was twistin' and a steady stream of twist records started to appear. Here are just some of them.

'The Twist', Hank Ballard
'The Twist', Chubby Checker
'Let's Twist Again', Chubby Checker
'Twistit', John Barry
'Twist Twist Senora', Gary 'US' Bonds
'Twistin' the Night Away', Sam Cooke
'Twist and Shout', Topnotes
'Twistin' and Kissin'', Ronnie and the Hi Lites
'It's Twistin' Time', Hank Ballard
'Frankenstein Twist', Crystals
'Dear Lady Twist', Gary 'US' Bonds
'The Twister', Bo Diddley
'Chuck's Soul Brothers' Twist', Chuck Jackson
'Fish and Twist', Flares
'Siamese Twist', Flesh for Lulu
'Good Twistin' Tonight', Hank Ballard
'Percolator Twist', Billy Joe and the Checkmates
'Twistful Thinking', Gary Edwards
'Twistin' the Mood', Joe Loss
'Twistwatch', String A Longs
'Double Twist', Howie Casey and the Seniors

'Viens Danser Le Twist' ('Again Dance the Twist' aka 'Let's Twist Again'), Johnny Halliday
'Pink City Twist', Fabulous Poodles
'Twistin' Postman', Marvellettes
'Slow Twistin'', Chubby Checker
'Twist at the Top', Howie Casey and the Seniors
'Twist Little Sister', Brian Poole and the Tremeloes
'Ya Ya Twist', Petula Clark
'Twisting by the Pool', Dire Straits
'Peppermint Twist', Danny Peppermint and the Peppermint Pigs
'Don't Stop Twist', Frankie Vaughan
'I've Been Twistin'', Jerry Lee Lewis
'Doin' the Twist', Emile Ford
'Twist Baby', Owen Gray
'Meet Me at the Twistin' Place', Johnny Morissette
'Christopher Columbus Twist', Firestones
'Newcastle Twist', Lord Rockingham's XI
'Bristol Twistin' Annie', Dovells
'Washboard Twist Blues', Eric Delaney
'Popeye Twist', Tornados
'Twist (Round and Round)', Chill Fac-Torr
'Twist My Wrist', Jess Conrad
'Twistin' Rose of Texas', Johnny Desmond
and that's your lot before I go round the twist.

The twist was once described thus: 'Imagine you are rubbing your back with a towel and stubbing out cigarettes with both your feet.'

Danny and the Juniors were originally lined up to cut a new version of 'The Twist' at Dick Clark's request. However, they were unavailable, so the almost unknown singer Chubby Checker stepped in instead.

■ THE HOUSE THAT JACK BUILT

One craze to emerge from the house music scene of Chicago was jackin'. Depending on whose opinion you seek, or how your mind works, 'to jack' can mean either to have sex, to masturbate or simply to dance. Here are several of the records you could 'jack' to.

'Jack Your Body', Steve 'Silk' Hurley
'Show U How To Jack (Jack Your Body Rock Your Body)', House Hustlers
'Can U Jack', Kenny 'Jammin' Jason with Fast Eddie Smith
'The House That Jack Built', Jack 'n' Chill
'Jack Mix', Mirage
'Jack Trax', Chip E In
'Jack the Groove', Raze
'Jackin', Homewreckers
'Jack Up Work Your Body', Raze
'White Knight Jacks', White Knight
'Tell Jack (Jack the House)', Denise Motto
'Jack Slick', Leroy Smart and Junior Murvin
'Don't Make Me Jack', Paris Grey
'The Jackin' National Anthem', Ramos
'Jack It All Night Long', Bad Boy Bill
'Jack Me Till I Scream', Julian Jumpin' Perez
'Jack Me Frankie', House People
'I Wanna Jack With You', Zinc
'Jack U Off', Prince
'Gonna Jack', White Knight
'Jack Le Freak', Chic
'Jack in the Bush', Patrick Adams
'Girls Can Jack Too', Zuzan
'Jack the Ripper', LL Cool J
'Jack to the Sound', Fast Eddie Smith
'Happy Jack' (How did this get in here?), the Who

■ RUDY'S ROCK

The rudys, rudies, or rude boys were Kingston, Jamaica's, wide boys and gangsters, the small-time crooks that earned a reputation as Jack the lads. They were to be sung about in many ska and reggae tunes such as the ones listed here.

'Rude Boy', Wailers
'Everybody Rude Now', Keith McCarthy
'Waiting for My Rude Girl', Prince Buster
'Rougher Than Rough (Rudies In Court)', Derrick Morgan
'Rudie Gets Plenty', Spanishtonians
'Rude Boys Outta Jail', Specials
'Rude Boys Are Back In Town', Boss
'Rude Girl', Sonny Burke
'Rudi's in Love', Locomotive
'Rudi Got Married', Laurel Aitken and Unitone
'Rude With Me', Dandy and his group
'Ruder Than You', Bodysnatchers
'Rude Girls', Doreen Campbell and Rico's Boys
'Rudy A Message To You', Dandy Livingstone
'Rudy Got Soul', Desmond Dekker
'Rudi Bam Bam', Caledonians
'Rude Boy Train', Desmond Dekker
'Rudi The Red Nosed Reindeer', Steam Shovel

The Wailers' 'Rude Boy' was the first rudy record while Keith McCarthy's 'Everybody Rude Now' is the rude boys' anthem.

■ PENGUIN TRIVIA

Now, as a tribute to my publishers (creep, creep), some Penguin-related music trivia. Doo-wop group the Penguins, recorders of 'Earth Angel' amongst others, took their name from the character Willy the Penguin, who appeared on Kool cigarette packets.

I can find few penguin songs, and those I do know seem to refer mostly to the Caped Crusader's arch enemy and can be found in the *I Spy For The FBI* section (p. 33). Only L. J. Reynolds' 'Penguin Breakdown' wouldn't seem to be about this villain, though what on earth it is about is quite beyond me.

Fleetwood Mac released an album called *Penguin* in 1973 and adopted that bird as a symbol for a while.

■ ANSWERS TO TITLES QUIZ

'Christmas Song', Gilbert O'Sullivan
'Picture This', Blondie
'Videotheque', Dollar
'Hollywood', Box Scaggs
'Police and Thieves', Junior Murvin, the Clash
'Tribute to a King', William Bell
'Sing Don't Speak', Blackfoot Sue
'Baby Take a Bow', Adam Faith
'Celluloid Heroes', Kinks
'Theme One', Cozy Powell
'Music and Lights', Imagination
'Sold My Soul for Rock 'n' Roll', Linda and the Funky Boys
'A Little Bit of Soap', Jarmels, Showaddywaddy
'Solid Bond in Your Heart', Style Council
'I Spy for the FBI', Jamo Thomas
'I'm the Urban Spaceman', Bonzo Dog Doodah Band
'Who Comes to Boogie', Little Benny and the Masters
'Puppet on a String', Sandie Shaw
'Movie Star', Harpo
'Put You in the Picture', PVC2, Rich Kids
'Saturday Night at the Movies', Drifters
'One Nation Under a Groove', Funkadelic
'Disco Beatlemania', DBM
'Facts and Figures', Hugh Cornwell
'Beer Drinkers and Hell Raisers', ZZ Top, Motorhead
'The Groover', T. Rex
'Don't Play Your Rock 'n' Roll to Me', Smokie
'Takin' Care of Business', Bachman-Turner Overdrive
'Sound Systems', Steel Pulse
'I Love My Label', Nick Lowe
'In the Studio', Special Aka
'Silence Is Golden', Tremeloes

'Short Cut to Somewhere', Fish and Tony Banks
'Like a Rolling Stone', Bob Dylan
'Give a Little Love', Bay City Rollers
'We Are Family', Sister Sledge
'All Around the World', Jam
'Classical Gas', Mason Williams
'Wild West Hero', Electric Light Orchestra
'Ain't That the Truth', Frankie Kelly
'Lies', Status Quo
'All-American Hero', Victorian Parents
'Press', Paul McCartney
'No One Gets the Prize', Diana Ross
'Radio Radio', Elvis Costello
'Stages', ZZ Top
'At the Club', Drifters
'The Great Gig in the Sky', Pink Floyd
'On the Road Again', Canned Heat
'Material Girl', Madonna
'I Like Sport', Stukas
'The First Time', Adam Faith
'First Cut Is the Deepest', Rod Stewart, PP Arnold, Cat Stevens
'In the Beginning', Frankie Laine
'King Rocker', Generation X
'Royal Event', Russ Conway
'Jail Guitar Doors', Clash
'They're Coming to Take Me Away HA-HAAA!', Napoleon XIV
'The Name of the Game', Abba
'The Name Game', Shirley Ellis
'Heroes', David Bowie
'Painter Man', Creation, Boney M
'Stand Up and Say That', Shadows
'I've Got Lots of Famous People Living Under the Floorboards of My Humble Abode', Splodgenessabounds
'We Love You', Rolling Stones
'Calling Your Name', Marilyn
'To Cut a Long Story Short', Spandau Ballet
'Who Can It Be Now', Men At Work
'Call Up the Groups', Barron Knights
'Something Stupid', Nancy and Frank Sinatra
'Hard To Say I'm Sorry', Chicago

'Who Are We?', Ronnie Hilton
'What's Your Name', Chicory Tip
'The Song of My Life', Petula Clark
'I Write the Songs', David Cassidy
'Your Song', Elton John
'Do It Do It Again', Raffaella Carra
'What Have They Done To My Song Ma', Melanie, New Seekers
'De Do Do Do De Da Da Da', Police
'Answer Me', David Whitfield, Frankie Laine, Barbara Dickson
'Laugh at Me', Sonny (Bono)
'Titles', Barclay James Harvest
'SYSLJFM (The Letter Song)', Joe Tex, the Q-Tips
'Cover Me', Bruce Springsteen
'Band Played the Boogie', CCS
'War', Edwin Starr, Frankie Goes To Hollywood, Bruce Springsteen
'Changes', David Bowie
'Bits and Pieces', Dave Clark 5
'D-a-a-ance', Lambrettas
'Listen to What the Man Said', Paul McCartney
'Sharing You', Bobby Vee
'Year of Decision', Three Degrees
'What's Another Year', Johnny Logan
'This Is England', Clash
'Mr Success', Frank Sinatra
'Power in the Darkness', Tom Robinson Band
'Drugs', Talking Heads
'Smoke Gets in Your Eyes', Platters
'Sing Little Birdie', Pearl Carr and Teddy Johnson
'Ghosts', Japan
'Tiptoe through the Tulips', Tiny Tim
'Electricity', Orchestral Manoeuvres in the Dark
'Cruel To Be Kind', Nick Lowe
'Dead Pop Stars', Altered Images
'Bang Bang', B. A. Robertson
'Gun Law', Kane Gang
'Rock and Roll Suicide', David Bowie
'Anything That's Rock 'n' Roll', Tom Petty and the Heartbreakers
'Waves', Blancmange
'The House That Jack Built', Alan Price, Tracie
'Rudy's Rock', Bill Haley and His Comets

FOR THE BEST IN PAPERBACKS, LOOK FOR THE 

In every corner of the world, on every subject under the sun, Penguin represents quality and variety – the very best in publishing today.

For complete information about books available from Penguin – including Pelicans, Puffins, Peregrines and Penguin Classics – and how to order them, write to us at the appropriate address below. Please note that for copyright reasons the selection of books varies from country to country.

In the United Kingdom: For a complete list of books available from Penguin in the U.K., please write to *Dept E.P., Penguin Books Ltd, Harmondsworth, Middlesex, UB7 0DA*

In the United States: For a complete list of books available from Penguin in the U.S., please write to *Dept BA, Penguin, 299 Murray Hill Parkway, East Rutherford, New Jersey 07073*

In Canada: For a complete list of books available from Penguin in Canada, please write to *Penguin Books Canada Ltd, 2801 John Street, Markham, Ontario L3R 1B4*

In Australia: For a complete list of books available from Penguin in Australia, please write to the *Marketing Department, Penguin Books Australia Ltd, P.O. Box 257, Ringwood, Victoria 3134*

In New Zealand: For a complete list of books available from Penguin in New Zealand, please write to the *Marketing Department, Penguin Books (NZ) Ltd, Private Bag, Takapuna, Auckland 9*

In India: For a complete list of books available from Penguin, please write to *Penguin Overseas Ltd, 706 Eros Apartments, 56 Nehru Place, New Delhi, 110019*

In Holland: For a complete list of books available from Penguin in Holland, please write to *Penguin Books Nederland B.V., Postbus 195, NL–1380AD Weesp, Netherlands*

In Germany: For a complete list of books available from Penguin, please write to *Penguin Books Ltd, Friedrichstrasse 10 – 12, D–6000 Frankfurt Main 1, Federal Republic of Germany*

In Spain: For a complete list of books available from Penguin in Spain, please write to *Longman Penguin España, Calle San Nicolas 15, E–28013 Madrid, Spain*